THE CRITICS PRAISE *WALKING SHADOWS*:

"A tingler from the outset...Fascinating."
—*Grand Rapids Press*

"Thoughtful, tricky, with surprise moves in store..."
—*The New York Times Book Review*

"The powerful conclusion reaches beyond fiction to the current British spy network and provides a chilling touch of realism. An impressive debut novel."
—*Booklist*

"A first-rate novel...one with good pacing and constant intimations of double- and triple-crossing."
—*South Bend Tribune*

"Taylor tells about one of the most dangerous and fantastic deals imaginable....He tells his story with great skill and leaves his readers guessing until they reach the dramatic denouement. One is well advised to immerse oneself completely in this exciting book."

—*Asbury Park Press*

"Dazzles the reader from first to last, it's something worth shouting about....It's all done with flair and believability that bodes well for Taylor's future in an already star-spangled field."

—*Knoxville News-Sentinel*

"Here's a dandy if you like espionage novels."

—*UPI*

Walking Shadows

FRED TAYLOR

ST. MARTIN'S PRESS • NEW YORK

For information, address St. Martin's Press,
175 Fifth Avenue, New York, N.Y. 10010.

Design by Paolo Pepe

ISBN 0-312-90377-4

Also by Fred Taylor:

THE GOEBBELS DIARIES 1939-41 (EDITOR AND TRANSLATOR)

Life's but a walking shadow; a poor player
That struts and frets his hour upon the stage,
And then is heard no more: it is a tale
Told by an idiot, full of sound and fury,
Signifying nothing . . .

Shakespeare: *MACBETH*

PHASE ONE:

'Sound'

December 1942–February 1943

1

It began, like any conspiracy, with a lot of talking between a few men, with meetings in rooms believed to be safe, in parks, nondescript hotels, neutral, apparently random places. Some of those involved thought that they could keep a hold on all the threads as time went on and the plot burgeoned, acquired life, complications and consequences. They were wrong.

'No matter how good we think we are,' said Bellingham once, 'it's a first principle that the only buggers we fool in the deepest sense—I mean, all the way—are our own sweet selves.'

He was well placed to judge and, on that particular occasion, he happened to be stone-cold sober.

With hindsight, one fact is certainly clear. The web of events that came to be known among Resistance circles in Berlin as *Plan Wintermärchen*—and later to a small group within the British SIS under the codename SIGNIFY—can be dated precisely from Wednesday, 2 December 1942. This did not rank as an eventful day by the standards of a world at war: in Russia, General Hoth's Fourth Panzer Division was placed on alert west of the iced-over Don and ordered to prepare for another futile thrust towards Stalingrad; Rommel's Afrika Korps, chased from the wreckage of the Agheila Line by the British Eighth Army, continued its retreat to Sirte on the Libyan coast; and in the capital of the Great German Reich, Arthur Nebe made a detour on his way home from the office.

He need not have walked a half-mile out of his way on that chill, damp winter evening, through the blackout with a briefcase that swelled plump and heavy with extra paperwork. Indeed, Nebe need never walk anywhere for, as the Gestapo's Reich Chief of Detectives and a Brigadeführer in the SS, he had an official car and driver at his disposal, but he spurned such privileges. He would tell anyone who dared ask that he was appalled that so many of the nation's leaders took no exercise, when it was their duty to set an example in their fitness and alertness. Even a small amount of exertion each day, say, walking to and from the office if one lived within reasonable distance, would suffice, he maintained. His obsession had earned him a minor reputation as an eccentric at Gestapo headquarters in the Prinz-Albrecht-Strasse, though no one would have told him so to his face: Nebe was respected as a tough customer, a man who had performed his obligatory service in charge of a killing-squad in the East with exemplary efficiency and who seemed to spare no effort, even his critics had to admit, in pursuit of the state's enemies. In any case, his fetish about fresh air and physical fitness was as nothing compared with the foibles of other SS bosses. The late Reinhard Heydrich's nocturnal whorings and drinking-bouts had become a scandal, and Himmler had his bizarre mystic interests. At least Nebe's passion was *healthy* . . .

The Brigadeführer's route this Wednesday led him from the Prinz-Albrecht-Strasse south into the Wilhelmstrasse, from there to the corner of Leipziger Strasse, where the famous Jewish-owned Wertheim department store had once stood, and then out of the government district altogether, into the network of narrower, seedier streets behind the Friedrichstrasse station. Suddenly he was skirting the fringes of Berlin's red light zone; already, though it was only shortly after six, painted women waited in doorways, whispering obscenely at the few passing men, and there were bars, illicit drinking clubs and blackmarket restaurants opening for business. Within a couple of hours they would be full, but Nebe showed no interest—personal or professional—in any of the dens along his way. He kept walking, pausing only to take his bearings in the darkness. After a while, he struck off left into a side street lined with more or less respectable tenement blocks. The gloomy, grey-brick building with its heavy Wilhelmine ornamentation lay some two hundred yards from the junction. Nebe quickly selected a bell push, pressed it and waited. He did not have to stand in the cold for long. A tall, fair-haired man answered the door and swiftly ushered him inside.

The apartment on the second storey into which Nebe was shown was decently, if sparsely, furnished. To a sensitive or well-trained observer, the place expressed convenience, transience, cold official hospitality. The living room was dominated by a huge window that would have brought light and a sense of space, at least, into the room had it not been covered by a large, heavy blackout curtain of thick felt.

'You'll be pleased to know that this place isn't on any of our lists. Yet,' Nebe said, casting an expert eye over the furnishings. He removed first his hat, then his leather gloves, and finally, still standing, his spectacles, which he wiped with a special cloth and then replaced on the bridge of his aquiline nose. 'I checked, naturally. Wild horses wouldn't have dragged me here if it had been known to my colleagues at the Prinz-Albrecht-Strasse.'

The man who had let him into the apartment was young, and he was alone. He cleared his throat nervously, uncertain how he should put his lugubrious guest at ease.

'Sit down, Herr Nebe,' he said. 'And don't worry. We use reliable nominees. The SS knows that the Abwehr rents many safe houses in Berlin. If they were to get wind of one more, it would hardly cause a sensation . . .'

'It might if I were seen coming here.' Nebe sat himself down heavily in an armchair, keeping on his thick overcoat and with his briefcase perched on his lap. The young man poured him a large schnaps. Nebe accepted it with a perfunctory nod.

'I've brought what you asked for,' he said shortly. 'I hope it will do for a while, because I've run some big risks in abusing my position.'

Oberleutnant Otto von Bredow raised his glass in salute. 'Here's to your courage. The nation will thank you one day—perhaps not so far in the future.'

The nation can go to blazes and probably will, thought Nebe. He gulped at his drink, unlocked his briefcase and produced a sealed buff envelope.

'A round dozen of photographic copies in all. I have disposed of the camera,' he announced. 'The material belongs to the Admiral now, to use as he sees fit. Quite frankly, I don't want to know what he does with it.'

Bredow smiled. 'Herr Nebe, he will be delighted. At last we have a lever on the British. No more pussyfooting, no more pleading for favours. For once we shall be able to name our price. It will be high.'

'I told you. I don't want to know, got that? In my position, the less I know, the better.'

'Very well. Then I shall say no more. We all understand your special circumstances,' the young man answered with a hint of irritation.

They sat in silence, their drinks still unfinished. The envelope lay on a low mahogany table between them. No man's land. Nebe's host was in his late twenties, fair hair and skin but piercing blue eyes, with the high cheekbones and square jaw line of a Prussian aristocrat and an air of idealistic intensity. He wore a civilian jacket and slacks for this encounter, but they sat awkwardly on him. He was the type born to live inside a staff uniform, Nebe thought; a typical Abwehr glory-boy of the kind who dreamed of riding to save Germany on a charger like the Teutonic Knights of old. The Brigadeführer summed him up quickly, and equally quickly decided that he did not feel like talking too such a young man tonight. His own reasons for being here had to do with blood spilt and bodies broken in the cellars of the Prinz-Albrecht-Strasse, and with wild days and nights in the East spent ordering an *Einsatzkommando* of two hundred men to kill, kill, and kill again for the same Germany about which Bredow cared so tenderly. Perhaps their country was past saving. Nebe wondered what the high-minded Oberleutnant would have done, if, to keep his job and maintain his usefulness to the anti-Nazi resistance movement, he had been forced to organize mass murder. Part of Nebe's instant dislike of him was based on envy. Bredow had never been faced with such a choice, and probably never would be.

'The envelope contains everything that was in the file. The last summary is dated 12 November. Now I must go,' Nebe said with brisk finality.

He got to his feet without ceremony, downing the remains of his schnaps as he stood, then retrieving his hat and gloves. He tucked his briefcase under one arm. In accordance with polite social usage, he offered Bredow his free hand.

'Goodbye, Oberleutnant. And good luck.'

They shook selfconsciously.

'With this in our pocket,' Bredow said, picking up the

envelope and tapping it affectionately with his forefinger, 'we may not need luck any more.'

Nebe, who had been about to leave, turned briefly on his heel and shot him a cold glance of disdain mingled with pity.

'Don't be a fool, Bredow,' he snapped. 'One always needs luck. Always.'

After Nebe had gone, Bredow went over to the telephone in the corner of the room and called a local Berlin number. Yes, the package had been delivered, all complete, he said. At last. He would be bringing it over to the Admiral's house in about half-an-hour. It was hard for him to keep the excitement out of his voice, though the phrases he used were cautious and elliptical.

Bredow put down the telephone. He placed the envelope in his own attaché case and put on his hat and coat. Before flicking off the light switch by the door, he glanced at his watch. A mere five minutes and forty seconds had elapsed since Nebe first entered the apartment block. He reflected that whatever else you might say about these SS characters—even the renegade ones such as Nebe—they certainly did not gild their lilies.

2

Bredow could see the man coming a way off on the steep, busy street that carved its way up from the port district to the Bairro Alto. No name or description had been vouchsafed by the British; they had merely agreed to send someone to the right place at the right time. Bredow felt energy prickle between his shoulder blades, flickering and flaring up towards the nape of his neck in little stabs and sallies like errant electricity. Three minutes to go. Everything fitted. He recognized the physical sensation as animal excitement leavened with fear.

The man approaching the hotel seemed to Bredow's eye almost a caricature of an English gentleman of a certain type and age, straight out of the pages of *Punch*. He looked to be pushing sixty and not encountering much resistance, pink-faced from the sun's action on a fair skin, a little paunchy, with greying hair and a salt-and-pepper moustache of the kind that would have been thought dashing in the First War. His long raincoat was ten years out of fashion and unbuttoned at the front, for winter in Lisbon was mild as well as wet. The ensemble was completed by a venerable trilby and a malacca cane. In his progress along the narrow thoroughfare that was fed, like hundreds of others, from the main artery of the Ruá do Seculá, the Englishman swung his cane from the wrist with a jaunty menace that belied his age and seemed to hint at an athletic, even dangerous, past. That also fitted.

Observing him from the window of his room, Bredow noticed that the Englishman began to pant slightly as he left street level and tackled the worn, uneven steps that led up to the hotel. The British had really sent a veteran, he thought, and if there was any muscle around to back the old man up, then it was very well hidden. Most probably they had decided to take a chance, for reasons which would have been made clear during the preparatory discussions.

A door banged against its hinges somewhere along the corridor. Bredow turned back into the half-light of his room and listened. A woman's voice squealed farewell in Portuguese, answered by a booming male laugh, rough endearments in a totally alien tongue. The sailors' whore along the corridor was parting from another client. A few moments later, her phonograph began to play a scratched recording of a *fado* song, sad, fiery music to lend retrospective nobility to the trade-off. Since Bredow had taken up his position two hours previously, the woman had received and accommodated two other men. Her routine had not varied that day: the half-hour session, the shrill parting, and the *fado,* and then the next . . .

One acquired a tolerance, even an affection for such places, Bredow mused, splashing his face with cold water from the solitary tap in the corner. It was something of a relief to move around the room and know that his contact was coming. He paused to study his reflection while his hands worked mechanically from the image in the mirror above the basin, straightening his tie and buttoning his double-breasted business suit. He had been twenty-seven last birthday. Perhaps there was a suspicion of pouches under the eyes, a few more lines around the corners of his mouth, but his overall condition was not bad—no wound-scars, or worse. In these times, he often reminded himself, he had been lucky. Eighteen of the officer cadets who had passed out at Potsdam in '36 were dead, another seven cripples, and only a few totally unscathed. He had heard those figures from his old instructor at the War Academy. It was confidential information, of course, but such things were confessed to an Abwehr officer.

A couple of paces to the window. A final glance outside. The Englishman had entered the hotel. Bredow pushed one of the pair of wicker chairs round so that it faced the bed, then took up his prepared position, standing facing the door with his attaché case alongside the bed, shielded by his legs.

He heard a murmur in the hall. The hotel porter croaking, '*Obrigado, senhor,*' and the discreet chink of coins changing hands.

The Englishman knocked and walked straight in without waiting for an answer. Once the door was shut behind him, he stopped and hovered a few feet short of Bredow, staring at the German as if making an initial judgment. Then he leaned his cane against the wardrobe with a discernible flourish, like a cavalier laying away his sword. He placed his hat on a hook on the wall, turned back to Bredow, thrusting his hands into his coat pockets to discourage physical contact.

'Good afternoon,' he said. He had a deep, gravelly voice; the sort that actors can spend a lifetime trying to acquire. 'Come to the right place, have I?'

'Oh, I believe so, Mister. . . ?'

The Englishman responded with a wintry smile and a 'never mind names for the moment.' He moved over to the chair indicated by Bredow, shifted it into the light, and sat down.

'You people do pick some places,' he said, staring around him with amused distaste. He focused on the garishly painted crucifix above the bed. 'It's my opinion that old bugger of a porter thought you were my fancy-boy. These places spring up like bloody mushrooms . . .'

'It is the war. Or, in Lisbon's case, should I say the lack of it?' Bredow agreed in his careful English, falling in with the conversational tone. 'The Portuguese benefit by catering for both sides; we are all the same in bed, and our money is equally good. As to the typicality or otherwise of such a hotel, I bow to your obvious superior knowledge.'

The Englishman laughed loudly, though he continued to stare in a puzzled fashion at the crucifix. Suddenly he leaned forward in his chair, clasping his hands together. There were grey hairs on the backs between the knuckles.

'So your lot are after some sort of trade, are they?'

He put the question with brutal directness. Gentleman he might be, but he clearly had no intention of getting too cozy.

Bredow shrugged. 'I thought that had been made quite clear.'

'Perhaps it was. But setting up this quiet little *tête-à-tête* in such a short time has been a headache. My chief doesn't like rushing, or bypassing the normal procedures. It had better be worthwhile.'

'I think you will agree that this is so, when you have heard what I have to tell,' Bredow answered. 'You see, we are in a position to help you with a grave problem, a breach of security of the most serious kind. In return for reciprocal actions of a highly specific nature. Hence the particular conditions, the . . . theatrical aspect, if you want to put it that way.'

The eyes of the man opposite him mocked Bredow and his elaborate, carefully-rehearsed phrasing.

'Actions?' the Englishman drawled. 'You want actions from us? My goodness, I can't for the life of me think what we can do for you, old chap. Got the whole war sewn up, haven't you? Still, no matter. Fire away. It's what I'm here for. To listen.'

While the man made his own little speech, Bredow took his cigarette case from his jacket pocket and flipped it open. He found himself automatically offering a cigarette in his guest's direction. The Englishman looked taken aback for a moment, then shook his head and patted his own pocket.

'No thanks. Pipe.'

The eyes were still playing on Bredow as he lit his cigarette. Bredow could see no weakness in the fleshy, professionally impassive features, but he thought he sensed a cynical empathy. There was subliminal signalling in full swing, and the message read: neither of us likes this job much, son, but I'm an ancient hand at it and you're just a young buck from the Tirpitzufer who's been despatched into the lion's den to do some fast talking. One word out of place, one false step, and I'll chew you up. I won't necessarily love myself for doing it, but I will . . .

'Very well,' Bredow said, brusquely to hide his nervousness. 'First our side of things. I will not beat about the bush. We have information from a wholly reliable source that the Sicherheitsdienst is maintaining a spy in London. This agent works in a very sensitive area of the Secret Service. In effect, he is a colleague of yours.' No reaction from the Englishman, not a glimmer. 'We know certain things about this man,' Bredow pressed on, 'including his codename. This is *Türkis*—turquoise. Appropriately enough, the information he is sending to Berlin concerns military planning in the Balkans and the Middle East.'

The Englishman, meanwhile, had taken out an old briar pipe. He nodded casually at Bredow's mention of the Middle East, then started scraping the bowl with a small, stainless steel device.

'Our reliable source has, in fact, managed to gain access to some of the agent's reports. Unfortunately, they do not indicate the man's real name or exact function in your network. It will, therefore, take some work to pinpoint him,' Bredow said. 'We are willing to supply that help.'

A raised eyebrow. The Englishman had been blowing into the briar's stem. Now he screwed it back together and began stuffing it methodically with a curly Virginia tobacco, shredding each nut-brown disc between thumb and forefinger before pushing it down into the bowl.

'And what form might it take?' he said, as if asking only from politeness.

Bredow knew full well that everything he said was being stored inside that square, greying head. 'We have access to the reports, as I said. We'll supply you with copies of the material. You should be able to narrow the field of suspects to a substantial extent by what you get from us. It should then be possible to manage the flow of material to those suspects in such a way that it will be apparent from the reports in the Sicherheitsdienst's files who the traitor is. Do you follow. . . ?'

'I understand well enough,' said the Englishman. He had the pipe, still unlit, in his mouth now and was looking at Bredow with a kind of condescending tolerance, even affection. 'I've seen it done before. You feed different stuff to each of the suspected naughty boys, then see which version comes out at the other end. Match your end version with the original, and there you are.' He frowned. 'Though I must admit that it's never been done with the actual connivance of enemy Intelligence. My God, your relations with the SD must have really hit rock bottom for you to do the dirty on them like that.'

'Our relationship with the SD is irrelevant,' Bredow cut in icily. 'This matter goes far beyond trivial rivalry between organizations.'

The Englishman snorted with amusement. 'All right, then. So why are you prepared to help us catch the SD's spy in London? That's presuming he exists, of course.'

'We are prepared to help in order to show our good will. And because we do not wish to lengthen the war unnecessarily. Your chief is aware of these things. He will also be aware that such a spy—who most certainly does exist—could cripple your war effort in certain crucial areas and cost you thousands of lives.'

'Umph.' The Englishman grunted, as if that one had hit home. His tone changed from one of amused banter to sharp enquiry. 'And what's in it for you?' he said.

Bredow cleared his throat. He could feel his heart in his own chest like a loud, intrusive foreign body. 'We want your active help in destroying Nazism in our country,' he said.

'What kind of flannel is that? Be specific. My chief'll demand precision.'

'Yes, of course.' Bredow paused to grind his cigarette into the room's sole ash tray. 'Then I will tell you that we want you to kill Adolf Hitler.'

The Englishman's eyes flashed. Then he looked down at his pipe, patted his pocket for matches. He lit the pipe, taking his time, losing himself for a few crucial seconds behind the match flame, the smoke, the two hands cupping around the briar in the manner of a man used to performing the operation in the open air. When he had the pipe burning to his satisfaction, he looked at Bredow again and had managed to remove any expression from his gaze.

'Why?' he said. 'You lot must come into contact with him every day. Can't you do the job yourselves?'

'We could. But we would rather not.'

'Aha.' A nod. Understanding? Scepticism? Playing for time?

'Yes,' Bredow said, warming to his task. 'We want the job done outside Germany by the notorious Secret Service. Hitler is planning to visit a remote part of the occupied territories this spring—where I cannot yet say, of course. With our aid, an assassination attempt would stand a good chance of success. Above all, we would not be blamed.'

The Englishman made a dismissive gesture. 'Not my business. I'm just a messenger-boy, here to listen to what you want and what you're prepared to give.' He allowed himself a smile. 'And the latter'd better be pretty damned convincing.'

'Of course.'

Bredow moved his legs and picked up the attaché case. He unlocked it and took out a sheet of pale grey, shiny photographic paper.

'This will give your chief a foretaste,' he said. 'It is a copy of a document originating from Bureau VI of the RSHA, the Sicherheitsdienst's department for foreign espionage. You understand German?'

The Englishman nodded blandly, reached over and took the paper.

'You may, of course, keep this document as proof of our good will,' Bredow continued. 'No doubt you will wish to satisfy yourselves as to its authenticity.' Suddenly he found himself cheap and absurd, like a backstreet pornographer working on a promising client, providing a 'sample' and promising stronger stuff to come.

'Have you got the original?' was the Englishman's sole comment when he had read through the paper. The door along the corridor slammed again. Another client arriving for the whore. The Englishman glanced automatically in the direction of the sound, then returned his attention to

Bredow, billowing pipe clenched aggressively between his teeth.

'No,' said Bredow. He had heard of *sang-froid*, but this was absurd. 'As you are doubtless aware, Bureau VI is part of the SS. We are attached to the General Staff of the Army, therefore quite distinct. The material was obtained in a clandestine manner, at considerable personal risk to the man concerned. He could only make a photographic copy.'

'And hence the reason why you can't actually tell me who the spy is and leave it at that?'

'If we knew the traitor's identity, we would tell you.'

'But, being noble souls, you're willing to assist us in tracking him down—provided that we play along with your private war aims.'

'I find this a distortion, but I suppose that it is one view.'

'Strikes me as the only view,' the Englishman growled. 'You've got your trusty burrowing away in the Prinz-Albrecht-Strasse, and you're perfectly prepared to sell out the SD's cloak-and-dagger merchants for your own purposes. Two birds with one stone: get us to bump off *Der Führer* without embarrassing involvement on your part, and discredit your rivals at the same time.'

'We are not "selling out" anyone,' Bredow snapped back. 'Our intention is to show that *our* Germany—the decent Germany—means well towards *your* England . . .' He shut up abruptly, realizing that he had been goaded by an expert.

Having successfully tested his host's mettle, the Englishman relaxed visibly. Nevertheless, he could not resist one final dig.

'Still,' he commented, 'it looks as though they've stolen a march on you. An agent at SIS headquarters. Quite a feather in Schellenberg's cap.'

'I am glad that you think so. That is why I am so astonished that you seem to take this entire matter so lightly.'

The Englishman looked pained. 'Lightly? Who said I took it lightly? Goes without saying that this information, if true, is of considerable interest.'

'It could determine the outcome of the war,' said Bredow.

'That will be for my chief to decide,' the Englishman retorted comfortably. He seemed to have a real talent for trivialization. 'In any case, this piece of paper won't get us very far. He'll want to know if there's more where this came from, and if so how quickly and reliably you can supply it.'

'There are two other documents, more detailed. Copies are in our possession in Berlin,' Bredow lied. 'We are trying to obtain more, but the circulation of the material is heavily restricted. We may have more for you when we meet again to discuss practical matters.'

The Englishman let the reference to 'practical matters' ride.

'I daresay that can be arranged,' he said. 'Depends on what my chief thinks. We'll be in touch through the usual channels if and when we decide another meeting's necessary.'

The vagueness was maddening. Bredow fought to contain a resurgence of irritation.

'Tit for tat. We are prepared to take risks if you are. I think that this spy is doing you a lot of harm, and will do even more. Tell that to your chief.'

The Englishman got to his feet without answering. He folded the photographic paper carefully and put it in the inside pocket of his raincoat, then stooped to retrieve his cane. When he faced Bredow again, he chose his words with deliberation.

'Don't worry. We're clear enough about what's at stake, and about the terms. There are areas in which we possess a community of interest, or at least that's my personal view. Clearly I can make no promises.'

'I understand that,' Bredow answered stiffly.

The Englishman acknowledged him in the form of a self-conscious, courtly inclination of the head, almost a bow. He was the complete gentleman as he smiled, hand on the door handle, and said: 'My regards to Herr Canaris, by the way. We never met—luckily for him—but one day in April 1917 we came pretty damned close.'

He walked out, closing the door gently behind him.

Bredow returned to the window, where he stood for several minutes, watching the raincoated figure's unhurried progress until finally the Englishman disappeared from view among the lengthening shadows.

Bredow felt a sense of anti-climax that shocked him slightly. The meeting had been so undramatic in style and feeling. Adolf Hitler's life offered on a plate . . . A master spy traded . . . Stuff that could topple empires. All discussed matter-of-factly, even a little hazily, in fifteen minutes in a seedy hotel room. It didn't seem real . . .

The thin winter sun was gradually settling over the estuary of the Tagus river. At this time of day during the summer months, the river turned into what the Portuguese called the 'Sea of Straw', a million stalk-like flecks of reflected light rippling across the water in the twilight. Once Bredow had settled his bill for the room, he had to make a long-distance telephone call from the central post office on the Praco dos Restauradores. Then, having used the correct form of words to indicate that the meeting had passed off safely, he was free until the night express to Madrid left at eleven. He would take a taxi down to the waterfront, perhaps buy some little souvenir to amuse his wife, and then treat himself to a supper of clams and *vinho verde*, forget the nameless Englishman, Canaris, and the rest of them for a precious few hours.

Bredow knew, of course, that what had happened was absolutely real—and that it meant he had betrayed his country. Even when a man knew his cause to be just, such a betrayal came hard. It was a pity that he was due in Madrid in the morning to report to the Admiral. Otherwise, Bredow would have been tempted to get himself quite thoroughly, solitary drunk.

Whenever, for his own reasons, Admiral Franz Wilhelm Canaris did not wish to advertise his presence in Madrid, he stayed at an apartment on the second floor of a house in the northern suburbs of the city which was registered as the Spanish headquarters of a German chemicals company, Burg-Chemie AG. The firm operated perfectly legitimately as a substantial importer of synthetic fertilizers and insecticides, but also received generous cash subsidies from the Abwehr's secret funds. In return, it took on several employees whose time was not wholly devoted to selling chemicals. Also, on occasion, Canaris was allowed to use the executive *pied-à-terre* above the offices.

Bredow had slept only fitfully during the overnight train journey. A taxi dropped him at the house shortly after eight in the morning. He was haggard and weary and longing for a chance to rest in a decent bed, even for an hour, but there was to be no respite. The receptionist ushered him upstairs into the company flat as soon as he gave his name. He found the Admiral sitting quietly by a log fire, a cup of breakfast coffee on the table beside him. Canaris had clearly been up waiting for some time.

'Ah, Otto,' he said, getting hastily to his feet, as if the younger man's arrival were a surprise. 'You look exhausted, dear boy. My apologies for forcing you to travel overnight, but . . .'

Canaris threw up his hands in a gesture of tongue-tied despair at the pace of life into which the war forced otherwise civilized human beings. His legendary concern for the health and well-being of his employees was one reason he could demand and expect total loyalty from them. Like so much about the man, it was impossible to gauge whether his thoughtfulness was genuine or at least partly assumed. Certainly, he rarely seemed to spare himself. He was constantly on the move from station to station, outpost to outpost, throughout Germany, the occupied countries and neutral Europe. This nomadic pattern had been established early in his career as head of the Abwehr. These days, though, no one was entirely sure whether he did it to keep ahead of the Allies or of his intimate enemies in Berlin—the SD, Reichsführer Himmler's own Intelligence Service, which was now openly challenging Canaris's authority. The joke at Abwehr HQ in Berlin went that the boss was everywhere—and nowhere. But then again, his restlessness contributed to the legend, and so perhaps was also calculation.

Bredow gratefully accepted some coffee from the pot, for it was freshly-made and real, from Brazil for once, and not *ersatz* from Chemnitz. He was forced out of politeness to stay on his feet. Now that Bredow had arrived, Canaris moved around the room as if incapable of remaining still. Dapper, completely grey-haired though still in his mid-fifties, the Admiral scaled barely five feet four in his neat suit and highly-polished shoes. As he fussed around the young officer, he resembled nothing so much as a diminutive clockwork toy set into action around the room.

Finally Canaris circled one last time and sat down in one of the fireside armchairs. Bredow did the same thing with a silent sigh of relief.

'Filthy weather, I'm afraid, unlike Lisbon,' Canaris said. 'Madrid, of course, has no sea to warm it. Fortunately the city still has charm, and it enjoys relative peace.' A pause and a grimace. 'Everything is relative, I suppose.'

Bredow nodded listlessly. Temperatures were only slightly above freezing here. He had seen civil-war cripples and shivering orphans crouched in their rags among the grand pillars of the Estacion del Atocha this morning, begging coins from the arriving rail passengers. Spain had kept out of the European war because she had already bled herself white. For many of her people, particularly those who had fought on the wrong side during the 'Glorious Crusade' that had brought General Franco to power less than four years previously, this was going to be a murderous winter, a winter distinctly without charm. Bredow drank his good, hot coffee and waited for the Admiral to drop the philosophy and get round to the debriefing.

'Well,' Canaris began hesitantly. 'How would you sum up the course of the meeting?'

'I think that the British will co-operate. We have the stick as well as the carrot. I can't see they have any choice.'

'No choice,' Canaris said.

The Admiral had a strange habit of repeating the last word or phrase of a previous speaker by way of reply, an unnerving device which absolved him from expressing an opinion of his own until he was ready to do so. It could also be used to wicked humorous effect. It was said that when reprimanded during his early naval career, the young Canaris had simply agreed with every statement his superior officer had made. Thus when told, 'Canaris, you are a blockhead!', he would reply: 'Blockhead, sir!' 'This report is shit!' would produce the response: 'Shit, sir!' Canaris liked to quote the Chinese Tao, which told the wise man to absorb an opposing force and make its strength his own.

'And their man took the document?' Canaris asked. 'Did he seem shocked, impressed, intrigued?'

'He tried not to show any clear reaction, and he was largely successful. A brusque, prickly old character. Difficult to deal with.'

Bredow described the Englishman and repeated his sly parting message.

After some thought, the Admiral chuckled drily. 'Yes,' he said. 'I think I know him from the First War, when I served in Spain. He was based in Portuguese territory, ran a network across the border that recruited local officials and paid them to disclose the movements of suspicious Germans. His name will be in the files.'

Canaris fell silent. Thinking this a signal to continue, Bredow took up his thread again, but he had hardly uttered half a dozen words when the Admiral spoke as if there had been no intervening pause.

'He operated in tandem with an officer named Stewart Menzies,' he said. 'They were friends. Menzies, of course, went on to become head of British Intelligence, while his comrade-in-arms continued in the wine trade which had been his cover and actually made quite a successful business out of it. This is very interesting, because as far as we knew he had been pensioned off by SIS years ago. That revelation must have been deliberate. A sign, sanctioned by Menzies, that he is taking this matter seriously, and also keeping it to himself. Excellent, if I am right.'

This time, he really did look enquiringly at Bredow.

'He seemed a very shrewd operator, Admiral,' the Oberleutnant said.

'He is. The pair of them were ordered to assassinate me—because I was offering bigger bribes and turning their agents. They very nearly succeeded.'

Canaris received the rest of Bredow's report in silence. He stared into the fire for long periods, nodding politely from time to time to show that he was listening. Though he tried to avoid showing it, he gave a distinct impression of being bored by the details. Bredow had to work hard to deliver a thorough, accurate account; preoccupied the Admiral might seem, but it was a fair bet that he would remember every word if the need ever arose.

'A promising enough beginning,' the Admiral said when the business part of their meeting was over. He looked away from the crackling logs and awarded Bredow a faint smile of approval, that of a benevolent but strict father-figure wondering how best to show his appreciation of a youngster's efforts without spoiling the lad beyond improvement. 'When you meet next, however, the discussions will be entering a very delicate phase. We must prepare thoroughly.'

'And how long does the Admiral think we shall have to wait?'

'A few weeks,' Canaris answered. 'Menzies will want what we have to offer, but he may also feel humiliated, resentful. He will try to think up some complication which will enable him to save face. I am certain of only one thing,' he concluded with a hissing chuckle of satisfaction. 'That is: he must respond in some way. What else can he do?'

Bredow nodded solemnly. 'What else indeed, Admiral?'

3

The driver, the man who couldn't run, snapped awake and looked at the clock on the bedroom mantelpiece. Just gone six and therefore all's not well, he thought. Must have dozed off again.

'Christ, I'd better get a move on,' he said aloud.

The driver immediately regretted his words, and hoped that the woman hadn't heard him. Ideally he would have liked to have simply left her 'ration', as she called it, on the kitchen table and disappeared. Until the next time. 'I get my ration, you get yours,' she had told him once after a few gins. Very coy, as if she wasn't really meaning it, but you just try forgetting to give her a little something for her trouble. Leaving the stuff the morning after like this helped her to believe she wasn't really a tart, just the kind of girl that men liked to leave presents for. As for himself, the driver preferred the relationship this way; commercial, free-and-easy, no untidy emotions.

He swung himself gingerly out of bed towards the chair where his clothes lay heaped from the night before. He shivered in the early-morning cold. It was still dark outside, but he didn't switch on the light. A man's eyes adjusted quickly enough. Then, when he had got as far as putting on his vest, a squeak of mattress springs told him he was unlucky. The woman had wriggled round. She lay propped unsteadily on one elbow, clearing matted dark hair from her forehead with her free hand and squinting at him through eyes sticky with sleep.

'What's wrong, Jimmy?' she mumbled hoarsely.

'Nothing, petal. Overslept. Time I wasn't here.'

He blinked when she turned on the bedside light. A smile hid his distaste for the vision of her puffy features and smeared lipstick. She was all right on the night with the lounge bar lights doing her a favour and a boozy bloom on her cheeks, but come the dawn she looked her age, and more.

'Oh, you do look funny, standing there with your dingle-dangle hanging down and just your vest on,' she giggled. 'Mind you, it's a nice dingle-dangle . . .'

She had woken up quickly—usually she just stirred in the mornings, accepted a kiss before he went. Now, though, she was staring at his groin with something close to a come-hither look on her face. She had moved cunningly so that the covers slipped down to expose her breasts, which was always the signal that she was hot. Those Bristols made a feast for a bloke's eyes, big and still firm, each a real handful, and she knew it. They were what passed for Maggie Austin's fortune. Poor cow.

Despite himself, the driver felt vague stirrings, the beginnings of engorgement. He put on his underpants, shook his head and laughed. Time for the rough treatment.

'You must be joking,' he said. 'Save it up for me, petal. Any more time on the nest and I'll be late at the depot. Get me wages docked. Then who'll buy a slag like you all those gin and limes?'

She tossed her hair, thought that one over. He had got

his trousers on and was doing up his braces when he heard her say: 'I don't know. Someone might.' All hoity-toity.

'Yeah. Maybe a Yank. One of them black ones. Those big buck niggers aren't too choosy . . .'

He ducked in anticipation. A pillow came sailing wildly in his direction and whacked against the doorframe a foot from him.

'Be a sport, petal,' he protested, changing his tack. The lovable cockney now. 'You know it's real love that draws me to you from the lonely reaches of the night and the open road.'

'Rotten sod.' She was laughing. He had won.

The driver finally walked out of the front door at twenty-five past six. She had insisted on making him a cup of tea, and he had forced himself to kiss her and touch her up a bit to show there were no hard feelings. He had avoided serious hanky-panky, though, because that would have cut things too fine. As it was, he had rushed the parting ritual; her shyly turning her back while he fished a seven-pound tin of Spam out of his duffel-bag and plonked it on the table. A bit more than usual, because it was the Season of Good Cheer. It was part of the routine that she didn't turn round again until he had gone. Then she would wave to him through the window, usually brandishing her 'ration' in triumph. Maggie was past caring what the neighbours thought, oh yes.

The house had been built during the slump, part of a drab, no-frills council development close to the main A5 trunk road some three miles south of St Albans. The driver had left his lorry parked in a lay-by a quarter of a mile away, though as far as Maggie was concerned it had spent the night at the local depot being unloaded. She was too pig-ignorant to know that drivers did their own shifting. The truth about the driver's work was more complicated. He did a run from the smoke to Liverpool and back—army contract stuff on the way there, American goodies for the return trip. His schedule allowed for an overnight stay in cheap digs in Liverpool, so what he did when duty demanded it was to drive straight back south again non-stop and kip at Maggie Austin's place, because that made things a lot easier.

His courting of Maggie—if that was the word—had

been designed to get himself a bed round here where he didn't have to register or leave his name. If she were to find her Yank and didn't want to be bothered with him any more, despite the 'rations', then he would get himself another bird. There were plenty of them around: widows, women scraping by on twenty-five miserable bob a week from the Public Assistance while the old man was off overseas fighting for King and Country, and they were grateful for the odd bit of company, not forgetting the contraband he picked up on the black market at the docks. He would never steal from his own lorry; that had been decided at the outset. The same-day dodge was acceptable because everyone did it now and again, to pocket the overnight lodgings allowance or because they had a bird somewhere on the route. Pinching stuff from your own load, though, that was both naughty and stupid. You might not get nicked, but you could get sacked or draw official attention to yourself. The last was unwise in the extreme. It interfered with duty.

The driver was thirty-one, heavily muscled, with broad shoulders and a narrow waist, the perfect build for a middleweight boxer. Old ladies had been known to come over to him when he was sitting down in a pub and ask indignant questions about why a fit young chap like him wasn't in the forces.

'I'm a Jehovah's Witness, darlin',' he would say, rattling an imaginary tambourine. 'We're conshies. Next time I'm in here I'll bring you a *Watchtower*. Save your raddled old soul.'

Later, when he stood up, they would see why he wasn't off fighting. The driver had a left hip joint that was out of true, been born with it, nothing the doctors could do. He walked with a splay-footed limp, an exaggerated version of a sailor's roll, and he couldn't run. Heavy work, lifting and shoving, was all right; since childhood he had learned to pivot on his good side and had developed the upper part of his body until it was very strong. He could drive a lorry as well as the next man too, though that had taken some very hard work. But he couldn't run. So he had been spared conscription in '39 and '40, when plenty of men who shared his political convictions had been dragged off to the war. They were dead now, many of them; the rest were weary cannon-fodder. He, though, had been given the opportunity to do something useful. His duty. If the driver had believed in God, he might have thanked him for that hip joint.

The lorry stood where he had parked it eleven hours before. The only trouble with this part of the scheme was that one fine night the whole shooting-box might get stolen by one of the gangs who worked the main roads in the blackout, but that was an unavoidable risk. The only one? He liked to think so. Using his powerful arms and his good leg, the driver heaved himself up into the cab of his pre-war Leyland ten-tonner with surprising ease. Being a bit of a cripple made you very aware of your body. In a funny sort of way you used it more efficiently. When it showed its limitations, you just fell back on basic animal cunning.

He pulled out onto the road and drove the eight miles south slowly, with the regulation masked headlights, because the road was slippery from the rain and there were nasty crosswinds. He carried on across the roundabout at Elstree. The transport café lay a couple of hundred yards from Stanmore station, the terminus of the London underground's Bakerloo line.

The café was a low brick building which puffed itself up with the 'roadhouse' tag that had been fashionable before the war, but really it was no more than the usual greasy spoon, making do with what customers it could get now that the private petrol ration had been abolished. Some kids from the suburb of Stanmore. Otherwise long-distance drivers like himself, the odd 'essential user' who could still get fuel for his aging bull-nose Morris, and of course the army. Not forgetting the Yanks, God rot 'em, who always seemed to have plenty of everything.

Inside in the warm, the driver ordered his usual tea and corned-beef sandwich. There was a party of glum-looking servicemen in the corner, a couple of older men in cloth caps, probably just come off shift work and having a cup of tea before walking to the station to catch the first tube train. The driver had visited the place often enough in the past fifteen months to draw a nod of recognition and a routine remark about the weather from the plump Welshman who owned it.

'Filthy out, in't it?' the Welshman said, shoving a steaming pint mug of tea across the counter. 'You'll have to hang on a minute for the sandwich. The missus is still makin' them up round the back.'

He had at least three chins, did the Welshman, and a mass of greying, greasy hair that hung down over his shirt collar. He probably thought it made him a ringer for old Lloyd George. To the driver he looked more like a great white woman.

'Yes, feels as though the winter's never goin' to end, and it's not even Christmas yet,' he agreed politely. 'As if the ruddy war wasn't enough to be going on with, eh?'

The driver's voice was surprisingly gentle, obviously cockney but not without culture. He spoke to Maggie Austin the way he did because she expected it, didn't know any better. In fact he was proud of his correct grammar; he had read books, if only people knew.

'Of course, there's some got it worse,' the Welshman responded eagerly. 'My son's on the Murmansk convoys, see. So cold you can't imagine. A U-boat puts you in the drink and you're finished. Freezing water kills you in five minutes. The missus can't sleep at nights for worrying about him, and that's the truth. She has nightmares . . .'

'Can't say I blame her, Taff. Still, look at the way the Russkies are givin' Hitler what for. That's thanks to blokes like your son, isn't it?'

Then, to the driver's relief, the sandwich arrived through the hatch behind the counter. He nodded his farewell, made his way over to a table well away from the other customers and the Welshman's whining tongue. The simple-mindedness of people like that had long since ceased to amaze him. They wanted a war where nobody got killed, a cosy, fireside war where all that mattered were the bulletins on the radio, like football results on a Saturday afternoon. All you had to do was use your loaf and say the right thing, even if it was obviously hypocritical or untrue, and you had them eating out of your hand. It was why these people were so easy to rule.

He worried at his sandwich, trying to stay outwardly calm. God knows why, but the few minutes beforehand always gave him a strange sort of thrill. Minutes passed.

At last it was time. He downed his tea, stood up, made for the Gents out the back.

'Blimey,' he said, grinning coyly at the Welshman. 'That's gone through like a dose of salts.'

'It's the ruddy bromide they put in it,' one of the servicemen in the far corner called out. Chuckles all round, anything to break the tedium.

The Gents consisted of a standup urinal and three cubicles. The urinal was filthy, the copper of the pipes mouldy green. Cigarette ends littered the concrete floor and clogged up the waste channel. Jesus, this place was what the upper class types he had met before the war would have called a bog, and no mistake. The driver came near to retching at the stench. He locked himself in the farmost cubicle, the appointed one, and was grateful for the small mercy of the door, which blocked out some of the stench.

Inside the cubicle, he listened. Then, satisfied that there was no one else about, the driver edged towards the back wall, raised one hand above his head and put his fingers over the left-hand rim of the cistern, holding on to the flush pipe for support. The oilskin wallet was taped to the inside by the ball cock. His fingers pressed against the wallet while his thumb prised off the tape, then moved down to give some extra purchase to his hold. Careful . . . don't let the bugger tip down into the water . . . With a practised upward curl of his fingers and a flick of the wrist, he hiked the wallet up over the edge of the cistern, then trapped it in the palm of his hand. The wallet, no longer than a tobacco pouch, went straight into the pocket of his jacket.

His hand was on the bolt of the cubicle door when he heard the sound of hinges creaking and steps moving across to the urinal. He paused, counted to ten, then coughed loudly, hawked a couple of times for added effect, and pulled the chain. He emerged to see one of the workmen standing at the urinal, idly humming to himself, preoccupied in enjoyment of an everyday physical function. Balding, about fifty, sturdy build.

The man glanced his way. 'Load off your mind, mate?' he said cheerfully.

The driver smiled and walked out into the café.

'See you, Taffy. Got to rush,' he called to the Welshman as he walked out through the door that led out into the car park.

Dawn was creeping timidly over the horizon, after the longest night of the year. Frosty, scarlet light. On his way back to his lorry, the driver experienced, as he often did afterwards, an almost overwhelming sense of elation. If he had been asked to describe the feeling, he would have said it was like being the only really free man left in England, the one who could cock a snook at that old bloodsucker, Churchill, his big-business friends, and the mealy-mouthed Labour politicians who claimed to speak for the British nation, for people like himself. By doing what he did, his duty, the driver was helping to ruin their little plans. Things would be different in a year or so; things would turn out absolutely different to what those bastards in power expected.

All the driver had to do now was to drop the wallet off at an empty house in Bedford. He would also collect the envelope that was waiting there for him on the table in the hall, with his expenses and the extra petrol coupons to compensate him for his detour. Then he would drive back to London and kill some time before clocking in. The man who couldn't run had never met any of the other links in the chain—for security reasons, naturally—but he knew the wallet always got to its far-off, alien destination. Meanwhile, he was well looked after for doing his duty. After all, the driver was an important man. A maker of History with a capital aitch.

4

Of course, he couldn't tell him everything, Sir Stewart Menzies reasoned, but it was time the ground was prepared for the next stage, after Lisbon. Even if Jackie Bellingham didn't know it yet, he was in deep. And, Lord help him, Menzies needed to use a man he could see as a friend, someone he could trust.

Menzies turned away from the window with the view of

the park and drained the last of his sherry, gesturing for his guest to do the same.

'Those were certainly the days,' he said. 'Old Quex ruled the Service with the proverbial rod of iron. He was the patriarch and we were all family—in some cases, literally. When he passed away to glory, d'you know who trudged round London, emptying his dead-letter drops? His faithful sister, Evelyn . . .'

Bellingham chuckled, took his pipe out of his mouth and obediently finished his drink. It felt good to be back in harness, if only on a temporary basis. The last few weeks, ever since Stewart had contacted him out of the blue, had been nerve-wracking. Nevertheless, he wouldn't have missed them for the world. His meeting with that young Abwehr buck in Lisbon showed that he had lost none of his skill, or his sharpness; and above all there was the joy of discussing things openly, of being himself and not some pompous expatriate port-pusher. Like a second chance at living, just when he had been about to give up, when he had felt himself drifting down the quiet stream to senility.

'I suppose you're awash with snotty intellectuals now,' Bellingham said. 'Always the same in the Service when there's a war on: the powers-that-be get in a panic and start buying up job lots from the universities and the merchant banks. They think the gentlemen can't manage on their own, got to get some players.'

'We've expanded a great deal since Quex died and I took over. Inevitable, and in many respects beneficial, but one does lose some of the sense of trust and community. In fact, Jackie old chap, that's more or less what I want to talk to you about . . . over lunch.'

They put on their coats and hats. Menzies pointed to a green, leather-padded door set in the far wall of his office. 'We shall go by the back door,' he said. 'The traditional path to enlightenment for our kind.'

It was an old joke, but Bellingham smiled dutifully. The rear entrance was a privilege of 'C' and of 'C' alone, permitting the head of the Secret Service to emerge into Queen Anne's Gate at a discreet distance from the ugly modern office building round the corner in Broadway that housed the headquarters of SIS. Like the privilege itself, the well-trodden stair carpet and rickety lift dated from the early years of the century, when the Service had been created in its present form.

They came out into the street through a door that was indistinguishable from a hundred others in the vicinity. With its coat of brown paint over oak and its ornate Victorian knocker, it looked like the entrance to the town house of a family roosting peacefully in the upper reaches of the British aristocracy, used perhaps when its members were in London for the social season or had duties at court to attend to. Indeed, Menzies himself had been commissioned into the Life Guards in the reign of King Edward VII, and had ridden escort to the coronation carriage of his successor; by birth and education he belonged to the tiny, exclusive élite whose village this square mile of London was, houses and clubs scattered between the twin castle keeps of Whitehall and Buckingham Palace. It had always been Sir Stewart Menzies' advantage that he fitted in. As he and Bellingham strolled through the light drizzle to his club a few hundred yards away, Menzies seemed the epitome of the man-about-clubland. Standing well over six feet, slim and imposingly handsome for all his fifty-two years, he towered above the fleshy, rubicund Bellingham, whose manner was appropriately, if subtly, deferential. Had it not been the taller man who held the umbrella for their shelter, an observer might have taken the pair of them for an ageing Bertie Wooster and his ever-faithful Jeeves.

Menzies' choice of club, White's, was convivial, close-knit, and High Tory, properly reflecting the image he liked to present, that of an affable drone with a family estate in Wiltshire where he passed his time riding to hounds, shooting, and cultivating very extensive gardens. After their coats had been taken and Menzies had picked up some messages left for him at the porter's desk, they walked at an easy pace to the dining room. On the way he exchanged carefully-modulated grunts of homage with other White's tribesmen who happened to look up from their crisp copies of *The Times* and the *Telegraph*. It may have been a criminal offence to disclose Menzies' position, or even the whereabouts of SIS headquarters, to the general public, but most of his fellow-members had a sound inkling of what Menzies did. Conversation, let alone speculation, was unfitting when he brought a stranger to lunch.

They were given a table well away from the other diners. Menzies smiled apologetically when the waiter brought the day's menu for the selection.

'Onion soup again, I see,' he sighed. 'I'm afraid it's pretty well standard these days. Two years ago, one couldn't obtain an onion for love or money. There was even an ode to the wretched vegetable in a popular newspaper. Now they've increased production twentyfold, and of course one can't get anything else. *C'est la guerre*. But I think,' he added with a wink, 'that the club's stock of claret might just outlast Hitler—provided we don't take too unconscionably long a time polishing the blighter off.'

They reminisced during the soup course and into the meat—no fish course to precede it these days, by law—with that brand of selective jollity that is usually possible a quarter of a century after terrible events, particularly if those events took place when life was youth, strength and idealism. The second bottle of Mouton Rothschild '34 had arrived before Menzies eased himself into serious business, moving smoothly from nostalgic recollection to the less rosy present.

He raised the first glass from the new bottle. 'Well, here's to that old devil, Canaris. Should auld acquaintance be forgot . . . He'll have remembered Jackie Bellingham.'

'I suppose so, Stewart. Perhaps after wracking his brains a bit, consulting his famous card index, and then consulting it again to make sure.'

'Oh, come on. You're too modest. You and I sent him scuttling out of Algeciras with his tail between his legs in '17. Gave him the fright of his life. He won't have forgotten that—or you—in a hurry.'

'Anyway,' Bellingham said, 'I wouldn't have minded being a fly on the wall when that young Prussian reported back to him after our meeting.' He toyed with his napkin, waiting for Menzies to get to the point. He had noticed the ground being prepared and knew that he would not be kept in suspense for much longer.

Menzies nodded slowly, leaning back in his chair with his hands planted on the tablecloth like a participant in a seance.

'Yes. Yes. Yes,' he agreed, as if Bellingham had said something very profound. 'Absolutely. It would make the decision about the Abwehr's offer a lot easier.'

'You're still thinking it over, then,' Bellingham said quickly.

'In a way. Though we can hardly turn Canaris down flat, for any number of reasons.'

Almost there. Bellingham frowned. 'So you're in, are you? I mean, in the game.'

'Yes. And I'd rather use the first person plural, Jackie. "We" are in. You and me. I want you to handle further negotiations. You did tremendously well in Lisbon . . . Ah . . .'

'All right. All right.' Bellingham was surprised and more than a little shocked at the irritation in his own voice, at the fear and confusion he felt well up inside at the thought of continuing to be involved in and responsible for this business.

'I want you to do it. I trust you, you see, Jackie.'

Bellingham nodded. 'Yes. Of course,' he said. There could be no serious argument when Stewart appealed like that. But the uneasiness remained.

'Stout man,' said Menzies with feeling. He looked more relieved than Bellingham would have expected. A sudden flash of humanity, vulnerability. 'I can see why you'd be doubtful, and I admire you for overcoming your reservations.'

They sat for a few seconds looking at—or rather, slightly past—each other, as if embarrassed by the intense little exchange. Bellingham thought he should say something in the way of explanation. This was an important step, for God's sake.

'It's not the practical aspect, really,' he murmured. 'That makes a kind of sense. And Canaris's young man wasn't particularly objectionable from the personal point of view, for all his Prussian airs . . . It's . . . well, just that I find it hard to accept that we can treat with these people. The affair feels unclean. I mean, even a completely lapsed Jew can't help baulking when pork chops are on the menu for dinner—' Bellingham shrugged at the incongruity of his own comparison. 'We've been stung before.' He looked up from the tablecloth, saw Menzies' eyes on him, curious, friendly, and also probing. 'I may have got out of touch with the inner workings of the Service,' he said with a sigh, 'but I heard about Venlo—it was the talk of Lisbon. And that, Stewart, was the last time we trusted a German bleeding heart—at least, so far as I know. Two valuable chaps ended up in a Gestapo torture chamber for their pains. How sure are you that this present offer is genuine?'

Menzies had winced visibly at Bellingham's mention of the so-called 'Venlo Incident.' In November 1939, two high-ranking British Intelligence officers based in the then-neutral Hague had been lured to the German border to meet a fake member of the German Resistance. They had been kidnapped in broad daylight, carted across into Germany. The fiasco had occurred within weeks of Quex's death, when Menzies had taken over as acting head of SIS, and had almost cost him confirmation in his job. The affair still rankled. His response when Bellingham had said his piece was slightly sharp.

'Venlo was engineered by Schellenberg and the Sicherheitsdienst—the exact same people that Canaris is out to dish at the moment. I can assure you there's absolutely no love lost between the SD and the Abwehr, none at all.'

'That may be true, but it doesn't answer my question,' Bellingham persisted.

Menzies smiled in reluctant recognition of Bellingham's stubbornness. 'Oh, believe me, Jackie,' he said, injecting some of the old warmth back into his voice, 'I have no rosy illusions about the Abwehr. It wouldn't be the first time they've tried to pull a fast one and sow suspicion in the ranks of the great and good of the Service. Nevertheless, we have to make some kind of a response, for if their story is true, then we have to set our house in order before considerable damage is done to the war effort. The thought of a traitor in our midst, occupying a position of responsibility and trust is appalling, almost inconceivable, but—' He threw up his hands in a gesture of despair.

'Worth a gamble, if need be,' Bellingham finished for him. 'A small investment of men and lives. And I'm referring to the second part of the proposed bargain. The real Greek gift.'

'I prefer to see it as a mutually advantageous agreement,' Menzies said with quiet firmness. 'I have the PM's approval for the project. We are in favour of any course of action, however drastic or unorthodox at first sight, which could save lives or perhaps shorten the war.'

Bellingham was tiring of this endless talking round the subject. A brief glance over his shoulder told him that there was only one member still at lunch in the club's dining room, a very elderly gent who seemed to have nodded off half way through his meal.

'Assassinating the Führer is drastic and unorthodox and that's for sure,' he said, partly out of devilment. 'But who'll be doing it for us—or should I say, for the Abwehr?'

Menzies did not react to Bellingham's rather adolescent indiscretion. He was aware that there was no one else within earshot. His answer rang hard and matter-of-fact.

'There will be no shortage of volunteers. There never is. We had no problem finding people when Heydrich was dealt with; this time, we'll use our own people, for a number of reasons.'

'You mean, SIS people?'

'Probably not, actually. Chaps from the British regular forces, with a smattering of special training and a few relevant skills. I personally don't want the Service directly involved, and neither does the PM. For security reasons. We don't know who the spy is, or where he is. Better to stick to Army men.'

'Who presumably will know what they're in for?'

Menzies nodded. 'When it really matters, yes. But these are early days yet, Jackie. We don't know the place where it will happen, either. For the moment, all you need concern yourself with is talking to Canaris's man. I'll be making one or two preliminary . . . ah . . . contingency arrangements via the Prime Minister's office. Our project isn't a Service affair, not in the usual sense. I suppose this counts as a warning of sorts.'

'Surely you can't ignore the Service altogether,' Bellingham said with mingled disquiet and awe.

'No. Certain individuals will be involved, but none of them will be more than partially aware of what the project concerns. In particular, no one will know anything about you or your role.'

Bellingham must have shown something of his disappointment, because Menzies softened his manner.

'I hope that's not too much of a blow, old boy,' he said. 'Stands to reason you'd be looking forward to meeting some of the old crowd again—those who are left—and wallowing in the *esprit de corps* . . . but I'm afraid it's just not on. Today's visit to Broadway was your last, Jackie. In future we meet elsewhere. Just the two of us. But there'll be plenty to keep you busy.'

The sparse remains of their chops and vegetables had been cleared away and the sweet course, apple tart, arrived. Ever the considerate host, Menzies topped up Bellingham's glass with more claret. It didn't do to waste good wine, he joked, and never mind prewar etiquette. That was suspended for the duration, like *habeas corpus*. However, he added only a little to his own glass; he had seen Bellingham's second look of dismay, this time the nervousness of the serious drinker who fears that the bibbing has to stop. So Bellingham had developed a weakness, he noted; but better it was a taste for the bottle than for women—or boys—or money, or the desire for notoriety. Jackie was apparently free of the more exotic vices. And he could trust him, at a time when he could trust few others. Menzies decided to tell Bellingham so.

'So. I may call on you to do some organizing as well as talking, Jackie. It'll mean some running about, and at our age this may seem a mite undignified . . .'

'Dignity be damned,' Bellingham said, sipping the wine with ill-concealed thirst. 'Though I thought you had young, fit minions at your beck and call. Continue.'

Menzies smiled, ladelling thin cream onto his pie.

'True, I have plenty of chaps. Rather more than I can easily manage, as I said. That's why you're so precious to me. Because our problem is an insider, and you—I hope you won't be offended—have been on the outside these past years.'

'Don't spare me, Stewart. I know,' Bellingham said. He laughed, really quite convincingly.

'And you're old school, Jackie. I know you won't let me down.'

Bellingham nodded in mild embarrassment at the compliment. 'That depends on the amount of physical exertion involved,' he warned. 'The spirit is willing, but you know how it is with the flesh.'

'No field stuff, no roughhouse. To tell you the truth, I'm not yet precisely certain what you'll have to do. For now we'll keep you meeting your young Prussian, and then we'll talk again when things have become clearer.'

Without waiting for Bellingham to answer, Menzies ordered brandy. He turned and cast an eye at the ancient diner whom Bellingham had seen asleep over his lunch earlier.

'That's General Speaight-Babbington,' Menzies explained with a chuckle, as if the other matter was now closed. 'Ninety-something, commanded a regiment in the South African War. Rumour has it that when Field Marshal Smuts flew in to visit the PM recently, the General was convinced he had come to beg for peace on behalf of the Boers. Ah, to have the luxury of a choice of enemies.'

'Not to mention a choice of friends,' Bellingham said.

'Harder to manage. A good deal harder.'

Jackie Bellingham might drink too much, Menzies reflected, but he had always possessed a talent for unconsciously saying the right thing at the wrong moment. He switched the conversation to personal matters. No point in risking things at this early stage.

'So, are you comfortable?' he asked. 'I'm told that Brown's is still a decent place to lay one's head.'

'Very good. No complaints. I gather they put on a good Christmas, shortages permitting.'

'I see. You won't be spending it with the family?'

Bellingham made a wry face. 'James is with the Lancers in North Africa. Charlie's spending some of his holidays with his mother, or with friends. I must say I couldn't face more rows with Charlotte and that frightful new husband of hers. Not fair on the boy . . .'

'He must be more than a boy now.'

'He's sixteen. Seventeen in April. Perhaps I might pop down and see him at school. Term starts a week next Monday, I think.'

'Take this opportunity to visit him,' Menzies suggested.

'I know that you haven't seen much of each other lately, because of the travel difficulties. I'm sure I won't need you for a little while yet, and I can always contact you should anything really urgent come up.'

Bellingham's pain showed. Both he and Menzies were divorced men. Sir Stewart's marriage, to the daughter of the 8th Earl De La Warr, had broken up in the mid-Thirties, with all the markings of a notable society scandal. Fortunately, the establishment had looked after its own, and the details had been kept out of the press. It was in no one's interests, after all, to have such a distinguished officer and leading figure at court forced to sue his wife for adultery. Menzies had licked his wounds and later remarried, apparently very happily. Bellingham's case was sadder. He had married at thirty-five to a girl just over half his age and whisked her off to Portugal with high hopes. She had borne him two sons, but then had begun to succumb to expatriate tedium, the disease that wilted so many English roses forced to root themselves abroad. Other men's wives gave in, lost themselves forever in organizing socially incestuous dinner parties, bullying the servants, living for their children, but not Charlotte Bellingham. She had issued him with an ultimatum: she and the boys, then nine and six, were off back to England, with or without Jackie. And he had stayed—he still wasn't sure why, because no one would have forced him to, not the Service or anyone—and by the time he considered changing his mind it was too late. His wife had met another man in London, where she had been living with the boys, and pretty soon she wasn't his wife any more. These were times when people moved quickly. Jackie Bellingham's marital history was commonplace and entirely preventable.

'Yes, perhaps I shall try,' Bellingham said. 'Charlie's at Radley, only about an hour by train from town. So long as you're not in a hurry.'

'Hurry?' Menzies said. 'Perish the thought. I know we've got to start the ball rolling, but on the other hand we don't want to appear too desperate. In any case, Canaris is a good Lutheran. He believes that one must suffer to attain one's goals. Let him work hard for his success.'

His concluding smile reflected a life in which very few things had not been attained with the very greatest of ease.

5

Shortly before midnight in the silver pine forest beyond the barbed wire, mean temperatures reached twenty-seven degrees below zero. Comfortable Western European man, who fancied himself civilized, could not imagine Russian cold such as this until he was forced to experience it; and when he did, it brought out the old savage. At his *dacha* headquarters three miles from the shattered city of Smolensk, Field Marshal Günther Hans von Kluge switched his liqueur glass from his right to his left hand to receive some death warrants. He signed the execution orders with a weary flourish and handed them back to his adjutant. Only then did it occur to him to ask the details.

'Partisans?' he said.

'Yes, Field Marshal.'

'*Francs-tireurs* are the scum of war. They shoot soldiers in the back. No one can blame us for acting severely against such people.'

'Certainly not, Field Marshal.'

'You may go.'

The commander of the Wehrmacht's Army Group Centre turned reluctantly on his heel and stepped back through into his living quarters, closing the door behind him. He had been called out in mid-conference to authorize the executions, but in a way the grim duty had come as a relief. Conference, indeed. More like an interrogation.

'So. Where were we, gentlemen?' he asked with the sardonic smile he used to hide his discomfiture, easing his tall frame down into a high-backed chair in front of the crackling log fire. 'I believe that you had done with the theoretical aspects of persuading a General Field Marshal to abandon his oath of loyalty and were proceeding to the precise mechanics.'

Major von Schlabrendorff shook his head. 'Field Marshal, others will deal with Hitler once he is here at your headquarters. Front-hardened veterans, members of Boeselager's commando squad. All we need is your support—even your tolerance would do. Once Hitler is out of the way—'

'Yes, yes. You've told me a hundred times,' von Kluge grumbled. 'When Adolf has finally got his come-uppance and lies in a pool of blood under my lunch table, then everything will be wine and roses, and I shall be the new Germany's man of the hour, et cetera, et cetera.'

He turned his leonine head to his right in appeal to Colonel Henning von Tresckow, his senior operations officer.

'Henning,' he said, 'I know you're one of these liberty-or-death characters yourself, but you'll back me up. We have exactly one hundred and sixty-seven tanks for the whole of Army Group Centre. Tell them: one hundred and sixty-seven! And you people sit here drinking my brandy and trying to convince me it's time we staged a civil war!'

Tresckow sighed. 'True, Field Marshal. But you must be aware of why we are so short of vital equipment. Vast resources are being transferred to support the activities of the SS murder squads. Incompetence and corruption in the party and industry, even in the Wehrmacht, are tolerated by Hitler in order to keep his henchmen happy. Under his leadership, Germany cannot win this war.'

There was a short silence. It seemed as if the colonel's argument had hit home. Then von Kluge chuckled slyly.

'Ah, but can we win the war without him, eh?' he said, helping himself to some more Cointreau from the bottle by his chair. 'When the Ivans threw us back in front of Moscow last winter, the entire General Staff were running around like demented chickens, squawking that the situation was lost. Our Adolf, though, just issued his lunatic orders and somehow, don't ask me how, the line held. The swine's got something. You can't deny it.'

'With respect, Field Marshal, I doubt if General von Paulus would agree with you if he were able to be here,' the third officer said quietly. Oberleutnant Bredow, conscious of his junior status, had let the others talk to the great man. He was an outsider from Berlin; Tresckow and Schlabrendorff had paid their dues in Russia, and had earned the right to beard von Kluge in his lair. For a moment the Field Marshal glanced at him in irritation, then nodded gloomily.

'Stalingrad. Yes, Stalingrad,' he muttered. 'Poor wretches.'

'And who will be next, Field Marshal?' Schlabrendorff said, swiftly taking his cue from Bredow.

This time, von Kluge did not reply. Upright and fit, a sixty-year-old whose impressive features might have been hewn from oak, he embodied the proud traditions of the Prussian warlord. At the front, striding from position to position, he was a great morale-booster, a heartening sight to his men. No one could accuse him of cowardice, stupidity, or lack of energy as a leader of men at war. It was only under these circumstances, faced with a moral and political decision, that the Field Marshal shrank to normal human stature. For a full minute he sat in silence with his fingers curled round a tumbler of liqueur, staring into the fire like any man who has lived most of his allotted life span and despairs of ever putting the world to rights.

'There is only one way to stop this criminal slaughter, Field Marshal. You know that,' von Tresckow said, breaking into von Kluge's thoughts. 'Without Hitler, there is a chance that peace can be achieved honourably, leaving the Germany we love intact for future generations.'

Von Kluge roused himself slowly. 'You may be right, Henning.' Suddenly he glanced at Bredow with a new interest. 'You are Admiral Canaris's representative here, young man,' he said. 'Are you here simply to listen to the old arguments? Or do you have something to contribute?'

Bredow glanced for support to the others. Tresckow nodded almost imperceptibly, looking down to light a cigarette. Schlabrendorff shrugged.

'The Admiral had indeed asked me to broach another line of attack,' he said. 'He permitted me to mention that some other method of . . . removing the Führer from the political scene might be a serious possibility. A method that would—will—not involve German officers breaking their oath of loyalty to their commander-in-chief, and that would leave intact the fabric of trust between the Wehrmacht and the German people. The Admiral feels that the Field Marshal could find this more tolerable than any previously discussed alternative, on both moral and practical grounds.'

'You mean: we get someone else to bump off Adolf?'

Von Kluge had taken several large gulps of Cointreau while Bredow was speaking. Now he was smiling incredulously, shaking his head like a raw subaltern being forced to listen to the regimental tall story. 'Who?'

Another check around the company. A deep breath on Bredow's part. 'The British, Field Marshal. The Secret Service.'

The commander of Army Group Centre reached urgently for the bottle, gesturing for Bredow to explain more fully.

'Thus,' Bredow said, 'we shall be able to assume power under very much more favourable circumstances, untainted by direct involvement in Hitler's death. Even the most fanatical Nazis will be convinced that all patriots must unite to save the Reich. And the SS, who are responsible for Hitler's personal safety, will be severely discredited. I am sure that the Field Marshal can work out further advantages if given time for thought.'

Von Kluge stared back into the fire. He was taking deep breaths, frowning.

'It is an outrageous notion,' he announced finally. 'But then these are outrageous times. And if it would save our resolve to fight on here being weakened by fears of another stab-in-the-back, a repeat performance of 1918.'

'It goes without saying that any government that came to power under such circumstances would stand a very good chance of British approval, Field Marshal.'

'Giving us a secure western flank. We could fight on here if necessary.'

'Churchill and his Conservatives were always strongly anti-Communist,' Tresckow cut in eagerly. 'Under favourable circumstances, they might quickly become disinclined to featherbed Stalin. They might even lend tacit support to an anti-Communist crusade, if it were to be pursued in a civilized manner.'

Von Kluge raised a shaggy eyebrow at Tresckow's bold suggestion. He was still a little sceptical, but he no longer dismissed such projections out of hand.

'Many things might be possible,' he said guardedly. 'Of course, the British may demand the return of Hanover or some such . . .'

Bredow smiled. 'A bargain is in the making, Field

Marshal. It may cost the SD a bloody nose, that is all. And the SD, along with the SS, will become defunct when the Führer becomes defunct.'

The Field Marshal slapped his thigh and let out a snort of amusement.

'Canaris and his skulduggery!' he said. 'I am a simple soldier. I tell you: I do not intend to break my oath and allow the Führer to be shot like a wild beast in my headquarters. But if he were to meet his end by enemy action, I would naturally support the reestablishment of order.' He winked. 'And like many senior officers, I would be only too delighted to deal with the SS if its leaders were to attempt to seize power in the wake of Hitler's death.'

'Do I take it, then, that the Field Marshal will take a positive view of the Army's assumption of ultimate authority in the state under such circumstances?' Bredow asked.

'Inevitable, my boy. Who else would be in a position to take over the country except Himmler and his butchers? We would have to step in quickly.'

'Thank you, Field Marshal.'

The gathering broke up twenty minutes later. Von Kluge needed his sleep, and he had already begun to show signs of back-pedalling. Tresckow, Schlabrendorff and Bredow paused outside the *dacha,* coat collars turned against the wind, voices as thin as the freezing air, to say their farewells. Bredow was due back in Berlin, while Tresckow had his reports to write up before the morning.

'Well, Otto,' the colonel said to Bredow. 'There you have it. Von Kluge is typical of his breed: order him to die at the head of his troops, and he will obey without question. Ask him to cooperate in ridding his country of a monster and he becomes a quivering mass of indecision. But this time he will stick with us, I feel it in my bones. So long as the British involvement doesn't backfire. Then we shan't see his highly distinguished person for dust.'

'The Admiral told me to mention the British only if I felt it necessary, colonel. I judged, during the course of our conversation, that the Field Marshal was about to escape us for good, pleading his oath of loyalty, blood under his lunch table, all the rest.' Bredow stood hunched. He smiled stiffly, swaying in the fearsome cold. 'The same goes for the other senior officers who play the loyalty card. They are not necessarily worried about failure, concerned for their own skins. Like von Kluge, most of them are brave men. But they are obsessed with their reputations. Their overriding concern is that the German people, not forgetting the history books of the future, should not be able to hold them personally responsible for the assassination of Hitler. Murder is a vulgar, even a squalid business. If the Secret Service does the job, the British can be blamed, and therefore all is well.'

Tresckow nodded, conceding the point. 'You were quite right to tell the Field Marshal. I find your arguments depressingly convincing.' His face was solemn and corpse-pale in the moonlight. He hacked moodily at the packed snow under foot with one boot heel. 'I will do my best to ensure that von Kluge is absolutely with us when the moment comes. Provided Canaris's plan works, he will be. And now I must go. *Au revoir*. Fabian will fix you up with a car to the airfield. And good luck . . .'

They touched hands like boxers rather than take off their mittens. The stocky colonel shuffled off towards his office in the low prefabricated block next to the *dacha*, huddling into his threadbare fur coat. Bredow and Schlabrendorff made their way back to the major's living quarters, where Bredow had been sleeping on a camp bed during his two-day visit.

The Russian stove in the hut had been stoked up by Schlabrendorff's batman during their absence. They stood for some while in the tiny room, luxuriating in the dry heat and the acrid-sweet ordour of woodsmoke after their walk through the snow. Schlabrendorff came back to life first. He coughed, motioned for Bredow to shed his coat, then pulled off his mittens and fumbled with the cupboard door of the locker in the corner, eventually producing a bottle of vodka and two glasses.

'The wine of the country,' he announced. 'Forget your namby-pamby headquarters drink, flown in from Paris. This is the stuff the Wehrmacht runs on in Russia.'

The vodka was an officers' brand, but it still burned the throat like a swig of petrol. After a while, Bredow noted, it also had a curious mixed effect, enlivening and anaesthetizing at the same time. Within a few minutes battle had been joined within his nervous system. Schlabrendorff, however, had already taken his glass and was pouring him another dose.

'Cheers. Merry Christmas. May it be the last under the Swastika,' the major toasted cheerfully. Then he turned to the telephone to see if he could arrange some transport to the airfield in the morning. After some argument and cajoling of the motor pool, he rang off. 'At six,' he said. 'Though God knows how long it will take in this weather. The only positive aspect is that the partisans may have decided it was too cold to bother mining the road.'

'Let's hope they're wise enough to stay home and drink this stuff,' Bredow mused. 'I can't see anyone wielding a paper clip, let alone a PPsh-41, after a couple of these.'

Suddenly, he realized, the anaesthetic effect was winning. After the initial surge of fiery energy, his body felt dreamily fatigued, as if he was being gently buried in thick, thick snow. His dissatisfaction with von Kluge despite the progress that had been made, his longing to get back to Berlin, even his commitment to the cause that had brought him here, were becoming vague abstracts, totally insignificant in the face of a simple urge to collapse onto the hard camp bed a few yards away.

Schlabrendorff clapped him on the shoulder; not hard, but enough to make Bredow come close to losing his footing.

'You speak from practical experience, I see,' he said. 'But please try to stay awake long enough to hear me out, Otto.'

Bredow nodded, fighting hard. Schlabrendorff's voice seemed to hum in his frost-burned ears like a swarm of bees.

'Tell the Admiral,' he heard Schlabrendorff say, 'that the price of failure with the British will be the loss of von Kluge. You must make that clear to him. Are you listening, Otto?'

'Yes . . . I'm listening . . .'

'You know, I call Tresckow the Field Marshal's watchmaker. He starts on him every morning, working to convince him of the need to overthrow Hitler. He winds him up all day, and we think we have the Field Marshal. Then, come the morning, Tresckow finds that von Kluge has been having doubts again, and so he patiently starts the whole process once more. If he can whisper in his ear every night, "the British are with us, Field Marshal . . ." then we shall be home and dry. We shall have the most powerful commander on the eastern front on our side. If not, the consequences could be disastrous. We shall be worse off than before you mentioned the British. Do you understand?'

'Yes, major. Absolutely.'

With a final drowsy whisper of assent, Bredow slumped down onto the bed, fully clothed, and was asleep.

Schlabrendorff poured himself another glass from the bottle and drank it slowly, gazing down at the still form of the Oberleutnant on the camp bed. He found himself hoping, for Bredow's sake, that his head for conspiracy was stronger than his head for the brutal wine of Russia.

Eleven hours after leaving Smolensk, Bredow landed at Staaken airfield, south-west of Berlin, where he was met by an Abwehr car. Shortly after six, he and Canaris were strolling along the Spree in the dull winter twilight. By contrast with the travel-weary Bredow, the Admiral seemed in lively, even ebullient form, intent on discussing the devil he kept in his office.

The devil had actually been presented to Canaris by the Japanese Military Attaché. It was a brilliantly-coloured painting of a grimacing *Dai Itoku Myo-o,* the wrathful aspect of the Buddha, and the Admiral counted it among the handful of possessions that he really treasured, along with his signed photograph of Generalissimo Franco of Spain, an old acquaintance from the First War, and the venerable army cot in which he often took a nap after lunch or slept the night when urgent business kept him from his home at Wannsee.

'My painting is grotesque,' he was explaining. 'But it is also ridiculous. That is all part of the artist's intention. Similarly, the Japanese as a nation are fanatical and cruel, yet they possess a truly cosmic sense of humour, a feeling for irony that goes beyond good and evil to the essential absurdity of the human condition. They will recover from this war more quickly than we Germans, you know,' Canaris said, wagging an admonitory finger at Bredow.

'They will accept the consequences of defeat—the humiliation, the blame and punishment—philosophically as their collective karma. And why not? To the truly religious oriental, there are no absolutes. That is why the devil, too, must have his funny side.'

He broke off to whistle his two dachshunds to heel. The small dogs followed him everywhere, scuttling around his office, dozing under his desk, even accompanying him to conferences of the High Command. To Bredow they often seemed like a kind of visual pun: tiny, bright-eyed, slyly inquisitive, contrary and stubborn in ways that the observer could never quite pin down, like their owner. Canaris's relationship with them was marked by an intensity of feeling absent from his attitude to all but a very few of his fellow human beings. Now that his wife and daughter had been evacuated to the peace of Bavaria for the duration, the dogs provided a fixed point in the Abwehr chief's life, around which all else could, and did, revolve as crazily as it wished. Bredow considered the weather mild after Smolensk, but the Admiral had wrapped up tightly against the cold airstream that funnelled through the streets of the Reich capital. The short, square figure beside the Oberleutnant bulged with sweaters under his naval greatcoat, and a thick red-and-blue knitted muffler protected his throat.

They had walked five hundred metres west from the Tirpitzufer headquarters to the Friedrich Wilhelm Bridge, and Canaris had talked about everything, it seemed, except the matter which had taken Bredow to Russia. It was his way.

The dogs ran back and leapt up playfully at the Admiral, who patted their heads and beamed paternally. As he did so he suddenly said, without looking at Bredow:

'I have decided to call this affair *Wintermärchen*. Heine rather than Shakespeare.'

He knelt and chucked one of the dogs in the soft folds of its throat, answering its friendly growl with a monotone greeting of his own, a low, gravelly sigh. Bredow lit a cigarette, shivered slightly in the damp atmosphere of the riverside. Perhaps the Admiral had been right to wear so many layers of clothes; here was a different kind of cold. *A Winter's Tale* was, in fact, a suitable choice for a codename. It referred to a bitter satirical poem by the great

Jewish poet and democrat, Heinrich Heine, who had been exiled from Germany by other oppressors a hundred years ago and had fought back with words, the only weapons that lay to hand—just as the Admiral's pressure on the British took the form of information, a story, rather than military force.

'Let's hope we have a reply soon,' Bredow commented drily. 'Otherwise the codename will no longer be so seasonable, Admiral.'

Canaris straightened up and turned to the promenade rail overlooking the Spree. He shrugged and thrust his gloved hands into the pockets of his coat.

'I allowed for delays. That is why we had to make the initial approach so quickly. Menzies has to tread carefully. He is a powerful figure, but he dare not proceed against the wishes of his political masters.'

'You think that they might tie his hands?'

'Unlikely in the extreme. But what of your own discussions at Army Group Centre?' Canaris asked, abruptly changing the subject.

Late homegoing commuters were hurrying past them on their way to the nearby Budapester Strasse underground station. Some were in uniform, but most were civil servants and clerks from the surrounding government offices. Their faces were drawn and anxious, grey amongst the grey, reflecting a new harshness in conditions on the home front as the third full year of the war neared its end. These people would be eager to reach the relative safety of their homes in the suburbs before night brought the threat of Allied bombers. Bredow waited until no one was in close earshot before he described the meeting at Smolensk. When he reached the point where von Kluge had referred to 'Canaris's skulduggery', the Admiral let out a snort of open contempt.

'Our pure-as-snow Field Marshal will be grateful one day for the dirty tricks we are preparing now,' he said with some force. 'We shall save him and his kind all manner of embarrassment—and hand them Germany on a plate. Until then, he knows that he can wait by his warm fireside in Smolensk, dreaming of his hour of destiny in the knowledge that all is being taken care of.'

'The Admiral will permit me to observe that the Field

Marshal does not appear the most decisive of men in political matters,' Bredow said stiffly.

Canaris glanced at him to check that he was serious. 'That, Oberleutnant Bredow, is an understatement worthy of an Englishman. I can see that you were born to deal with such as Mister Bellingham.'

'Bellingham?'

'Your sparring-partner in Lisbon. I have looked him up in my files.' Canaris had his hands behind his back and was tapping one foot like an impatient schoolmaster. 'John Charles Darius Bellingham, known as "Jackie". Born Bridport, Dorset, 1885, son of a country priest. Commissioned 1914, served in Egypt until 1916 when recruited into MI6. Active in Spain and Portugal 1916–21 as an officer on active list, after 1921 as civilian employee. Thought to have been retired on pension 1931 as a result of departmental economies. Languages: Spanish, Portuguese, French, German, Arabic. Divorced—no adultery. Weaknesses: alcohol since retirement. No sexual or political deviations known.'

'I am surprised by the alcohol. He seemed very self-contained,' Bredow remarked. He had joined Canaris at the promenade rail because the Admiral seemed to be inviting a certain kind of intimacy.

Canaris smiled. 'When he is busy, he doesn't need the bottle. When he is bored, feels frustrated and useless . . .' He did not finish the sentence, merely made a throwaway gesture. 'Menzies would not risk employing him, in any case, if he were a complete, uncontrollable drunkard.'

'For old times' sake? They worked together in the last war in Spain, you said.'

'Menzies is no sentimentalist. He has faults, but that is not one of them. The recall of Bellingham to active duties must be the result of careful calculation. He needs a man who is not part of the present Intelligence establishment, who no longer has any close friends in MI6, who will not gossip, who has no political affiliations in the department. Above all, a man without ambition.'

Bredow would have liked to know precisely what Menzies' weaknesses were, but such a question might have been reckoned impertinent. Instead he said: 'Why without ambition, Admiral?'

'Because only a man who expects no personal advantage will follow Menzies with absolute loyalty,' Canaris explained, pleased at the opportunity to show off his understanding in matters of human behaviour. 'The ambitious man will be ruthless, but he will always hedge his bets in case things go wrong and his protector is discredited. Bellingham knows that whatever happens he will go back into retirement when this is over. He will do precisely what Menzies tells him to do, and then disappear obediently.'

To Bredow, Bellingham's fate sounded intolerably sad. He stood for some time in silence, staring down at the grey-green surface of the river and wondering if he would live long enough to be as useful—and as dispensable—as the Englishman, Bellingham.

After a while, Bredow glanced to his left and noticed that the Admiral was staring upwards at the darkening sky with a hint of the unspoken fear that oppressed everyone in Berlin these days. The light faded early in December, and any time soon the radio might announce that enemy bomber formations had been sighted crossing the Dutch coast in the direction of North Germany. 'Reich capital among possible targets'. Despite his unquestionable physical courage, Canaris had been known to admit that he loathed the random slaughter of air raids more than any other aspect of this war.

'A fairly clear night in prospect, I'm afraid, Admiral,' Bredow commented, for something else to say. 'But the RAF has been hitting us hard lately. Perhaps tonight it will be Hamburg's turn.'

Canaris said nothing. He turned away from the rail, embarrassed that Bredow had noticed his mannerism, and whistled to his dogs to show them that the time had come for them to return to the Tirpitzufer.

'You will remain in Berlin until we see some movement in *Wintermärchen*,' he announced when they had covered a part of the distance. 'I gather Colonel Oster has found you a plausible job, something to keep you out of harm's way?'

'Yes, Admiral. Using my Russian experience to collate reports from short-range line-crossing units. I seem to have ended up as a glorified filing-clerk, but the work means that I can be flexible in my arrangements.'

'Good. I shall have to ask you to be very flexible as *Wintermärchen* proceeds. Any problems, inform Oster. If he can't sort them out to your satisfaction, then inform me.'

'Thank you, Admiral.'

Canaris nodded benignly. 'Try to enjoy what there is left to enjoy in Berlin.'

He had switched to the familiar 'du' form, showing that he meant to speak as man to man. The serious talking was over.

'None of us can do very much until Menzies replies,' Canaris added. 'So relax. He will have to speak to us, for any number of reasons. There are wheels within wheels, my boy.'

They passed a newspaper vendor, and Canaris stopped to buy a copy of the *Berliner Nachtausgabe*. It was his invariable habit to stop at the news-stand while walking the dogs in the late afternoon when he was in Berlin, and a curious one for a man who knew so much that neither this nor any other newspaper in Hitler's Germany would ever print. The headline trumpeted a new 'defensive victory' on the Stalingrad perimeter. That meant a retreat. An 'ordered withdrawal' was really bad; it meant a massacre. The Admiral glanced impassively at the front page, permitted himself a shake of the head, then rolled up the newspaper and slipped it under one arm in a motion that was almost furtive.

'Some coffee, I think. To warm the blood,' he said, and headed across the cobbled street towards the Abwehr headquarters with his dogs, and Bredow, trailing in his wake.

Bredow had been able to ring his wife from the airfield earlier that same afternoon. As promised, he arrived in time for dinner at the rented villa in Dahlem that had been their home since their marriage in the spring of 1940.

He walked up the slightly overgrown path to the front door, paused on the porch to fumble for his key, and found himself blinking in a sudden flood of light as the door swung open. His wife stood in the hallway, smiling.

'Come in before the *Luftschutz* people have us shot,' she said. 'My God, Otto. I thought the Abwehr had priority. You look as though you *walked* from Smolensk.'

'All tourist flights were fully booked. I had to hitch a lift in one of Herr Mayer's flying cattle trucks.'

At the beginning of the war, Reich Marshal Goering, head of the Luftwaffe, had rashly declared that if even one Allied bomber managed to desecrate the holy soil of Germany, then 'my name is Mayer'. Sure enough, he was now known throughout the air force and elsewhere by that name alone.

Gisela drew Bredow in and slammed the door firmly behind him. He eased off his trench coat and dropped his bag, then shuffled through into the living room. His wife unhooked the telephone with unhurried efficiency. A large glass of schnaps appeared on the low japanned table by the sofa, where Bredow had collapsed, still in his heavy boots.

'Dinner will be ready in twenty-five minutes precisely,' Gisela announced. 'Does the Herr Oberleutnant wish to take a bath before he dines?'

Bredow shook his head, swallowed some schnaps, then lay back to luxuriate in the warmth of the fire. They had hardly touched yet, he and Gisela. She was wearing the white cocktail dress that he had bought for her at the Galaries Lafayette in Paris the previous summer and looked unimaginably blonde, pale and fragile, as if she would fall apart on contact. Beautiful.

'I love you,' he said after a short while.

Gisela did not answer, just knelt and began to tug at his boots. One, two, off they came, and then her grey-green eyes appraised him quizzically.

'Perhaps you do,' she whispered. 'We shall see.'

His smile anticipated the next step in his homecoming. They had played this game before. Getting used to each other again, re-inhabiting 'their' world.

Her fingers inched up on to his thighs, then moved with teasing slowness up towards his groin.

'Let's see,' Gisela said, and started to massage his genitals through the thick cloth of his uniform trousers. 'Aha . . . the possibility becomes a probability, Herr Leutnant . . .'

As she felt him swelling, her free hand went to the first button of his trousers.

'He loves me . . . he loves me not . . .'

The preliminaries were long and lazy, but when they made love, tumbling together onto the Astrakhan rug in front of the fire, his climax was almost immediate, a fierce, uncontainable explosion of stored tension. They lay for a long moment afterwards, he still inside her, she with her best Paris dress up round her waist and beyond all hope of elegance.

'Blitzkrieg,' Bredow panted.

Gisela giggled huskily and tossed her hair, then leaned over to plant a damp kiss on his mouth.

'First dinner,' she said, squirming gently free. 'Then comes the real battle, and I shall demand my reparations.'

She had laid out a celebration table in the dining room, but in the end they decided to eat off trays by the fire, sprawling on cushions as they had done so often during their courting days. Then Gisela had been studying Fine Arts at the Humboldt University. Like other bright, middle-class girls in an age when the Nazis discouraged education of women beyond the confines of bed, marriage and children, she had sneaked in on the pretext of majoring in Domestic Science, the loophole that had become known as 'pudding matriculation'. It was the way, the way people learned to use the system. She would joke, not without bitterness, that three years as a student had taught her to garnish salads beautifully, to arrange dinner-party flowers perfectly in accordance with the principles of the new 'German' art. Tonight, however, there were no sarcastic asides, only veal cooked in wine with fresh buttered noodles, the result of a month's hoarded ration coupons and a tacit agreement that for this hour they could be back in her lodgings in the Kantstrasse in peace . . .

After they had eaten they sat drinking Crimean champagne that Bredow had brought back from Russia, laughing a lot because Bredow had surprised her with the news that he would be based in Berlin for some time, a matter of weeks, even months. He did not talk about the eastern front except to say it was cold, or about Headquarters Army Group Centre except to say that Generals were boring human beings, and he decided to mention nothing at all of his meeting with Canaris. Gisela told drily funny stories about her part-time work as a telephonist at the local air-defence headquarters. The place was ruled by an incompetent Ortsgruppenleiter who had been shunted off there as too stupid even for party administrative duties. The women who worked with Gisela called him 'the troglodyte', because he spent most of the time hiding in the air raid shelter, dead drunk, while they did the work coordinating emergency services. Gisela and Bredow finished the bottle of champagne and took off each other's remaining clothes. She got her reparations in full.

The air-raid sirens sounded not long before midnight, but by then they were too drunk and too tired to get dressed and scuttle down to the cellar. In any case, Dahlem had never been subjected to serious bombing. The RAF usually went for the centre and the eastern industrial suburbs, or sometimes the huge Siemens plant at Spandau, and tonight was no exception. When they heard the dull drone of planes, the crump of anti-aircraft fire, Bredow merely got up and switched the radio on to a forces' request programme to cover the noise.

'The girls can manage without me tonight,' Gisela said. 'It's all futile, anyway. There are so many bombers . . .'

Bredow nodded.

'God, the world is mad,' she continued matter-of-factly. 'And we can do nothing about it, only turn up the volume on the radio.'

Bredow felt an urge to look at her face, her whole body, everything changed by nakedness and love, and commit it all to memory. She lay with her head back, smoking a cigarette, and the skin of her breasts and rib cage was stretched taught, marvellously clear and white. He leaned over to kiss a tiny lacuna of perspiration that had become trapped along the bone of her shoulder blade. He could not, at this moment, imagine a world where he would never again be able to do that, or hold her close, or hear her cry out in pleasure, or simply look at her. His mind told him that such a reality could too easily exist, but for now he kept his eyes on that skin and let the radio play over his mind.

From Heidemarie in Wunstorf, for her man who is serving with our brave U-boats in the far Atlantic, the orchestra brings the theme from that great epic of German heroism, 'Baptism of Fire' . . .

'Then we shan't talk about the world,' was the only comment Bredow could bear to make.

6

Bellingham realized after about ten minutes in his son's company that the decision to visit Charlie had been a mistake from almost every point of view, certainly as far as his own morale was concerned. The realization left precisely six hours and ten minutes during which he could chart the complete boundaries of his error.

Charlie met him at Oxford station. They had agreed on his housemaster's telephone that a day out in the city would be better than wandering round the grounds or—the ultimate horror, it seemed—another boring session at some teashop in Abingdon, the closest town to the school. Oxford was 'special', a few more miles away and across the county boundary from Berkshire, and it held promises of adulthood and metropolitan excitements. Before the war, boys of Charlie's age from Radley would have looked on a trip to Oxford as a chance to size up the place and its university, where it was quite likely that they would spent three years or more as students in the not too distant future. Now, of course, most of them would be commissioned into the forces instead, and anything else was too much to think about, but a trip to Oxford was still the mark of a proper parental visit, a slap-bang treat.

In the event, the day was wet and overcast, and Oxford itself inconceivably drab when measured against Bellingham's pre-war memories. He saw more young men in uniform than wearing undergraduates' gowns; someone had told him that only science students stood much chance of exemption from the military, and even they ran the risk of being called up if their examination results were considered unsatisfactory. The lucky survivors got a strait-laced parody of the 'best years of one's life': forced study and compulsory ARP duties.

Charlie was another matter. Three months short of seventeen, he was now a full inch taller than his father, a long-legged monster where the last time they had met, in the spring of '39, he had still been a boy with an unbroken voice in flannel school shorts and a cap. He had also filled out, so that he had developed his father's squareness of build and slightly fleshy nose. Unfortunately he had acquired his mother's capacity for wounding, too.

'Hello. It was terribly good of you to take the trouble, father,' he said when they found each other on the station platform, and they shook hands carefully. He wore a brocade waistcoat and a topcoat with a velvet collar, and he seemed totally sure of himself. Luckily he had a spot on his chin, which he kept picking at, or Bellingham would have been at a complete disadvantage right from the start.

They wandered in damp, wary tandem along Park End Street and up through Gloucester Green into St Giles'. There they toured a couple of colleges. There were onions and parsnips planted in the fellows' garden at St John's, Bellingham noted in wonder. His son, when he remarked on the fact, smiled loftily.

'Oh, everything's being dug up now, father,' he explained. 'I suspect they'll be starting on the war cemeteries next. Plenty of nitrogen and humus. This is, after all, a country at war . . .'

The sly digs at Bellingham's failure, as the boy undoubtedly saw it, to come back from Portugal and 'share' England's trial, were mounting up. Oh, father, what brings you here . . . just a business trip, naturally, yes . . . do they have bananas in Portugal, I suppose they do . . . mother says the Portuguese like the British so long as they can make money out of them . . . naturally one couldn't expect them to come in on our side . . .

Bellingham tried to field it all with dignity. He would have had no problem facing up to that sort of thing from a stranger—he had never, unlike some chaps in the Service, had the urge to confess and say: 'Look, I'm not really the idiot or the liar I seem to be'. Coming from Charlie, though, it caused him pain. Bearable, but pain nevertheless. From the outset he had decided to treat today as an exercise in self-restraint. Charlie had to be dealt with according to the way things were, not as either father or son would have liked them to be.

They took a quick turn around the University Parks. By now it was almost mid-day. Bellingham found himself wishing that it were peacetime and the cricket season and that he could sneak himself a drink in the spectators' tent, offer Charlie a gingerbeer shandy to show that they were grownups together these days. He had sworn, though, that he would lay off today, so it was just as well that no such opportunity presented itself. With iron discipline he marched Charlie into Fuller's tea room in Cornmarket at a quarter-to-one and there, amid the oak panelling and general tone of maiden-auntish, strictly nonalcoholic indulgence, he ordered the most expensive thing on the menu for them both: a roast beef salad and a pot of tea for two.

'Well, the tide seems to be turning, Hitler on the run,' he said when the waitress had gone. 'Come the peace, we'll have to fix up for you and James to come over and have a boys-together session, like the old days. Relax in the sun and all that.'

Charlie sat rubbing the pimple on his chin, realized that Bellingham had noticed, and stopped, pushing his hands down onto his lap with an uncomfortable grimace that he tried to disguise as a superior smile.

'Do you really think so, father? The war, I mean? Jimmy doesn't seem so confident, and he should know. He says there's still plenty of fight left in the Germans he's come up against. And he's seen the Yanks in action in North Africa. He reckons they haven't got a clue.'

That use of Jimmy, and not James, put it in a nutshell. It brought home the continuing intimacy between his two sons, growing up together over the past eleven years without him. Now his elder son's name was no longer that of a nice middle-class child but belonged to a man, who swore, drank, fought, womanized . . .

'Oh, he may be right,' Bellingham said. 'But I remember the last war. The Americans weren't too bright then at the beginning. They're not used to fighting wars. Have to work themselves into it, and then they're very useful, I can assure you.'

'Pity they always join in a bit late, isn't it?'

'I suppose so. But don't forget they're not part of Europe.'

The waitress came with their meal. She was a kindly, broad-beamed matron who, to Bellingham, looked absurd in her starched cap and white apron, like an adult dressed up in doll's clothing, but he was grateful for the smile she gave him when she set down her tray. Her smile was one of complicity and understanding, and it did something to raise his spirits; she must be used to these gruesome encounters between absent fathers and their public-school offspring.

He tried to get back to safe ground. 'Old Joaqim—you know, the cellar foreman, the one with the beret and the long white beard—he sends his regards. Always had a soft spot for you. He used to give you wine to taste. You got quite sick once . . .'

Charlie smiled politely. Goodness, smiles were a complicated language, harder to fathom than were words.

'Yes. Of course.'

'We could have a whole summer together,' Bellingham suggested. 'I expect James . . . ah, Jimmy . . . will be back here finishing his degree, and with any luck you'll be here too—unless you betray the family and go to the other place.'

'The other place?' Charlie began, then realized that his father had been referring to Cambridge. 'Oh, I don't think either of them. And I'm not so sure Jimmy will be coming back. He wrote to me last month and said he fancied seeing a bit of life if he got through all right. He thought he might go out to Rhodesia or somewhere and have a crack at farming. There won't be much to do here, he reckons. Not if a fellow wants a bit more out of life than nine-to-five.'

'Ah,' Bellingham said. Another generation made restless by war. He couldn't blame them. Why had he stayed in Portugal? It hadn't just been out of patriotic duty. He wondered why the thought of his sons taking the same path—minus the professional complications, naturally—disturbed him as it did. Perhaps he was frightened for them. Then again, it might just be creeping old age.

'He had tobacco in mind,' Charlie confided in earnest hero-worship of his elder brother. 'You can make pots of money and live like a king. Hard work, goes without saying, but then you can get servants out there to do all the routine stuff, and labour's cheap.'

'Well, if that's what he decides on after due consideration, I'll give him every help. He'd need to get his produce out through Beira, which is in Portuguese East Africa. I've got good contacts in the Mozambique Railways, you know. People I dealt with in the home country who were later posted out there.'

Charlie nodded listlessly. The sudden outburst of enthusiasm, which had briefly brought the two of them into communication, ended as quickly as it had begun. The vize eased down, putting back the distance.

'And how about you, Charlie?' Bellingham asked, grimly determined not to let go now.

'Oh, the forces I suppose. Even if you're right about the war, I shall be eighteen next year. And you're forgetting the Japs. They've got to be beaten as well as the Germans. If I've got to be cannon-fodder, I was considering the RAF, actually. It's the least stuffy of the services, I'm told.'

Bellingham frowned. 'You'll never be cannon-fodder, my boy,' he said gently. 'We've got our faults, but we do care about human life on this side of the divide, you know.'

'So they say.'

'And they're right. I don't think you realize what the Nazis are like.'

'Why, do you?'

'I know what they've done, and I know our people would never do those things. That's all I can say.'

Bellingham ached to say something concrete, based on his own experience. He knew he could not and that he should therefore shut up before the afternoon went sour. The special set of rules that he had made for today didn't include these issues. All he hoped was that Charlie would never need to fight. And that no one would ever let him down.

'So. Possibly the RAF. They're doing a useful job,' Bellingham continued, trying to be matter-of-fact. 'Or I could fix you up in the Royal Sussex, my old outfit . . .'

'Of course, father. But I'd like to fly. It's the independence apart from anything else.'

For a moment there was a glimmer of respect in the boy's eyes. However long ago, Charlie's father had fought in a real war.

'And after that?' Bellingham asked, pushing home his advantage. 'This business really isn't going to drag on for ever. Good Lord, if it lasts much longer, they'll be calling on old buffers like me.'

He needed to make that little private joke. It made him feel better. The boy, of course, didn't even hear it. He was staring dully around at the other customers, obviously hoping for some diversion from this relentless parental cross-examination.

'I really don't have very much idea about jobs and stuff,' he mumbled, looking back at Bellingham but avoiding direct eye-contact. 'Jimmy says I can help out if his farming project gets going.'

'What's the opinion about that at home?'

'Well, mother doesn't really approve. She doesn't like anywhere that's Abroad, even though Africa's sort of English . . . My stepfather doesn't approve of most of what goes on in this country, let alone anywhere else.'

Bellingham noted the strange formality of 'my stepfather'. Charlotte had played safe the second time round and married a comfortable, unadventurous solicitor named Parker. He got no more adventurous as the years passed, but apparently he could be distinctly uncomfortable these days. Parker, at least, could be discounted when the emotional battle lines were drawn up; if anything, he thought with perverse satisfaction, the boys seemed to despise him more than they did their natural father.

'I want to know your opinion, son,' he said, sensing the chance of a real conversation for the first time. 'I want to know how you see your future.'

Chewing mechanically on the last of his gristly beef, Charlie shook his head. 'I don't know at all, father. One can't say, can one? I mean, England's going to be back to more of the same once the war's over, isn't it?'

'Is that such a bad thing?' Bellingham said with feeling. 'There are plenty of nations on earth who would envy even the worst features of our life here. In fact, I would guess that the numbers of the envious are growing by the hour . . .'

Charlie, who was not quite seventeen and had probably never met anyone from Germany, let alone the Abwehr, who could not conceive—thank God—what drove that young Prussian in Lisbon, and who saw life as an oscillation between extremes of tedium and excitement, answered with a smirk.

'Come on, father,' he said. 'You have a rosy view of the old country. One chap at school who reckons he's a communist—rot, of course, his parents are rich as Croesus—says that the Yanks will own us lock, stock and barrel pretty soon, so you can forget your Land of Hope and Glory. He argues that the choice is either soulless transatlantic capitalism or socialist revolution—which at least offers some hope of keeping our British identity.'

Bellingham controlled his irritation with difficulty. Only the young could be so smugly self-opinionated. The most pompous of middle-aged blimps had enough experience of life to harbour secret fears that he might be mistaken, but these children had been brought up in an age of extremes, of fors and againsts, and that made it worse.

'Political systems don't make people, Charlie,' he said. 'It's the other way round.'

As he said it, he knew it wouldn't satisfy the boy. It wasn't even wholly true, or at least not nowadays. What had made him, Jackie Bellingham? Or the Prussian in Lisbon? Cause and effect was a minefield that you entered at your own risk. What mattered was that some societies were built on laws, sanity and tolerance; others foundered in cruelty, madness and terror. Charlie knew only the first sort, however distorted by war, and it was the sort you didn't value, like good health, until it was too late. Try explaining that to a sixteen-year-old who read the newspapers and saw what went on.

'It's raining even harder now,' his son remarked, shifting position so that he could stare out of the tea shop window.

Bellingham decided to abandon the unequal struggle. 'So it is,' he agreed cheerfully. 'Then how about a visit to the cinema this afternoon? I think they were showing *In*

Which We Serve somewhere. Unless you've seen it already, of course . . .'

'I haven't,' Charlie said firmly. Bellingham had a strong feeling that he would have said the same thing even if he'd already sat through Noel Coward as the improbable commander of *HMS Kelly* a dozen times that week, but perhaps he was being over-sensitive.

'A film's the thing, then. So long as it leaves us time to get you back to school before the witching hour.'

And so they spent the afternoon watching others do the talking. At five they parted at the bus terminal, where Charlie had to catch a local service back to the school. He unfroze a little while they were saying their farewells. Perhaps he also regretted that nothing had been resolved between them. Again, Bellingham may have imagined a certain wistfulness in his son's eyes. He promised, anyway, that if he should visit England in the spring, which was on the cards, they would meet in London, have a proper lunch somewhere a bit ritzy, see a show in the evening. With Charlie so grown-up now, they would be able to do all sorts of things together.

'All right, father. I'll write to Jimmy and tell him I've seen you. He'll be interested,' the boy said.

'I'll drop him a line as well. Mention the Mozambique Railways.'

'Oh yes, the Mozambique Railways. Thank you for the lunch and the cinema. Goodbye.'

'Goodbye, Charlie. God bless.' There was a glimmer somewhere, he could have sworn it, but no longer time to kindle it. A plump young bus conductress had just swung herself up onto the rear platform of the double decker. Charlie, obviously practised at the mechanics of catching buses by the skin of his teeth, made a hop and joined her. She rang her bell, tossed a burning cigarette end so high and so hard that Bellingham had to duck for fear of catching it in his face. When he straightened up again, the bus was moving away. Charlie was staring at him with an undeniable look of longing. Bellingham called out: 'The future's not so black, you know. There's such a thing as decency!'

Menzies rang him on the following Wednesday morning

at his hotel in London and suggested that they meet in St James's Park. They were ready for the next stage.

7

As had become the pattern, some mysterious service department of the Foreign Office fixed Bellingham up with a seat on the Lisbon plane. Travel documents were delivered to his hotel four hours before departure time. He was able to spend Friday night at his own villa near Santarem, enjoy a leisurely lunch in Lisbon the next day, and then take the train twenty-five kilometres down the coast to Estoril. Menzies had insisted that they meet outside the capital in case either embassy's busybodies had got wind of the first encounter. The Germans had concurred immediately. Bellingham arrived at the magnificent station directly on the seafront at three-fifteen, which left him with two hours to wander around the town and regain his bearings before he was due to see his Prussian.

Bellingham first stopped off to confirm his overnight booking at the *Palacio* hotel, where the meeting had been fixed, and then took the bracing Atlantic air along the Grand Esplanade. He could not escape a sense of extreme loneliness. The Prussian, he thought enviously, would probably be travelling on offical cover with all the trimmings, Abwehr passes and safe houses at his command, a reliable communications system, proper briefings. For his part, Bellingham felt as if he were at the end of an enormously long, thin string that could be cut—or fray—at any moment without his realizing the fact for some time. The responsibilities were enormous, the support minimal. Except for the fact that he was about to negotiate with the representative of an enemy power, he remained no more than Jackie Bellingham, retired wine shipper, failed husband and father, pillar of the Anglo-Portuguese community, master of nothing.

Heading past the casino and the hotels, Bellingham saw a modest café that he knew from the holidays with

Charlotte and the children years ago. The sight of it brought a slight but crucial lift in his spirits. In those days, Estoril had been a really grand place—home to a gaggle of former crowned heads, plus a veritable pride of Archdukes—but never any the less Portuguese for that, and therefore a very human place to be. He wondered if the café would be open, and it was; it might need a lick of paint, but people here were valiantly determined to do business even in the second week of January.

Bellingham walked into the café, sat down and ordered a *galão,* white coffee in a tall glass. He had to keep a clear head. To his surprise and pleasure, he recognized the proprietor as the same man who had served them with sweet pastries on those hot afternoons almost fifteen years ago. He was a good deal fatter, greyer, and a shade less jolly than Bellingham remembered him, but the welcome was no different, and he had a rather pretty daughter now who worked in the kitchen. Bellingham was the only customer. He spent an hour there, chatting in a desultory way about pre-war days and thinking about the boys in their shorts and singlets, about buckets and spades and shrimping-nets. At a quarter to five he decided he ought to make for his rendezvous, paid his bill and said a reluctant goodbye to the owner. The man wished him well. Nothing unctuous or self-serving about him. He would have wished the same to a fisherman or a millionaire. Bellingham was reminded of some of the reasons why he liked this country so much, and the reminder did him good.

The bar of the *Palacio* had the advantage of being a great cavern of a room, with small private booths arranged round the edge. Bellingham had thought of the place because its clientele had always been predominantly 'international', rich exiles and birds of passage. Two foreigners drinking together, even in wartime, would not attract undue attention.

There were no more than half a dozen customers in the bar when Bellingham arrived, ten minutes early by design. The interior was so large that the customers looked like bumpkins at a failed country dance, despite the elegant decor and the expensive clothes. Two waiters dived towards Bellingham as he walked through the door, and the winner escorted him to a round, polished table in one of the booths with a grin of triumph. Within thirty seconds he had his whisky and soda by his side and a clear view of the door.

In tune with every cliché about German regularity, his Prussian was on time to the minute. He wore a homburg and a trench coat, and under that a well-cut dark suit and a tie with a diamond pin through it. Presumably he had been advised by the props department that this was a good-class watering-hole. Bellingham thought that he looked extraordinarily blond and Aryan, like one of those propaganda pictures, even more conspicuous than in Lisbon and by the looks of him anxiously aware of the fact.

'Hello,' the Prussian said as he sat down. 'This hotel is very fine. I will admit that you have a better taste in meeting-places than we, though it does seem a little . . . prominent . . .'

Bellingham chuckled. 'Best thing, my dear fellow. You can see exactly what's going on and who's doing it. Drink?'

The Prussian said that he would have what his host was having. He lit a cigarette immediately, a Balkan brand from a silver case bearing the initials 'OB' engraved in italics.

'A good marque,' he observed when he tasted his whisky. 'Though I am no expert. I drank it not very often before the war, and since 1939 it is not generally available, for obvious reasons.'

'The situation in England isn't that much better, I can assure you, though the reasons are less obvious.'

The Prussian smiled and Bellingham smiled back. An exchange of vital economic information, the availability of decent hooch on either side of the battle-line. Bellingham realized that he actually liked this earnest young man, and that he did not feel inclined to give him a bad time as he had in Lisbon. Watch your step, you rubber-toothed old lion, he told himself.

The Prussian opened the bidding, in his diffident way. 'I would guess that your chief has made his decision, yes?' he asked simply.

'You'd be right,' Bellingham said. 'I am authorized to make it clear that in view of the information you have supplied to us during our discussions, and of his own soundings, he is favourably disposed to the plan. But my chief wants some real, hard details now. It'll be a delicate operation. Our side has to start making arrangements.'

'We understand that, naturally. From now on, you will be doing most of the work.'

'Too true.'

Bellingham made a wry face. The Prussian shrugged, as if to say: 'We've done our share'. Then he took a sip of whisky and nodded appreciatively.

'I have some more information,' the Prussian said. He lowered his voice a fraction. 'Just before we part, I shall hand it over to you. It has been reduced in size to fit in a small packet.'

'I hope it's good stuff.'

'I think so. It includes references to *Turquoise*'s background which are still inconclusive but nevertheless helpful.'

'Whoopee. Just what we need. Should narrow things down a bit.'

On impulse, Bellingham gulped down the remains of his whisky and waved at the waiter who was lounging over by the bar. Damn sobriety. He'd bet he had a stronger head than the Prussian, and things could do with a touch of oiling. While the drinks were being organized, he asked: 'And the second half of the bargain?'

'That we should also discuss.'

'Then fire away. You're the one with the tale to tell.'

The Prussian lit a second cigarette from his monogrammed case, waited until the waiter had come and gone.

'Since the situation in Africa became critical—that is, I suppose, since Berlin realized that Rommel's defeat at El Alamein was more than a temporary setback—the Führer has been under pressure to meet Mussolini in secret,' he said. 'For a thorough discussion of the Mediterranean situation, you know. Africa, the Near East, the Balkans; obviously, it is all strategically connected, and both German and Italian troops are involved. Anyway, the chief problem has been that secrecy could not be guaranteed either in Italy or in Germany. Therefore a place has been sought that would be . . . away from . . .'

'Off the beaten track,' Bellingham suggested, then motioned with his whisky glass for the other man to continue.

'Exactly. Various places were rejected as too isolated, others were too obvious, or there was the danger of guerrilla activity—this applied particularly to Corsica and the Adriatic. Finally they decided on the island of Rhodes.'

'Italian possession, largely Greek population. Quite a fashionable resort before the war, I seem to remember, but pretty remote when you come down to it. Just off the coast of Turkey.'

The Prussian nodded. 'There is a good airfield. And the nature of the island is such that it can be sealed off for forty-eight or seventy-two hours, until the conference is over. Hitler flies in . . .' He made a whistling noise, imitated an aeroplane landing with the flat of his hand. '. . . He talks, maybe gives Mussolini a piece of his mind. Then he flies out again—or perhaps he does not . . .'

'Ah. Yes.'

'Indeed. You will already have men on the island. You can do that fairly easily, I know. We will supply you with precise information that will be known only to those immediately involved with Hitler's safety: routes, times, nature of the vehicle he will be travelling in to the conference, and so on. Of course, these details may only become known a matter of hours before his arrival. Security will be very heavy. For Hitler to set foot outside continental Europe is really quite remarkable. I would be inclined to believe that providence is on our side.'

'I wouldn't put too much trust in that sort of thing,' Bellingham admonished him mildly. 'Better to keep matters on a businesslike footing and not get too airy-fairy.'

'But you must see what this could mean: a chance of peace without further bloodshed on the battlefield.'

'I most certainly see all that. But we're not bosom pals yet, ourselves and your Abwehr. The way you've started to talk, anyone would think we've been holding hands these last few years instead of stabbing each other in the back,' said Bellingham, wondering whether he was mixing his metaphors or mashing them, and not really caring too much either way. 'We have to ask ourselves: What if you change your mind about Hitler? Or what if you're out to make bloody fools of us in front of our allies?'

The Prussian snorted in exasperation. 'I think that if we wanted to do that, we could achieve it more quickly and with a lot less trouble,' he retorted archly. 'Men on our side have been putting their lives at risk for this project. It goes beyond simple self-interest.'

'There's a war on. People do that all the time. While we discuss the significance of bits of paper and haggle in the comfort of a hotel bar in a neutral country, men are being slaughtered in their thousands for no good reason most of them can think of. Many more could end up dead if I make a misjudgment.' Bellingham realized with a shock that he was almost losing his temper.

'We have given away a lot without any guarantee. Does that not prove our good faith?'

Bellingham nodded wearily, made a dismissive gesture. Perhaps he couldn't bear to think of the other side as idealists; it would make life too damned complicated. He had felt angry with the Prussian because when he saw him he saw clarity, honour, a kind of old-fashioned rightness. Why couldn't the man be as murky as everyone else, even himself and Stewart Menzies, and most assuredly that old cannibal Canaris? He hadn't meant for the conversation to go this way.

'We're prepared to work with you,' he said. 'That's what matters.'

'Good. That I shall tell to my chief.'

The young man was clearly ready to take his leave. The bar was beginning to fill up, and the big picture window on the seaward side of the room was almost dark.

'Come on, one for the road,' Bellingham said, regretting his previous ill humour. When it came down to it, there was no reason why they shouldn't behave like normal human beings.

The Prussian nodded assent and took an envelope out of his inside jacket pocket before Bellingham could call the waiter. He pushed the envelope across the table to the Englishman, who slipped it away into his own with practised smoothness. The entire process took perhaps two or three seconds. Immediately he had the material, Bellingham turned casually and signalled for more whisky.

After that they sat quietly, drinking their last drink. The atmosphere was surprisingly companionable, but since there was also a limit to the small talk you could exchange under such circumstances, neither put any pressure on the other to communicate. Their glasses were almost empty when a sizable group of men invaded the bar, chattering and joking noisily in German. Bellingham looked nervously to his Prussian, who grinned and shook his head.

'Have no fear,' he said. 'I recognize the dialect. They are Swiss, quite clearly to my ears.'

'And what on earth are they doing here?'

The Prussian listened in to the loud conversation at the bar. 'Oh,' he muttered after a few moments. 'I think they are a club or something similar, on holiday together. Imagine that. They have travelled across half of Europe just for a few chilly days by the sea. One forgets that people still do such things for no urgent reason.'

'Doesn't one,' agreed Bellingham.

He insisted that it was his turn to settle the bill, and the young Prussian left.

When Bellingham went up to his room to change for dinner an hour later, the Swiss were still going strong in the bar, back-slapping and bawling at each other in their harsh sing-song voices. Abroad on holiday, letting their hair down, jolly times of ease. Imagine that, as his Prussian had so rightly said.

Sturmbannführer Gronheim looked at the luminous dial of his watch, then tapped some ash from his half-smoked cigar into the ash-tray before it fell and marred the cloth of his good civilian trousers. The car windows were misted up, but in this cold he had no intention of opening them even a centimetre to air the interior. Gronheim shivered, consoled himself by thinking of his mistress, who was waiting for him back in Stockholm. He was due to land in her bed at about two in the morning, provided that Lunde didn't choose to be late tonight. His mistress did not mind the hours Gronheim kept. He would tell her he had been out touring the city's wickedest places; this often excited her.

He heard the crunch of car tyres on frozen earth. Another vehicle was approaching along the forest track. Gronheim ran the wipers over the windscreen again, rubbed the inside with one gloved hand. For a moment the oncoming vehicle's headlights dazzled him, but then they dipped, flashed twice in quick succession. It was Lunde all right.

The Swede cut his car's engine as Gronheim emerged from his own plain DKW saloon. It was a clear, cold moonlit night, and now utterly silent. Gronheim waited, arms akimbo and cigar still clenched between his teeth, but Lunde did not get out.

Lunde's window was being rolled down. The Swede stuck his head out into the chill air. 'Good evening!' he called out to Gronheim, in German for the SD officer's benefit. 'I am in a hurry. I have an engagement. Do you mind if I don't get out?'

Gronheim shook his head, tossed the smouldering cigar to the ground and squashed the stub beneath his heel. The floor of the clearing was like concrete. Nothing else had passed through this godforsaken spot for days. Gronheim walked over to the Swede's car and stood looking down at the man in the driver's seat.

'On the contrary. I don't mind at all,' he said. 'And how was London?'

Lunde laughed. 'Terrible. The British have been reduced to eating whale meat. Their children are having to go without shoes. Shall I stop before I make you cry?'

Gronheim forced himself to smile. He often wished that someone else could act as Lunde's controller. He disliked the man, thought him inherently corrupt. Any field man worth his salt preferred to work with people of his own choice, not self-appointed mercenaries such as this man. On the other hand, Lunde's material was absolutely superb; it had rarely been faulted in almost three years. It was hardly surprising that Gronheim's bosses in the Prinz-Albrecht-Strasse never paid any attention to his complaints. The much-travelled Swedish bank official was their star agent.

'I shed all my tears a long time ago,' Gronheim told Lunde. 'All right. Ready for business when you are.'

The Swede nodded, reached into the glove compartment, held out an oilskin wallet through the car window. Gronheim bent down, took it, replaced it in the Swede's open hand with a packet. Then he stepped back, clicked his heels and bowed, playacting the correct Teuton.

'Charmed, *Herr Baron.*' Lunde's command of German

was excellent but somehow he wore it badly, like a tramp who has found some expensive clothes among the garbage cans. He had a plump, very pale face and red hair, which was uncommon enough in a Swede. At home in Germany, redheads were investigated for Jewish blood. Gronheim would have been delighted to investigate Lunde.

'The usual payment. You won't starve,' Gronheim commented, unable to hide his resentment.

'I run risks,' said the imperturbable Swede. '*Auf wiedersehen*, my friend. I shall see you again soon. My employers are sending me to London for a week in February. More trade negotiations, arranging of credits. The British are eager to buy Swedish goods. Especially ones that kill Germans.'

Lunde turned the key in the ignition. His farewell guffaw was lost in the racing roar of his car's engine.

Gronheim granted him a perfunctory wave, then turned away and trudged back to his own DKW. As he reached it, he saw the Swede completing a fast, tight turn that set him ready to leave the clearing nose-first and at his usual breakneck speed. Lunde, like so many spies, was a middle-aged adolescent, and a particularly greedy one.

'*Arschloch,*' Gronheim muttered to himself. He made sure that the oilskin wallet containing the *Turquoise* material was securely lodged in his inside coat pocket, then opened his car door and eased himself into the driver's seat.

Tonight, he decided, he would tell his mistress he had been with a negro woman. She would go crazy for him.

8

'You're doing a marvellous job, Jackie,' Menzies said. 'The stuff you acquired in Estoril was top-notch. All very exciting.'

'Glad to hear you're pleased. Managing to narrow the field, are we?' Bellingham asked.

'We're doing all right. We've had to spread our net a little wider, just in case the Abwehr people were wrong in their assumption that he was a specialist—we've included selected liaison people at the War Office, the Cabinet Office and the FO, and we've reckoned Turkey and Hungary into our suspect's possible area of work.' Menzies shrugged. 'Amazing—and really rather frightening—when one starts tracing through who's seen what file, and often for the most tenuous of reasons. I'm rather glad we don't have to sack everyone who's broken the registry rules, or we'd have no one left come Monday morning.'

'Well, yes. So what are the numbers involved?'

A wry smile. 'A dozen or so possibles. Three or four probables—presuming that all Canaris's details are correct.'

'Service chaps?'

' 'Fraid so.' Menzies took a couple of paces, unlocked a drawer in his desk. He took out a thick, loose-leaf folder. 'They're here, both categories. Without fear or favour. Take a glance, if only for interest's sake,' Menzies said. 'No one you'd know, of course, old boy. All recent vintage. Make sure you don't mix the pages up.'

With a terse little wave, 'C' disappeared through into the living room to make a telephone call, leaving Bellingham alone holding the folder. Since it was icy outside, too cold to consider another meeting in the park, Menzies had delayed going into Broadway this morning and invited Bellingham to his town flat in Belgravia. A week after his return from Estoril, Bellingham was still no wiser regarding the specific nature of the documents he had picked up there. Instead, he was being placated with a brief guided tour through a wad of material regarding people he did not know and would almost certainly never meet. These were copies of personal files, plus the usual official mugshots of the men involved, mostly taken when they had joined the Service. In the majority of cases, that meant the photographs were no more than two or three years old. They were all the new intake, often anti-fascist idealists; one or two, he noted, had even been to Spain during the civil war, and they were Oxford and Cambridge to a man, with a strong sprinkling of junior dons. Average age in the early thirties. Bellingham saw that there was a certain sameness about them. The task Menzies had taken on was by no means impossible, but neither was it easy.

'Seems funny, doesn't it?' Bellingham said when 'C' came back into the study. 'All these earnest pinko types, and one of them presumably a secret Nazi. One wonders how a chap like that would manage to juggle everything and stay sane. Must be able to divide his tiny mind up into separate compartments.'

'I presume so, Jackie. Whether he's a Nazi or not is a moot point. He might just be doing it for the filthy lucre, or because his section head doesn't make him feel wanted. In a way, I hope so. These ideological traitors you find nowadays, the ones who do it out of cold intellectual conviction, give me the heeby-jeebies. Not our style of spy, eh?'

Bellingham shook his head. Most emphatically not. He was about to ask some more questions about the men in the files when Menzies looked at his watch and raised an eyebrow.

'Good Lord, is that the time?' he murmured. 'I've an appointment at the Foreign Office at eleven. There's a lot to be sorted out before I leave for the conference with Roosevelt in Morocco. We'd better get down to serious business.'

He leaned over, picked up the folder from where Bellingham had put it next to himself on the small sofa, spirited it back into the drawer, and locked it away.

'Right,' Menzies said then. 'Rhodes is fine, for all sorts of reasons. We've got excellent local contacts, and one could conceal a small army in those mountains there. The Greek population is vehemently anti-wop—and anti-German inasmuch as the Third Reich is allied with Mussolini.'

'How long do you think our people will have to be there before they can finish the job, Stewart?'

Menzies pursed his lips thoughtfully. He sat down, crossing his legs, a habit that Bellingham was beginning to recognize as an unconscious signal of tension. The younger Menzies had always sat square and open, before middle age and responsibility gave his body something to hide.

'Depends,' he said. 'I think we'll land the men on the island some time before Hitler's due to turn up, as Canaris's man suggested to you. On the surface—I mean, so far as people in London are concerned—they're going to be a partisan liaison-cum-reconnaissance team, sent in amidst much secrecy and to-do, because we're seriously thinking of using Rhodes as a springboard to the invasion of the Balkan mainland. They will accordingly send perfectly genuine radio messages back to London, which will be used to "feed" the main suspects and set our process in action. The marked fiver factor . . .'

'Am I to assume,' Bellingham interrupted his flow, 'that you are using the same team for the . . . marked fiver . . . as will carry out the attack on Hitler?'

'Absolutely. No point in having hordes of chaps wandering around the Eastern Med, all doing different little jobs. That would only arouse German suspicions, increase the chance of their realizing something was up. One small team in and out. The marked fiver just involves sending routine messages.'

Bellingham pressed on with his devil's advocate role. 'And the Germans won't get cold feet when they know there's Brits in the area? They won't call the Führer's visit off?'

Menzies smiled and shook his head almost imperceptibly, more a flick of the cortex. 'Oh, I don't think so, so long as we keep things low key. They know we're constantly sending commando groups in and out of the islands, to their intense irritation. If they're prepared to allow Hitler to go there in the first place, they must have taken that into account. And, of course, how's the Führer to know we've got informants in the heart of his own security services?'

'I suppose you're right,' Bellingham said, and lit his pipe, hoping that it would help him to think. 'Comparatively low-risk and cost effective.'

'That is, as the Americans would say, the sign of a real pro, which is what I like to think I am, despite some opinions to the contrary,' Menzies retorted with a certain waspishness. Now and again he showed that the widespread view of him as a foppish amateur hurt. 'The rumour of the so-called reconnaissance project will be irresistible for our spy. He'll have to feed it straight to the SD in Berlin; it's right in his special field and exactly the kind of thing his controllers are panting to hear from him. It will also be a very effective cover, enabling us to keep the real—not to mention lethal—object of the mission secret until the last possible moment. Until well after the men are established on the island, in fact. Clear?'

'I think so.'

'Good-oh. Then you just nip back to Portugal and tell the Abwehr all's well and that we'll deal with things from now on.' Menzies looked at his watch again, realizing that the meeting was nearing its end. 'I'm relying heavily on you, Jackie.' He touched Bellingham's shoulder in a gesture of affectionate intimacy that would only have been possible in private. 'And I'll be fashioning further burdens for your broad, uncomplaining back before this business is over. Would that there were more where you come from. I fear the breed's fast becoming extinct.'

'Our sort are working animals, but at least we're thoroughbreds.'

'Very true. I hope you don't mind too much. You're the only fellow I can trust to be in on everything.'

'So when do you want me to talk to my Prussian?'

'As soon as possible. We'd better swap the rendezvous again, just in case. You choose somewhere, will you,' Menzies said. He laughed. '*Your* Prussian, eh? Not going soft on the Abwehr are you, Jackie?'

Old friends, loose ends, thought Bellingham. Twenty minutes after leaving Menzies' flat, he still had no clear sense of what to do with the rest of his day. While he had been closeted with 'C', the sun had come out, and he had tried wandering along the river. Now the game was up. *Damn it, a drink.*

Bellingham found a news-stand not far from Cleopatra's needle, bought an early edition of the *Star,* then headed purposefully up into the network of streets surrounding Charing Cross station, in search of a pub and company.

He found a reasonable-looking place and without thinking ordered a double whisky at the bar. Mine host chortled richly.

'My word, where you been these past few years, sir?' he said. 'Single's all you'll get, worse luck. We got plenty of beer at the moment, though. Just had a delivery.'

Bellingham smiled weakly, rubbed his numbed, cold hands. 'Then I shall have a pint of beer with a whisky chaser of regulation size, if that's all right.'

'They can't stop you, sir, though I reckon the buggers would if they could.'

Bellingham took his drinks and found a bench seat by the window. At his villa in Portugal he would have a large whisky at his elbow this time of day, no question. Since he had retired from the day-to-day running of the business and left the donkey-work to his Portuguese partner, he was in a kind of limbo there, too. Pleasant enough: old copies of the *Illustrated London News, The Times* a few days late, books from the British Council Library in Lisbon, and pottering in his garden, but nothing like home. The trouble was that this wasn't home either. He probably had a couple of days before he went back to Lisbon, forty-eight hours to kill. Funny the way the English language talked about 'killing' time, as if capital punishment were all it deserved instead of careful nurturing, infinite care to make it grow and provide a rich harvest, because you would never get it back. Even Menzies must sometimes be plagued by a sense of loss, of time wasted. Even 'C' must have some of an ordinary mortal's desires.

He turned to his newspaper and read it slowly, knowing it would have to last him through the afternoon, though it was down to four pages now because of the paper shortages. At a nearby table, two soldiers were discussing a recent football match in which, apparently, Brighton had lost eighteen-nil to Norwich.

'Must've been about five hundred people there,' one was saying. 'And, you see, Brighton had their entire first team called up. They had to borrow two reserves from Norwich and rope in three blokes from the crowd to make up the numbers.'

His mate nodded. 'And that's our national sport . . . Mind you, the Germans don't seem to be too short of players for theirs, do they?'

That got a laugh all round the bar room.

Even Bellingham smiled. Everyone was in a limbo of sorts in wartime, including young men who demanded no more than the basic pleasures.

9

Tra-bloody-la, sang the driver to himself. *Spring is nearly sprung.* Duty could be pleasure as well. At twenty to seven of a mild February morning, it was good to be out and about.

Into the satellites of the city, the outer suburbs, cosy and peaceful. He drove into the parking space next to the café and sat in his cab for a few moments with his window down, savouring the first good morning air of the year, fresh but not chilling. Then he lowered himself down onto the cinders, swinging out to one side of a large puddle.

One of these days, he thought, he'd be tempted to come early, really early, and try and catch a glimpse of the character who made the drop. It got boring, it started to feel sort of pointless, when all you did was pick up, drive off, dump it, collect your coupons and your bit of expenses. He hadn't actually spoken to or seen anybody for, what, eighteen months? Then it had been some peculair sod, all nicotine-stained fingers and food down his old school tie, and he had given him all the instructions he needed for the duration, or so he had said. They'd warned him that things would be difficult—a lot of people had to put up with it, only seeing a kindred spirit (nicotine-stain's words) once in a blue moon. Since then, of course, it had been a case of working on his own, unthanked and unrecognized as far as he could tell, no contact with the others because that was strictly against the rules. That was right, and the driver could see it would be stupid, that you had to make sacrifices. Still, sometimes he felt like being a bit wicked and taking a dekko at the bloke who made the drop, just to see what he was like, watch him and think: good on you, mate, you're one of us. He wouldn't ever, not in the end, though; they trusted him to do his stuff for the new Britain and he wouldn't let them down.

The greasy Welshman started pouring his tea the moment he spotted him coming in through the door.

'Morning. Good to see you back round here again,' he said.

The driver grinned. 'I'm a sucker for punishment, as they say.'

Some people's lives ran like ruddy clockwork. The Welshman, for instance, he must think like a machine, a trained dog. Same old routine every day, same jokes and chat, same bloody customers most of the time. Those two old boys drinking their tea and ogling *Jane* in the paper. Machines, yes.

The Welshman laughed. He seemed very cheerful this fine morning. The driver told him so.

'Well, I told you about my son,' he said. 'The one on the convoys. He's home on leave, you see. Fast asleep now, of course, getting his strength back. They're pulling him off the Murmansk business. He can't say where he's supposed to be off to next, but I'd guess the Mediterranean. Not so bad there. The missus reckons it was her prayers as brought him through his ordeal . . .'

Ordeal? What did these people know about ordeals? Stalingrad, that was something, but they'd never understand that. They understood fuck-all. Only what the tame-dog gutter press told them, and the politicians.

Nevertheless, it was interesting what the Welshman had to tell. You learned a lot just by listening to individuals, because like the little waves if you looked at them closely enough you could have a good guess at the way the sea was going. His son being pulled off the Arctic run to the Russkies and probably heading to the Med. That could mean there was something else happening down there, that they were building up, reckoning the situation in the East wasn't so desperate, or just transferring resources down there and letting the comrades in Moscow go hang. Old Chruchill had only helped Stalin out of necessity, hadn't he? No honour with those thieves . . . He'd wanted to have a go at Europe before Uncle Joe started trying to move west. Thinking that way, though, just increased the driver's frustration. Having thoughts like those and having no one to tell them to was terrible. He decided to chat the Welshman up, to pass the time.

'Glad he got through it all right,' he said. 'Plenty of poor buggers didn't, excusing my language. Reckon your boy'll be in on the big one? Second Front Now, all that malarky?'

'I suppose he might be. He's on a frigate, you know . . . I suppose they might be escorts, like with that North Africa business before Christmas.' The Welshman sucked in his cheeks, suddenly concerned. 'I suppose it wouldn't be too dangerous, like. I mean, not as if he was going in with a gun against the mines and the barbed-wire and all that. Mind you, his ma'll have a fit if she hears he might be getting bombed and shelled and everything.'

'Bound to, but I bet your boy's not that fussed, eh? He's been through it all.'

'I should say so. Some of the things he told us about those bloody convoys . . . blokes bein' fished out of the water frozen stiff . . . hundreds of them when a ship went down, and them havin' to sort 'em like at Hull docks when they bring in a catch from the Iceland grounds. I ask mesself whether it's worth it. The way they got treated by the Russians when they got to Murmansk or Archangel or wherever was just shocking . . . you'd think they'd welcome our lads with open arms, but they just took the cargoes and didn't even offer 'em a cup of tea . . .'

'Terrible, terrible. Hard to understand, innit?'

The conversation lost its interest very quickly, but the driver decided to stay at the counter and switch off his attention, simply nodding or agreeing, 'terrible' or 'yeah' between mouthfuls of sandwich. It helped to keep him calm before the pick-up, which somehow he needed this morning. The irritation of the Welshman was like a smaller pain that distracted you from the greater one, as you might bite your lip hard when you'd twisted your ankle.

'I'll tell you, it don't make sense,' the Welshman was saying as the driver finished his sandwich. 'They're talking about the Beginning of the End and all, but the rationing's getting worse, not better. The trouble I have gettin' just ordinary ingredients to feed my customers, you wouldn't believe it. Where's it going to end?'

'Usual place,' the driver quipped, pointing in the direction of the Gents. 'That's where it all ends up. Which reminds me . . . I've got a long drive ahead. Won't get much of a chance to answer nature's call.'

'Anyone would think you only came here to . . . you know,' the Welshman said with a smile.

'Well, it's one pleasure in life they can't put on coupons, in't it?'

'I've heard of others.'

'Rubbish. Bit of skirt'll cost you, even if you're married to it. Maybe especially.'

With that he made his way casually to the door of the Gents. No interruptions, couldn't have been easier. He had the wallet in his pocket and was out again in just over two minutes. This time he stopped and bought a packet of Woodbines from the Welshman, and he even nodded in the direction of the regular customers. Not that anyone seemed inclined to be friendly back. Miserable, stupid sods.

The driver opened the door and went out into the open, and then the old walking-on-air feeling hit him like something entering his blood. As if he'd suddenly swallowed half a bottle of whisky and he just got the warm, good sensation without the drunkenness. When he reached his cab, he clambered up in his usual way, lit a cigarette to calm himself a bit before turning the engine over. Then he cursed. The lorry coughed noisily like his old mum on a bad morning, then died, just as she had eventually done, and he knew he was going to have to crank it.

He was busy starting his lorry, and so he didn't notice the two regulars come out of the café, the two workmen in flat caps who were there every morning. The pair noticed him, though. They didn't really look at him very long, and they certainly didn't react, but they slowed to a saunter where before they had been walking quite briskly, as if in a hurry. A few yards short of the main road, one of them took out a pipe and stopped to light it, and it looked as though he was making heavy weather of the procedure.

Finally the driver's lorry did a laborious turn and eased its way out of the car park, turned right to take the truck route northwards to Bedford and the safe house where he would deposit the wallet. He saw the two workmen, thought nothing of them. It meant nothing to the driver that the balding, older one took off his cap and scratched his pate with slow deliberation. Someone else, however, saw the signal. A black Austin Twelve saloon with a bold printed sign saying, 'DOCTOR ON URGENT CALL' displayed on its windscreen pulled out from the kerb fifty yards away and drove off in the same direction as the lorry.

'Regular as clockwork, isn't he?' said the balding workman to his mate. 'You could set your watch by him.'

The two of them watched the lorry and the following car disappear round a bend in the road.

'We'll have to be careful we don't come out too soon next time,' the younger one muttered. 'Got to give him leeway. He sees us watching him, we could be in trouble.'

'Bugger it, I say. Atkins has got him all the way to Bedford now.' The balding man frowned. 'Same routine every time. Some foreign gent comes and fetches it from there. After that, the issue gets mysterious. Impossible to find out what it's all bloody for or where the stuff eventually goes. Someone must know, I suppose.'

His companion nodded. 'Must do. I can't understand why we don't just pull the bastard in and give him a going over, you know.' He was muscular and had big knuckles, which he cracked as he reached his conclusion.

'Orders from on high, apparently. Old Grainger's got the fear of God in him and no mistake. Word has it that "C" might be involved.'

A whistle through the teeth at the mention of the Service's All-Highest. 'Then it's ours not to reason why, eh?'

'Too bloody right. Come on, we're on top allowances—I'll buy you another tea.'

10

The black internal telephone on Bredow's desk at the Tirpitzufer buzzed and would not stop. Eventually he gave in and found himself speaking to Colonel Oster's secretary. The Herr Oberleutnant was requested to present himself in the colonel's office as soon as was convenient.

Canaris had travelled to Hamburg that morning and was not due back from his visit to the Abwehr training school there until the next day. His absence put Oster, as Director of Central Bureau Berlin, in charge. Relations between Oster and Bredow had cooled slightly these last weeks, for reasons that Bredow could not quite fully understand, and the Oberleutnant felt some irritation at being summoned to the acting chief's office so late in the afternoon when he had been hoping to be home with Gisela at a reasonable hour. She had been needing him lately; the raids had been bad, and she had been feeling none too well. Bredow's resentful mood lifted a degree when he walked through the door into Oster's office and saw Captain Hans von Dohnanyi perched on the desk. The bespectacled lawyer-turned-Intelligence officer smiled a greeting. This was Resistance business.

Oster, who was in the act of returning a file to the massive steel safe in the corner, acknowledged Bredow's arrival affably enough.

'Good afternoon, Otto,' he called over his shoulder. 'Not too bored with our mundane little shop after your first-class touring of Europe, I trust?'

'On the contrary, Colonel. I find it very soothing.'

Oster locked the safe and turned to face him. 'Hans and I have been talking. We decided that we don't see enough of you at the moment,' he said. Dohnanyi nodded silent assent.

Their manner put Bredow on his guard. He muttered a meaningless phrase to the effect that the Admiral kept him busy.

'He does indeed,' said Oster. 'I read your excellent report on your meetings with Mister Bellingham of the Secret Service. Very interesting. Very impressive.'

'Thank you, Colonel.'

'You're welcome,' Oster replied. 'However, while I am aware that the Admiral intends that we should wait for his return from Hamburg before we all settle down to plan the next move, I thought it would be pleasant to have an informal chat now, just the three of us.'

'If the Colonel deems it necessary,' Bredow answered stiffly.

'The Colonel asks only, in a friendly manner. For God's sake, Otto, make yourself comfortable and stop behaving like a constipated officer cadet.'

Bredow obeyed with a sheepish smile. He stood easier, but remained cautious.

'Now, Otto,' Oster continued. He snapped open an elegant silver case, offered Bredow a handmade cigarette before fitting one into his own ivory holder. 'Let me see if I understand the implications of your report fully,' he said. 'Correct me if I'm wrong, but the British have swallowed everything. They are a hundred per cent committed to the *Wintermärchen* proposals. Yes?'

Bredow nodded. 'They have raised no major objections. They seem pleased with the idea.'

'And so von Kluge and all the other doubting Field Marshals will be made happy.'

'I believe that they will. Such was my clear impression in the case of von Kluge.'

'Thank you. We were not treated to an account of that particular meeting, though it was before Christmas.'

'It was.'

Bredow found himself reddening. If he was honest with himself, he had been expecting an encounter of this sort with Oster for some time. Oster knew only too well that Bredow was the Admiral's protégé: his father and Canaris had served together in the First War and still met socially from time to time. He owed his transfer to a job with the Abwehr, a posting much coveted by ambitious young officers, to that connection, and the fact had been noted. Nor was Oster's resolute jokiness an indication that he did not take every word he said to Bredow very seriously. The colonel was notorious as a social butterfly, a quicksilver opportunist from all surface appearances. At forty-eight he was still a handsome man; he wore exquisitely-tailored uniforms and affected that cigarette holder; the whole package marked him as a lightweight, the charming spymaster who could dazzle generals' wives at parties, who knew everyone, who never went deeper than the skin. The impression was quite misleading, however. If Canaris, from his lofty eminence, was the guardian angel of the conspiracy against Hitler, then its moving spirit could be no one but Oster—or rather, the other Oster, the high-minded desperado behind the smokescreen of charm, the conspirator ready to countenance any double-dealing in a just cause. Sometimes he frightened Bredow, though he had always treated the junior officer with kindness and mildly condescending affection, as a little brother who still had much to learn. Bredow found Oster incalculable.

And his stonewalling attitude seemed to be affording Oster amusement.

'And how long do you think this entire project will take, Otto?' he asked. 'You are not permitted to telephone the Admiral in order to be told what to say. This is an initiative test, if you like.''

'Colonel, that is an unfair question.''

'Perhaps. But your assessment does not have to be correct. All I want is an opinion from you. Hans and I feel that we have not really spoken to you for months, since you have been involved in *Wintermärchen* as the Admiral's emissary. Just give us an idea.'

'Another ten to twelve weeks. That is purely my personal opinion—'

'Thank you. No one will hold you to that estimate. It is, however, very good to have some idea. I will be frank and tell you that the Admiral has not been keeping us very well informed. He lets us have this and that report—such as your accounts of the negotiations in Portugal. When we manage to trap him for a moment and tackle him about the timescale and the way in which it influences . . . other matters . . . we find him evasive.' Oster shook his head. 'Ten or twelve weeks. That is a long time, Otto.'

Bredow noticed that while Oster, though clearly concerned, was quite calm, Dohnanyi had suddenly become pale and was fiddling with his tunic collar.

'For such a complex and crucial matter, not so long, Colonel,' Bredow said. 'We discussed all this at the outset. The Admiral and myself were given a free hand . . .'

Oster shrugged. 'The situation has changed. You tell him, Hans.'

'The Gestapo is nibbling away at the edges of our territory,' Dohnanyi told Bredow with an embarrassed sigh. 'They have been trying to worm their way into the Tirpitzufer for years now, and at last there are indications that they may be getting somewhere. It does not help that so many people are now involved in our work. Paradoxically enough, the more successful a conspiracy is in gathering support, the more vulnerable it becomes . . .'

'What he means, Otto,' Oster interrupted with uncharacteristic sharpness, 'is that we may not have as much time as we thought. If there are any changes in plan, snags, mistakes, in the *Wintermärchen* process, it will cost us dear. Can we rely on the British? Should we rely on the British? And Hitler may not go to Rhodes—he is constantly changing his mind. There are so many imponderables, and meanwhile the Gestapo are not sitting idly by. I don't think I need to be specific about their activities.'

'No, Colonel. You don't.'

Bredow could feel himself weakening. He knew why Dohnanyi had paled at the mention of the timescale, for the shy, scholarly captain was one of the most vulnerable of the conspirators. Now and again the Gestapo, sniffing on the heels of dissident groups and individuals, followed through a trail that led them close to the Abwehr, and Canaris had to organize a protective smokescreen. Recently Dohnanyi, with Oster's blessing, had extended a small sideshow network that he ran into Switzerland. Before long, word had somehow got around that the operation—codenamed *Kaspar*—involved an extraordinary number of Jewish agents. The SD was by now almost certainly aware of this interesting fact. Whether the Prinz-Albrecht-Strasse had also worked out that the apparatus was little more than a disguised escape-route for the Nazis' racial victims, paid for out of Abwehr funds, was not quite so certain, but the likelihood was worrying enough. Dohnanyi, drawing on his lawyer's cunning, cooked the books with great skill, and every time there were suggestions that the figures might be made available for an outside audit, Canaris used his authority and influence to prevent it. He manipulated Wehrmacht-SS rivalries to ensure that the High Command never sanctioned such a move, and so far this had succeeded in every case, but his task was not getting any easier. Neither, therefore, was Dohnanyi's position regarding *Kaspar*. Yes, Hans would be giving a lot of thought to the Gestapo . . .

Oster, meanwhile, was leaning forward urgently. 'Listen to me, Otto,' he said. 'I was at a party the other night, a diplomatic reception for the Slovak Foreign Minister. We ended up in the cellar, hiding from the RAF. But while we sat there, passing round the caviar and trying to pretend that the bonbs were no more than a minor inconvenience, like bad plumbing, a Hungarian military attaché buttonholed me. He was drunk as a pig, and he told me: "My dear Hans, we'll soon get rid of our own fascists and put an end to this futile slaughter. When will you people summon up the courage to do the same? I hear rumours, I hear rumours . . ." Then he winked and lurched off to renew his pursuit of someone else's wife. Dear God in heaven, if those chocolate soldiers know what's going on, then you can be sure that the Gestapo do too, and they're just biding their time—while we canoodle in this leisurely fashion with Sir Stewart Menzies.'

The colonel's Saxon accent, usually no more than a suspicion, a quaint affectation, had come through strongly, transforming his voice into a sort of passionate squawk. Dohnanyi peered anxiously at the door and pursed his lips in disapproval.

Oster, who had started pacing the room during his monologue, sat down again and smiled. 'The least we can do,' he said in a more normal voice, 'is to allow alternative plans for the elimination of Hitler to proceed, rather than placing all our eggs in one basket. Otherwise we shall be totally at the mercy of the British. We should make this clear to the Admiral. Agreed?'

'All the neat footwork in the world won't save us if the Gestapo manage to penetrate the Tirpitzufer,' Dohnanyi commented. 'And neither will Sir Stewart Menzies—no matter how much he may come to love us.'

Bredow nodded, but he said: 'I'm sure the Admiral has his reasons. Perhaps we should wait and see what he suggests tomorrow. We'll have the opportunity of discussing the issue then.'

Bredow's words were those of the loyal junior. Dohnanyi's latest mention of the Gestapo, however, had chilled him deeper than any before. He had always been aware of the hazards, naturally, but he had been so busy running around Europe on Canaris's behalf that somehow fear had receded into the background. The whole thing had become absorbed into routine. Bredow had served an apprentice year in France after the capitulation in 1940, part of a control team sending agents into the unoccupied Vichy zone. He had followed that with a six-month tour attached to the German embassy in Berne, ferreting out details of Swiss exports to Allied countries. He had witnessed a hundred meetings in station restaurants, in safe houses, hotels, serviced dozens of dead-letter drops. From a strictly practical point of view, his encounters with Menzies' man had been no different. One became accustomed to behaving as a member of a charmed élite that made and enforced its own rules, as the military caste in Germany had done for the past two hundred years or more. The Nazis, they told each other, were a passing phase, while the Army went on forever. Until the realization crept in that officers, even Abwehr officers, were mere flesh and blood, no more or less mortal than the Resistance fighters murdered by the Gestapo in the occupied countries, the Jews, Gipsies and Slavs sent to concentration camps; they had flesh that could be scarred and hurt, blood that could flow at the flick of a scalpel, the pressing of a trigger, the drop of a headsman's blade. Perhaps Oster knew that too. Perhaps that was why he always seemed so relentlessly superficial, so full of sour humour, so eager to recount battlefield gossip, and the inside stories of bloody failures with such apparent relish. It occurred to Bredow that by reducing everything to squalid farce the colonel hoped to escape the cold touch of evil, like a man who is constantly mocking the body's malfunctions in a dismissive, familiar way to conceal his fear of the cancer that may already be in him and growing.

Oster and Dohnanyi gave up. The talk of Canaris and his plans grew desultory and finally they turned to the war situation in Russia. Stalingrad was clearly doomed, and the only question was how to counter the powerful Soviet offensive that would undoubtedly follow the final fall of the city. Manstein, appointed commander of the Southern Front in November, was performing miracles of organization, while at Group Centre von Kluge of the famous hundred-and-sixty-seven tanks sat tight and waited. Sure enough, Oster had the latest details, which he related with enthusiasm:

'Von Kluge is refusing to risk his precious armour

around Orel, which forms the hinge between the two commands, therefore one of the Red Army's main targets once they have poor von Paulus and his boys in the bag. Von Kluge wants the new Panthers when they come, but Manstein is getting all the nice toys at the moment. Von Kluge is therefore refusing to play, sulking in Smolensk. Hoppla! These are heroic times we live in . . .'

Bredow listened with disgust to Oster's descriptions of the bickering between the two most senior commanders on the Eastern Front. Men responsible for the lives of millions, whose decisions would probably decide the outcome of the war, were expending most of their energy on exchanging snubs and telling tales on each other, like siblings contending for a patriarch's favour. The patriarch was, of course, Hitler. Bredow understood why von Kluge would only move in favour of a new, non-Nazi régime if someone else—preferably a complete outsider—stepped in and eliminated Hitler. At the moment, the Field Marshal was extracting too much grim enjoyment from the situation; he had too much invested in Hitler and Nazism to give it up of his own volition . . .

At a quarter to six, when he considered that he could leave without appearing rude, Bredow made his excuses. Oster and Dohnanyi were extremely friendly—perhaps more friendly than he deserved, Bredow reflected. He would be glad when all this conspiracy finally bore fruit; at the moment the plotters were irritable, divided amongst themselves. Nevertheless, he felt that he had to remain loyal to Canaris. He could not give in and join the Oster-Dohnanyi camp. Let them fight their own battles.

It had begun to snow outside, tiny flakes as yet because the temperatures were only slightly below freezing. In the blackout the snow felt almost a comfort. Then the mass of commuters at the underground station swallowed up Bredow, uniform, briefcase and all, for which he was also grateful.

Bredow arrived home an hour later, and at first he was worried that Gisela had had to go out for some reason, perhaps because they were short-staffed at the Air Defence Centre. He went into the living room, calling his wife's name, then saw that she was sitting on the sofa in the light of just one table lamp, oddly flushed and nervous-looking.

'There's only soup and sausage to eat. I hope you don't mind, Otto,' she said incongruously as he halted at the threshold of the room. She had her knees closed tight together, and her hands were folded in her lap like a thirteen-year-old who has brought home a poor school report. 'I had the afternoon off, you see, but I had to go and see Dr Baerlein in the Lützowstrasse . . .'

Bredow warily put down his briefcase. 'Why? What's wrong?' he said, trying to keep his voice calm. He evidently failed, because Gisela moved hastily to explain.

'Nothing's wrong, Otto. I . . . I'm pregnant. I'm going to have a baby. You've gone white as a ghost—'

Then, at long last, she smiled.

Bredow walked over to her, knelt and kissed her on the cheek. The damp iciness of his greatcoat made Gisela shiver and giggle.

'It's due in August,' she whispered, burying her head in his shoulder. 'It will be hard to look after a small baby in the winter, with the fuel shortages and everything, but I'm sure we shall manage.'

'Yes, we'll manage.'

'I haven't telephoned mummy and daddy yet, or your parents, because I wanted you to be the first to know.'

'Of course.'

Suddenly she shifted position so that she could see his face. 'Are you happy, darling? You don't look it,' she said.

'I'm sorry. I'm very tired. But your news is wonderful, really wonderful.'

He told her that she must phone her parents immediately, and forced himself to sit holding her hand, nodding and smiling encouragement while she made the announcement to the prospective grandparents, discussed where the baby would be born, what it would wear . . .

And all the time he felt the weight of Dohnanyi's quiet, ominous words: 'All the neat footwork in the world won't save us.'

Us. First person plural. Himself, Gisela, and the baby.

The summons from Canaris came at a quarter to seven the next morning. Bredow padded out of bed in his pyjamas to answer the telephone, cursing sleepily and hoping that it was not family bad news, then registered the Admiral's voice, brisk and extremely awake.

'You are at the Tirpitzufer, Admiral?' Bredow mumbled. He struggled to recall something Dohnanyi had mentioned, about the first train from Hamburg not arriving until eight a.m. 'So early?'

Canaris chose to ignore the question. 'I have been considering the situation and would like to discuss it with you personally. The others are due in at about eight-thirty, so if you could come into the office immediately . . .'

Gisela had stirred when Bredow first got out of bed, but she had drifted off again by the time he went back to the bedroom to dress. He was relieved to be absolved from explanations. A scribbled note, as usual left propped against the alarm clock on the bedside table, gave the bare information that something had come up at headquarters. The difference on this occasion was that he addressed it to 'both of you'.

Bredow arrived at the Tirpitzufer less than an hour after Canaris had rung him. He had travelled on an early workmen's train, and there had been no raid, therefore no transport disruptions. Canaris had obviously been in the building during the night. Glancing through the half-open door that led to the small room beyond the office, Bredow noticed that the army cot he kept there had been lain on, but that the covers had not been turned back. The admiral stood gaunt but bristling with nervous energy, hands in his tunic pockets and his devil at his back.

'My apologies,' he said. 'I had to see you, Otto. The evening conference in Hamburg ended early and I was offered a car back to Berlin. It occurred to me that there were urgent matters awaiting my attention here—and the communications section is open all night . . .'

Bredow hung up his greatcoat and cap, took the seat the Admiral offered, and lit his first cigarette of the day. Canaris remained standing, careful to explain that he needed to stretch his legs after the car journey and the hours spent at his desk.

'I have been busy ensuring that all is well on Rhodes for the *Wintermärchen* work there. We cannot afford delays or mistakes on our part—or problems with our local agents,' he said to Bredow, as if thinking aloud. 'No. I realize that

Wintermärchen entails risks, and they must be minimized. We—should I say the British—will be granted only one bite of the cherry. If we fail, we shall have wasted time, energy, and probably lives.'

Canaris sounded slightly gloomy, but Bredow found his concern comforting. The Admiral had anticipated the problems mentioned by Oster and Dohnanyi, it seemed, and was taking action. Bredow therefore decided not to mention his conversation with Dohnanyi and Oster. But he did say: 'I think that the Admiral's expression of his clear intentions regarding *Wintermärchen* will be generally appreciated.'

Canaris stared at him coldly. 'Anything I say to you, Otto, is for your ears only. Understood? *Anything*.' He glanced at his watch. 'We shall be meeting Colonel Oster in about twenty-five mintues. Until then, we shall speak alone, and you will repeat nothing of what I tell you.'

'As you wish, Admiral,' Bredow answered, reddening. This was a peremptory Canaris that they rarely saw.

'Yes. As I wish.'

Canaris's habitual mildness of tone remained; but there was a glint of tempered steel in his grey eyes. Bredow's father had warned him, only partly in jest, that his old friend Franz Wilhelm was not quite the cuddly type he so often appeared to be. The previous evening, when they had spoken on the telephone about the baby, he had told Bredow to 'give my regards to the old crocodile'. Well, here was Canaris showing his teeth, and they were obviously still in serviceable condition. It was not prudence and consideration alone that had taken him to the top of the Abwehr's greasy pole.

'I shall inform the others of any specific actions undertaken as part of *Wintermärchen,*' the Admiral continued. 'You will discuss only what is contained in your reports, which will continue to be vetted by me personally.'

'Yes, Admiral.'

'Good. As a result of my investigations and conversations with our people in the area, I feel confident in saying that things are looking up. In particular, Menzies has taken a step which I expected and consider makes our position much easier.'

A pause.

'In fact, Otto, he has played precisely into my hands, by activating a double agent on the island of Rhodes—a man whom he believes he controls but who is actually one of our most loyal collaborators there. He informed me immediately, of course, when SIS contacted him and asked that he act as local liaison man for the mission. This gives us extra security, Otto. A second line of defence against betrayal or deception. This is always useful, don't you agree, Otto?'

'Yes, Admiral.' Bredow took a deep breath, decided to risk it. 'What I don't understand, however, is why Colonel Oster can't be informed of this very favourable turn of events, this happy coincidence . . .'

'Coincidence?' Canaris hissed. 'Nonsense! I have worked for it. Oster found our man—Stavros Ioannides is his name—before the Italians even entered the war. However, he hired him as a simple informant, a relayer of harbour gossip. *I* have turned him into something more, and set a trap for the British that they have not been able to refuse. *I* instructed Ioannides to offer himself to SIS as a double agent, through channels of my own. He is one of several that I have planted on the British in various vulnerable parts of Europe—in every case, without the knowledge of Oster, who for all his brilliance talks too much and takes too many risks. Does that help you understand? Is your curiosity satisfied?'

Bredow nodded slowly. Canaris was looking at him with a kind of angry affection, and also with an element of defiance, as if to say: I will burden you so heavily with the truth, my boy, that you will have no choice but to obey me totally, be the Admiral's Man.

'The Admiral is very frank. Very frank indeed,' he said, because Canaris obviously demanded an answer.

'Yes. You should also know that I am aware of the Gestapo's investigations into Dohnanyi, and therefore into Oster. All the more reason for restricting both their knowledge of *Wintermärchen* at this stage.'

'Is there a real danger for Dohnanyi, Admiral?'

Canaris shrugged. 'I have been successful in keeping the Gestapo away from our affairs, and I have every reason to believe that I shall be able to do so for as long as necessary. But one can never be certain. So . . .' He let out a shallow sigh, as if releasing a last remainder of emotional pressure from his body. 'Let us return to present practicalities. Your next meeting in Portugal. Happy?'

'By the sound of it, there will be relatively little to discuss with Mister Bellingham, Admiral.'

'A little more information. Not too much, not too little,' Canaris said with a laugh. He was relaxing visibly. Here he was on ground where he felt sure of himself. 'So that they arrive tantalizingly close to friend *Turquoise*. Sir Stewart Menzies will be anticipating a *grand coup* . . . and that is what he will get. Everyone will get what he wants. Except the enemies of decency.'

The last word was unexpected; it dropped into the conversation like a pinch of spice. Bredow wasn't sure how to handle it.

'Is there anything else we should discuss, then, Admiral?' he asked, checking the time by the walnut veneer clock on Canaris's desk. It was twenty past eight.

Canaris shook his head. 'Nothing that can't be dealt with in company.' He sat down, showing that they were returning to normal, and his manner softened. 'You look tired, Otto,' he said. 'I'm sure that this next trip to Portugal will be the last. You must take some leave then. I shall ensure that you do.'

'Thank you, Admiral,' Bredow said. 'My wife is expecting a baby. She told me last night.'

'My goodness, congratulations,' Canaris said, shaking his hand. 'Yes, then in that case you must spend some time with her as soon as it can be arranged. Pregnancy can be a rocky period in a young couple's life,' he commented sagely. 'Women change, you know. Something to do with disruption of the hormone balance.'

'It will make no difference in practical terms—I mean to my role in *Wintermärchen*,' Bredow said, suddenly fearing that in some obscure way Gisela's pregnancy might reduce Canaris's confidence in him. The naïvety of the remark earned him a bemused glance from the Admiral, who had been thinking nothing of the kind. 'I told my father. He was delighted, of course,' Bredow added quickly. 'He sends you his best regards.'

They were interrupted then by Canaris's secretary, a tall, handsome young war widow of thirty who was known to the younger officers at the Tirpitzufer as 'the Amazon'. The nickname was pure sour grapes, because she refused to flirt with them, but it suited the brusque ruthlessness with which she organized her boss's day and protected him from the trivial bureaucratic demands of his position. This morning, because Bredow was in the office at Canaris's express invitation, she flashed him a demonstrably feminine smile. Colonel Oster was in the building, she said, and she believed that the Admiral wanted to see him first thing. Should she call his office and have him come up?

'After we have discussed my immediate appointments, my dear,' the Admiral told her. 'All in good time.'

Canaris and his secretary went through his diary for the day while Bredow smoked another cigarette. The Amazon went out to buzz for Oster, leaving Bredow and Canaris alone. Nothing more was said about the Admiral's secrets. Canaris got up and stood under his devil again, rocking on his heels and nodding. Several times he repeated, 'That was kind of your father to remember me at such a time, Otto. Most kind,' as if kindness were really the most important thing in the entire world.

11

Brigadeführer Walter Schellenberg strode along the wide corridor like a conqueror. He acknowledged as his due the salutes of the men, the smiles from the women, stopping shortly before his destination to check his turnout in a half-length gilt mirror between high windows. Satisfied, he turned the corridor corner smartly and approached the oak double doors that marked the entrance to Kaltenbrunner's office suite.

A curt 'Heil!', a languid raising of the arm, and the two SS guards stepped aside to let him through. No need even to break his stride. At her desk in the corner of the imposing anteroom, the cool, blonde secretary looked up and waved. Schellenberg was popular as well as admired and feared, and to prove it he swooped towards her, bearing an imaginary bouquet of flowers, apeing the lovelorn swain.

The young woman giggled, patted her braided fair hair. It was the sexy peasant girl look. *Blut und Boden* chic. 'Charmed, Brigadeführer. But alas, I am a married woman . . .'

'Nothing's impossible. I should know,' he said, and carried on with the 'presentation' until she was helpless with laughter. Then he perched on the corner of her desk. 'Must I go straight in, or am I permitted to loiter here with you?'

'I'm afraid he's expecting you at any moment, Brigadeführer. And I warn you: this morning his mood is not good.'

'I'll soon change that. Or rather, this will.' He smiled broadly, indicated the contents of his kidskin briefcase. He slid off the desk. 'Nothing's impossible.'

Nevertheless, Schellenberg composed his handsome, if slightly puffy, features into a businesslike mask before knocking on Kaltenbrunner's door. Flirting with a pretty, empty-headed secretary was one thing; an interview with the Reich's chief of security was another. If Schellenberg had really examined his own feelings—something he rarely, if ever, did—then he would have been forced to admit that he was frightened, irrationally frightened.

Kaltenbrunner did not rise when his visitor entered the room. He simply waved Schellenberg to one of the Louis Quinze chairs scattered around the room and finished scratching at some paperwork. Almost a full minute passed before he said a word.

'More material from England, you said?' he asked quietly, without looking up.

'Correct, Gruppenführer.'

'Well?'

'It seems that, should the British succeed in clearing our forces from North Africa, they will make a stab for the Aegean. The evidence for a proposed invasion of Greece—perhaps with Turkish aid if Scaroglü and his government can be bribed into joining the Allies—is accumulating. *Turquoise*'s information is very good, and it fits other evidence that we have been receiving from a variety of sources. What is more—'

'All right, all right!' Kaltenbrunner made a dismissive gesture, indicating that he was not up to too many details, and drank deeply from a glass of water on his desk. Then he stood up slowly to his full six feet three, half-turned, winced, and walked into the centre of the room, careful to keep his eyes away from the direct sunlight. The nation's secret-policeman-in-chief was suffering, Schellenberg realized, from nothing more dramatic than a severe hangover.

'Gruppenführer—'

'So long as it's not chickenshit gossip, Schellenberg, you can circulate it to the Führer,' Kaltenbrunner growled. 'And so long as you're certain of its accuracy.'

Schellenberg sudenly shifted uneasily in his chair. He had been intending to flow easily from one marvellous piece of news to another. Kaltenbrunner's attitude was making the process difficult. The Gruppenführer might be an Austrian streetfighter, and he might lack the suave intelligence of his predecessor, the late Reinhard Heydrich, but he knew when to ask an awkward question. Low cunning. Survival.

'Absolutely,' he said with an assurance that was not entirely felt. How could it be? The whole affair had an element of the gamble in it, like everything else in this game.

'You're certain? Happy with every aspect? His sources, methods . . .'

Schellenberg dared to interrupt, before he had time to know what he was doing. 'Our Swede and *Turquoise* have a close, direct relationship. It seems they drink and womanize together. *Turquoise* is a free spender on a limited salary. He needs his share of the proceeds.'

'That may be true. It does not change the fact that no one has met him apart from the Swede.'

'You have made that point before, Gruppenführer,' Schellenberg said with a prim, martyr's sigh. 'I must tell you that such a situation is not uncommon when an agent is recruited in enemy territory during wartime.'

'Still, we have no proof. I *like* proof. I have been on both sides of the law in my time. I know the importance of proof.'

'The quality of the information is superb—'

'It has never seriously been tested.'

Kaltenbrunner had played this game before. He enjoyed fixing Schellenberg with that baleful stare, seeing him squirm like a trapped insect. But this time the young Brigadeführer had something up his sleeve. He had been hoping to choose his moment during the interview to reveal it, but clearly he couldn't wait.

'Then—as I was about to tell you, Gruppenführer—why does he warn us of an assassination plot against the Führer?'

The time had not been of his choosing, but the effect of his words was even more profound than Schellenberg had hoped. Kaltenbrunner's expression changed from one of threat to one of confusion, then to urgent interest. 'What? Elaborate, man!' he snapped.

'*Turquoise*,' Schellenberg said, rolling the word luxuriously off his tongue, 'has information that the British Secret Service is planning to kill our Führer. He does not yet have all the details of time, place, and so on, but he is prepared, our Swede claims, to hazard a great deal to find these things out. In return for an increased consideration, of course.'

'Of course,' Kaltenbrunner echoed with a hard smile. This was the kind of situation he could grasp and follow. He had stepped out on to the ten metre square Isfahan carpet in front of his desk and stood with his big hands behind his back, feet apart, square as a bull facing a matador as he looked at Schellenberg. A highly intimidating sight. The black uniform fitted his powerful physique perfectly. Only the face was out of place, Schellenberg mused; it was a battered, second-hand head topping an immaculate tailor's dummy of a body.

Schellenberg had to lower his gaze to avoid feeling physically overwhelmed by his superior.

'In fact,' he said, 'I have already taken the liberty of informing *Turquoise*, via Gronheim and the Swede, that he will be fabulously rewarded for more specific information.'

'I'd bet a year's salary he already has the details and is holding back to push the price up,' Kaltenbrunner said, pacing the floor. 'The question is, do the British still have connections in Germany, or are they going to try to catch the Führer in the occupied territories, as they did Reinhard?' His bruiser's features tensed with the weight and worry of it all.

'It seemed to me, Gruppenführer, that we had little

choice except to demand more information, whatever the price . . .'

'Yes, yes. Of course. But we must get it quickly.'

Schellenberg nodded obediently. 'We shall, Gruppenführer. And when we do, the Abwehr—who know nothing of the affair—will look very foolish. We, on the other hand, will have come out covered in glory, as we did in '39 after Venlo.'

'I remember. Don't worry,' rasped Kaltenbrunner, taking another swig of water. 'Everyone remembers your triumph then. But this had better work out, too. Our uncovering an unsuccessful British plot against the Führer's life would be the stuff of dreams; to find out about one that then proves successful, however . . . I need not go on, I think.'

'No, Gruppenführer.'

'Well, I shall strengthen the security precautions around the Führer—without informing him for the moment. For the present, all will proceed normally—or what passes for normally in the Führer's life—and you will do your job.'

'Certainly.'

'Action that immediately. We shall meet later in the week when I am better prepared.'

The SD boss was looking somewhat fragile again after the enlivening shock of Schellenberg's revelations. He put out his hand for the folder of material that the younger man had brought to the meeting and then tossed it onto his desk for later examination. 'I'll sift through this stuff from London,' he said and then nodded, clearly a dismissal.

Schellenberg, for his part, did some fine calculations on his chances of pushing his superior too far, decided to take the risk, and stayed seated.

'I was also going to ask if the Abwehr investigations were still proceeding in a satisfactory fashion,' he said, braving Kaltenbrunner's glance of irritation.

The response was not immediate. Kaltenbrunner, who had been about to sit down at his desk once more, glowered at him, then shrugged. 'Yes.'

'Close to a successful conclusion, I hope, Gruppenführer.'

'It seems so. The boys at the Forschungsamt are slow,

but they're as thorough as any academic when it comes to heaping up their facts . . .'

Schellenberg cleared his throat. 'Naturally, as head of the most interested department—'

Kaltenbrunner's features cracked. The final result was rather more than a grimace, not quite a smile.

'Don't worry, little Walter,' he interrupted, using Schellenberg's first name to gently diminishing effect. 'Once we've sorted out the Abwehr and brought everything under our control, you'll get your share of the pickings. It will take time, but we should be ready to move in on Dohnanyi and his Yids by the spring. If we can get just one of the bastards down to the Prinz-Albrecht-Strasse for interrogation, we'll be on our way.'

'Such measures are long overdue, Gruppenführer. For German officers to behave in such a way is scandalous.'

'More than that, it's downright illegal, and that's how we're going to nail them and put them where Canaris can't lift a finger to protect them. Now, if you'll excuse me, I'm busy . . .'

Well satisfied, Schellenberg saluted smartly and turned to go. As he reached the door, he heard Kaltenbrunner's voice again. He swivelled on his heel.

'Spies are your business, Schellenberg,' Kaltenbrunner said, in a voice like iron filings. 'This *Turquoise* is becoming more and more crucial, more and more informative. If you are right, he could be the most important Intelligence coup of this war or any other. If you are wrong about him . . . well I hope not. Because, as I said, he's your business.'

'Yes, Gruppenführer.'

'Good hunting, Schellenberg.'

Outside in the anteroom, the blonde had a mirror set up on her desk and was repairing her makeup ready to go out for lunch.

'How was he?' she asked.

'Not so bad,' said Schellenberg, switching on a confident smile. 'Look, are you sure you're married?'

'Of course I am!' she protested. 'Mind you, he is in the Ukraine or somewhere. Special Duties, he says. That's an awful long way away.'

Schellenberg could take a hint. 'You're lucky, darling,' he said, nodding in mock sympathy. 'My wife lives a mere three streets from here. Still, nothing's impossible . . .'

This time they met by the beach at Carcavelos, nearer to Lisbon. The small, unfashionable resort was almost deserted, as Bellingham had known it would be. They climbed down from the town and took a blustery walk across the beach, coats flapping in the brisk westerly wind.

'Always I forget that this is not the Mediterranean but the Atlantic,' the Prussian said, waving one hand in the direction of the sea, which had retreated out a good half mile. 'Tidal, you see. Just like Sylt, or Travemünde, or . . . Brighton . . .'

Bellingham grunted wordlessly.

'You don't seem very talkative,' added the Prussian.

'Well, you're making up for it. Chatting away gaily, more than enough for both of us.'

'I apologize. I have recently had some good news for a change. My wife is expecting a baby.'

'Ah.' Under these circumstances, Bellingham thought, what precisely was the etiquette? It seemed unfair for the Prussian to suddenly spring a personal happiness such as that on any enemy, but perhaps one shouldn't be too churlish. Sod it. In a way, they were both in this together, equally powerless in the face of their superiors' demands. 'Very nice. Congratulations,' he said, and smiled.

They changed direction and wandered a way towards the sea before they stopped to begin their business talk. The ridged sand, only recently exposed to the drying action of the wind, was still distinctly wet under foot.

'It seems that everything has been arranged to our chiefs' mutual satisfaction,' the Prussian said.

'Certainly looks like it. No last-minute problems.' Bellingham stroked his coat pocket where he was carrying the small package that he had received from the Prussian while they were still in the shelter of the rocks. It contained the final batch of the *Turquoise* material, the Germans' 'advance payment'. 'There'll be no necessity for another meeting until you provide the details about Hitler's visit to Rhodes.'

'True. You will have the most work to do in the meantime, I think.'

'I suppose you'll just hang around Berlin keeping your ears flapping,' said Bellingham in an attempt at jocularity.

The Prussian missed the finer implications. Perhaps irony is a British specialty. 'Are you optimistic?' he asked.

'Well, yes, old boy. Nothing's certain, of course . . .'

'You kill Hitler, and we'll be able to fish the swine's name out of the SD files at our leisure. Schellenberg and company will be far from the Prinz-Albrecht-Strasse, either drawing their pensions or preparing their defences while waiting to stand trial for crimes against the German people!'

'I see what you mean,' Bellingham said, feeling that he had to match the younger man's vehemence somehow. 'You'll be the masters, eh?'

'Yes. When we are in charge, and provided your government has the sense to make peace with us, you can have your pick of the SD files, I think.'

'But not the Abwehr ones.'

'Unlikely,' the Prussian agreed with a laugh. The mood was easy.

After a pause, Bellingham said: 'I know that our doing away with the Führer is the most important part for you, but my chief specifically asked me to make sure that you were aware of the stress we place on the radio messages and the resulting information. We call that bit "the marked fiver". It's our insurance policy. In case . . .'

'In case Hitler survives yet again. All right. We are quite clear about our promise to help you catch this spy. We understand fully the way the system will work—radio messages leaked to the three or four suspects, with subtly differing key information in each, and then we see which version comes through. Simple, good, like tracing forged money, as you say. So long as the choice of suspects, the—shortlist?—is correct.' The Prussian's mood had darkened again. He was nodding gloomily as he spoke. When he had finished, he stared down at the damp toes of his shoes. 'I hope that all goes well for you,' he added incongruously.

Bellingham wasn't sure who the 'you' referred to, and so he simply shrugged and answered: 'Likewise'.

The Prussian absently brushed one heel across the sand, scouring out a short line, a barrier. 'So we do not have much to say to each other today. More another time, perhaps.'

'Another time. It's possible. One never knows in our profession.'

'No. Goodbye, then.'

'Goodbye.'

Bellingham rubbed his hands together, retreating as he did so. Then he turned and walked the two hundred yards to the steps cut in the high sea wall. He did not look back until he had reached the promenade at the top. Panting from the climb, he rested on the iron rail there for a while and gazed out over the long, curving beach. It took him a few moments to identify the Prussian, who was striding energetically to the west, head bowed, at a speed that Bellingham found puzzling. His shoulders were hunched against the rising wind as he walked, and occasionally he would hold up one hand to prevent his hat from blowing away in a particularly strong gust. The Prussian looked as though he intended to walk for hours like that; as though he needed to work something out of his system on the beach at Carcavelos.

After he had watched the dwindling figure for a minute or so, long enough to fix the image in his memory, Bellingham thought how short the meeting had been on this occasion. With a start of irritated surprise, he realized that he would miss these encounters; perhaps because he was chary of what the next stage of the operation would bring. He had been invited to Menzies' place in Wiltshire for the weekend, a fact which served only to increase his apprehension.

The Prussian had become almost indistinguishable from the grey rocks of the headland to the west. Bellingham shielded his eyes from the afternoon sun with one hand, looked hard and fancied he saw him again, standing motionless against the headland and staring back towards the town. Then he—if he it was—clambered up onto the rocks and over, and Bellingham took himself and his precious package off to catch the train to Lisbon, first step on the route back to England.

12

Menzies led the way as he and Bellingham trudged up between the tall, bare beech trees to the brow of the hill. They turned to look down on Bridges Court, his country home, half a mile below them where the Wiltshire Downs dipped into the valley. The square Queen Anne House, sheltered to the north by a wide crescent of trees and with parklands rising west and south, was the colour of pale honey in the sunlight. A retriever sniffed the dead, frosted leaves a few feet from them; both men carried double-barrelled guns, beautifully-balanced hunting pieces from James Purdie and Sons.

'There's a view that hasn't changed for two hundred years—and never will if I have anything to do with it,' Menzies said. 'We're lucky today. Sometimes on a winter's morning, the mist gathers on the low ground, and you can't see a darned thing of the combe or the house.'

Bellingham nodded appreciatively, his hands thrust deep into the pockets of the padded shooting-jacket that Menzies had lent him for their outing. 'Glorious,' he agreed.

So far, Menzies had hardly referred to the real purpose of his visit to Wiltshire. They had spoken on the telephone when Bellingham arrived back from Portugal; Bellingham had outlined the substance of the Carcavelos meeting, arranged to drop the package of material. Then, when he had arrived from London the previous evening, there had been the business of becoming acquainted with the second Lady Menzies, playing the role of the old war chum, making anecdotal small talk. Bedtime had been ten-thirty, sharp. After breakfast today, Menzies had suggested that they go out for a gentle stroll with the guns and perhaps have a casual bang at some end-of-season pheasant—no loaders, just a couple of keepers to do the beating and Laddie, Menzies' favourite dog, to fetch for them.

Menzies stood with his gun tucked under one arm and prodded thoughtfully at a fallen tree trunk with one gum-boot. His breath steamed in the clear, cold air.

'I hope you don't mind spending the weekend simply *en famille* with us, Jackie,' he said. 'Better than loitering around St James's Park like a pair of ageing pederasts, don't you think?'

'Don't worry, Stewart. This is perfect. I'm flattered that you and Lady Menzies should be prepared to put up with my company for a whole two days.'

'I stood it for a number of months, twenty-five years ago,' Menzies chided gently. 'Strikes me you're suffering from what those modern quacks call a sense of inferiority.'

'Inferiority be buggered. I'm coming up to my second decade of enforced bachelorhood. It makes you crusty, hard to cope with in a civilized household.'

Menzies laughed. 'Rubbish. You're not for the breaker's yard yet. You've got important work to do, and you're going to need all the native guts and intelligence you can summon. I know the old spark's still there. I've seen it.'

Bellingham said: 'Brass tacks, then, Stewart?'

He had to wait for his answer. Menzies had spotted a pheasant rising a hundred yards away. He raised his gun and fired. The bird carried on into flight, but others had begun to take to the air. A second shot brought one down. The retriever bounced joyfully away, plunging down the hillside towards his master's victim.

'Inelegant, to say the least, but there you are,' Menzies commented, setting down his canvas game bag by the tree trunk and preparing to reload. 'Next one's yours, so keep your eyes peeled.'

'I'll have a go.' Bellingham paused. 'Now, what exactly are you driving at? What do you want me to do? Apart from massacring the wildlife, that is.'

Laddie was racing back with a plump bird gripped gently between his well-schooled jaws. The dog dropped the pheasant at Menzies' feet, earning a pat and a tickle behind the ears.

'It's pretty straightforward. The Rhodes business needs someone reliable to oversee it, and you're the only chap I can think of who'll do,' Menzies answered slowly. 'That means an end to your travelling back and forth to Portugal. There's no need for you to be involved in that aspect any more. We've finished the part where your wise head was required. From now on, it's a question of getting specific information through as quickly and as safely as possible, and for that the Vatican connection will do very well. I want you for Rhodes instead, Jackie.'

'Lucky me.'

'Oh, I considered one or two Service veterans,' Menzies continued, impervious to sarcasm. 'Men with good records, too. But I couldn't get away from the problem of security. In any case, whoever's running the show needs to be able to put up a good front, to organize well, to be aware of exactly what he's up to, and—above all—to react quickly and calmly to whatever situation arises.' He smiled, transmitting his feelings in advance. 'That means he has to be in the know, as you are, because you've been handling the negotiations with Canaris's man. You're the only candidate, really.'

Bellingham mused that Charlie must have felt like this during their day out together in Oxford. This was Menzies' equivalent of the slap-up treat, and big softening-up exercise. It was the same spiel, whether it consisted of a café lunch and a bad film, or a ration-straitened weekend at the family seat with Sir Stewart and Lady M. In his increasingly frequent moments of self-examination, Bellingham knew only too well what he wanted from Charlie and was prepared to bribe him for: the gift of unconditional love. As for what Stewart was working to draw out of him now, it was a related quality. Call it loyalty, patriotism, also of the absolute kind.

'Um. Tell me what it means in practical terms,' he said.

'First thing: you'll have to be commissioned back into the army.'

'Christ, Stewart. I'll be sixty in two years' time.'

'There are octogenarians serving happily with His Majesty's Forces. They lie about their age. It's frightfully easy to have people posted on the General List. We can have you made a major inside a fortnight. Stranger things happen every day, I assure you.'

'That's not what I mean. I mean, I don't know anything

about the way those things are done these days. All my experience is a quarter of a century old, Stewart.'

'You'll have experts to help you,' Menzies continued, implacable. 'Your job will be to sit in an office somewhere in the Middle East, as they say, and be an administrator, keep an eye on the technicians. Nothing more adventurous than that—except for some recruiting.'

'Recruiting?'

'I intend to train volunteers taken from army units already serving in the Eastern Mediterranean. I've been in touch with a chap in Cairo who's agreed to assist us in that respect . . .'

'Wait a minute, Stewart. The Service is packed to the gunwales with fit, highly-trained young men, all raring to be off to occupied Europe to give the Nazis a bloody nose. What's wrong with using a few of them?'

'Nothing,' said Menzies placidly. He waited a beat for effect. 'Under different circumstances, nothing at all, but this is a very special case. First of all, to have you toddling around Cairo calling for volunteers adds a nice touch of conviction. The mysterious major . . . Second, I feel safer with soldiers. They accept orders, do what they're told, and then, when it's all over, they go away again, none the wiser as to the greater significance of the whole affair. Lastly, if the worst happens and they fall into enemy hands, they will be able to tell their captors only what they know from us—which means you.' Menzies wagged a long finger. 'No question of their divulging any Service secrets, or pretending to be other than what they are: serving soldiers. Of course, since they will wear uniform, there will also be less likelihood of their being shot as spies, if that helps you to feel better about it.'

'That'll do, Stewart,' Bellingham drawled. He had taken a seat on the tree trunk, and his briar was filled and lit, so thorough and lengthy had Menzies' apologia turned out to be. 'I can grasp the advantages well enough. Presuming that these officers can be sufficiently well prepared.'

'They can. The commandos turn them out in no time, and we shan't be so demanding. An intensive course. A very small group. Our people will be chosen for their existing skills and abilities, further reducing the time needed to train them.'

'Nevertheless, it seems you're asking me, an instant major, to tell lies to young men who have volunteered to risk their lives, and I don't like the sound of it much,' Bellingham said.

'Tell *lies*?' Menzies gave every appearance of genuine surprise and hurt. 'You will assume a cover, admittedly, and the men involved will not be told of their work's actual objective until as late in the day as possible. And they won't know the identity of their target. This is partly for their own sake.'

'Really?' Bellingham continued to look sullenly doubtful.

'In this field, one has to tell people to do extreme things,' Menzies said with an exasperated laugh. 'If an explanation becomes necessary, one gives whatever reasons appear plausible and expedient at the time. They may be strictly true, and they may not be.'

'I realize that, but under these particular circumstances—'

'Jackie, I want you to imagine you order someone to go and dig a hole in the ground. If pressed for an explanation of why, you say that you wish to trap a savage tiger. Are you listening?' Menzies waited for Bellingham's assenting nod. 'There are no tigers in the vicinity, in fact,' he continued. 'Your real aim is to bury a hoard of gold doubloons. Is that not a white lie, at worst? It makes no difference whatsoever to the actual process of digging, and therefore none to the individual carrying out the work—so long as he is not disabused of his original notion in a dramatic fashion. He performs the service, receives his reward, and goes away innocently content. You see the parallel with our chaps' situation, surely?'

'But they're going to kill Hitler!' Bellingham bellowed.

One of the estate workers beating the copse down at the bottom of the hill looked up for a moment, startled by the unexpected noise. Menzies waved to reassure him and said to Bellingham without even a glance in his direction:

'Do you think we'll be short of volunteers under those conditions? Advertize it thus: "Mission to kill prominent enemy official. Dangerous, uncomfortable work. You won't even be told who he is until afterwards. Capture means a good chance of being shot out of hand. Success, though, means a chestful of medals and something rare and absolutely wonderful to tell your grandchildren.'' See the response, Jackie. We'll find ourselves inundated, don't you agree?'

Meanwhile, the retriever, lost for a while on some truly inexplicable canine errand among the beeches, had re-appeared and was sniffing the air, every muscle tensed.

Bellingham did not reply to Menzies' rhetorical question. He stood up without bothering to take his pipe out of his mouth, waited impassively. After a few moments, he swiftly lifted his gun and took aim. A pheasant that had just taken off from the edge of a ploughed field below to their left skewed over in flight, then dropped like a soft, fluttering missile into the mud between the furrows. Because the hillside was so quiet and the ground so icy-hard, the sound of the fall echoed gently, almost sadly.

Menzies whistled between his teeth. 'I told you, you haven't lost it, Jackie. You can still pick 'em off when you decide to.'

They watched Laddie's progress down the slope towards the corpse of the hapless bird. Less than three weeks and it would be close season. A classic case of being in the wrong place at the wrong time, at least from the pheasant's point of view, Bellingham thought.

'It's those ruddy grey areas,' he said to Menzies. 'They worry me. They worry me a lot.'

Menzies was busy popping the second pheasant into the bag. One each, which meant honour satisfied.

'It's after twelve,' he announced. 'Time we were getting back for lunch.'

'Make mine a double. I think I need strength.'

'Does that mean you're willing to give the Rhodes project a spin?'

'Did I give the impression that I wouldn't?'

Menzies whistled to his dog. 'I think you might rather enjoy it. You always were adept at entering into a role. In fact, if I dare say so, it's what makes you such a darned good liar.'

'I'd rather you put it some other way, but never mind.'

They walked in silence to the bottom of the hill, crossed the muddy field and clambered over a stile in the hedge that bounded the grounds of Bridges Court. Bellingham thought a lot about Cairo. He had spent a year there during the last war in a nice, undemanding staff job, after his spell on the Western Front had cured him of any grand ideas about the nobility of suffering. Halcyon days, an interlude hanging out at Shepheard's and the Turf Club, when all he'd had to do was look smart and say the right thing to anyone over the rank of captain who happened to glance in his direction. It had ended suddenly, when some Smart Alec had recommended him to MI6, on the grounds that he had something of a talent for languages and that he was—as Stewart had said, actually, all too rightly—capable of lying with fair conviction in every one of them.

The study at Bridges Court made no concessions to passing fashion. Its owner's tastes were solidly Edwardian and male: a large oak desk with a leather top facing the window, framed portraits of long-dead thoroughbred hunters on the walls, and deep armchairs that invited man-to-man conversation over cigars and vintage port. No cigars this evening, but port, plenty of the real stuff, laid up in better times.

'I must say Lady Menzies is admirably tolerant,' Bellingham remarked, watching Menzies draw the curtains. A fire had been lit by the maid before dinner, ready for their withdrawal here. 'But then I suppose this sort of thing must be becoming part of her routine.'

'Oh, really only since Quex died and I took over the bed of nails. There's so much to do, and one can't fit it all into the week in London. We have people down about one week in three. It's her contribution to the war effort, she says, acting the gracious hostess and knowing when to make herself scarce.'

'Marvellous woman, Stewart.'

'Yes. Yes indeed,' Menzies agreed, pouring them both large measures of port. Perhaps he was conscious of Bellingham's envy, but he did not invite further conversation on the subject. 'You know,' he said, 'I can understand why you might have felt a spot of apprehension when I outlined the Rhodes jaunt, Jackie. It's not the way things are done these days, more's the pity. Personally, I find it comforting to think that one can still cut corners, rely on friends, get away from all the dreadful red tape we seem to be afflicted with, and pull a quiet fast one while the bureaucrats and the better-safe-than-sorry crowd aren't looking. But we have full support from the PM, so don't worry, if that was the problem.' He unbuttoned his dinner jacket and smiled comfortably. Somewhere out in the park an owl screeched. This was a hungry month for them, when their prey, like the fox's, became scarce and elusive.

'I'm all right,' Bellingham said. 'I've been thinking about the traitor, and finding him hard to understand. It makes the entire situation . . . uncanny is almost the right word. In our war—I mean, the first lot—we had Roger Casement, but he had the excuse of being an Irishman . . .'

'Simple patriotism's on the way out, Jackie. The world's dividing up: left, right, anywhere but the old British golden mean. The revolutions of the past twenty or so years threaten to make our type redundant. We're moving into the age of the turncoat, and his opportunities are infinitely increased, because our methods of waging war are so much more sophisticated and therefore more vulnerable,' Menzies said. 'I see this quality even in Canaris.'

Bellingham looked at him sharply. 'If what his young man said is true, he is set on overthrowing a beastly system. I find that hard to fault.'

'Quite. Those Germans are idealists,' Menzies said. 'And that is precisely why they are dangerous. Useful, but dangerous, differing from our own traitor only in as much as we find their action laudable. The principle of their betrayal is no different. Where does it end when one starts putting conscience above country?'

He leaned forward to pour some more port. A slap-up treat, you're a big boy now, Jackie, Bellingham thought irreverently. You shall want for nothing, not even special confidences to flatter you.

'You see,' Menzies continued. 'The Abwehr has been giving away secrets in a fairly systematic fashion for some years now, since before the war. Representatives visited distinguished politicians here at the time of Munich, to promise a military putsch if we stood fast and forced Hitler into war over Czechoslovakia. Winston was one of the few who took them at all seriously. Colonel Oster, head of Berlin Centre, tried to warn us of the beginning of the German offensive against the Low Countries in May 1940—and unfortunately the attack was postponed so often that when he finally got it right, everyone of importance had stopped listening. They're determined to dish Hitler, all right; and if they can't kill him, they have to ensure his military defeat, whatever the cost.'

'I'm sure that if I were in their position, I would find it difficult to think differently,' Bellingham said.

Menzies pursed his lips thoughtfully, with a suggestion of disapproval. 'Thank God that neither of us is so placed,' he murmured. 'Imagine, if you can, that Hitler had invaded Holland and Belgium, and Oster had got it right first time, which might well have meant that we were properly prepared. Thousands of young German soldiers might well have been slaughtered, because one individual—for highly-tuned moral reasons—had decided that his notions of freedom and justice transcended any narrow duty to his country . . .'

'Right or wrong?'

'One's country is rarely either of those things,' Menzies retorted blandly. 'One's country . . . is one's country.'

'I'm beginning to wonder why you're prepared, in that case, to play fast and loose with those doubtful individuals, Stewart. Don't you feel some slight, sneaking sympathy?'

The leg-crossing routine came immediately. Really, one day he must tell Menzies about it.

'I do,' Menzies said. 'I should hate to live in Nazi Germany, and I should certainly feel outraged at the horrors being committed in the name of my country, but I could not justify what I—we—undertake on those grounds alone.' He smiled almost painfully and shook his head. 'No, I have entered into this *imbroglio* because I see solid benefit in it for my country's righteous cause and for the work of the Service I have the privilege to command. At no time, I might add, do I forget that Herr Canaris heads an organization which employs some fifteen thousand men and women whose task is to do us down whenever and wherever they can, and of whom the vast majority have never heard of any plot to overthrow their Führer.'

'If,' Bellingham suggested drily, 'the manager of a slaughterhouse is converted to vegetarianism, it makes no difference to the wretched animals.'

Menzies nodded enthusiastically. The analogy pleased him. 'Ah, Jackie, but if handled correctly, it may be of some use to the commercial opposition, don't you think?'

They laughed together, and it dispelled some of the tension between them. From there they moved away from uncomfortable theories and on to brass tacks. They would begin with the detailed planning straight after Menzies' return from Casablanca. He would talk to the PM there, obtain his final approval, and with that in his pocket he could begin to prepare the ground for Bellingham's trip to Cairo. Jackie would need credentials, an office, a place where the volunteers could be trained—in fact, a small-scale empire. When Bellingham asked him if this wasn't going to mean leaving an active and extremely dangerous spy at large for rather a long time, Menzies assured him that this aspect was being covered, efficiently and unobtrusively. He would not elaborate, even after their fourth glass of port, and in the end Bellingham had to accept that the chief knew best. It was Menzies' plan, after all, and 'C' was entitled to play it as close and mysterious as he chose. If only he would uncross his legs, Bellingham found himself thinking. If only he would uncross his legs.

13

The plump, almost hairless figure seated on the canvas stool held a long brush ready. The famous jaw jutted forward in fierce concentration, the free hand signalled for his audience of one to keep patience. There . . . a gentle sweep of ultramarine set off against the azure, so that it should not be too monotone a sky.

'I have a confession for you,' came the announcement when the stroke had been completed. 'This is the first picture that I have painted since the fateful day in September 1939 when I was summoned to join the War Cabinet.'

Sir Stewart Menzies stooped politely to view. 'The . . . ah . . . Atlas Mountains, is it, Prime Minister?'

'What do you see all around us but their glory?' Churchill said, rising impetuously to his feet to glower the better at his creation. He gripped Menzies' arm. 'There is only one thing that has never failed to make me paint. Africa, man, Africa! One could go mad attempting to describe this brooding, cruel, majestic continent in pale words. One must reproduce it raw.'

'Quite so, Prime Minister,' Menzies answered, glancing away towards the mountains and then back at the canvas, as if checking that his leg was not being pulled. 'I do rather like the play of light where you've administered the various . . . shades of yellow . . .'

'Spoken like a true courtier. What you and I need, however, is not aesthetic reflection but a stiff drink, and that, Stewart, is what we shall damned well get!'

Releasing Menzies, he clapped his hands like a pasha. An orderly came scurrying through the open French windows onto the terrace of the villa.

'Two brandies and a soda syphon, my dear fellow,' Churchill commanded. 'And kindly make 'em Yankee measures—like the ones last night.'

Britain's war leader collapsed into one of the latticework chairs nearby, stretching out his bare legs to the sun's attentions. They waited for the drinks. He had risen from a short siesta to finish his painting: though it was four in the afternoon he wore his favourite silk dressing gown emblazoned with red dragons, and underneath it a singlet and a pair of silk shorts. This vision of the great man at his ease might have shocked those used to the propagandists' stirring images, but personally Menzies found the real, private Churchill more appealing. Sprawled in his chair in his brash gown and underwear, he resembled a brooding aristocratic rake in an engraving by Hogarth, grand and yet gross, high and low life in one. Perhaps something of a throwback to the old, terrible England that had boozed, whored and gambled while seizing a quarter of the earth's surface for itself without scruple. Certainly not the watered-down modern version, the country of 'democratic' righteousness and mealy-mouthed sweet reason.

The brandy arrived promptly. Churchill splashed a token jet of soda into his glass. Menzies, judging the quantities of spirit involved, was more generous in his mixing.

'To Marrakesh. Escape from the silken prison,' Churchill toasted with an extravagant gesture. 'To painting in a scented garden and to victory!'

'Indeed, Prime Minister,' Menzies answered. 'To all those estimable things. I hope that you were pleased with the outcome of the conference.'

'In measure, Stewart. The only pity is that FDR's advisers whisked him away so quickly. He could spend only one night here with me away from the razzamataz of Casablanca.' He sighed. 'I had been hoping to bend the presidential ear a little more thoroughly on the subject of the Mediterranean, but it was not to be. He and George Marshall still demand a landing in France, and we must let them have it . . . So let the preparations commence.'

'They are already in hand. But first we must sort out Rommel in Tunisia.'

Churchill chuckled mischievously. 'We sit here staring at his behind, while over on the Libyan border Montgomery peers keenly at his groin. The Fox does not know where the next blow will strike his sensitive parts.'

'Indications, sir, are that he will try to pre-empt us very soon,' Menzies said. 'He knows very well that if a junction is affected between the Allied armies to his east and west, he is finished.'

'Oho. Yellow box?'

'I have the latest summaries with me, Prime Minister.'

The 'yellow box' which appeared mysteriously in Churchill's office most working days was marked strictly for his personal attention. Even members of his immediate staff, supposedly intimate confidants of the PM, were unaware of its contents, for the box was the most closely-guarded secret of the war. In it were summaries of information culled from German radio traffic throughout the main theatres of war, which the British had been able to decode with increasing success since the fall of Dunkirk, and without allowing the enemy to know his ciphers were vulnerable. The Germans, it seemed, continued to consider their code unbreakable; they named it 'Enigma' after the sophisticated machine that generated it. The officials who ran the huge monitoring and decoding establishment at Bletchley Park in England labelled the material 'Ultra' and made it available only to a tiny circle of ministers, Intelligence officers and generals serving in the field. In Churchill's and Menzies' private language it was 'yellow box' or 'the secret source', filtered through the SIS headquarters at Broadway to Downing Street via a tight courier system. Occasionally Menzies would deliver it to the Prime Minister in person, to put his own department's stamp on the information or, as now, because it was safer to use the SIS diplomatic bag facilities than to rely on the notoriously unreliable international communications system.

'When I have run an eye over it, we must discuss the implications with Ismay,' Churchill said. He called for more brandy. 'The Axis must be cleared from the North African shore before we can lunge at its belly. I thank God for our source. And you, Stewart, for the practical part . . .'

Menzies nodded coolly, waiting for the orderly to finish refilling Churchill's glass. He was glad that they were here in the foothills at last, freed from the barbed wire, the exaggerated security, the oppressive, backslapping atmosphere that seemed to affect any conference at which the Americans called the tune. Here one could talk frankly, make real decisions. Nevertheless, it was necessary to tread carefully.

'A propos, Prime Minister,' he said when they were alone again. 'The . . . other business is proceeding seamlessly so far. All concerned have taken their baits like good boys. We are almost ready to move on to the next stage.' Suddenly he felt a twinge of apprehension, and a glance at the Prime Minister told him that the old man's sensitive antennae had not missed the hint.

Churchill had been about to drink. He set down his glass without a drop having passed his lips and fixed Menzies with a stare of mild reproach.

'We have discussed this SIGNIFY many times, Stewart,' he murmured. 'We have considered this response, that response, or no response at all, to the opportunity with which the Abwehr has presented us. We have considered the possible cost—trivial though regrettable—and the probable benefit—inestimable—and we have determined to press on along the path that we have chosen. Or rather, which we have had forced upon us. Now, do I sense lurking, insidious doubts, spymaster?'

'There are always doubts, Prime Minister,' Menzies said slowly. 'Doubts both about what is possible and what is right in an affair of this kind.'

'You are still uncertain that we have backed the right horse?'

'There is . . . discomfort. Canaris is, by the standards of these terrible times, a decent man. Shall I say that my heart occasionally comes into conflict with my head?'

'Stewart,' Churchill said, leaning over to pat Menzies' arm, 'I understand your feelings. I love you for your gentlemanly virtues.' Then his voice hardened a fraction. 'And yet, I must remind you that it was you who, after much agonizing, settled on the path we should take—particularly in the light of FDR's refusal to even consider cooperation with the conspirators, and the fact that Stalin would probably declare war on *us* on the spot . . . I quote your own words, Stewart. You convinced me that you could nevertheless weave a rich tapestry of benefit for our cause from the materials with which fortune had presented us. We agreed: Better the devil we know . . .'

Menzies sighed. 'Of course, SIGNIFY makes perfect sense, Prime Minister,' he admitted. 'But SIGNIFY still represents what we *must* do rather than what we would *like* to do.'

'Well said, as ever. That's what being a soldier is all about, and in a way we are both soldiers. I also have my regrets. I hate that swine Schickelgruber, but I reckon your head's got the right answer. Brother Canaris, our little Admiral without a navy, and his plotters will have to be led as far up the garden path as our interests demand, and that's that.'

'Yes, Prime Minister,' said Menzies, deciding that agreement would close the subject.

'Good. Now, tell me what we do next.'

Menzies smiled like a schoolboy acknowledging the encouraging words of a chum. 'The good Bellingham goes to Cairo, Prime Minister, and finds us a selection of brave chaps willing to undertake dangerous work. He kits them out, trains them. I have already found some technicians, Prime Minister.'

'Good, good.'

'On the island itself, we have a trusted agent who will act as a liaison for the last-minute details. He will also be responsible for shipping our chaps off the island if possible after the . . . the crucial event. His codename is *Dancer*.'

'The presence of such a fellow must reassure you, Stewart.'

'Of course, Prime Minister. Although very precise timing will be required. Neat footwork that makes his codename most appropriate.'

'Clearly.' Churchill grimaced. 'Failure is, of course, always harder to organize than success.'

'Quite so.'

Churchill sighed, heaved himself out of his chair, clutching his brandy glass tightly in one chubby fist, and moved ponderously forward to gaze out over the town of Marrakesh below them. White roofs; jutting minarets; blood-red bougainvillea trailing everywhere; ripe green palms; all softened by the dusty haze of the afternoon. The Prime Minister stood for some time in silence with his back to Menzies, a still volcano. 'C' half-turned to watch him, waiting for an eruption, but it did not come.

'These businesses. These deceptions,' Churchill said at last, facing Menzies once more. 'They fray an old man's nerves more than a hundred battles. Covert. Unseen. A hundred years from now it may all seem so clever, even comical, to some prurient history writer.' He gestured violently with the now-empty glass. 'We know the cost and the risks as well as the possible benefits—and nevertheless we must act . . . What is that saying: "In the country of the blind, the one-eyed man is king"?'

'A firm axiom of my trade, Prime Minister. Canaris sees very clearly all that is in his field of vision, and he uses it as best he can. I see more. Therefore I have him exactly where I want him.'

'Unless he sees more than you think!'

'He must have Hitler dead for his plan to succeed. That is his weakness.'

'Yes, his weakness,' Churchill was forced to agree. He began to pace the terrace, shaking his head emphatically as he padded backwards and forwards over the same stretch of terracotta tiles. 'I would not like to be in his shoes, a victim on such a grand scale.' He stopped suddenly, threw back his head and laughed a big belly-laugh. 'One day we shall tell the Americans about this, the way we bamboozled poor Canaris. Roosevelt and his Unconditional Surrender! He thinks that is the way to beat the Germans—to tell them there can be no negotiations!'

Menzies smiled frostily. 'I must admit, Prime Minister, that the President's demand for the enemy's unconditional surrender—which you endorsed at the press conference yesterday—hardly enhances our chances of convincing Canaris of our good faith. I can see the principle behind it, but it comes at a poor time for SIGNIFY.'

'You can lie! You will lie!' Churchill exclaimed. He pounced without warning on the seated 'C', lunged so close that Menzies could smell his brandy-breath. 'The statement yesterday was words, Stewart,' he growled. 'Lie to your Germans if necessary: say that the terms Roosevelt laid down apply only to Hitler and his gang, say anything. War justifies any words, and most deeds, as you should well know.'

'Yes, Prime Minister.'

Mollified, Churchill straightened up and went back to his pacing. 'You are right, of course,' he said. 'I did not want the Unconditional Surrender declaration. FDR was speaking out of his cigarette holder, and not for the first time. However, I could not gainsay him, Stewart.' He stared at Menzies almost plaintively. 'Do you know that the whole long road from Casablanca to this place was lined with GIs when we travelled it yesterday? That was FDR's show of force—of arms, men, and money, where he is strong without equal in human history. And he will not always listen to me. That is why we wise, sad old Europeans must go our own way from time to time . . .'

His voice died away. He nodded heavily, staring down at the town. The light was fading, and the distant mountains glowed orange. There was nothing more of substance to be discussed.

'I shall sit here for a while alone, Stewart,' Churchill said. 'And then I shall proceed to the contents of my yellow box. It is the delight of my days, and I have been missing it. To see into the enemy's heart and mind, into his very being. A gift from God . . . Perhaps we shall talk more after dinner about SIGNIFY.'

Menzies got to his feet, less than completely happy but relieved that the Prime Minister had not chosen to pick a fight.

'As you wish, sir,' he said.

Churchill had returned to sit on his painting-stool, his great, melancholy baby's head sunk between his shoulders.

'One thing applies to all of us, you know, Stewart,' he said softly. 'Canaris, Hitler, Stalin, FDR, you or I . . . There comes a point when the talking is over and men must prove themselves. We must all do that some time, eh?' A big Havana was extracted from its box, ready to be lit as an accompaniment to Churchill's evening meditation. 'We must press ahead with what we have decided to do, though never knowing what the eventual outcome will be.'

'Never knowing, Prime Minister,' Menzies agreed with unusual fervour.

14

Bellingham had been provided with a brand-new major's uniform, a paybook that dated his return to the army from February 1940, a variety of intimidating documents that seemed to give him the power to do whatever he darned well pleased, and a spare seat in a Liberator carrying a party of British Members of Parliament out to Egypt on a fact-finding junket. This had meant that the journey, via Gibraltar and Malta to avoid the fighting still going on in the Tunis Pocket, had been comfortable, with proper seats, food, drink and so on. The price had been twenty-one hours in the company of fools.

'Of course, we should've kept the blasted place under our thumb. A protectorate, wasn't it, in the first show?' his neighbour, a pear-shaped Tory peer was telling him as they came in over the Delta. 'That fat boy of theirs, Farouk, is a pro-Nazi. Quite notorious. His court's a hot-bed of spies. If anyone had any idea what they were doing, he'd have been packed off to premature retirement in Monte Carlo years ago, and his doxies with him . . .'

Bellingham nodded politely and let him drone on. It was better, and in most ways safer than the territory covered by the previous monologue, on how his lordship had caught a whiff of gas at Passchendaele and how otherwise, it went without saying, he'd be back on the active list as well . . .

The plane landed ten minutes later at Heliopolis airport. Their RAF steward had told them to set their watches at five past two, which meant that they would be disembarking into an Egyptian day that had only just passed its torrid peak. As they taxied in, Bellingham managed to ignore his companion for long enough to take a good look out of the porthole by his seat. He could see rising haze in the distance, where the main tarred road to Cairo seemed to shimmer and eddy like a black river. Close up, he noticed, even in February, the sunlight picked everything clean, sharpened tones and lines until the effect was almost unbearable. The yellow of the sand, the dazzling whites of the buildings, the browns and flurries of winter green where bushy vegetation had taken hold, had not lost their capacity to excite him. His last introduction to Egypt, from a steamer at Suez, had been slower, dirtier, more chaotic; it had been days before he had escaped from docks and dusty streets and managed to look at the country in the way he could now from his privileged seat. Flying was an old man's luxury.

The VIP group were herded out, and Bellingham shuffled down the gangway steps at what he fancied to be a safe distance with the travelling bag containing all his precious bits of paper gripped firmly in one hand. He was to be met by an Intelligence officer from Cairo, Menzies had told him, and when he reached the bottom of the steps he stared around in the still heat, blinking in the light, and waited. Within seconds he had been swamped by a crowd of British and Egyptian officials and journalists and general hangers-on attached to the parliamentary delegation; someone tried to grab his bag. He fought his way towards the edge of the mob, lashing out furtively where required, then found himself being manhandled by a man in a khaki uniform, who ignored Bellingham's astonished protests until they were in the clear.

'Sorry, sir,' his attacker panted. 'Christ, I mean, you are Major Bellingham, aren't you.'

'Yes, indeed.' Three pips up and hardly out of rompers. 'Captain. . . ?'

'Rogerson, sir. The Colonel had a conference this afternoon, so he sent me to collect you. I'm the outfit's liaison man.' A self-deprecating but sly smile. 'Which means I spend most of my time setting up smokescreens.' Rogerson glanced over to the belly of the plane. A Sikh the size of an industrial chimney was scrapping with a gaggle of Egyptian porters by the cargo doors, bellowing insults in a mixture of Punjabi, kitchen Arabic and English. 'Ah,' he commented. 'I see our driver's managed to rob up your luggage. We usually pick him for airport jobs. He can handle himself rather well.'

Bellingham nodded approvingly. The Sikh giant had emerged bearing the visitor's trunk as if it were a Christmas parcel, tucked under one arm, dealing blows to his left and right as he made a stately exit from the free-for-all.

'Let's go then, shall we, sir?' Rogerson said.

The young captain's fresh, freckled appearance reminded Bellingham at first impression of a figure out of *Tom Brown's Schooldays*—one of the hero's friends, a little less peerlessly moral and muscularly Christian than Brown himself, but nevertheless a trier and a good egg. He can't have been much more than twenty-four or twenty-five, and second thoughts told you that he had probably always been cheerfully, deviously capable of anything. Or perhaps it was something one learned; Bellingham couldn't remember.

'Lucky we got here on time, sir,' Rogerson said as they walked over to the waiting jeep. 'Otherwise you'd probably have ended up being swept off to the Mena House for a six-course lunch and a lecture on "The Eighth Army: Britain's Fighting Machine".'

'Fortunate indeed,' observed Bellingham. His military alter ego, he had decided during the flight, was going to be a man of few words, most of them rather pompous.

Rogerson ushered him into the back seat, where they hunched leaning against the luggage, and then he bawled at the driver not to spare the horses. Accordingly, the jeep accelerated across the tarmac and headed for the airport's perimeter gate like a mare in heat.

After a brief stop to have their papers checked, they were out on the Cairo road zig-zagging in and out of the military traffic in a way that was all the more terrifying for being awesomely precise.

'Do you want to go straight to the Shambles, sir, or would you rather sort yourself out at Shepheard's first?' Rogerson asked, shouting to make himself heard above the growl of the engine.

Bellingham conquered his horror for long enough to say that he would appreciate a bath and a chance to take a nap.

'Right-ho, sir! I think the Colonel had in mind dinner somewhere later on.'

The 'Shambles', Bellingham had learned during a briefing session with Menzies, was the headquarters of 'S' Force Middle East. The nickname had something to do with self-mocking humour and with a place in Tunbridge Wells. It was also, he had been warned, ultimately highly misleading.

Shepheard's, the most famous hotel in the Middle East, had changed remarkably little since 1916. There were still the patient *safragi* in their Turkish pantaloons waiting on the guests' whims, still the delightfully immodest bronze Venuses lining the corridors. The place was relatively quiet these days, now that the war had moved west to the frontiers of Tunisia. The previous autumn, when the fighting had been less than fifty miles from Cairo, the place had been raucous with young subalterns on forty-eight-hour leave from up the Line, thirsting for excitement and alcohol and, where they could get it, sexual relief. Rogerson said that they had been sleeping in the lobbies, on camp beds in the ballroom, even on the billiard tables, thanks to the indulgent and patriotic management. There were plenty of other hotels that would have taken them in under more comfortable circumstances, but then a leave in Cairo wasn't the same without Shepheard's, was it?

Bellingham undressed in his single room on the second floor, lay down and immediately went to sleep. He awoke at half-past-four after exactly an hour, because he had always been able to pace his sleeps, ever since the First War, when it had come in very useful. Down the corridor for a bath and then a change and he was fit for the evening. Welcome to Egypt and God alone knew what. It was nice to know, in one's fifties, that one's body was still a machine that would do what was required of it, never mind how reluctantly.

The Long Bar was open. Rogerson had called out something vague along the lines of 'don't call us, we'll call you' when they had parted outside the hotel earlier in the afternoon, and so Bellingham simply left notice of his whereabouts at the reception desk. Then he went for his drink. He had been very modest in his consumption on the plane, which was more than could be said for most of the politicians, and now he reckoned he deserved a quick snort and a chance to think.

It was a delight to walk into the bar and order a double Bell's, which he received within seconds, with a smile and a delicate request for a little chit to be signed. The place was already filling up with an assortment of rich Cairenes, journalists, diplomats, military gadflies. Nothing much changed there, Bellingham reflected, eyeing a young staff officer chatting languidly with a civilian further along the bar. The boy could have been himself twenty-five years ago: elegant uniform, wet behind the ears and eager not to show the fact, loving the cachet of the whole thing. Could have been his Prussian, too, if you changed the uniform and the accent. Bellingham was separated from the staff johnny by time, his Prussian by geography, but then all accidents involved time and geography, not least the fatal ones.

He was well into his second double whisky, beginning to turn his attention to what exactly he was going to say to this famous 'colonel' that Rogerson had talked about, when a well-modulated voice next to him asked: 'Whisky, is it, Major Bellingham?'

The man who slid onto the stool next to his was in his mid-forties, with a pleasant, open housemaster's face and two crowns on his shoulder. Bellingham did not need to enquire any further: if Rogerson was a friend of Tom Brown's, then here was the good Doctor Arnold of Rugby School, to the life.

'Edmund Dulac,' the colonel introduced himself, pausing to light a solid, straight-stemmed pipe. 'I keep a *pied-à-terre* at Shepheard's myself, and since we were due to meet later this evening in any case, I thought I'd just potter over and see if I could find you. You were, of course, where any civilized Englishman would be found at this time of day.' He was on first-name terms with the plump Arab assistant barman, and the drinks appeared very quickly. 'Cheers, Major. Very interesting to meet you. Sir Stewart was very complimentary.'

'Most kind of him, I'm sure.'

'I thought I might stand you dinner. I've booked a table in the restaurant. Is that all right, or are you still rather weary?'

'Absolutely not. Dinner's an excellent idea, sir.'

'Call me Edmund, for goodness' sake,' the colonel said, in a quietly insistent way that made Bellingham feel oddly deflated, as if the man had instinctively decided to ignore his cover. It shouldn't have, but it did. This was clearly one of Dulac's talents.

They weighed each other up in amiable silence. An American was arguing with the young British staff officer now, yelling: 'Bastard! She hasn't got a twin sister! I happen to know that . . . there are no coincidences in Cairo!' The Englishman was laughing nervously, signalling for another round.

'I'm afraid the boys get a little rowdy sometimes, but there's never any fights,' Dulac said. 'But then Sir Stewart said you were here in the last war?'

'For slightly less than a year, more or less by accident. It was much the same then, except for the Americans. And there were even fewer girls to bicker over.'

'And a different kind of war to fight, I daresay.'

'Oh, some would say that the likes of us don't fight a war at all . . . Edmund.'

Dulac continued to puff placidly on his pipe. 'Don't they always,' he said. 'Personally, I've long since stopped apologizing to the hairy-chested, up-and-at-'em crew about my way of doing things. I'm in the business of ensuring that when they have to fight, they win. Here's to that. . . ?' He paused enquiringly. First names, of course.

'Jack. If you prefer it. Call me Jack.' 'Jackie' somehow didn't sound right for a second-hand major.

Bellingham had been briefed about Dulac and 'S' Force during a very full weekend spent with 'C' at a draughty country house north of London after Menzies' return from Casablanca. That time had been an eye-opener; there had been hard-looking men patrolling the grounds and manning the gates, quite a little private force built up there, all for the purpose of the catching of the spy in MI6, and clearly quite thoroughly concealed from the rest of the Service. Menzies had named the project SIGNIFY, he had told him. Bellingham had been reminded of some oriental potentate, threatened in his own capital, withdrawing in a drastic huff outside the walls to lay siege to what was already his.

He had been informed rightly regarding Dulac, anyway. The colonel, so it went, was an eccentric, and also one of the cleverest men in the British Army, an institution where neither quality was very highly prized. It explained why he was still a colonel, but also why he could claim to be an extremely important colonel. You had to be careful not to tred on his toes: he had built up an efficient Intelligence machine, and he guarded its integrity with absolute ruthlessness. He commanded an extraordinary 'phantom army'. 'S' Force controlled whole battalions of fake units throughout the Middle East, from Cyprus to Basra, including tiny signals units pretending to be busy regimental, Brigade, even Divisional HQs, and then rubber tanks, plywood aeroplanes and fleets of vehicles that simply drove around different areas, changing their number-plates and insignia to give the observer an impression of enormous and varied military activity where there was virtually none, rather like bit players in a crowd scene at a provincial playhouse, who keep disappearing stage right and rapidly re-appearing with different helmets or banners seconds later. With the aid of these props, Dulac's organization could and did make fools of the Abwehr controllers in Athens and Sofia, Bari and Istanbul, using captured and turned, even imaginary Axis agents to feed the Germans exaggerated and subtly misleading information about Allied strengths in the region and of those forces' ultimate military purpose. So far 'S' Force had played a major part in achieving victory in the Middle East, and its importance had increased as the Allies prepared to clear Rommel from North Africa and jump off across the Mediterranean. Dulac's 'notional' forces were to be moved around according to what the High Command's strategists wanted the Germans to think, and his agents—most of them actually in prison, or kept under heavy guard—were to report accordingly, so that when the Allied blow against the southern part of Europe came, it would arrive where the enemy least expected it.

Dulac's operation was an enormous, high-class confidence trick, and it took some tight organization, as Bellingham had been warned. If the enemy had cause to suspect that the information their faithful spies in the Middle East were providing was planted by the British, then the whole stratagem would collapse. The colonel had to be very sure that any outsiders who began working in the area would not interfere with his plans—their deceptions contradict his deceptions—and hence the cosy dinner at Shepheard's. It was Bellingham's first test, because with only a matter of weeks to organize the business end of SIGNIFY, he needed Dulac's active good will badly. Tonight would probably determine whether or not he got it.

They talked for the moment about Cairo as it had been, and about London as it was now.

'I spent some time in France towards the end of the last show, but missed the worst—if that's the word,' Dulac confided. 'Sweet nineteen and office boy to a Tactical Intelligence team in Flanders. We had a lot of plucky Belgians counting troop trains behind the German lines. And then, for reasons which continue to escape me, instead of being demobbed I was sent off to Turkey when the army moved into Constantinople in '19. Ever since, it's been the exotic byways for me; I'm afraid it's spoiled me irrevocably for anything else at all, military or civilian. That's the way it so often goes with chaps like us, doesn't it?'

He smiled faintly at Bellingham's understanding nod, looked at his wristwatch and said: 'Aha. About time we stopped gossipping like old women and got something to eat. I believe dinner is being served . . .'

Dulac caught the barman's eye, slid an Egyptian note under his empty glass.

''Bye, Hussein. May you prosper.' The barman acknowledged Dulac's tip with a solemn, almost magisterial nod. 'The likelihood of our friendly barman's being reduced to penury is so small as to be immediately discountable,' Dulac murmured to Bellingham. 'He owns three tenement buildings in the east of the city, all of them purchased with huge mounds of fifty-piastre notes. Come.'

Neither did Dulac choose to show his hand during the course of their excellent dinner. Perhaps the restaurant was too crowded for him, and then again perhaps that was why he had chosen to bring Bellingham here to dine. The availability of suitable army candidates for the new 'box of tricks' was touched on in general terms, and there was chat about the situation in the Aegean, which Dulac knew well. He had relations with MI9, the escape and evasion people, who ran caïques to the Greek islands to ferry POWs, service personnel on the run and so on out of enemy-occupied territory. He would put Bellingham in touch with them and drop a diplomatic word. That was about all. Dulac steered the conversation to stories about King Farouk, about the Anglo-French tiffs in Lebanon, a Cook's Tour of local gossip to which Bellingham listened with polite boredom. He was tired now, and had half a mind to disengage and make an appointment for the next day when Dulac suggested they take a turn round the garden. It would be quieter out there in the winter chill; no dances, no boozy parties this time of year. Have a look at Kléber's Tree, the ancient sycamore which marked the spot where Napoleon's commander in Egypt had been assassinated a century and a half before. Ten minutes, Bellingham thought, ten minutes more chat, then bed.

They stood in one corner, watching a patient *safrag*

clearing away some tables and chairs. Dulac laughed suddenly and said:

'Sir Stewart will wonder what I'm doing when you get on the telephone in the morning . . . Jack.'

'He might. Yes, he might. Well?'

'I like to get to know a chap first, and dinner was a good opportunity. If I might be so bold, you're tense, you want to get this job over—a job that, on the face of it, most time-servers worth their salt would relax and enjoy. No questions about that aspect,' Dulac said, looking up at the stars. 'I suppose you could call this an apology. For boring you witless.'

'Oh, I don't know . . .'

'The straight bat, Jack. Good. You're going to need that. There are two styles: as little explanation as possible, or an awful lot, most of it totally irrelevant. You're in the former category, while I, as you have most certainly realized, tend to adopt the latter approach. With me so far?'

'Yes.'

'Then I'll be frank. According to Sir Stewart, you are to set up a nice little special ops unit for his own purposes, which he assures me will not conflict with my own humble activities. Maybe. There are, after all, majors with strange labels all over the Middle East and elsewhere with offices and telephones and forgotten orders, on full pay and allowances, pursuing all sorts of weird, wonderful empire-building schemes. Personally I don't believe a word.'

Bellingham nodded vaguely. 'Rather unflattering, old boy.'

'You're plausible enough,' said Dulac, touching his shoulder conspiratorially. '"C" is sick of SOE—you can see them in the Long Bar any evening, brandishing their credentials, saying: look at us, we're the boys who hit the Nazis where it hurts. Sick of intrigues in his own house, everyone knowing everyone else's business. Sends over an old trusty with an army background to produce a bit of spit-and-polish order. A private army that behaves like an army. Plausible enough. Why not?'

'Why not, indeed.'

'Because to me it doesn't feel right,' Dulac answered. 'You don't feel right, Jack—not for what you're supposed to be doing.'

Bellingham decided he must try to keep in character and said huffily: 'Oh, that's useful to know. But there's not much I can do about it, I'm afraid. I've got my orders . . .'

'I'm sure you have. I intend to help you in any way I can, because I promised Sir Stewart I would. What you must give me, however, is your assurance that you'll be in and out with as little trouble as possible. That's the one thing that I really must insist on, if you don't mind.'

Someone, Bellingham thought, should invent a new tense to describe the way people like Dulac issued an ultimatum: perhaps 'imperative conditional' would come close.

'It goes without saying,' he muttered. 'That while I am carrying out the duties incumbent on me here, I shall endeavour to the best of my ability to avoid putting my foot in it. Such an undertaking does not, of course, in any way imply that I confirm the statements you have just made.'

'Dib-dib, dob-dob,' said Dulac. 'Good scout.'

There was irony but no rancour in his voice, which surprised Bellingham, as did the fact that the colonel extended his hand. It was the first physical contact, indicating that Dulac felt they had made a breakthrough of some kind.

They began to walk again, strolling along the fifteen-foot high trellis work screen thickly threaded with greenery that divided Shepheard's from the sight and sound of the Cairo slums, Gezireh and the real world. An occasional snake might manage to slither through or over, but never a human being.

'Don't mind me,' Dulac continued mildly. 'We get a little suspicious sometimes, because we're strictly army and operational, despite the glamorous trimmings, and the thought of having things messed up by your lot—I don't know, trying to poach our agents or whatever—is a bit of a nightmare. Most times that we look after a bird of passage for "C" it tends to be some genteel thug in a linen suit routed via the embassy and the adjacent fleshpots. If we haven't liked the look of him, we've tended to freeze him out, and I don't think Sir Stewart has really minded very much when we have.' He sighed. 'In your case, though, I think he would mind, and I'm not disposed to cause trouble. I hope you'll approve of the setup in the mountains,' he added.

'I look forward to seeing it. When I've done the necessaries in Cairo.'

'Alan Rogerson's seeing to that. He knows an awful lot of people. Rather unhealthy in one so young.'

'My thanks. You've obviously put in a great deal of work on my behalf,' Bellingham conceded. Let Dulac niggle; clever, nervous men had to find their ways of appearing to keep control. Stewart must have come on pretty strong in his approaches, used his muscle. For his part, Bellingham knew he had to keep up what was left of his façade, for form's sake and because if Dulac found out what was really going on, the hobnobbing with Canaris and the rest, he would probably cheerfully strangle his visitor with his bare hands, here in the garden of Shepheard's no more than fifty yards from Thomas Cook's.

'Well, I should imagine that we'll have a list of lambs for you by tomorrow evening. You can use one of our offices for the interviews if you like,' Dulac suggested. 'After that, it's your show.'

Bellingham tried to smile and almost succeeded. 'These volunteers I want will be well looked after if I have anything to do with it. They're not sacrificial offerings, you know.'

'No, but they'll have lost their way. Bah, bah, bah . . . Cairo's full of them, looking for a good shepherd,' Dulac retorted with disturbing relish.

Had he not already been assured to the contrary, Bellingham might have concluded that Colonel Dulac, in his quiet way, was distinctly unbalanced. Instead he contented himself with the observation that the prevailing mode of thinking in 'S' Force appeared to combine Baden-Powell and Machiavelli, with a pinch of Wodehouse thrown in as a civilizing influence.

'We shall see about that,' he said.

Dulac nodded thoughtfully. 'So you will. Choose carefully, old boy, won't you? Once they're off that caïque, they'll be on their own and you never quite know what they'll get up to.'

It was some time later that Bellingham had cause to remember what the colonel had said and to reflect that

Dulac was not only eccentric and clever, but wise. A bloody prophet, in fact.

Headquarters 'S' Force took up most of a requisitioned building in the Kasr-El-Nil district, not far from the British embassy. The place, as Dulac had revealed with some pride the previous evening, had been a high-class brothel until taken over by the army, and when Bellingham saw it in the morning he could believe it. The duty sergeant downstairs sat surrounded by heavy, ornate plush wall coverings behind a reception desk that could have come off a Hollywood film set.

'Major Bellingham,' he announced. 'Colonel Dulac is expecting me.'

'Ah, yes,' the sergeant said. 'You're staying with us for a few days, aren't you, sir? I'm afraid that the colonel has to convey his apologies; he's been called away, but he has left instructions for you to be given a desk and a telephone and everything. You'll be in the bar.'

'I beg your pardon . . .'

'The bar, sir. That's what it was before we moved in here.'

'Of course.'

He told Bellingham where to go, and he went there and sat in the strange room for several hours, twiddling his thumbs and studying the decor, while a silent Indian mess orderly appeared every couple of hours with a cup of hot, sweet tea. He went out for lunch and came back. Finally Captain Rogerson walked in through his door at twenty-to-three in the afternoon, carrying a fat briefcase.

'Hello, Major,' he said cheerfully. 'Sorry the Colonel's not here. He had to clear off somewhere at short notice. I don't know when he'll be back, so you'll have to make do with me. I've got something for you to be getting on with. Like this place?' he asked, fishing out a thick wad of files bound together with rubber bands and dumping them onto the desk top in front of Bellingham.

'It's unusual, I'll grant you.'

'The Colonel is particularly fond of it. For the first six months that we were here, he allowed Madame and her girls to continue working on the top floor, because he is a very considerate man, but GHQ found out about it and forced him to chuck them out. Pity. They brightened one's day.'

'I suppose the top brass were worried about the security aspect,' Bellingham said.

'Doubt it. I think they were probably all regulars before, and miffed that they couldn't use the place without being spotted. Madame has re-opened two streets away and continues to flourish.' He smiled cherubically. 'If you're interested, mention my name, by all means, sir.'

Bellingham stared at the fresh-faced figure leaning against the empty bar in front of him, wondered whether he was serious, and decided there was a good chance that he might be.

'Thanks for the files,' he said. 'I'll read through them and make up a short list. Mind if I consult you further when I reach that stage, captain?'

'Be my guest. All the chaps seem to have the kind of itchy feet that might help them view your approaches favourably. They've got reasonable records, no rubbish, and I think there's a few Greek speakers into the bargain.'

Rogerson saluted and left. Bellingham heard the sound of laughter in the corridor outside as he opened the first folder and got down to work. Eeny-meeny, miney, mo . . .

15

The face that wouldn't go away belonged to Lavinia, his fiancée, broad and healthy and accusing, the face of an athletic madonna. The lips were moving. The terrified observer squeezed into the cell of his unconscious mind strained to catch what she was saying and realized that Lavinia was calling him a coward, a swine, a filthy lecher, and more. She was using the most obscene army language, and he knew he deserved it . . .

Gerald Ambrose Xavier Meyerscough had no choice in the matter but to wake up.

Clean sheets. A shout from the barrack square. So far, so good. Then, as he forced one eye open, the sun crept a fraction of a degree higher and a merciless shower of light filtered through the blind on his window. Meyerscough groaned, flopped back and buried his head in the pillow. The full storm of the hangover had yet to hit him, but he knew it would come soon, just as the images of the previous night were beginning to tumble around in his head, still coded like a dream.

Boredom, the ancient enemy, had been to blame, more than lust and the rest. You see, other officers came and went, were sent off to do this and that in the real world, the shooting war, but he was a fixture at the barracks. Sometimes it seemed a conspiracy existed to keep him out of the war. So he had been persuaded to abscond with some of the chaps for a few drinks, a night-club, belly-dancer and so on, and he'd ended up separated—Mother of God, he hoped he'd got separated—with that girl. He dimly recalled meeting her and a gaggle of other floozies in the bar with the dancer; there had been a lot of boozing, off-colour jokes, dares, and then a stumbling, giggling walk through dark streets and up some steep stairs. She had been a little coptic girl, moon-faced, stupid, eager to please and justify her hire, and she had kept her jewellery on even in bed. Clank, clank, those cheap chain bangles had gone while she panted and fumbled and pawed at him, vainly trying to rouse the beast. A blank after for a while. Finally Egyptian banknotes scattered on the wall, the girl cowering in the corner of the nasty little room, headlong down those stairs and staggering around looking for a taxi, shouting.

What had he been shouting? Holy Mary, mother . . . forgive . . . And perhaps she had, because he had made it back to here at some stage. Meyerscough shaded his eyes with one hand and risked a glance at the clock on his bedside locker. It was a quarter to eight; before collapsing back beneath the covers he told himself that honour demanded he put in an appearance at the Mess for breakfast. It was not to be, however. The sleep that came was more like a short-lived coma, happily dreamless. When he next acknowledged the world it was in response to a gentle knock at his door, and three-quarters of an hour had passed. Meyerscough sat bolt upright, wild-eyed, and listened while the sound was repeated. The discreet quality indicated that it was probably Stevens, his batman.

'Enter.'

A brilliantined head peered round the door. 'Good morning, sir,' Stevens said warily, edging his way over the threshold.

Meyerscough grunted. The man carried a tray with a glass containing a viscous-looking yellow liquid.

'An egg flip, sir,' Stevens explained, struggling to keep a straight face. 'Compliments of the gentlemen in the mess, who wish you a speedy recovery. And a communication, sir, what arrived this morning by messenger.'

'Put them down on my locker, Stevens,' Meyerscough murmured. 'Please present my apologies to the mess for my temporary indisposition.'

A ghost of a smirk. 'Natcherally, sir. Will there be anything else?'

Yes, go jump in the Suez bloody Canal, you little cockney sewer-rat, Meyerscough thought. But he spoke in the dignified fashion that went with the ritual.

'Be so kind as to come back in twenty minutes and lay out my uniform, will you?'

'Oh, yes, sir.'

Stevens lingered, his bright, ever-wandering eyes examining the litter of clothes surrounding the bed with a keenness that would have done credit to a forensic expert.

'That will be all, Stevens.'

When he had finally got rid of the batman, Meyerscough set about pushing the previous night from his mind and facing the day. He had to be out and among the chaps within the hour or be called a pansy who couldn't take his drink. Accordingly, he leaned painfully over and sniffed the egg flip, only to feel his stomach tighten in protest and a bitter smack of bile hit the roof of his mouth at the back. Moving gently away from the glass, he recalled the envelope Stevens had also delivered. A letter by messenger. Should have been exciting, or at least intriguing, but at the moment it had about the same effect as the egg flip, which meant that he had to reach out for it blindly, chewing back the vomit as he did so.

The grey envelope was addressed to Lt. G. A. X. Meyerscough, 2nd Battalion Norfolk Light Infantry etc. etc., *MOST CONFIDENTIAL AND PERSONAL* and adorned with an ugly black seal showing that it came from

G.H.Q.M.E. After a short struggle, Meyerscough succeeded in lacerating the envelope sufficiently to extract the contents, which he read once, then again. He was, the letter said, to be so kind as to telephone a certain number in Cairo and ask for Department 'E', because the officer in charge there would like to speak to him about a confidential matter. The contents, or even the receipt of this letter were not to be vouchsafed to any other personnel, military or civilian. End, with illegible signature. No heading, no reference or unit number, nothing.

Meyerscough lunged at the locker and seized the egg flip. He downed it in one gulp, but if he had hoped to catch his digestive system by surprise he was out of luck. He was still throwing up noisily into the porcelain basin by the window when there was a sound at the door. Stevens had returned to lay out his uniform. After a few moments' silence he dimly heard footsteps receding. Stevens may have been born in the gutter, but he knew when not to disturb an officer and a gentleman.

Meyerscough telephoned 'Department E' at eleven after appearing in the mess to drink some black coffee and staggering through some of the arrangements for the football match he was supposed to be organizing for the lads that afternoon. The man who answered, who gave his name as Major Bellingham, was most polite and apparently in no hurry. Could Meyerscough manage an appointment during the next few days? It was always best to have initial discussions over a relaxed snifter, didn't he think? There had been nothing very relaxed about the letter, but Meyerscough thought it best to agree. He did some swift calculations and reckoned that he could get away from the hated soccer in time to make it today. Six-thirty would be fine.

He had been to Shepheard's only occasionally before. The last time, in fact, had been duty, attending a party given by a brother officer to celebrate his engagement to a nurse from the British Hospital. That would have been before Christmas, and the last time he had done any serious drinking—with the exception of the previous night. He had spent quite a lot of time complaining to anyone who looked influential and who would listen about the fact that he never seemed to have much to do. Perhaps this appointment this evening was the fruit of that party. Meyerscough, spruced-up complete with swagger-stick, made his way through the crowded lobby of the hotel at twenty-five past six, feeling that his hour might have come at last.

A flunky in a fez and pantaloons showed him up to the major's room, which seemed to be about a quarter of a mile away. To tell the truth, Meyerscough was relieved that the meeting was in private and not down in one of the lounges or bars; standing at the reception desk and casting an eye over the motley crowd of officers, hangers-on and really rather brazenly-dressed women, he had felt conspicuous and vulnerable, unable to suppress a fear that the coptic girl might pop up from somewhere to cause a scene. Shepheard's was, of course, much too posh for the likes of her, but nevertheless there was something *decadent* and unpredictable about the place. Here they were in the middle of a war and there were Swiss receptionists reeking of eau-de-cologne and fawning wogs in fancy dress showing one about . . .

The major opened the door, slipped the Egyptian a coin, and ushered Meyerscough in without saying a word.

The room was luxurious enough but oddly bare. There were several cut-glass decanters filled with various spirits and sherry, a jug of water and a bottle of Indian tonic water, all supplied by the hotel. The only thing belonging to the major seemed to be a dog-eared copy of the *Sporting Life*, and it sat on the table like a theatrical prop.

When Meyerscough saluted, the major looked slightly surprised, then returned it rather sloppily and waved him to one of the pair of armchairs by the table. 'Er . . . let's not stand on ceremony, Lieutenant,' he said, and asked him what he wanted to drink.

He had what the major was having, which was whisky, and steeled himself for the hair of the dog. In fact, his system had made a decent recovery, and the whisky was an excellent malt. One up to the major: none of your *White Horse*, your bookies' tipple.

As for Major Bellingham, he struck Meyerscough as a companionable, straightforward sort. He wore the ribbon of the M.C. on his chest, probably gained in the last war.

He had done his bit in the rough and tumble then, Meyerscough guessed, and now he was entitled to his comfy niche, the *Sporting Life* and the kind of rates of pay and allowances that made possible the old malts. There were plenty like him around, the modern equivalent of grizzled veterans guarding the tribe's baggage waggons, and he for one did not resent them.

'Thank you, sir,' he said politely. 'I needed that.'

Bellingham smiled. Meyerscough was momentarily disconcerted by his eyes, which were friendly but somehow opaque, like the silvered glass of a mirror. Then the major said: 'Thought you looked a mite frazzled, old boy. Hard night? This is just the stuff. Many's the time in my younger days . . .' Problem solved. Meyerscough had come across that quality before: the walled-off look of the mild alcoholic who's concentrating on getting the first couple of drinks down.

The major waxed enthusiastic about the delights of Cairo, in response to which Meyerscough, as was his acquired habit when the subject came up, simply smiled and agreed with everything said. He had mastered the appreciative leer; to do otherwise in one of the most corrupt cities in the world was considered impossibly wet. Another unwholesome aspect of this conscripts' war, in Meyerscough's opinion, was that most men would brag endlessly about sexual exploits, even with bought flesh, but were reticent on the matter of death and killing, which was, when it came down to the basics, the point of the whole darned operation.

'So,' said Bellingham eventually. 'You're probably asking yourself why you're here, captive audience to a chap you've never seen before in your life. Well, I'll get to the core of things in a minute, but first can I ask you a question?'

Meyerscough nodded. 'Fire away, sir.' Holy mother, at last.

More whisky from the decanter. Bellingham scratched his nose. He reminded Meyerscough strongly of his own father, wondering what to say when he was preparing to sack one of the labourers on the estate.

'Are you . . . ah . . . prepared for a change, quite a drastic change, Lieutenant?' he asked.

'If it means getting away from organizing football matches, then I can answer you in the affirmative, sir.'

'Oh, it would certainly mean that.'

Meyerscough decided to prod him along a bit. 'I don't expect you to explain everything at once, sir, but do you think you could give me a rough idea of what you're driving at?'

The major put down his tumbler and nodded energetically. 'Absolutely,' he said. 'I'll put my leading cards on the table. No names, no pack-drill, but the people I represent want some reliable chaps for special duties in the Med area—leading small armed parties into occupied territory, linking up with local partisan fighters, performing . . . a few important odd jobs. Including attacking installations and, ah, key personnel on the Axis side.' He smiled paternally. 'Really rather risky, I suppose, but rewarding. The sort of thing that'll enable you to say you had a "good war", as they say.' An easy pause. 'Now, tell me, are you game? No one will think the worse of you if you say no, believe me. We'll just part amicably and forget all I said . . .'

Meyerscough felt a prickling sensation begin in the back of his neck. This was it. Someone had heard him sounding off at that party here. He took the war very seriously, not as a political cause, for he had no sympathy whatsoever with the ideals of democracy and equality, but as an activity in itself, a proving-ground. After all, his family had it in their blood from William the Conqueror's time; only their stubborn Catholic faith had barred them from service for two hundred years, but what was a couple of centuries to a Meyerscough? His own father, squire over fifteen hundred acres in Norfolk, had long been an ardent supporter of Mussolini—at least since the fascists' Concordat with the Vatican, and had been inclined to give the Third Reich credit for the way it dealt with the godless Reds, but he had listened in solemn silence the day in September 1939 when King George had come on the radio—Neville Chamberlain would not have sufficed for the old man—and instructed his subjects to buckle on their armour. 'Ah well, Gerald,' he had told his son afterwards. 'It looks like a fight, so we'd better get on with it. Could have thought of a few better people to pick a quarrel with, but ours not to reason why.'

'No question about it, sir,' Meyerscough said to Bellingham. 'The sooner the better.'

The major smiled. 'I can see from your record that you've been no slouch. Rather the other way. France. The Desert. I really can't think why you haven't been transferred to more suitable duties before.'

Meyerscough reddened. 'My C.O. has blocked it repeatedly. He thinks I'm headstrong, sir.'

'The bugger. Well, we need no-nonsense, honest fighting men like you, chaps with no special axe to grind except wanting to get to grips with the enemy. Too many people these days insist on mixing politics with duty, which just complicates the issue where irregular and partisan forces are concerned.' The major raised an eyebrow. 'I can take it, therefore, that you are at our disposal?'

'Of course, sir.'

'Jolly good. Don't worry about clearance for your transfer. We do have influence in certain quarters. We'll call you when the time comes.'

Meyerscough noticed that Bellingham's tone was becoming perceptibly crisper. He did seem to be very confident of himself and of his power to get things done, more so than either his rank or first impressions would have implied. The major had seemed like the monkey to someone else's organ-grinder; now it was beginning to look as though he owned the ruddy instrument outright.

'So . . . that's it, is it, sir?' he said.

'For the moment. Less said the better at this stage, don't you agree? That's our policy, anyway, and I can't emphasize too strongly that we're relying on your absolute discretion.'

'Absolutely, sir.'

'All will be revealed in the fullness of time, I assure you. Here's mud in yours.' Bellingham's eyes twinkled as if by remote control. 'Welcome aboard.'

'Irene, it's nothing to do with whether I love you,' Mark Patos Knox was saying for the umpteenth time that morning. 'I am, appearances to the contrary notwithstanding, a soldier, subject to the usual military discipline. I have work to do. A conference at eleven. There's a war on, for God's sake, or I wouldn't be in Cairo at all . . .'

The telephone rang.

Knox moved over to the table by the open balcony door and picked up the receiver, turning his back on her. The last was done with no malice, but out of necessity, because he found it extremely difficult to conduct a conversation, particularly an official one, while having to meet the eye of a pouting, shameless female sprawled naked on his bed. Since his flatmate had been called up to Jerusalem on a course, Irene had made a habit of staying there all morning, often until past lunchtime, and rarely seemed to put on any clothes except to go out.

'Hello,' he said. 'Knox here.'

'Captain Mark Patos Knox?' the voice on the other end of the line enquired. There was a distinct emphasis on his Greek middle name, which whoever it might be pronounced correctly, with the accent on the second syllable.

'Yes. Whom am I speaking to, please?'

'The name's Bellingham. Major Bellingham. Actually, I'm ringing to ask if we might meet. It's army business that I can't discuss on the telephone.'

Knox frowned. 'Well . . . sir,' he said cautiously. 'I'm rather busy at the moment. Is it important?'

Irene was giggling, and he was beginning to suspect that this might be some kind of practical joke. His flatmate, a signals man, loved playing pranks. Once, the previous autumn, he had rung Lambert up from a public kiosk putting on a thick Central European accent and claiming to be a Panzer Hauptmann who had just arrived in the suburbs after a push through the Alamein Line and wanted to rent a room. On the other hand, this might have something to do with that unpaid mess bill he had left behind in England two years ago.

Major Bellingham, it soon became clear, was neither a joker nor a debt-collector.

'Yes, it is rather important,' he said, in a firm but matter-of-fact tone that Knox was beginning to be impressed by. 'It is also secret, and you will doubtless understand that I cannot disclose much on the telephone, particularly here in Cairo. May we discuss a time and a place for a meeting?'

A bewildered Knox found himself agreeing that they could. The major said he was only in Cairo temporarily, which left them the choice of his hotel or Knox's flat.

'Oh, I think Shepheard's would be best,' Knox said quickly, inwardly cringing at the thought of trying to remove Irene from the flat long enough to conduct a secret conversation. He explained that he had a conference on today, but that he would be free tomorrow afternoon. The dry major confirmed that tomorrow would be satisfactory and suggested Shepheard's terrace for tea at five.

'All right. I'll be there, sir. And, yes, I do understand that the matter is absolutely confidential.'

'I mean that. Goodbye until then,' the major said and rang off.

Knox put down the telephone and reached for his briefcase without turning round, hoping for a quick getaway, but Irene was in no mood to be easy on him.

'Who was that person, Mark? Must you go away again?'

He pretended to finish checking the papers he needed for the conference, then snapped the briefcase shut.

'Of course not. I've got to meet some fellow on army business, that's all,' he said.

He heard Irene snort, a brief, explosive expulsion that tailed off into a keening Slavonic sigh.

'Bloody war. Bloody army, always bloody army,' she recited. 'Why do you not fight the communists? They are as bad as Nazis, even worse maybe. I would say this means you will not take me out tonight to the cinema at Jimmy's. Always this happens . . .'

Knox picked up his briefcase and his cap before facing her. Indications were not good. She had got onto her two favourite topics—the inadequacies of British war aims and his neglect of her social life, not necessarily ranked in order of importance. And she had lit two cigarettes, one of which was being offered in his direction between the long fingers of one outstretched hand.

'Tonight's still on,' he said, instantly despising himself for playing her game again. 'You know I always try to take you somewhere on your nights off. That's why I said I'd see the man tomorrow. And for goodness' sake, Irene, I'm due at this blasted conference in an hour. You know what it's like trying to get a taxi . . .'

By the time he finished speaking, however, he was already smoking the cigarette and had sat down on the edge of the bed.

'You are a beautiful man,' Irene said, stroking his thigh. 'I knew you would not leave me in the lurch.'

She laughed huskily, then swallowed some smoke and began to splutter.

'Thanks for the compliment. You are not without charms yourself,' Knox returned, feeling helpless.

When he had found this place in July of the previous year, newly posted to Cairo, he had wondered what the outgoing tenant had meant by sly comments about the hired help being worth the rent in itself. The penny had dropped when Irene had turned up the next morning in a headscarf and apron and begun to make strong coffee and wield the carpet cleaner like a woman possessed. Within half an hour she had made rather more mess than she had found, had told Knox for the first time that he was beautiful, and had delivered a lengthy lecture on the evils of Bolshevism, with which the foolish British had allied themselves and which would prove their downfall.

Irene Kontiak, he learned quickly, was a White Russian, and the daughter of a Czarist general. She never tired of recounting how her parents had made their way down through the Caucasus in 1920, carrying tiny Irene, selling their jewels on the way for food and visas, never again to return to their estates near Tsaritsyn—try calling it Stalingrad within her hearing—where there had been dinner parties every night, dances once a week, handsome young officers, willing servants, grace and elegance beyond bourgeois westerners' imaginings . . . All that, of course, came from her father's descriptions, because Irene had been less than two years old when they arrived near-penniless in Cairo, having buried her poor, delicate mother up on the Syrian border. Not that the image of pre-revolutionary Russia seemed to lack magic for that: she always spoke as if the Czar's time were an arcadia that she herself had inhabited, loved to distraction, and lost.

Opinions differed when it came to deciding how General Kontiak had kept himself and his daughter since their exile. Someone had once told Knox that the old boy used to own a run-down antique shop near the Continental

Hotel, a precarious living that he had supplemented by selling stolen tomb artifacts through a network of Egyptian crooks that the police had never been able to trace back to him. Others claimed that he, along with a group of fellow-exiles, had been involved in smuggling arms to the Arabs in Palestine before the rebellion there. All Irene would admit, with a haughty toss of her long, dark hair, was that 'papa lowered himself to trade, for the sake of my education'. The last had always puzzled Knox, for she was one of the most profoundly ignorant people he had ever met. Her general knowledge seemed confined to the history and geography of Russia, and her view of the world was based on the existence of a Jewish-Bolshevist conspiracy of breathtaking deviousness and inconsistency, which led her to comments such as: 'This man Churchill is all very fine, but his mother was American, I think, and everyone knows that Americans are Jews who have changed their names from Goldberg . . .' This facet of her character was so comical and pathetic that Knox had grown to discount it, assuming it to be yet another legacy from Kontiak *père*. Certainly since her father had died, just before the war, she had been adrift. At the moment she worked evenings as a cigarette girl at a night-club and added to her earnings by 'doing' for the military occupants of flats in the block. Knox suspected that if it hadn't been for her sinecure here, she might have been forced on the streets. She would certainly rather sell her body than the last family heirloom, a pair of gold-and-diamond cufflinks that her father, she said, had won from the Grand Duke Constantine thirty years ago in an epic game of *vingt-et-un*.

'One day,' she mused when she had stopped coughing. 'When you take me to England, I will find my relatives. Papa always said we had some people there. A far-off cousin—'

'Distant,' Knox corrected her.

'As you wish. Anyway, when you take me to England . . .'

Knox surreptitiously checked his watch. A couple of minutes. He knew where this conversation was leading. She was sitting with her long legs crossed, those surprisingly voluptuous breasts quivering gently as she reached out to keep hold of him. In a moment she would force him to look into her eyes, and she would ask him if he loved her and wanted her to be happy. He would say that of course he did, and then there would be questions about how the British gentry lived, and how many servants they had, how big his father's house was, and whether they danced a lot. He would do nothing to destroy her fantasies. Neither he nor she had ever mentioned marriage: despite everything, Irene was too proud, and when it came down to it Knox knew he was too much of a coward to make the impossibility of the situation clear. And too much of a bastard, too, or he would have fended her off the first time she had said, 'You are a beautiful man'.

'Irene, my love, I really have to go,' he interrupted. 'If I'm late, I'll get one hell of a rocket.'

He stubbed the cigarette out in the bedside ashtray, stood up and recovered his cap and case.

'Bloody, bloody army,' Irene hissed balefully, sliding towards the edge of the bed. 'You do not even fight, you are an officeboy.'

'Sorry. I'll see you this evening. And for goodness' sake do put some clothes on,' Knox muttered, heading for the door.

He reached the street and looked up at the balcony. Irene was standing three floors up, hanging over the parapet and wearing just a brassière and a contemptuous smile.

'Modesty is for peasants!' she shouted.

Knox noticed an urchin lounging against a fire hydrant across the street. The boy grinned broadly at Knox and made the obscene sign of the fig—'male' thumb in 'female' clenched palm. Knox continued on his way without looking back at the balcony, but before he reached the main avenue and started looking for a taxi, he slipped his own thumb between the fingers of the hand that carried the briefcase and smiled sourly to himself. In parts of the Aegean it was a sexual insult, too, but curiously enough it was also a way of warding off the evil eye by shocking the devil. To see the full logic of that, you had, like Knox, to be born of a Greek mother.

Major Bellingham sipped at his lemon tea and smiled comfortably.

'War hangs rather sadly here,' he said, waving a hand

across the crowded terrace. 'Not much time to appreciate the finer aspects. The only thing that hasn't changed is the horde of characters down at the bottom of the steps, still trying to sell the most unlikely things to the rich Europeans.'

Encouraged by Knox's earnest nod, the major decided to expand on the comment.

'One of the nicest stories I ever heard was about Harry Boyle, the Oriental Secretary at around the time Egypt was a British Protectorate,' he said. 'Apparently, he was a very scruffy dresser, and he was sitting out at one of these tables one afternoon in a straw hat, baggy trousers and a threadbare jacket when a perfect stranger came up to him and whispered: "Sir, are you the hotel pimp?" Boyle, unruffled, replied: "I am indeed, sir, but the management, as you may observe, are good enough to allow me the hour of five to six as an interval. If, however, you find yourself pressed for time, perhaps you will address yourself to that gentleman"—which saying, he pointed to a large, burly, English baronet sitting further along the terrace—"He is taking my duty, and you will find him most willing to accommodate you in any little commission of a confidential character which you may see fit to entrust to him." Boyle then swiftly settled the bill for his tea, and was already half way down the steps when he heard the loud thud of a body hitting the marble floor . . .'

Knox found himself liking Bellingham. Tha major might look the perfect blimp, but he seemed to possess an acuteness and a sympathy that one rarely found in such characters. He would have liked to find out more about the man, but realized that Bellingham was moving smoothly onto the subject of his guest's background.

'Of course, I gather your father was also a distinguished diplomat,' he continued with a smile. 'I daresay he could cap that story and provide a few others.'

Knox knew he was under the microscope from now on, and suddenly felt an irrational and ill-defined guilt, a desire to hide his past, such as one felt when a policeman looked hard at you in the street.

'Oh, my father is a rather more serious character altogether, sir,' he answered rather lamely, though on the whole the judgement was true. D. L. Knox—even his family called him 'D.L.'—could be called a kind, clever, even an interesting man, but off-the-cuff fun was hardly his style. As far as his son could ascertain, his marriage to the daughter of a Greek trader had been the only uncalculated, passionate act in a singularly conventional, hard-working life. It had also undoubtedly cast a subtle shadow over his career at the Foreign Office, though he had never seemed to regret the step, nor show any bitterness at never quite rising to ambassador status. Knox often wished he knew his father better, and sometimes suspected that he did not know him at all. It was the English middle-class way: there had been boarding-school, a year at Oxford before inessential students were called up, and then the army.

'I suppose,' Bellingham said, offering him a cigarette from a silver case, 'that as this century has progressed we have found more reason to be serious. A pity. "The gods save us from living in interesting times", as the Chinese sage said. And it must have been difficult for him, bringing you up single-handed after your mother died.'

'Yes, I'm sure it was,' Knox answered, intimidated rather than offended by the fact that he had known this man for ten minutes and that his family background was already an open book.

Bellingham picked up on the look and smiled like a good uncle. 'You must excuse me. I've had access to your file, of course, and I'm bound to use it. These kind of conversations are rarely self-starting.'

'I understand that, sir. One has to find points of contact.'

'Exactly. And I'll confess that it is your family history that interests me, from a professional point of view. My people, you see, need bilingual chaps. Tell me . . . ah . . . do you know the Aegean Islands pretty well?'

Softly, softly, thought Knox. What on earth he might be letting himself in for in response to this man's gentle interrogation, he had no idea. The worrying thing was that he was beginning not to care.

'It depends which islands, sir. My mother's family were—are—Chiots, from the eastern end. I visited them often as a child, less frequently after mother's death, though father ensured that we didn't lose touch, because of his own affection for Greece. Chiots, sir, will travel far on business, but for pleasure they stay at home . . .'

Bellingham chuckled. 'Well, it's a kind of broad knowledge of the islands off Anatolia I'm looking for at the moment. How about Kos, Leros, Rhodes?'

'Those are Italian possessions, sir, and not exactly places a good Greek would honour with his presence unless strictly necessary,' Knox said. 'I remember we went to Rhodes when I was nine or so; I thought it was rather like a white-painted Brighton, and the ice cream was super. Father, who wanted to see the Street of the Knights, claimed it was full of ageing Italian gigolos—which passed over my head at the time—and mother was furious at the way the local Greeks were treated.'

'Quite rightly,' Bellingham agreed solemnly. 'And Crete?'

'I was there for exactly a week, sir, in May '41. On liaison duties with the Greek king's headquarters at Heraklion. When King George left, I went too. Well before seeing hide or hair of a German parachutist,' Knox added with recalled bitterness. He might have been new to the game, but he had been astonished that the king agreed to flee the last remaining part of his realm still in Allied hands before the issue had been decided. Surprising how such resentments could lie dormant in the mind, ready to come to the surface when a stranger touched a nerve. He felt angrier about it now than he had at the time.

'Nasty cockup,' Bellingham said. 'Your only combat experience?'

Knox laughed. 'You've read the file, sir. Unless you count the Greek royal visit to the front line last November. Most of the time I was helping to sort out the catering.'

'So you've been doing this sort of job for nigh-on two years. Do I detect boredom?'

'You might, sir.'

The friendly questions followed each other in precise, unswerving sequence, like hard bowling from a team-mate in the cricket nets at school. Every time you hit one back, there came another ball straight down the wicket, and at the end you knew your tormentor would still be there, smiling and fresh.

'Oh, one gets into a rut, sir,' he was saying. 'I certainly

wouldn't want to be transferred to some even more tedious corner of the machine.'

'I quite understand your point of view, and that's not what I had in mind. Interested?' the major asked.

Knox considered for a moment. 'Why not?'

Bellingham pushed his tea-glass gently to one side and leaned across the table. He spoke in a strange, whispering bass voice.

'The job I want you to consider is covert stuff, with a deal of danger involved. You'll be asked to run very real risks in occupied territory, possibly with Axis forces on the lookout for you. On the other hand, your work will be of crucial importance to the war effort in general and to enslaved Greece in particular. And it will take you away from Egypt for some time.'

'I can understand why you can't be *too* specific,' Knox murmured.

'Good Lord, I've gone as far as I can. *On s'engage, puis on voit,* as the French say. Of course, if you don't feel suited, say so now. I don't want any half-hearted recruits.'

The last, lofty sally was skilfully aimed. Knox tensed and said: 'Perhaps I should discuss things with my own boss . . . discreetly, of course . . .'

'Oh, never mind that,' Bellingham said quickly. 'Discussion is generally kept to the absolute minimum. When we put in a request for a chap, it's all over in a day or two. No arguments. Top level. It's got to be your own decision, Captain. I think you'll do, and now I want to hear your opinion.'

The avuncular smile had returned to the major's face. Knox nodded, despite the fact that he had been thinking with the suppressed Greek part of his mind: when a British officer is apologetic, you can bet your boots he'll trample over anything to get what he wants.

'And when will I be transferred?' he found himself saying.

'Oh . . . a couple of weeks' time . . . three at the outside. We're still setting things up. It's a very small group, because we're a new outfit. You'll be in very much at the ground floor.'

Knox listened to the major's dark-brown, capable voice

and wished to Christ he could get Bellingham to do the explaining to Irene while he stole away like a thief in the night . . .

Bellingham's walk back to the Shambles took half an hour or so; a taxi would have taken him there in ten minutes, but he wanted to be alone. He had seen a short-list of eight officers in all, met with two outright refusals, rejected another three as insufficiently qualified or otherwise blatantly unsuitable. One more, a Lieutenant Jessup, was going north to the mountains as an outside chance, to make up the numbers. They probably wouldn't use him, but he'd be there just in case of accidents. Meyerscough and Knox were the prime choices: the first for brawn, the second for brain. The two men should balance each other. In any case, Bellingham had to hurry, and he couldn't be too choosy. Less well-suited teams had been sent into the field and done good jobs, he told himself, because the keys were training and motivation, and thank God he hadn't lost the capacity for the latter. Menzies' men would have to deal with the former. The rest, the small but all-important percentage, was luck, and there was buggerall you could do about that.

Rogerson breezed in shortly after he had arrived back at his temporary office.

'Well?' he said. 'How was today?'

Bellingham prodded the heap of files. 'We've got ourselves a Greek-speaker at last. I was going to have to draw up a secondary list, but that won't be necessary. The nucleus is there now.'

'Jolly good.'

'Yes, and thanks for your help.'

'So you'll be off up to Lebanon soon, then?' Rogerson asked. There was a mirror behind the desk, a remnant of the bar's fittings, and he seemed to be preening himself in it. Bellingham guessed from that and his cheerfulness that the captain had a date with a girl.

'I suppose I shall,' he said. 'Any chance of seeing our elusive Colonel before I go?'

Rogerson wrinkled his forehead thoughtfully. 'Depends when you're planning to leave. He had to clear off up north himself, as I told you, and sometimes he can be away for a couple of weeks. He's a law unto himself, sir, I'm afraid. If it's anything specific you want to discuss, there are other chaps around who could help apart from myself . . .'

'No. It's all right.'

'Happy then, sir?'

'Certainly, certainly.'

'Then, I'll see you tomorrow. Have a think and if you want any more practical assistance I can usually rustle up someone. Amazing who's tucked away in dark corners round here,' Rogerson said.

'Thanks.'

Rogerson opened the door to leave, saluting as he turned. Another officer not much older than the captain was waiting outside in the hall, looking bored. He glanced away when Bellingham met his eye. Before the door shut again, Bellingham heard the faint noise of a typewriter coming from one of the other offices, like very distant small-arms fire. One finger. Click. Click-clack. Pause. Click-click. Clack.

'S' Force had helped him, and now they were easing him gently out into the big world again. Bellingham thought that it was fair enough, took a sheet of paper, and began to draft a telegram that he would be sending to Menzies at the house north of London when morning came. It read: 'TWEEDLEDUM, TWEEDLEDEE, PLUS FRIEND, NOW SAFE. AWAIT FURTHER INSTRUCTIONS BEFORE PROCEED NORTH'.

This time, he would take a taxi back to Shepheard's, order up a bottle, and then take off this darned uniform and drink himself to sleep. Booze was the foremost, perhaps the only weapon of the exile.

16

'Now, tell me, Otto,' said Oster with a hard edge to his voice. 'You have been talking to Menzies' poodle. In your opinion, are the British absolutely committed to *Wintermärchen*?'

Bredow, who had seen the question coming, took refuge in lighting a cigarette. Oster recognized the ploy.

'Come,' he urged, 'Hans, Henning and I have been perfectly frank about our personal situation. Please be so kind as to be equally forthcoming.'

'The Englishman in Portugal seemed trustworthy enough. He certainly carried out his task with a degree of good will,' Bredow said eventually. 'Further progress depends on two factors: a final decision by Hitler on the date of his spring meeting with Mussolini; and the ability of the British to train and transport their commando group. These are both outside our control. We have done all we can. What more is there for me to tell you?'

Oster looked at him carefully, weighing him up as a teacher judges a clever but devious child. 'That,' he said, 'is what concerns us. An awful lot of things have passed out of our control as *Wintermärchen* has developed.' He looked away. 'Henning!'

Colonel Henning von Tresckow, on leave from Russia and the ostensible cause of the select little celebration at Oster's flat, had been keenly studying a grotesque erotic drawing by George Grosz that hung on the wall to the left of the fireplace, part of the chief of Berlin Bureau's proud collection of degenerate art. Perhaps Tresckow had been hoping to escape becoming involved in this conversation. He turned back to face the party, shrugged.

'I admire your loyalty to the Admiral, Otto,' he said. 'But Hans is right, I'm afraid. *Wintermärchen* represents the Best of Possible Worlds, it is true—the British doing our dirty work for us and all the rest. But perhaps the Admiral is a little dazzled by its symmetry and beauty . . .' He smiled in diffident apology. '. . . Otherwise, he might realize that opportunities must be seized wherever they arise. We must, in the end, have a free hand to kill Hitler, and to blazes with Canaris's clever diplomacy.' The plump, balding colonel punched the air to add substance to his point. He was moving into his stride. 'You see, there is little point in our beavering away in Russia if the Abwehr falls apart before Hitler dies. And it seems clear that Kaltenbrunner and that oily swine Schellenberg have you fixed in their sights. By any rational standards, we should be acting as soon as possible. If the

SD were to move against you with Hitler's support, the very best we could hope for would be to ride a damaging body-blow to the Berlin apparatus. At worst, if arrests were widespread and prominent individuals were involved . . .' He gestured helplessly. 'I think you can imagine. Every man jack who ever even thought of opposing the Nazis would end up in the Gestapo's cellars. Otto . . .'

'Gentlemen, I am not the mover of this project,' Bredow murmured in something approaching desperation. 'If you are so worried, then you must ask the Admiral.'

Oster snorted impatiently. 'You know very well that he is in Norway this week!' he snapped. 'Next week he will be in Copenhagen, then in Kiel for some meeting he has arranged with *Grossadmiral* Raeder. The Amazon will protect him if he is forced to spend a day or two here within hailing distance of ordinary mortals, and then he will be off somewhere else before we know it . . . I suspect that if we had an outstation in Timbuktu, he would suddenly discover some urgent reason why he had to inspect it. Do you really believe that he is prepared to explain himself?'

'I don't know. But I can only tell you what I have done, and how I feel about my part.' Bredow had made a decision, and he passed on quickly to the resulting lie. 'He does not confide in me any more than he does in the rest of you.'

Oster looked at him in disgust. 'Perhaps. I confide in you: we shall act precisely as we see fit. We have no choice. There—you are welcome to that secret information!'

Sarcasm of this kind had become increasingly characteristic of Oster during these past weeks; the only expression of his internal rage and fear that the Abwehr's charmer would allow to surface. And there were other small hints: perhaps two cigarettes slipped into the holder in an hour where before it had been just one: and a touch more champagne taken on board during occasions such as this.

Bredow found Oster depressing. The worst thing, however, was the expression on Hans von Dohnanyi's face. The quiet lawyer, dressed in a dark civilian suit and subdued tie, had said almost nothing during the course of the evening. And he, too, had been drinking heavily by his usual spartan standards—perhaps seven, eight cognacs. He sat now holding a half-empty glass, examining Bredow from behind his thick spectacles. After Oster's bitter little outburst he shook his head almost imperceptibly, his eyes still fixed on Bredow, and the tiny motion conveyed a hidden mass of pent-up despair. For him, more than for any of them in this room, time was beginning to run very short. Arthur Nebe, their man inside the SD's apparatus of terror, had apparently heard rumours to that effect. Had it been his boys who were in charge of the investigations, he might have been able to put a few devious spanners in the works, slow things down. But the case against Dohnanyi and the *Kaspar* network was above Nebe's head: it was a pet project of Kaltenbrunner, he said, and the Gestapo plain clothes chief cum conspirator had enough risks to cope with in turning up the information on the English spy without putting his head on the block for Dohnanyi's sake as well. The SD's case was being put together by Kaltenbrunner, a special Judge-Advocate, and Gestapo-Mueller himself, with Schellenberg bouncing like a fawning puppy-dog at their heels, eager to pick up whatever scraps might be available after the bloodletting.

At that moment of tension, the air-raid sirens sounded across the city.

'The RAF has heard our plea!' Tresckow announced with an impish grin. 'They have decided to catch the Führer on the outside lavatory in the Chancellery garden and save everyone an awful lot of trouble! They know his movements—pun absolutely intentional, gentlemen . . .'

The laborious joke unleashed the healing laughter it had been intended to arouse. The sirens screamed and they chuckled and slapped each other on the back until the tears ran down their faces. 'It's true!' Tresckow insisted whenever the hilarity showed signs of flagging. 'I swear it, Otto vouchsafed this to me after his hush-hush meetings with Menzies' man!'

Then, seizing on the new mood of frenetic good cheer, Oster collected two bottles of champagne from the refrigerator in his kitchen, told the others to bring glasses, and bellowed: 'To the cellar! Henning must have a good time on his leave in beautiful, peaceful Berlin!'

He led the way down, swinging the champagne bottles like Indian clubs. The big flak gun above the Zoo, a few hundred yards from Oster's apartment, was already in full, deafening operation as they tramped down the stairs, and points of flickering yellow from the searchlight beams, let through by chinks in the blackout curtains, played eerily on the walls of the landings. Every night, Bredow thought, is *Walpurgis-nacht*. Every night a bomb party.

They reached the cellar entrance to find the janitor of the apartment building, who doubled as air-raid warden, preparing to close the heavy, flame-proof steel doors that had been installed. The man saw Oster coming and paused in his work, but the Abwehr colonel, for whom this was not enough, made a spectacular lunge for the opening, calling out: 'Don't shut us out, Herr Dahnke! Germany needs us far more than you can know!'

'Herr Oberst,' the long-suffering janitor acknowledged with a wan smile and a nod. When the four officers were safely inside, he listened for the sound of any more footsteps on the stairs, heaved his shoulders wearily and eased the door shut. 'That's it,' he said to no one in particular.

Some quiet murmurings in the corner, a baby crying. It was a big cellar, with only a couple of dim emergency lights. The forty or so tenants of the building who had taken refuge in there had tended, by some quirk of the psychology of fear, to make for the walls, away from the light, so that the faces that greeted the new arrivals were half in shadow. The crump of the flak was very faint now, deadened by the concrete ceiling and the reinforced steel.

They stayed by the door, away from most of the others, and Oster said: 'Warning, ladies and gentlemen. I am about to open a champagne bottle. The noise you will hear has absolutely nothing to do with the RAF.'

The cork shot up and bounced off the ceiling, the champagne, shaken up by Oster's mock-gymnastics on the way down there, poured out loudly onto the floor, leaving the bottle half-empty. With great aplomb he handed it to the nearest officer, who happened to be Bredow, and repeated the operation with the second bottle, with the same results, carefully explaining that such otherwise unforgivable barbarism of opening it before they could drink it was out of consideration for the other occupants of the cellar. He sat the second down, retrieved the first from Bredow, and began to pour, not at all put out when a seismic tremor went through the cellar and the emergency lighting flickered dangerously. Another bomb followed, and another while they squatted there drinking, mainly in silence, under the gaze of the rest of the cellar. Some were too wrapped up in their own misery to bother with the four officers, others smiled nervously. The janitor sat in solitary state on a small chair with his head in his hands, trembling slightly every time the cellar shook. Once he looked over at the incongruous champagne party by the door, and Bredow caught his eye. Before the janitor looked away, Bredow sensed a wave of concentrated, sullen resentment, close to hatred, and realized with a shock that it was directed at him. His attention was diverted again when Oster decided on another joke to raise flagging spirits.

'Gentlemen,' he confided in a stage whisper that must have been audible everywhere in the cellar. 'If we are killed tonight by the British, we have absolute proof that "C" cannot be trusted. I have every reason to believe that he knows my home address . . . and his arm is long . . .'

The wit was laboured and adolescent, the indiscretion foolish though certainly harmless, and the fizz had gone out of the evening, as it was slowly disappearing from the wine. Bredow laughed least of all. He was thinking of that janitor, who was probably sick of war and Hitler, but who found it easier to hate men of their stamp in their polished boots, with their smart uniforms and well-cut suits and mannered indifference, than any shadowy Nazi criminals. To the janitor, Hitler was a concept, a figurehead, while they were immediate, the war's privileged élite, and never mind the fine points of freedom, tyrannicide and high politics. If they succeeded in killing the Führer, millions of ordinary Germans like him would need a lot of convincing that they offered something better, while if they failed the ensuing witch-hunt would give the masses perverse satisfaction—the arrogant 'vons' and the champagne-drinking patriots dragged in the dirt for betraying their country . . .

The raid was by recent standards a small-scale one. Shortly before midnight the all-clear was sounded, the janitor shuffled over to open his door, and the cellar began to empty. Oster and Tresckow seemed keen on opening another bottle of something upstairs and making a real night of it, but Dohnanyi insisted that he must go home to the south-western suburbs. Since he lived not far from Dahlem and had brought his car, Bredow was quick to accept his offer of a lift. With the public transport system unpredictable and taxis hard to find after an air raid, he was prepared to risk the lawyer's being a little drunk.

The others came down to the street to see them off. The Tiergarten district was fairly quiet, without serious damage, though a fire-engine raced across a nearby intersection while they stood smoking a farewell cigarette on the pavement. The biggest fire seemed to be somewhere over by the Reichstag.

'Maybe they have hit the Prinz-Albrecht-Strasse,' someone said. 'And Gestapo-Mueller was working late.'

'That bastard only ever does overtime in the interrogation cellars. He would survive even a direct hit down there, God rot him.'

Oster made no more mention of the Admiral's Plan *Wintermärchen;* only his farewell to Bredow was a degree or two cooler than usual. He kept his final sally until Bredow was seated next to Dohnanyi in the front of the car. Suddenly there was a tapping on the passenger window. Bredow saw the colonel's sardonic face at the window and wound it down.

'Yes, Colonel?'

'Take a tip from an old hand, Otto,' Oster said. 'Ask more questions. The right questions, I mean.'

He stalked off back to the pavement, took Tresckow's arm and led him back into the apartment block. Dohnanyi pulled cautiously away from the kerb and drove slowly with muted sidelights in the direction of the Kurfürstendamm, heading for home. They were held up by police at a road block by the Kaiser Wilhelm Memorial Church, showed their Abwehr passes and were waved through. For some minutes after that, Dohnanyi stared ahead at the road, his gloved hands gripping the steering wheel tightly like a racing driver, though they were travelling at no more than thirty kilometres an hour.

'Are you all right, Hans?' Bredow asked.

Dohnanyi started visibly, as if being torn out of a meditation. 'You mean, have I had too much to drink? Yes . . . a little too much. And I dislike driving in the blackout. Don't worry, though, I'll get you back to Gisela in one piece.'

'Oh, she's working tonight, at the air-defence place. I've tried to tell her she shouldn't work irregular hours, but she insists that it's all right for a while yet. When the spring comes and the baby starts to show, she will give it up . . . How is Christine?'

'Managing. It's not easy for her,' Dohnanyi said. 'Our wives have the hardest time of all, don't you think? They sense problems, but they know they must not ask what's really wrong. And sometimes even I don't know.'

'Yes,' Bredow agreed lamely, feeling the accusation in Dohnanyi's words. Two municipal ambulances, one behind the other, sirens shrieking, overtook them on the broad highway through the Grunewald. They were heading south-west, towards Dahlem or Zehlendorff. Dohnanyi kept up his sedate pace; on the forest road there were few buildings and not even the dim emergency streetlighting that was permitted elsewhere, and accidents were common round here at night.

'Oster was hard on you tonight. He thinks you are holding back out of loyalty to the Admiral,' Dohnanyi said. 'I have to say that I share his opinion. What is going on, Otto?'

Bredow glanced at him, saw tiny beads of sweat on his forehead. The talk this evening had cost the man dear, and the question just now even dearer.

'You know what's going on. Canaris is wooing the British . . .' he answered.

'While we mark time and wait for the Gestapo to make their move. I don't think he realizes that Kaltenbrunner's bloodhounds are sniffing close to the Tirpitzufer, closer than ever before.'

'The Admiral is a powerful man. He and the Wehrmacht High Command would never allow . . .'

'They are living in the past,' Dohnanyi interrupted with sudden force. 'When the army was a law unto itself, because Hitler needed the generals. I never thought I would have to say it, but the Admiral is a fool. No one—but no one—is immune these days. I fear we shall all find that out for ourselves.'

'Hans, you're frightened. I understand—'

Dohnanyi thumped the steering wheel with one hand in anger and frustration, causing the horn to beep.

'Of course I'm damned well frightened!' he said. 'You know what those Gestapo animals are capable of! Canaris and the people who think like him believe they can cover all their options and act like a state within a state. Can they really? Are the Nazis that stupid? Once the Gestapo have their evidence, the witch-hunt will start.'

'But they have no evidence, Hans, that's the point—'

'They have. A few weeks and I'm finished, Otto.'

Dohnanyi's voice was sad, quiet and matter-of-fact, and brought a shocked silence. Outside it was beginning to rain hard. He reached over and switched on the electric windscreen-wipers. They began to clear the glass in front of him, squeaking gently as they moved backwards and forwards, hypnotic.

'What on earth are you talking about?' muttered Bredow. 'What can possibly go wrong?'

Dohnanyi hunched forward over the wheel. 'They picked up one of my Jews at the border. A routine check, they said, though I am certain that they had been waiting for him since before Christmas. Of course, he was carrying more than the permitted amount of currency, as they knew he would be. A serious offence. Twenty-four hours ago, three senior officials from the Prinz-Albrecht-Strasse travelled to Munich to take charge of the interrogation. Mueller will follow.'

'You and Oster didn't mention this earlier. Why not?'

'Oster does not know yet,' Dohnanyi said. 'I decided to try to involve him only if absolutely necessary. It's possible that the Jew, to save his own skin, will lead them on to Schmidhuber, my man in Munich, and then sooner or later they'll get on to me. Oster might do something stupid if he knew.'

'Such as?'

'Trying to protect me. He feels responsible as my immediate superior, because he gave the go-ahead for *Kaspar*.'

'This is pure speculation. I tell you, the Admiral will not allow things to get that far,' Bredow insisted.

'He may delay the Gestapo for a while, true,' Dohnanyi answered. 'So long as he is in Berlin at the time. And so long as the High Command backs him . . . et cetera et cetera . . .' He took his eyes away from the road for an instant and shot Bredow a completely humourless smile. 'I think that you have spent too much time scuttling around on Canaris's business, Otto,' he said. 'If you had your ear to the ground you would realize that there are rumblings. The balance of power is changing. In very high places they are beginning to ask why our beloved Abwehr makes so many mistakes—why the information is never quite good enough; why, for instance, there was no warning of the Allied landings in North Africa, and why we cannot say where the next blow will fall . . . Soon they will be wondering whether it is a matter of incompetence or deliberate sabotage of the glorious Greater German war effort, and whichever conclusion they arrive at, the Admiral will suddenly find that he has very few friends. Do you understand what I am saying?'

'Yes, yes. Of course I do. This has always been a risk.'

'A calculated risk, until now. No longer, Otto.'

Bredow swallowed hard. Oster's tough approach had been relatively easy to resist, but Hans Dohnanyi's combination of deeply-felt fear and irresistible reasoning left him helpless. He was talking to a man who stood within sight of the Gestapo interrogation cellars. That changed the rules, somehow.

'Why are you telling me if you will not confide in Oster?' he asked hoarsely.

Dohnanyi thought for a moment before replying. They were passing under the commuter railway that ran down to the Nikolassee, and soon they would be on Bredow's home ground in Dahlem, towards the rim of the sprawling city. Despite the rain and the darkness, he could pick out familiar landmarks, but tonight it gave him little comfort.

'Because, I suppose, you need shock treatment,' Dohnanyi said. 'I'm not asking you to betray Canaris, only to try to make him see reason. You have a personal connection, and he trusts you in a way he would not trust freer spirits. Forgive me for putting it that way, but it is a fact that you have always done strictly as he has instructed you. If you were to start questioning, it might bring him to his senses, too. At least in time to retrench and ensure that no more damage is done.'

Bredow saw the bizarre cottage construction of Dahlem U-bahn station, with its whimsical thatched roof, built at the turn of the century when English bucolic had been all the rage, right up to the Crown Prince Wilhelm's mock-tudor Cäcilienhof palace. Another three or four minutes.

'You talk,' he said, 'as if your arrest and the subsequent damage to the Abwehr were an accomplished fact.'

'They are probable. There is nothing I can do.'

'Nonsense!'

'Not nonsense. I ask you to challenge the Admiral. You may hint at my situation, but you must not reveal everything. I'll tell him if I feel I must, in my own way.'

There was something Roman in Dohnanyi's manner, the senator waiting for the Emperor's assassins to come and calmly putting his affairs in order. First sending messages to his friends . . .

'I have already spoken to him,' Bredow said. 'He is quite adamant. He wants the British to kill Hitler. He believes this to be the perfect solution, and he won't be swayed. I can try again—'

'Why not?' Dohnanyi said. 'But I warn you: Canaris is a man of personal charm and integrity; he is also quite ruthless in doing what he believes to be right. You will see, Otto. Compared with Canaris, even Oster is as a little child.'

Bredow could only nod dumbly and stare back at the road ahead. He caught sight of the road block an instant before Dohnanyi stepped on the brakes.

They came to a sliding emergency stop a few feet short of the striped barrier poles laid across the highway. A gaunt, hard-faced policeman in a high, peaked cap and cape squelched over to shine his masked torch at the car. Dohnanyi wound down the window and flashed his Abwehr pass at the cop. The magic wallet did its work for the second time that night.

'Herr Hauptmann,' the policeman explained carefully, 'you can't come through this way. You must drive back and take the road around the rear of Museum. Bad business. The RAF chose to give our Dahlem a real pounding tonight.'

Gisela will be busy, run off her feet, Bredow thought guiltily. He must—must—really insist that she give up this auxiliary work, perhaps suggest that she moved out of Berlin altogether. Her parents would be delighted to have her with them; their place near Neustrelitz was plenty big enough, and he could visit her at weekends. He would manage much better if he knew that she and the baby were safe. What possible place could there be for an expectant mother in a city under attack?

A moment later he heard the policeman say in answer to a question from Dohnanyi: 'Yes, bad, Herr Hauptmann. A dozen houses in this one street—and a direct hit on the air-raid centre. An incendiary. Leaving us with no switchboard, no organization . . . the chaos has to be seen to be believed. We've had to call in help from the central area. They got off lightly tonight. Usually the boot's on the other foot . . .'

Dohnanyi, his reactions still slightly slowed by alcohol, made the connection too late. He started, twisted round in his seat, barked: 'Otto!' But Bredow had already opened the door and was out in the road. He ran towards the police barrier, ignoring the driving rain and the warning shouts of the guard on duty there. Someone made a grab for him and he squirmed away, slid on the greasy cobbles and almost fell, then straightened up and vaulted the road block, clumsily but effectively. He panted on past a steaming fire engine, saw that the policeman had not been lying. On the far corner of a familiar street a hundred yards away, past the glowing shells of buildings that were of no importance to him, he saw a mass of smoke, swirling and eddying uncontrollably in the downpour.

They told Bredow some time later, when he could be told such things, that the astonished firemen had been forced to knock him unconscious in order to drag him from the burning air-raid centre. He had been trying to fight his way towards the cellar steps, one arm thrust up in an ineffectual attempt to protect his face, screaming like a maddened animal: 'My wife and child are in there! My wife and child!'

When Otto von Bredow returned to the Tirpitzufer, weeks later, it was officially spring. The burns, the outer wounds, had almost healed. He accepted the Admiral's heartfelt condolences. He spoke to him face to face about *Wintermärchen*. By then, however, the world had moved on, as it does. Menzies' commando group had been trained; the murder of Adolf Hitler was being actively planned; the breathtaking project Canaris had worked and schemed for was nearing fruition. And Hans von Dohnanyi, Captain of the Abwehr, had been detained by the Gestapo for interrogation. 'Under strict conditions', the arrest order said. That meant torture.

PHASE TWO:

'Fury'

March—April 1943

17

One moment the driver's world was as ever; the next it had changed—he saw it completely differently, though for the moment he didn't know why. Call it instinct, sixth sense, any of those names, but he felt suspicious of the two regulars in cloth caps from the moment he walked into the café, and the apparently irrational feeling of threat persisted and even grew when he went out to fetch the wallet from its usual place in the Gents. Perhaps it was because these pick-ups had become more frequent lately—two since Christmas where before they had been three, four months apart. There had to be something important going on for so much material to be passing along the chain. Anyway, by the time he got back out into the fresh air, every part of the driver seemed to be tingling with suspicion, fear, and a kind of defensive anger. He was alert as an animal that knew it was being stalked.

So it happened that he started up the lorry, waited a moment, saw the two cloth caps standing in the café doorway. Then he pulled out carefully, pretending he was having to make a difficult manoeuvre to avoid another five-tonner that was parked at right angles to him, all the while snatching quick glances at the cloth caps as he checked his rear wheels. Yes. The two of them were coming out, strolling across the cinders of the car park towards the main road. He had a dim recollection of their having done the same last time, in February; the memory just bubbled up into his conscious mind at that moment. Pity it couldn't have bubbled a bloody sight earlier, he was to tell himself in the bitter weeks to come.

Hullo, my son, the driver said to himself. *Hullo, hullo.*

The driver passed them without looking at them, reached the road. Then he pulled out into the main road without indicating—there was never any traffic, anyway—and accelerated away as fast as the lorry's ageing engine would stand. He checked his rear-view mirror when he had driven fifty yards or so and, sure enough, one of the men from the café was making a gesture that was a shade too frantic to be innocent. Now the driver was certain. He had never thought this would happen—how the hell had they got on to him?—but he had to believe his own eyes, didn't he?

Whatever was happening, he thought quickly, it was bad news. Maybe a hijacking gang, but more likely the Old Bill, probably the Special Branch or whatever they called them these days. Oh, he knew those bastards of old, from when he had organized rallies and meetings before the war; they had never been far away, always checking on his private life and his movements. Trouble was, he'd been led into a false sense of security after being a different person for the past two years. He'd thought they would never find him with his new identity, that the system was foolproof.

A quarter of a mile on, short of the turning he intended to take, the driver saw the car following him. It was a black Austin, with a card stuck in the windscreen that he couldn't decipher through his mirror at a distance of a hundred yards or so, but it rang a bell. Last time it had been closer for a while and he had noticed that card, a doctor's identification, and he remembered thinking idly that those blokes had it good, they got petrol. The Austin had been behind him most of the way then—not surprisingly, because when he took the usual route he stayed on the main road until he was a couple of hundred yards from the safe house.

The driver felt his palms going sweaty on the steering-wheel and realized that he was more than just scared. He was beginning to be gripped by a dominant, chemical fear, and there was no way of getting rid of it.

The turning was due, a narrow road, hardly more than a lane, going left into wooded countryside that would eventually bring him out at Radlett Aerodrome after a few twists and turns. See if the Austin followed him. If it did, the case was clear-cut.

He turned with a shriek of brakes and a clamour of protesting gears. Then he was motoring slowly along the unmetalled minor road between tall, tunnel-arches of trees, peering in his mirror. Within seconds his anxieties were confirmed. He was being followed. Definite.

What to do, though? From now on, the Austin—and who knew what else?—was going to be on his tail. Whether he made the drop now or not, he would never be free of these people, would never be sure if he was betraying his comrades the moment he tried to make a telephone call or send a message to warn them. And they must already have tabs on the man who delivered the wallet to the café, had probably been breathing down his neck for months and the stupid bastard never noticed. The driver knew he had to tip his comrades the wink, though, by hook or crook; there was a number he had been told to phone in emergencies, real emergencies. His linkman, the man in the pub with the nicotine stains, had told him it was safe, a sweet little granny who ran a telephone answering service: you told her you wanted an appointment with Mr Brown of Brown Contract Cleaning, and every day they rang in to check with her. Just the fact of your 'phone call was the alarm signal. And everybody was beautifully untraceable . . .

But all right, the driver thought then. So he could phone the emergency number and warn them, but that didn't do a lot for him, did it? The rest of them would be all right. Great. He'd almost certainly be for the high jump, though, because the people following him wouldn't let go of him now, like a big cat with a very small mouse. He'd get a lifetime in chokey or even worse, because this was wartime and they weren't too fussy with spies.

And so he did his level best to throw the Austin off. And he failed. Twelve, fifteen miles along lanes until he didn't know where he was. His petrol was getting low. He had no coupons to get more, because he hadn't made the drop and picked some up. He couldn't go on like this all bloody day. The black saloon dawdled, kept disappearing and re-appearing, and he wouldn't maybe have noticed it if he hadn't already known, but it stuck with him. It was always there. And he was going mad, stark staring.

That was when he made his decision. He speeded up, putting a little distance between himself and the Austin, and carefully chose his moment to stop. Once he had made his decision he felt calmer, colder.

By the time the Austin came round the bend, only fifty yards behind him, the driver had the lorry parked at a cunning angle so that the other car couldn't squeeze past between the hedge and his near side. The driver was sitting waiting with his cab door just open, checking in his mirror, watching the look on the bloke's face. The Austin stopped abruptly. When it tooted its horn, the driver pushed his door to full open and monkeyed down onto the road, doing his level best to look scared himself, then relieved, as he stumbled towards the Austin, exaggerating his limp. That helped to lull people; without even consciously thinking about it, they were never so wary of a cripple as of a whole man.

'Thank God, a doctor!' he said, hobbling over to the driver's window of the Austin.

The man in the car didn't know what to do. He wound his window down a couple of inches and squawked: 'What is it? I've got an urgent call, man! Kindly move your vehicle!'

He was a square sort of chap with one of those Ronald Coleman moustaches, wearing a mackintosh and a deerstalker hat, pretty much the part. And at that moment he was confused and worried sick. Not that he was a bad actor; the bluster was quite good, but the driver could smell the man's fear.

'You don't understand,' the driver said. 'My mate's in the cab. He's suddenly gone all blue. I think he's had a heart attack. I stopped and tried to do something for him. Quick, doctor, please . . .'

The man in the Austin was stymied, wasn't he? He couldn't admit that he knew the driver didn't have a mate with him. The driver guessed he was just supposed to follow the lorry and see where it went. If that was so, then to give himself away now would ruin the whole act. And there was another factor. The driver could see that the man in the Austin, because he was human and all humans doubt, was beginning to ask himself if this hadn't all been a terrible mistake, and had he been following the wrong lorry all this time?

'I see,' the man said. 'Er, I suppose I ought to see what I can do . . . just a minute.'

He cast an anxious look behind him at the road, very quick and hardly noticeable, as if he was half hopeful, half worried that something would collide with his rear coming round the corner. Then he reached into the back seat of the Austin. Blimey, the driver thought when he saw what the man was doing. They've even supplied him with the little black bag. Nice touch.

'Hurry, doctor. Please,' he said, injecting a whine of desperation into his voice. 'My mate could be dying at this very moment. Hurry, sir . . .'

The man in the Austin put the bag down on the seat beside him to unlock the door. He had one hand in his coat pocket, though, and that gave the game away for certain. The driver would do what he had to do next with a clear conscience, because it was obviously him or the 'doctor'.

The driver opened the car door for him from the outside, still staring straight at the man with frightened eyes—which in a way wasn't hard. And in the moment when the door swung open, and before the man could possibly do anything, he thrust his left hand round the rim of the door and grabbed the man's arm where it disappeared into the coat pocket. Elbowing the door fully open, the driver held on and tightened his grip, dodging a wild punch that the man tried to swing over the top of the steering wheel. When he had room to manoeuvre, his free hand shot inside and went straight for the throat, sliding for a second over the stiff collar and the tie before he felt his fingers pressing savagely against flesh and cartilage, already beginning to ache. It was then that he knew it was all over for the man in the Austin. Those arms, hands, fingers, were extremely well developed, you see, because he couldn't depend on the power of his legs like other people. His arms, hands, fingers, were strong on their own, working muscle, lethal miracles of engineering in flesh and blood. He had worked so hard at it, and it was paying off, saving his skin at the price of this enemy's life.

The man in the Austin would die soon, because the driver was not just cutting off the air flow; he was crushing his windpipe, causing terrible physical damage that was beyond repair.

The effort hurt like hell, though. Even muscles like the driver's were pushed to the limit by such use. His left arm, especially, was having to work superhumanly hard to keep the man's hand in his pocket, away from the weapon concealed in there. He could tell that the man in the Austin was concentrating all his strength to get that weapon out, because he was experienced and aware enough to realize that he wouldn't get the driver's hand away from his windpipe while the driver was alive. He had only a few seconds, though, and he knew it. The man's eyes were turning big and red-veined, his face was going puce, and there was a surprisingly faint, harsh sound coming up out of his oesophagus, like a distant crow on a telegraph wire. No chance. He was a goner now.

The man in the Austin went limp quite suddenly. One moment he was still struggling, and the next the life went out of him. To be on the safe side, however, the driver didn't relax his grip for ten or fifteen seconds. His caution cost him precious time.

The van came round the corner fast, and slammed its brakes on even faster, so quickly that the driver only had time to let go, not to get away or start trying to prise the dead man's hand out of the coat pocket to get at the weapon. He was still thinking, 'I'll say the bloke's had a heart attack. Most people wouldn't know the difference', when a door slammed and he turned to see one of the workmen from the café moving towards him with a gun in his hand.

Of course. And he couldn't run.

The driver spun round and got behind the bonnet of the Austin, shouting, 'Keep away!' in the kind of voice that might make them think he had a shooter, too. He didn't, fuckit, because they'd told him not to carry one in case of random road checks, the Old Bill searching lorries for black-market stuff. That had happened once, and he'd been clean as a whistle, and he'd been grateful for the advice. Not now.

The man, who had been joined by his mate, stopped and went full-length on the road, his gun trained at the Austin, steadying himself like a target marksman. These people were pros.

'I should come quietly if I were you!' a voice yelled. 'You can't get out of here!'

But the driver wasn't listening. He was for the chop either way, unless he got to the gate ten yards or so away, by where he had stopped the lorry. From his cab he had been able to look over the hedge when he had stopped, and he had seen a copse a short way across the field, cover, where speed wouldn't be so important. He peeked round the side of the bonnet and saw that the marksman's mate had gone again, probably trying to work a flanker. Make it snappy, his instincts screamed at him.

He went, loping at first like an animal, scooping himself forward with his arms and hands, because he could move faster that way and present a limited target. He had a few yards' grace, thanks to the position of the car, before the marksman could get a sight of him, and if he got through that he'd be between the lorry and the hedge, a narrow corridor that led to the gate.

A shot went off before he reached the back tailgate of the lorry, and he heard the thumping clang of the bullet against steel. Then the driver was into the gap between the lorry and the hedge, half on and half off a slippery grass verge, with stray branches from the uncut undergrowth whipping across his face and wetting him with morning dew. He was almost upright now, going into a fast shamble for the dash to the farm gate. The bloke on the road shouted something he couldn't catch, and he was at the gate, up and over in a vault and dropping slightly awkwardly onto the surface of the ploughed field, down on his hands and knees for a second before lurching on.

The driver started to move diagonally across the field, which meant that the bullet from the second man, who was approaching along the field side of the hedge, hit him side-on in the thigh. The driver kept on, but it was very painful, and his trousers were getting wet. Must be blood, dear Christ, and what strength he had left seemed to be ebbing very fast. He didn't look round—no point unless he was willing to give himself up—but kept his eyes on the copse of beech trees ahead, which was coming on all too damned slowly. For a while now he had been hearing heavy breathing and the sound of boots slipping and splatting on the earth close behind. Then, finally, the sound was on him and something kicked him hard in the arse, sending him head first down with a piercing yelp, and he was being battered round the head while he lay in the mud, with the heavy weight of a man squeezing the breath out of him and a voice bellowing: 'Bastard! Bastard!' until he lost consciousness.

'Jesus,' said Barraclough when he arrived at the scene in the middle of the field. 'You wouldn't believe the bugger could shift at such a rate, would you?'

Kelly had calmed down sufficiently to get busy. He was kneeling on top of the driver, fixing a pair of handcuffs round his wrists.

'Shit, shit, shit,' he muttered, repeating the word like an incantation. 'A proper, grade A, twenty-four carat foulup . . . What's the position with Atkins?'

'He's had it,' Barraclough said simply. 'Very nasty. And we're right in the soup. "C" will have our guts. There'll be blood in the out-trays at Broadway when they hear about this, old boy.'

Kelly nodded and stood up, cautiously prodding the driver with one foot to check that he was really out for the count. He had lost his cloth cap at some stage in the chase, and a long hank of brillianteened hair from his balding head had fallen and was sticking to his forehead. He kept it carefully brushed to hide his hairless patch, and violence had found his vanity out. Kelly swept it automatically back into place.

'I've got a shocking stitch. Getting too old for this kind of thing,' he panted.

'This kind of thing wasn't supposed to happen,' Barraclough reminded him. 'What a bloody, bloody mess . . .'

'You speak the truth, O chief. Still, it was lucky we decided to get after poor old Atkins in the van.'

Barraclough sighed. 'We'll have to own up, get on the nearest blower and ask Grainger for new instructions, pretty bloody pronto . . . First, though, we'd better get Atkins into the van and sort this bugger out before he comes to.'

Kelly grimaced with a kind of bleak relish. 'He won't do that in a hurry,' he said, fondly patting the cosh he had stuck back into his belt. 'Lost my rag with him more than somewhat over Atkins. Hope I didn't do for him, because it's my guess that "C" will want him for interrogation, to see what can be salvaged.'

He leaned over the unconscious man and tossed Barraclough the oilskin wallet that he had retrieved from the driver's jacket pocket. Barraclough caught it and put it safely away without comment in his own overall. He scratched his head.

'Come on, then,' he said. 'Let's get a move on. We'll carry him over as far as the gate, then leave him there while we put Atkins in the van. If we're unlucky and anyone happens along and asks, he's a crazy, homicidal deserter and we're carting him off back to the glass-house. All right?'

'Right. He's also a big chap and all dead weight, damn him.'

'Aren't they always?' Barraclough grumbled, squatting down to take the driver's shoulders and motioning for Kelly to take his legs. 'Bleeding like a pig from that leg, too. Oh my gawd, the fur will fly tonight. Oh my bloody pension. Hup . . . Christ, you're right about the size of him.'

The driver inspected the room through half-closed eyes. The left one was actually near-blind, swollen and raw. That chap in the field had given him a hell of a beating in a comparatively short time, but the strange thing was that he felt no pain, only a slight heaviness. He guessed that he had been given some sort of injection—morphine or similar. He was entitled, he reckoned, to pretend to be not all there when they tried to threaten him and ask him questions. He intended, if possible, to buy time until the situation got clearer.

What he had managed to glimpse of the room told the driver several things. Firstly, this was not a police station, because there was ornate plasterwork on the ceiling, including some delicate golf leaf. The room had a sense of space. He was handcuffed to an armchair with wooden arm rests. So a private house. Secondly, he had been conscious since mid-afternoon and it was dark, seven o'clock or so; he could tell that, because long pencils of light had been thrown on the facing wall from chinks in the curtained window behind him, but they had disappeared with the darkness outside. Thirdly, there was no traffic noise, which meant he was not in London. Therefore the place must be a country house well away from the nearest road, most likely set in extensive grounds. A real hide-away. Lastly, the men guarding him were waiting for something or somebody. They had made no attempt to revive him or talk to him. They just kept on whispering to each other, going outside and then coming back in, though always leaving two men in the room to keep an eye on him. They all had guns. In fact, they were a right villainous-looking mob, not that much different to the razorboys he had grown up with in the East End. They'd do you as soon as look at you, that much was obvious. The driver felt physically strange because of the drug, but he knew he was thinking good and clear, that his old cunning hadn't deserted him.

A distant hum from outside the window broke into the driver's thoughts. As he listened, it got louder. A car was coming up the drive, fast. He closed his good eye fully and concentrated. Powerful engine: four- or even six-litre job, he realized when it got closer. Slowing down in front of the house. Stopping. Door slamming. Footsteps on gravel. One voice very level and authoritative, another hoarse and jumpy.

Several minutes went by. Then the driver heard the door of his prison opening and his guards getting hastily to their feet.

'Good afternoon, sir,' one of them said. His voice was soft, respectful in the extreme. The newcomer, it occurred to the driver, must be a very big wheel indeed. He opened his good eye a fraction and peered, saw a tall man in his early fifties with a thin moustache, a right nob type, wearing a nicely-made double-breasted whistle with a hankie in the top pocket. Dapper was the word. From his napper to his feet, as the song said.

While the driver was still watching, the tall man signalled to one of the guards, who moved in the driver's direction. Time to shut the eye again. The driver then felt himself being shaken, which actually brought a faint surge of pain. God knows what it would have been like if they hadn't dosed him up. He hated to think what state his body was in.

'Wakey, wakey! We know you're in there somewhere,' the guard hissed in a loud whisper, like he was in a church or a hospital operating theatre. 'Someone very important indeed wants to talk to you. You really ought to listen to him, because otherwise you'll end up on the butcher's slab, mate.'

The shaking went on for a few moments more, until the driver thought he would have to scream. Then the guard left off him, moved back a couple of paces, muttered something. Soon there was a much lighter pressure on the driver's shoulder, more like a comforting hand. The voice was different—cultured and controlled—and its tone was almost friendly.

'Listen carefully,' it said. 'I am the man he was referring to, and I have a proposal to put to you. Understood . . . Finch?'

The driver tensed so quickly and so tight that it must have been noticeable to the others. Christ, no one had called him by his born name of Finch for years now. They knew who he was all right, and a lot more besides . . .

'As you must realize, we are very well-informed, so don't think you can spin us any yarns,' the voice went on. 'You are in a very perilous situation, because this morning you murdered a servant of His Majesty's Government in cold blood. That is a capital offence under any political system—and particularly the one that you have chosen to serve in preference to ours.' The voice came closer to his ear. 'Do you want to die, Finch?'

The driver waited, did not move. He wanted to hear a proposal.

'We don't even need to go through a trial in order to deal with you,' the voice resumed. 'This is wartime, and the usual legal processes don't necessarily apply. In short, you could just disappear from the face of the earth, depending on how the mood takes us. Nevertheless, there is a chance that we might . . .' There was a short, slightly embarrassed interval while the toff searched for the kind of sordid phrase that the driver would understand. '. . . There is a chance we might go easier on you,' he said. 'And the more you co-operate with us, the greater is that chance.'

The driver could feel his heart beating like a tribal drum. Some bastard had shopped him, one of his so-called comrades. Must have for them to be taking this attitude. The hand came off his shoulder, and the posh voice said to the room in general: 'He's shamming all right. He can understand every blessed word I say.' Then, to the driver again: 'Think about it. I shall be back in a few minutes.'

A silence followed. They were all waiting for him, the driver thought. Sod them. He felt a sudden surge of defiance, then a sour satisfaction as the toff murmured something in an irritated voice and walked out of the room. The door closed behind him. Another pause. Then renewed movement as one of the guards came over. When he heard the man's voice, he realized that it was the one who had spoken to him before.

'The chief was really serious about all that,' the guard said. The driver could smell strong traces of recently-drunk beer on his breath. The aroma was sour, but the driver would have liked a beer for himself, very much. 'And I'd like you to know,' the guard continued, 'that if you don't do what he says and he decides to get rid of you, I'll be volunteering for that job. The fellow you murdered on the road today was a friend of mine. He had a wife and kids. It would be a pleasure to watch you die, believe me.'

The guard reached down and touched the driver's thigh. The driver became aware of the bandage wrapped tightly round his leg. The numbness was going; he was beginning to feel his body. Then the guard delivered a swift, skilfully-calculated punch right onto the wound with his balled fist. The driver opened his mouth wide, cried out in unashamed agony.

The guard laughed. 'There you are,' he commented aloud to his friends. 'It talks. It doesn't walk, but it talks.'

Sir Stewart Menzies closed the door behind him and beckoned to the man who was waiting for him outside the room where they were keeping Finch. He said nothing. Together, Menzies and the man walked a short distance to a small sitting room, where there were easy chairs and a tray laid out with refreshments.

'Sherry, please, Grainger,' Menzies said, mechanically checking his watch. He took the drink but remained standing. Grainger, who had been about to sit down, was forced to do the same. 'Five minutes we shall give him. Though I don't think we shall get him at this stage. It may take a while.'

They both turned when they heard the prisoner's bellow of pain, dulled by the intervening walls, but nevertheless unmistakable. Menzies clucked disapprovingly.

'They have been ordered not to do any lasting damage, sir,' his companion was quick to explain. 'They're all well trained in that sort of work.'

Grainger wore a creased dark suit and the old boys' tie of a decidedly minor public school. Surprisingly, his plump, middle-aged face, with its perpetual expression of worried concern, resembled nothing so much as that of an overworked physician who has seen a lot of suffering but has never quite come to accept it. He was known to the few who were aware of his department's role—or even of its existence—as 'Butcher' Grainger.

'I see,' said Menzies.

'It's just that it seemed proper to reinforce the message. We do have to try to bring him round to our point of view as soon as possible. You said so, sir.'

'Yes. I did.'

'I . . . ah . . . presume then, sir, that your intention is to keep him here until needed. Providing, that is, he agrees to co-operate.'

'That is so.'

'Well, I'm sure he'll break some time. Let's just hope it's soon, eh?'

Menzies nodded curtly. 'It is up to all of us to ensure that he co-operates, thus undoing the damage inflicted by today's fiasco. It was fortunate that your chaps were able to drop the material off and give us a breathing-space.'

'I suppose you have considered the alternative, sir? We could round up the entire ring tonight, sir. If you were to give the word . . .'

'I'm afraid that's not on. The matter is very much more complicated. I must remind you yet again that Finch is indispensable to a very finely-balanced plan. He must be kept alive and persuaded to co-operate. That is all.'

'Of course. It's your decision, sir. I dare say we can manage the necessary arrangements here.'

The atmosphere between the two men was already distinctly chilly. In the silence that followed, it slipped another couple of degrees. Menzies cleared his throat.

'I sincerely hope you can,' he said tartly. 'Perhaps this mess might be put down to sheer bad luck, but it mustn't happen again . . . Tell me, how seriously injured is Finch in your estimation?'

'Oh, he's not as bad as he looks,' Grainger answered, keen to turn away the implied rebuke. 'Our pet quack patched him in a jiff. Reckons the blighter'll be able to get around, after a fashion, inside ten days. With the proper care, of course. Mainly loss of blood and bruising, perhaps a spot of concussion. The chap's got the constitution of an ox, though I wouldn't like to . . . ah overstrain him.'

'No. I'm allowing you to rough him up a bit today, but until I get back from abroad, I don't want any more of that.' Menzies sighed. 'I wish I didn't have to go tomorrow, but I can't avoid it now. Bloody nuisance a complication such as this occurring at this stage.'

'The problem, the real problem, sir, is lack of funds and therefore of men. We simply haven't the resources to train and equip them, what with all the cash going to the glamour-boys and the cloak-and-dagger merchants. I know it's no excuse for slip-ups like this one, but on the other hand our allocation doesn't permit the kind of operational efficiency . . .'

Grainger's plaintive voice died away. Menzies was staring into space, swallowing hard as if finding it an effort to keep his temper in check. This was obviously not time to complain to 'C' about the department's share of the budget. Silly of him to think otherwise, Grainger told himself. He hurriedly finished his own sherry and eyed Menzies' drink meaningfully.

'Another, sir? Perhaps a small one?'

Menzies let the silence speak for him for another moment or two, then shook his head.

'I think not,' he said. 'Rather check up on our friend in the interrogation room, if he's still in one piece. Goodness, this is a distasteful affair, but one can't baulk at such duties.'

'Indeed not, sir.'

Grainger was by no means sure whether the reference to

'such duties' concerned the prisoner specifically or his own department's activities in general. Quite possibly both, knowing the way 'C' expressed himself. When in his cups with trusted employees, Grainger liked to draw comparisons: where the rest of the Service fancied themselves as fox-hunting men, in it for the colour and the thrill of the chase, Grainger's department were mere vermin-control operatives and therefore looked down on, like the farmer who dug up the foxes' earths and slaughtered the creatures with his twelve-bore. Very infra-dig. Not quaite naice. Grainger was still faintly astonished that 'C' had involved the department in this business he was pursuing, but he was also flattered and delighted. Menzies could rely on Grainger and his lads to keep mum and do their jobs, which was more than could be said for most of the rest of the Service.

They spent half an hour in the room with Finch, who continued to hold back on them. After the doctor referred to by Grainger as 'our pet quack' had been called in and had declared the man unfit for further severe interrogation, Menzies decided to call it a day. He left the room and called for his hat and coat. They had not secured Finch's co-operation, but Grainger was relieved to see that 'C' was, if not happy, at least philosophical about the situation. He saw him to the main door of the house.

'Shall we continue to interrogate him, sir? See if we can break him—without going too far, naturally.'

Menzies thought it over, shook his head. 'No. On the contrary, give him whatever he needs or asks for. Nurse him back to fitness. Make him feel we care about him. All right? He's not the type who responds to the physical approach.'

'He's a thug, sir,' Grainger said testily. 'His sort has a very strong sense of self-preservation . . .'

'I said no violence while I'm away, Grainger. I'll be back in four or five days. Then I'll try again.'

'Well, everyone wants to survive, sir, don't they? I mean, after a fashion?'

Menzies' chauffeur was standing by the open door of 'C''s Bentley, making a face that showed he had no desire to wait around on a cold, windy March night. Menzies nevertheless stood for a short while more in the doorway, hat in hand, looking very thoughtful.

'Yes, I suppose we all do,' he said at last. 'And so we slaughter each other. Something of a paradox.'

Then he stooped and entered his car. It would be midnight before he got back to his office at Broadway.

By that time, in the curtained room on the second floor of the big house, the driver had already long succumbed to a dark, dreamless sleep. First, however, he had asked for and received a small glass of beer, and they had unhandcuffed one of his hands so that he could drink it properly himself.

'My, you're a lucky murderer, old son,' the guard had told him. 'Someone up there's decided he needs you. I can't for the life of me fathom out why, but he does. So you're in clover. For the moment, at least.'

The driver felt confusion, surprise, an almost religious awe of the man with the cultured voice and the beautiful suit. That bastard knew everything, even how to break him.

Because the driver could withstand anything except gentleness.

18

'Dohnanyi was standing over there,' Canaris said, pointing at a scorched patch of wall in the corner. 'Next to the safe, while Judge-Advocate Roeder removed the last of the papers. Oster was here, behind the Gestapo man; and I was in the doorway, watching everybody. I saw Oster make his move to secure the *Kaspar* file from the heap on the desk. I couldn't stop him . . . and neither could I intervene when the Gestapo man turned around.'

The Admiral shrugged sadly. He and Bredow stood in the middle of the charred shell that had once been Hans von Dohnanyi's office. The air raid two weeks previously had ended an era; the Abwehr was now in the process of moving from Berlin to Zossen. They had come here for Bredow's benefit, so that he could hear the full story of the

Dohnanyi Affair and pay his final respects to what remained of the Tirpitzufer.

'I still can't believe that you allowed the Judge-Advocate and the Gestapo man into Hans's office,' Bredow said.

Canaris kicked half-heartedly at a sliver of plaster that lay near the shattered window.

'It was a miscalculation. I assumed that Dohnanyi would never keep such incriminating material in his office safe, and I looked forward to sending Kaltenbrunner's bloodhounds away with a flea in their collective ear, never to darken our doors again. God in heaven, I accept that he could hardly have kept the file at home, but there are other places of safety . . .'

'He was desperate and confused, Admiral. On that last night . . . before Gisela . . . he told me. I could have warned you.'

'Past,' Canaris told him sharply. 'Spilt milk. Sometimes, Otto, I almost believe in the famous teutonic death-wish.'

Salvage gangs had already cleared these upper storeys, where the bomb-damage had been worst. This part of the building was cold and eery, whipped by the wind despite the rough hard-board sheets nailed to the window frames. And everything was so quiet, so still apart from the wind's howl. Such a contrast with the way it had been. Bredow felt an involuntary shiver. He drew his leather coat more closely round his shoulders and wished that he had not come here.

'How bad a time will they give Hans? Will he break?' he asked.

'Nebe, who hears what goes on but can do nothing, says that they are still proceeding with relative caution in their interrogations. Dohnanyi is clever and brave, and a trained lawyer, and they are still bogged down in the currency violations charges.' Canaris laughed bitterly. 'The Gestapo must pretend to observe the legal niceties at this stage. For all it matters, they could have arrested him for jaywalking, or for allowing his pet dog to foul the streets. The important thing for them is that they have him in custody. Oster is a cause of equal, if not greater concern.'

'Oster?'

Canaris nodded, put a hand on Bredow's shoulder. Much had been kept from the Oberleutnant while he had been in hospital. It was hard not to break it all in a demoralizing rush.

'Colonel Oster behaved nobly, as usual, but with overweening stupidity. Now he has been suspended from the Army, accused of attempting to impede the Judge-Advocate's investigations.'

'But surely you still have influence, Admiral?'

'Our friends in the High Command would dearly like to save him, but it will need a miracle, for the regulations are quite clear, the procedures laid out. Oster is almost certain to be discharged with ignominy, which means that he too will be at their mercy. Soldiers have few enough rights in this Germany,' Canaris observed. 'But civilians, my boy, have none. Sooner or later, they will take Oster also. And to think that only a few days later, the British came along with their damned bombers and blew this office to bits. Late, as ever. Dohnanyi's files would have burned beautifully. Everything else here did. I'm sorry—'

Canaris had seen Bredow turn away and bite his lip at the reference to the bombers. It was six weeks since his wife's death; this was his first outing since his discharge from the clinic at Wannsee. He walked with a slight limp, and a linen patch still covered his right eye. Under the coat, one forearm was in plaster, a reminder of how he had tried to barge his way through blazing masonry that night, before the fire-fighting team had got to him and dragged him away. Much had happened since so far as Canaris was concerned. He had been busier than ever, fighting doggedly to maintain the high-wire act that was *Wintermärchen* while at the same time coping with the loss of the arrested men and the temporary absence of Bredow. It was easy to forget personal matters under those circumstances, including the fact that Bredow would never again be able to conceive of fire as a saviour.

'No apologies, please, Admiral,' Bredow said, though the surge of pain was still etched on his features. 'These issues must be discussed. We cannot afford to be oversensitive. What is to be done now? Am I to have a part in it?'

Canaris took him gently by his good arm and led him

out onto the landing, away from the bleak sights of the office. In any case, it was draughty in there. The boy must be looked after still.

'We go on, with *Wintermärchen* as the lynch-pin. I have activated the Vatican channels for further contacts with the British. I foresee no problems there. A matter of simple communication rather than negotiation.'

'Admiral—?'

'The answer is, yes. I shall put you formally under the command of Pieckenbrock at Zossen. He is a reliable man, as you know. Less temperamental than poor Oster. But you will be on duties in the occupied territories.' Canaris continued to hold Bredow's arm. 'Give yourself another ten, fourteen days to recover more fully. Then we shall talk again.'

'May I ask you what these duties will involve?'

'You may, but I will not necessarily answer you. Suffice it to say that the Mediterranean heals many wounds, and that its islands are a long way from the Gestapo,' Canaris said, his dour face softening. 'We cannot go back now, however great the temptation. We can only go forward, survive, and if possible gain our end. Any withdrawals will be purely strategic. You will continue to play an important part in *Wintermärchen*, wherever you are, for as long as you are fit and willing. And I never doubt that you will be the latter. It is, after all, largely due to your work with Mister Bellingham that we have gained what we now possess—a direct channel to the heart of an England that may be our enemy at the moment, but should be our friend.'

Bredow was moved. 'It will be a fine thing to prove that humanity counts for something, even in these insane times. We must show that men of good will can make agreements and keep to them . . .'

They set off down the patched stairs, their footsteps reverberating into the empty corridors. A small kitchen-cum-canteen remained open in the basement, to cater for the few key Abwehr personnel who had not yet moved to Zossen. Canaris had promised coffee with real strawberry cake, made with cane sugar, as a special treat to commemorate Bredow's return to the fold.

'Such an agreement is a rare thing,' he commented

while they rested for Bredow's sake on the fourth-storey landing. He spoke with some passion. 'Certainly the last of its kind, unless together we and our British counterparts succeed in salvaging something of the old values. In Germany they put their gentlemen in prison, while in England these days they make them responsible to parliament. The result is the same. The nation's natural moral and political leaders are rendered powerless, and the sweepings of the gutters are permitted to control the destinies of whole empires!'

Suddenly Bredow felt his mood changing. He was struck by the arrogance in the Admiral's words. He had never before questioned that men such as Canaris and the others—humane, patriotic, cultured and clever—were entitled to represent the 'real' Germany. Yet while Canaris had been delivering his short political lecture, he had found himself picturing the face of the janitor in the bomb-shelter, the hate he had seen there during that last, crazy night of revelling—the *Walpurgis-nacht*—with Oster and Dohnanyi and Tresckow, the night that Gisela died. How often had he, or Canaris and the rest, really tried to understand ordinary people's dreams, fears, hopes and longings? The German military caste had tolerated Hitler, because in the early days of his power he had seemed to offer protection for 'values' threatened by communism and democracy. They had invited the Nazi cuckoo into their nest, and when the Führer had shown himself to be a monster, they had begun to prepare to expel him—falteringly, guiltily, and at times with shameful incompetence. When Hitler really was gone, they would have to face ordinary folk like the janitor, give their reasons, offer them some kind of decent life. Then, of course, the 'gentlemen' would have to seek their agreement, not with the likes of Sir Stewart Menzies, but with the despised masses to whom Canaris referred with such easy, paternal contempt.

Bredow did not dare contradict, however, at this moment. And soon his dour, disturbing new thoughts were swept away—by nothing more earth-shattering than the prospect of company, coffee, and real, honest strawberry cake.

19

The trainees were still about a mile from where their Dodge truck was parked on the mountain road. Knox clambered to the head of the gorge, looked round quickly to see if either of the sergeant-instructors was in sight, saw they were not, and sat down on a rock, resting his Sten by his side and leaving the face of the precipice to take some of the weight of his fifty-pound pack. It was filled with stones, to simulate the kind of load he might well be carrying on Rhodes on outings with the local guerrillas. Knox shifted position until the pack no longer tore at his shoulder muscles. Never mind ashes to bloody ashes, he thought. I'll give 'em rocks to rocks when my number's up.

One of the sergeant-instructors appeared within seconds, as Knox had half-expected. His name was Watts. He came from Dorset and was built like the proverbial brick shithouse; his experience included blowing holes in mountains in South America for open-cast mining and two years' extremely active service with the Commandos. Knox admired and loathed him simultaneously.

'Aha, sir,' said Watts, staring up at the officer. 'Taking an illicit breather, I see?'

'Waiting for the others. Using my initiative. Preserving my strength. All good survival technique . . .'

'Bollocks, sir,' Watts commented mildly. 'You went wandering off while they took a more direct route to the top. They're waiting for *you*.'

'I see. I'd better shimmy down then, hadn't I?'

'Yes, sir. Once we're all up there, it's downhill to the lorry,' Watts assured him as he picked up his Sten and scrambled wearily down the slope. 'Been a good day's hiking, I reckon. You're all getting much fitter, more used to the terrain. Not much to choose between you now.'

One of them usually got lost for a while on these mountain hikes. It had become an incestuous joke in the small group, accompanied by accusations of shirking, blindness, inability to cross the road without taking a wrong turning, and so on. Captains Knox and Jessup were the main offenders, naturally: Lieutenant Meyerscough never deviated from the projected route, just as he never dropped his weapon, or complained, or got faint from the heat, or failed to look anything less than a hundred per cent fit and raring to go. Since they had been informed that the Rhodes operation was going to be a 'two-man show'—two officers, that was, plus one of the sergeants—Meyerscough had become even more intolerable in his persistent efforts to show willing, and he was not, being the sort of man he was, aware that by this stage both Knox and Jessup were secretly rather wishing that they *wouldn't* be selected to go on a mission that sounded more dangerous the more they heard about it.

The second sergeant-instructor, Darling, and the other trainees were resting on a ridge facing west, eating chocolate.

'The prodigal returns!' Meyerscough bellowed amiably. 'I'm surprised we didn't hear you'd been shot while trying to escape!'

Knox smiled weakly. 'I wanted to. Escape, I mean. But I didn't have the energy.'

Nevertheless, Watts had been right about their fitness. Knox felt stronger, could go harder and longer than when he had arrived in the Lebanon two weeks ago. They had all improved. If necessary, any of the three officers would be able to cope with a pretty tough environment. They could even conduct basic repairs on a radio transmitter. And, with luck, kill an enemy with their bare hands. This outfit they had joined was definitely very curious, but it seemed to deliver what it had promised.

While the three young officers sat and stared out over the valleys far below, Watts and Darling put their heads together. They were both short, barrel-chested men whose extraordinary physical prowess and technical expertise combined with ignorance of all aspects of philosophy, religion, politics or culture to produce the perfect soldier. Such characters, Knox thought, had probably done far more to conquer Britain's empire for her than all the Clives, Kitcheners and Rhodeses and the like put together.

And they did so like to make officers suffer, when they got the chance, as if to prove it.

'Right,' Watts announced when his conclave with Darling was over. 'Because we've all had a nice long rest, we're goin' to run down the jolly old hill to home.'

Knox, Jessup and Meyerscough stared down the stony, narrow track that wound towards the foothills and to the Dodge, which they could just make out as a tiny toy an unimaginable distance down and away. Even the spring anemones seemed to be clinging to the path for dear life. Nevertheless, they heaved themselves to their feet, packs and all, and shouldered their Stens. For once, even Meyerscough's jaw was a little slack at the prospect.

'I'll follow behind to make sure no other bugger loses his way—though if any of you do, it's a long drop,' said Darling with a joyful leer.

'Into the sunset, my mountain goats, the luvverly Lebanese sunset,' Watts declaimed into the clear, thin air.

'Can't see the ruddy point of it,' Jessup complained. 'You're nothing but a ruddy sadist.'

Watts looked at him innocently. 'No, sir. C of E. Anyway, don't forget—even brave boys have to run away sometimes. This is a good practice. Off we go . . .'

Meyerscough scrambled off over the rocks towards the path ahead of Knox, who heard him mutter as he went: 'Run away? Speak for yourself!' It confirmed what Knox had been thinking about him for some time, which was that he might be big, he might be good, and he might be a hell of a chap in a scrap, but G. A. X. Meyerscough lacked appreciation for the finer points of tactics. In fact, he was proving himself to be what they called in the trade a mad bastard of the first order.

The sun had all but set when the Dodge halted at the gate to the villa on the Beirut-Broummanna road where they were quartered—or, some would say, imprisoned. The group in the back of the truck waited while Watts showed his pass and swore cheerfully at the Sudanese sentries who had been on twenty-four hour guard duty here ever since Knox and the others had arrived. Two black faces appeared at the tailboard and peered in. One of the Sudanese poked his bayonet in, prodding the floor a few inches short of Knox's left foot, making sure they had no stowaways. The Dodge's passengers were used to the routine, which was invariable and had become almost a comfort. Perhaps, they speculated, all white men looked alike to these guards. Knox did not move his foot, for he knew that the soldier's touch with his blade was very sure. Jessup merely grinned and said: 'Thank you.' The Sudanese politely answered likewise and proceeded to jab dutifully in his direction, to show there was no question of favouritism.

'Monkeys. Just monkeys,' said Meyerscough quite loudly when the gates swung open and Darling, who was driving, wrenched the truck into gear for the steep climb up to the villa itself.

The main door was open when they jumped out, lugging their packs and weapons. They saw Elliot, the civilian instructor, lounging against the trellis work of the narrow terrace that ran along the front of the building. He was drinking wine, as he did in the evenings, but tonight he had someone with him, a tall, muscular-looking type in a double-breasted jacket and trousers that were uniform and yet not military. There was a big Armstrong Siddeley saloon parked a little way away, a smart, black coupé.

'Worked 'em hard, have you, Watts?' Elliot called out, raising his glass in wry salute. 'We've got guests to impress . . .' He indicated the muscleman, who frowned and inclined his head.

For his part, the sergeant nodded, po-faced, and waited for Darling to climb down from the driver's cab. His normal good humour evaporated at the sight of Elliot. The civilian, who gave them lectures on the politics, language and people of the Eastern Aegean, was good-looking in an epicene way and possessed a fine head of fair hair. Watts had been overheard in conversation with Darling referring to Elliot as 'Goldilocks' or, even more unkindly, 'Jean Harlow'.

When the two sergeants had gathered themselves, they led their trainees past Elliot and his unknown companion and into the house for their evening meal.

'And watch out where you go!' Elliot said as they were about to disappear into the house. 'Major Bellingham is walking in the Monastery Garden, and he walks with God himself!'

The 'Monastery Garden' was their nickname for the walled garden at the back of the villa.

'He's pissed as a ruddy newt,' said Meyerscough enviously. 'And a blasphemer,' he added with rather more genuine disapproval.

'In its way, it's perfect here,' Bellingham said. They stood still for a moment and listened to the sound of men's voices. The trainees had come back from their day in the hills. 'We're nicely secluded, convenient for the mountains, but all the basic creature comforts are seen to. Colonel Dulac may be a rum sort, but he can pick a hidey-hole, I'll concede him that.'

'Yes. He's had plenty of experience. Your chaps happy?'

'They don't have time to get dissatisfied.'

Sir Stewart Menzies nodded, walked on, enjoying the cool of the evening, for they had suffered a hot drive up from Beirut in the late afternoon.

'*And the righteous shall flourish like the palm tree; he shall grow like a cedar in Lebanon,*' he quoted with a wan smile. 'Very heartening, the Psalms, Jackie. Not that they're much of a guide to real life. That sort of homily's nice to bear in mind, but if it were really so, we'd be out of a job, don't you agree?'

Menzies' lightweight suit hung perfectly on his willowy frame. That perfection, combined with the freckled celtic pallor of his face, made him look as though he had been dropped out of the sky to this spot from some high-class celestial body bank, a Fortnum and Mason of the human animal. In fact, he had been in the Lebanon so far for a total of seven hours, checking up on his investment, and he was due to fly off again that same night. To Bellingham he seemed slightly restless, cynical, irritable. Perhaps it was the day's heat, from which it took a European—particularly a Scot—a few hours' cooler night air to recover.

'Well, we seem to be flourishing,' said Bellingham.

'So. Happy with progress?'

'No complaints about practical aspects.'

'Good, good. I think you've done an excellent job on the organizing side. You always were rather good at anything that required a spot of amateur dramatics.'

Bellingham relit his after-dinner pipe. He longed for a whisky or two. Perhaps when Menzies had gone. 'Oh, it's usually a matter of finding the right approach. *Fingerspitzengefühl*, as the Germans say. For the rest, you can thank "S" Force for the loan of the props, and if our volunteers do their stuff without a hitch it will doubtless be due to the instructors' teaching skills.'

'Excellent chaps, aren't they?' Menzies said.

'Efficient,' Bellingham answered cautiously. 'The two sergeants are good sorts, but Elliot is . . . shall we say . . . a touch prickly. I suppose he's all right. Bit full of himself.'

'Yes, I think his time attached to the Athens Embassy gave him a rather fancy notion of his importance, but against that he's genuinely very well-informed. He'll do his job and disappear the moment your chaps are safely on the island. He's a technician, an artisan like the others, whatever he may think.' Menzies touched Bellingham's shoulder, as if feeling and envying him the cloth of the uniform tunic he was wearing. 'You're much more than that,' he said. 'You're my eyes and ears, and above all only you know what this is all about. Elliot is aware of what I told him, which is more or less nothing. And he's under your command, whether he likes it or not. Don't let him forget the fact, Jackie.'

'Speak roughly to your little boy, and beat him when he sneezes . . .'

'That's about the size of it,' Menzies agreed with a faint smile. 'Elliot is inclined to tease.'

He seemed not the slightest put out that Bellingham had thought it appropriate to choose a quote from *Alice in Wonderland*. When they had walked on a few yards, however, he mopped his forehead with a silk handkerchief, poked it back into his breast pocket, and looked at his watch, made a noise indicating faint concern. Somehow everything, and especially his Olympian calm, appeared a shade studied.

Turning to stare in the direction of the garden gate, Menzies said: 'It won't be long. Word came through just before I left London that Hitler has agreed to a provisional date for his arrival on Rhodes. April 17th. Less than a month from now. And, of course, we want the party *in situ* ten days or so before then. So I'm very, very glad that everything's going well. When the final order comes, it will be short notice, I warn you.'

'That's all right, Stewart. Provided no one breaks a leg, the group will consist of Meyerscough, Knox and Watts. The sergeant's a fine chap, and as you, of course, know, he's handier with explosives than just about any man alive.'

'Good, good,' Menzies said. 'Well, soon I'll have to be making tracks. I have this blessed appointment to keep . . .'

Menzies had, so he said, arranged a meeting at Bir Hassane aerodrome with an assistant to the British Resident, to discuss the political situation in Syria and Lebanon and the Service's role in the area. Tedious, but one had to keep up appearances. Nowadays, even 'C' had to have an excuse of some sort for being on what was technically foreign soil. The sensibilities of the Free French—not to mention other British government departments—were easily bruised. One had at least to pop by and say 'hello' to someone official.

'So, I take it everything's fine your end?' Bellingham asked while he still had the chance. 'The channels open, obviously. All else smooth-running?'

'We're ready. No problems of note,' Menzies said casually, starting to walk back towards the house and forcing Bellingham to move too. 'What you're doing here is the real key, you know.'

'By the way,' said Bellingham, catching him just before they got to the gate, where he had posted a sentry to prevent anyone bursting into the garden and disturbing his talk with 'C'. 'The commanding officer of one of our volunteers is still kicking up a bit of a fuss. He says he needs the man, something about a football team. I told him to contact the War Office, as instructed. I presume there'll be no more problems.'

Menzies consented to pause. 'Quite right. If he does get in touch with the War Office, he'll be connected to a speak-your-weight machine, and the machine will tell him in no uncertain terms: Sir, you are very healthy at the moment, but if you persist in making life awkward for Major Bellingham, then you will become lighter to the extent of an entire command at some date in the very near future. I think that will shut him up.'

'He seemed to think he had some influence at G.H.Q.M.E.'

'Don't they all? It doesn't matter even if he's Alex's best friend, actually. Anyone will get the same dusty answer. And I can't see any general wanting to collide with Winston over a few spare officers who decide to volunteer for a spot of action,' Menzies assured him. 'Now look, I absolutely must be going, I'm sorry to say. It's such a long, roundabout flight, and I don't want to be away from London for more than a few days . . .'

'Yes. Forgive me for being such an old woman, Stewart. It's just that I don't want to cope with any last-minute spanners in the works after everyone's done so much for . . . SIGNIFY,' Bellingham said, nodding to the Sudanese corporal on duty at the garden gate and producing his security pass.

'I quite understand,' said Menzies. 'Can't have us stumbling in the final furlong. But don't worry. We won't.'

They waited while the corporal subjected Bellingham's pass to a thorough inspection, despite the fact that the 'major' had been here for two weeks. When his pass was handed back, Bellingham said: 'Thank you'. The corporal repeated: 'Thank you'. Bellingham had not yet grown used to the parrot-like responses of the dozen or so guards that Dulac had supplied for the villa. They were colonial troops from a remote region of the equatorial province close to the Ugandan border, and they spoke only an obscure dialect of Swahili impenetrable to anyone but a scholar of African languages. Apart, that was, from elementary army commands and the words 'please' and 'thank you'. 'S' Force apparently used them to guard some of their shiftier double-agents, who were also kept under guard in villas among these mountains; Dulac praised the Sudanese as perfect watchdogs, since they were unable to gossip except among themselves, were absolutely loyal, and were fierce enough to make mincemeat of anyone who attempted to enter the grounds without being in possession of the appropriate pass, or being accompanied by an inmate, or both.

They walked quickly through the villa, passing the kitchen, where the trainees could be heard eating supper, and out onto the terrace. Menzies paused, motioned his driver, who had come over with him from London in order to transport 'C' around the Lebanon in perfect discretion. The man got obediently to his feet and walked over to the car, opened the door and waited.

'Goodbye, Elliot,' Menzies said in a vague gesture. 'Do your best, there's a good chap.'

'I'll see you in London, sir,' the civilian instructor said, his speech slightly slurred but his manner respectful.

'Yes. Of course.'

Menzies turned away from the man on the terrace and offered Bellingham his hand. They shook.

'You just ensure you do your bit, Jackie,' he said quietly. 'That's all that matters. The rest's out of our hands. *Au revoir.*'

Then 'C' walked over to the car, turned to wave once more, and climbed into the back. Once in his seat, he was invisible in the darkness.

Bellingham then had to descend to the gate on the Beirut-Broummanna road to ensure that the guards allowed Menzies' car to leave. The Armstrong Siddeley finally made its way out onto the serpentine, pot-holed highway a couple of minutes later, with one last, lordly wave from Menzies. Bellingham watched it disappear in the direction of the capital and set off back up the hill towards the villa.

The place had been built by a rich Maronite merchant at the turn of the century and had apparently last belonged to a French police chief. He, it was said, had retired here for the entire summer every year, and with Gallic concern for his creature comforts had carried out his essential duties by telephone and, if necessary, by messenger, on the simple assumption that any civilized criminal would also be taking an August break. *Monsieur le Commissaire* had chosen to return to France when the inconsiderate British had invaded Vichy-held Syria and Lebanon in '41, and the newly-established 'S' Force had snapped the place up for the duration. They had converted the stables block into a lecture-hall, but otherwise the villa was as it had been left. Other people's houses, Bellingham reflected during his climb. One spent the war in other people's houses . . .

It was extraordinary, perhaps even unnerving, how quickly one could set up a cosy minor empire in wartime. Once the initial authorization had been given—in this case originating from Churchill's private office and laundered through the war ministry—then no further explanations seemed to be required. One simply waved the crested bit of paper, looked confident, demanded stores, equipment, premises, personnel, and very few people were disposed to argue. So many strange and improbable projects were being undertaken, there were so many grey areas, that one more, or a dozen, went more or less unnoticed. Such an addition was the tiny outfit that had come into being under the aegis of 'Major' Bellingham (G.S.L.) in the foothills of the Lebanese mountains. The organization had been christened 'IFCU' by Menzies, the initials standing for 'Irregular Forces Communications Unit'. That 'IFCU' consisted of a minute staff in a pokey villa, seemingly responsible to no one, need attract no adverse comment or even attention. After all, had not many powerful military fiefdoms been established by just one resourceful officer who originally possessed no more than an office, a telephone, and, most important, an allocation of funds? Dulac had loaned them another empty villa half a mile from here, for appearances' sake; after all, 'IFCU' would be preparing for expansion . . . Bellingham had motored over there a couple of days previously out of curiosity; they would never use the place, but ambitious profligacy was, he had been told in Cairo, the order of the day, the norm, the perfect cover. The last thing one wanted to appear was *timid*. That was really the way to get into trouble.

Bellingham felt his mouth already drying in anticipation of the large tumbler of Bell's that he had decided to grant himself when he got back to his office in the house.

Elliot, however, was still in position on the terrace when Bellingham arrived at the top of the drive. The Service's former young-man-about-Athens was looking slightly the worse for wear, too.

'Evening, Major,' he said, without rising from the step.

He toasted Bellingham unsteadily with his half-full glass of red wine. 'Did we see Sir Stewart off all right, and do we now have our final orders—whatever they may be?'

'I saw him off. The rest's none of your bloody business,' said Bellingham. 'And I'd deem it a compliment if you'd stand up when we're conducting a conversation,' he snapped.

Elliot obeyed with the cool insolence that had become his trademark. From a distance, his slightly over-long fair hair and blue eyes might have lent him a sexually ambiguous air, but at closer quarters observation revealed a controlled brutality that was unmistakably, if unpleasantly, male. The unsettling aspect of the man's looks was precisely the contrast between appearance and character, the face of a fallen angel. Bellingham judged that a certain type of woman might find Elliot quite irresistibly attractive, and at first he had tried to make allowances, suspecting that his personal dislike was founded on envy. Soon he had decided that a bastard was a bastard, and a bastard Elliot most assuredly was, and strangely enough it made dealing with the younger man easier.

'The good Sergeant Watts popped out to say he'd put the kettle on while you were saying your farewells,' Elliot said. 'Wanted to know if any of us would like to join them. Democratic outfit, this, in tune with these heroic times. Very laudable and progressive. My own pleasure, Major, is watching Wattsie at work with the sentries, coping with the white man's burden. He's becoming a past master at getting the buggers to do what he says, and all through sign language and tone of voice. Reminds me of my late mother training red setters.'

Bellingham looked at him with a combination of pity and disgust. It wasn't the drunkenness—that would be the pot abusing the kettle all right—but this man's loathing for others, which was clearly based on a self-hatred of the most extreme kind.

'They're fine colonial troops, the Sudanese,' he said. 'They don't need to be laughed at—or patronized.'

'Absolutely,' retorted Elliot slyly. 'Splendid fellows. Willing. Intelligent. What have you. All the things mama used to say about red setters. It's just that the communications problem is rather entertaining. About the only thing in this hole that is at the moment, if you don't mind my saying so, Major.'

'I don't care what you say, so long as you get on with your job.'

'Fair enough. If only the world were fair.' Elliot had found some sediment among the dregs of his glass of cheap local wine. He tossed the remains onto the gravel in front of the steps, made a face. 'I mean,' he continued, 'there I was settling into a well-earned spell back in Blighty, a chance to sleep in a decent bed—with some company if I was lucky—knock around a bit in the wicked city or enjoy the season of the earth's renewal, according to taste, when the call comes from upstairs.' Elliot's voice contorted into a cruel parody of 'C', slow and drawling. 'My boy . . . I would like you to slope orf to the jolly old Levant again and give a pal of mine a helping hand in a project he's setting up on my behalf. Abso-lutely hush-hush, pack your toothbrush, you leave at dawn and all that . . . Intrigued, I was,' Elliot said in his normal voice. 'Thought it might involve exotic dancers, swarthy villains in dark glasses, the thrill of the Orient. In fact, apart from the duskies I might as well be helping run a training course somewhere in the Home Counties. Now that, Major, is not fair,' he concluded with a crooked smile.

'I don't know. Look on it as a holiday from the flesh. Relax. Enjoy yourself.'

'Enjoy myself, Major?' Elliot said. 'Don't you know there's a war on?'

'Excuse me. I have work to do,' Bellingham muttered, moving past up the steps. He was at the door when Elliot called out: 'I say, Major!' He turned reluctantly.

Elliot had put down his glass on the bottom step and was standing with his hands in the pockets of his cotton slacks, head cocked to one side.

'Major,' he said. 'Now that the boss has been and gone, can we clarify a couple of things?'

'If you insist.'

'The fact is, you don't like me very much, do you, Major? I mean, we don't get on.'

'It's irrelevant, if true,' agreed Bellingham. 'But you said there were a couple of things.'

Elliot looked both cunning and sad. 'Yes,' he said. 'I

know you don't like me, and I don't think much of you, either. And in a way that's a pity. D'you know why?'

'No. Really . . .'

'Because,' Elliot pressed on mournfully, 'we've both been sent out here for some very peculiar reason. P'raps to get us out of the way. "C" didn't want to come out here at all, you know,' he said. 'Too busy at home. Some frightful hoo-ha, his driver told me—we used to drink together, y'know, in the pub round the corner from Broadway . . . Some frightful hoo-ha. "C" didn't want to come.'

Bellingham knew he would have to tread carefully—Elliot knew that the group was being sent under Menzies' particular supervision, though he didn't know why, and nor should he. But this was interesting.

'Pull yourself together, man,' he said sternly. 'Now what's all this about "C" not wanting to come here?'

Elliot shrugged, poured himself some more wine out of the bottle.

'Well,' he said, 'you know he's been spending a lot of time out of town lately. Strange errands. Almost no one knows what's going on, but a little bird told me that he's become a regular visitor to some ghastly Victorian mansion in Hertfordshire that's run by Grainger's mob—you know him, dubious character, strong-arm stuff and all that—and that's funny, because apparently Grainger's happy band of bruisers had a bad cockup recently, one of their chaps got killed arresting someone.' He gulped down some wine. 'Beginnings of a big hoo-ha, as I said, but Menzies stepped on it personally.'

'An arrest?' Bellingham asked. 'In connection with what?'

'Oh, I don't know . . .'

Bellingham moved several steps towards Elliot and said sharply: 'Surely that sort of thing's done by the Special Branch, or at least by MI5?'

'Well, yes. I mean, I don't know exactly what was going on,' Elliot said hastily, aware even in his half-drunk state that he had passed the limits of what could be said safely in front of a superior.

'I want to know more, Elliot!'

'It . . . it must have been something close to "C"'s

heart, not to be vouchsafed to the hoi-polloi. That's as much as I heard, old boy. All I'm saying is that I was surprised to see "C" here on a courtesy visit with—rumor has it—so much on his plate *chez* Grainger. That's all . . .' Elliot looked at the expression on Bellingham's face, smiled weakly. 'I say, I wish I knew what's going on.'

If he expected a rocket or even a rebuke from Bellingham, he was, however, wrong.

'I have to confess, Elliot, that I agree with you for once,' Bellingham said. 'But if I were you I'd keep your mouth shut and your head down . . .'

The younger man nodded. 'Got carried away. Hate this bloody place. Could do with some leave.'

At that moment, Sergeant Watts appeared. He was in shorts, sandals, and an open-necked shirt, puffing contentedly on his habitual brand of full-strength cigarette.

'Tea, sir?' he asked Bellingham with a smile that froze into embarrassment when he realized the delicacy of the situation. 'Oh, excuse me—'

'Don't worry, Watts,' Bellingham said. 'Mr Elliot and I were having a chat. It's finished now. I don't want any tea, thanks. Perhaps Mr Elliot should, though.'

'Ah. Right, sir.'

'Good day, Sergeant?'

'Passable, sir. I'd reckon the gentlemen are in reasonable condition compared with when they arrived from the fleshpots.'

'You'll permit them to accompany you, then?'

'So long as they stay out of the way when it matters, sir.'

The sergeant grinned, acknowledging his joke, which was also not a joke.

After his blasting experience, which had taken him from the West Country of England to South America and Southern Africa, Ron Watts had joined up in '39, been snapped up first by the Commandos and then the Long Range Desert Group, from where he had been plucked by Menzies on some sort of secondment arrangement that amounted to permanent loan. His face had the colour and texture of seasoned old leather, and he sounded and looked like a Dorset yokel, but he was a jewel of an all-rounder—explosives, survival in extreme conditions, radio use and maintenance. His expert knowledge had been acquired in a variety of hard schools, most of them even tougher than anything the military could provide. Bellingham was extremely glad to have him.

'I think that's probably the only essential training they need,' said Bellingham with a laugh. 'Finished supper?'

'Almost, sir. A day's stroll with a pack on their backs seems to give 'em an appetite and a half. Troughin' away still, as if 'twas their last meal on earth.'

'Beers all round tonight. Nice cold ones from the refrigerator. Perhaps I'll drop by and join you a bit later, after I've got some paperwork out of the way.'

Watts nodded. 'That'd be favourite,' he said as they do in Dorset and Somerset. He was his own man. The L.R.D.G. had suited him well because of its lack of bull and rank distinctions, and 'I.F.C.U.' seemed to do the same. If Watts felt any curiosity at its lack of size or, at this stage, definite purpose, he failed to show it. Bellingham had the feeling that the sergeant was impressed by very little in life, and surprised by even less. All these aspects of his character fitted Watts for a crucial role in 'I.F.C.U.'—read: SIGNIFY.

20

'Back to basic principles, Menzies,' Churchill demanded, pointedly using 'C''s surname and thereby making it clear that he was here as the government's servant. 'Regale me item by item, and do not spare my feelings—or anyone else's—in the telling, I beg of you.'

Outside it was a brilliant afternoon, sun shining through showers, with a rainbow visible to the south, across the river from the Prime Minister's office in the Palace of Westminster. Menzies had slept little during his circuitous flight home. He was becoming wearily certain that rest would be in short supply until SIGNIFY was concluded one way or the other.

'Let me first explain that there is very little cause for

concern, Prime Minister,' he began patiently. 'I intend to deal with Finch, the courier, immediately our interview here is concluded. I thought it best to come straight from Croydon to you for reasons of pure prudence, because I was aware that the situation had been causing you concern.'

'No flannel, please!'

'Quite. Now, there are two potential problems, Prime Minister. One is Finch. I really don't believe he represents a real threat. The other has been always with us, and concerns the Abwehr's access to the Sicherheitsdienst's files . . .'

'I fear the warning was transmitted too early. Canaris's burglars may find it in Schellenberg's files and smell a rat.'

'Unlikely, Prime Minister.' Menzies folded his hands, nestled more deeply into the armchair opposite Churchill's desk. 'May I explain?'

'You better, as the Americans might say.'

Menzies smiled thinly. 'The worst, sir, that can happen is that the Abwehr goes into a big panic and starts frantically flashing signals to the effect that our spy is leaking material about a proposal to kill the Führer. After all, *Turquoise* has not been specific; he has merely offered a piece of gossip, as spies will. Such a discovery might, in fact, come as a boon of sorts to Canaris; it would raise the risks so far as he is concerned, but he would also fancy that it tied us to him more firmly. Do you . . . ah . . . understand that, sir?'

'Yes, yes.' Churchill, who had been standing, sat down heavily at his desk and peered at Menzies suspiciously over the tops of his half-moon spectacles. 'However, the broth is thickening alarmingly; new ingredients are being added daily by alien hands; soon we must eat the damned concoction or it may be too rich to stomach, possibly even poisonous. Be truthful,' he asked. 'Is it worth the risks?'

Menzies paused for no more than a moment. He nodded emphatically. 'SIGNIFY is very precious, Prime Minister. The potential cost is small, the potential gain inestimable. Nothing has changed since our last discussion. There are practical difficulties to be overcome, of course, but then these will always occur. It is my task to gain our object despite those difficulties. In this I am sparing no effort; I believe SIGNIFY will work, but I cannot *guarantee* complete, unmitigated success. That only God can do, sir.'

A moment's silence while Churchill absorbed Menzies' arguments.

'Chance is cruel, as I know too well,' he said then. 'And the world grows madder by the day. By all that remains sacred,' he mused. 'What I would give to be a fly on the wall in your prison mansion, to see the face of this courier, this Englishman who has lost the right to be called an Englishman. Try to describe to me, Menzies, what such a man is like—a man who will sell his country in time of war . . .'

The request was doleful, almost plaintive. Churchill's subtle, penetrating intellect could reason out the motives for treachery. His problem was that his emotions could not grasp them; so elemental and inborn was his patriotism that he lacked the capacity to *feel* what could lead a man to betray England. Churchill was an old man. He had grown to adulthood in the reign of Queen Victoria, had served as a cabinet minister when Adolf Hitler was still a tramp wandering the backstreets of Vienna, and when Josef Stalin lived in precarious exile, a refugee from the Czar's secret police.

Menzies found himself, as always, embarrassed and lost for words when asked such a question, like a policeman suddenly forced to ascribe moral qualities to a road accident.

'The courier, Finch, is—if I may use the word—an idealist, Prime Minister,' he answered gently. 'Throughout his career of treachery, he was undoubtedly acting according to principles of a kind—ill-considered and violent, born of envy and malice, but principles for all that. Moreover, let us remember that he could not know the real destination of the information he carried.'

'And how will you ensure that he does us no harm?'

'By offering him a respite, a life of sorts so long as he cooperates with our work on SIGNIFY.'

Churchill frowned. 'I cannot sanction a reprieve. Please understand that.'

'I can offer him a respite. He knows what he has done. He will be grateful for what he can get, for permission to live day by day. Perhaps he will respond when offered a final chance to redeem himself. Men can be approached thus.'

'Such a person, however,' Churchill muttered, his rich voice thick with contempt, returning to his original preoccupation. 'He serves an idea. Not a place, or a people, or any real, human things, but a cold book of revealed truth. May he be damned for it. And you believe, Stewart, that this man, placed in your power by an unfortunate chance, will do all you require?'

'It has been made clear to him that the alternative will be swift, hard and inevitable, Prime Minister.'

'A man will not choose certain death for a cold book. Not a sane man.'

There was a knock on the door. A private secretary looked in and reminded them that Churchill was due to meet Clement Attlee, his Deputy Prime Minister, in five minutes. Churchill scowled, then let out a deep chuckle.

'Tell Mr Attlee that I am engaged in foreign affairs discussions of the most confidential and vital kind, and that I shall see him in fifteen minutes. He only wants to nag me about his national insurance scheme, whatever he may claim to the contrary. I am dealing with the only national insurance scheme that really matters: winning the war against the Nazis!'

'Shall I tell him that, Prime Minister?'

'Don't be a bloody imbecile.'

'Yes—I mean, no—Prime Minister,' said the secretary, withdrawing with a tight-lipped sigh of mortification.

'So,' Churchill continued when the man had gone. 'That leaves only one remaining factor to keep me awake of a night. I refer, Stewart, to the fate of our gallant volunteers. I want to know that we are doing for them all that can be done.'

He leaned forward as he spoke, and Menzies could not help noticing that the bulging curve of his spine where it joined the shoulder-blades was becoming appreciably more grotesque, as if his head was being forced down, causing the muscles of his shoulders to swell. Age and the responsibilities of his office were turning the greatest living Englishman into a hunchback.

'C' stiffened. 'Provided that they obey instructions and

use what they have learned in their training, they will be able to survive until X-hour arrives,' he said. 'And afterwards, sir, it will be a question of how quickly our agent can get them off the island. These are provisions we would make for any commando group undertaking a project of such magnitude; in purely practical terms, there will be no difference. Hundreds of men must hazard their lives every day for lesser causes, Prime Minister. I don't wish to seem heartless, but—'

'Enough!' Churchill growled. 'I understand. You are right. That brute chance yet again.' He raised one plump hand and patted the air, a gesture indicating both helplessness and farewell, but his eyes were already on his notes for his meeting with the stolid Mr Attlee.

Menzies' Bentley was waiting for him in Palace Yard with his usual chauffeur, who had accompanied him to Lebanon, at the wheel. The man was almost as weary as 'C', but he absorbed his chief's terse instructions, moved out onto the Embankment, turning eastward in the direction of Vauxhall Bridge and from there north to find the trunk road to Cambridge. Menzies dozed off while it was passing through the north-eastern suburbs of London.

The car travelled on, carrying the sleeping Menzies. It went beyond the edge of the city and into the countryside, through pretty villages and neat hamlets, until the land began to turn flat and featureless. Dusk was gathering when it stopped in front of a high, wrought-iron gate festooned with a sign that read: WAR OFFICE PROPERTY. STRICTLY NO ADMITTANCE TO UNAUTHORIZED PERSONNEL. The chauffeur woke up 'C' as two men carrying pistols and clothed in uniforms that lacked insignia of rank or unit came out of the lodge and stared in through the windows with a brand of coldly aggressive curiosity that identified their occupation more exactly than any badge.

'Oh, welcome back, sir,' said one of them when he recognized the Bentley and its passenger. The gates swung open, and the car accelerated up the long drive towards the house, ignoring the stated speed limit of five miles per hour.

Grainger must have been tipped off by the thick-ear specialists stationed at the lodge, because the guard who opened the main door to Menzies simply said: 'Good evening, sir. Captain Grainger is waiting in the rest room to brief you.'

There was the refreshments tray, the chairs.

'A long flight, I dare say, sir,' Grainger said by way of greeting. 'Not much to report, actually. Except that Finch seems to be mending well, and that we've had no problems with the dead-letter drop. Hunky-dory so far as we can tell.'

'Good,' Menzies said, cutting him short. 'I want to see Finch. When will that be possible?'

'Any time, sir. He's taken a little light exercise in the garden yesterday and today, meek and quiet as a lamb. Under close supervision, though, goes without saying.'

'I'll wait for a few minutes,' Menzies said. 'In the meantime, I want him handcuffed securely to a chair. I want to talk to him alone, without your fellows looming around.'

'Certainly, sir. If you wish.'

When Menzies entered, Finch was seated in the middle of the room, which was lit only by an old-fashioned standard lamp against the far wall. He wore a clean, open-necked shirt with the sleeves rolled up so that his bulging arm muscles were exposed, and a pair of trousers that hid his wounded leg. On Menzies' first visit the previous week, he had looked bad, a mass of blood and bruises, but now he exuded returning physical power. The unit's medic had been right in his prognosis. Finch smiled faintly when 'C' came into the room and rattled the handcuffs that restrained him, as if the procedure was part of a harsh private joke between the two of them.

A deep, chintz-covered armchair had been pushed to within a few feet of where Finch sat. Menzies walked over and lowered himself into it.

'Have they been treating you well?' he asked, his tone coaxing and firm at the same time, like that of a man talking to a cowed but still savagely unpredictable animal.

'Oh, handsome,' said Finch immediately. 'They've even brought Teddy to keep me warm at nights.'

Menzies smiled, more out of relief than amusement. The first hurdle had been crossed; no more stubborn silence. 'You seem to be taking all this very philosophically,' he said.

'Have to, don't I?'

'And you're on the mend, I'm told?'

'Not so bad.'

The captured courier's voice was a pleasant tenor, though he whistled strangely while he talked, because of the two teeth that he had lost during the course of his arrest. Before, fresh from that beating-up, he had sounded and looked like a punch-drunk boxer; now he possessed a kind of command, a rough fluency that marked him as more than a plain thug. He had dark, thick hair, a square and superficially open face. Menzies had seen hundreds of young men with faces like that go into the trenches to die during the First War, the flower of the English working class. Almost thirty years ago. What had gone wrong?

'I want to talk to you. A little about facts, but much more about larger things,' Menzies explained.

Finch's eyes narrowed and he pursed his lips sullenly. 'Yeah. I was wondering when you were going to start again.'

'Quite. Facts first, then. Now, you receive your instructions in coded form, by letter. Am I right?'

A shrug.

'*Am I right*? We've done our homework, Finch.'

A nod.

'And you never had any personal contact with the man who dropped the wallet at the café? No one gossiped to you about his identity?'

'No.'

'No what? To the first or second question?'

'To both,' Finch said reluctantly. Then he took a deep breath: 'Only personal contact for almost two years now was a bloke I met in a pub . . . middle of '41 . . . that's the last time. Everyone else . . . people I knew before the war . . . they're all working for the glorious victory, aren't they? In their fashion. I stopped being an activist . . .'

'On orders from above, yes. And you never saw the man who dropped the wallet at the café, either?'

'No. Though sometimes I got curious. I'd have liked to have had a dekko.'

'I understand. Boring business, being a traitor,' Menzies said.

Finch looked at him, thinking: *I just said something very important. He relaxed in a funny sort of way when I said I'd never seen the fellow.* 'All depends what you mean by the word "traitor", doesn't it?' he said eventually by way of an answer.

'Well, I have no doubts about what I mean, Finch. You're the one who's confused.'

'Come on. When it comes down to it, we're fighting the same enemy . . .'

Menzies laughed contemptuously. 'Is that really what you think? Good Lord.'

'It is, yes. And so far as I'm concerned, our brothers-in-arms are entitled to know anything that comes through my hands!' Finch persisted. Then he fell silent and stared angrily at Menzies. 'C''s cold ridicule was riling him, wearing him down.

After a while, Menzies said: 'So you thought everything went off to Mother Russia, eh? Extra information to help the comrades gain a clear picture of what we were up to in London. Some useful, light reading matter for Uncle Joe Stalin of a winter's evening?'

'You know my political record. It's your class we'll have to fight after the war. The skirmishing's started now,' Finch snapped.

'Rubbish! I'll tell you where your wallet and its information came from and where they were bound,' Menzies said, speaking slowly and evenly. 'Listen: the man who delivered it to the café for you was employed in a sensitive area of Military Intelligence. Our Military Intelligence. He stole the information from our government files.'

'Look—'

'Don't interrupt! You collected it, delivered it to the house in Bedford. There it waited for a while until it was collected by one Vassily Marenkov, who has the gall to call himself a cultural attaché at the Soviet Embassy. From there it went by diplomatic pouch to Stockholm, where a Swedish agent whose cover is that of a businessman offered it for sale, claiming that the information had been garnered from a "friend" in London whom he met during business trips there. I think that you might be surprised to learn the identity of the man to whom our Swede sold the material—particularly as this was not the first time.'

'Go on, I'm waiting to be amazed!'

'Really? I don't think you'll like what you hear. You see, the man who bought information—and who has been buying similar information for years past, thanks to you and your friends—was a high official of the Nazi Secret Service, and he took it home, chortling all the while, to the nest of the fascist hyenas in Berlin.' Menzies' voice became deceptively soft. 'Hitler's had access to some crucial British military documents, Finch, thanks to you,' he said. 'The kind that can decide not just battles but entire campaigns. How do you feel about that?'

'Come on. The Soviet comrades wouldn't do that. Why should they?'

'Because, Finch, at this stage they want to sabotage certain aspects of the British war effort. Because, though they're still supposed to be our allies, they want to stop us from getting into Europe, particularly Central Europe, before their own steamroller can really start moving westward. They'd see our boys—your workers, your political supporters and friends—slaughtered rather than allow us that advantage. Because Stalin knows the war's well on the way to being won, and the question is: who gets the spoils? How . . . do . . . you . . . feel?'

Finch was trying to cut off, retreat into his habitual shell. Menzies sensed that this was his final defence, always had been. He pressed quickly and hard.

'You have murdered for it. I want to know how you feel,' he said.

'You can't fool me.' Finch tilted back his head and stared upwards.

Menzies got immediately to his feet, moved forward so that even when the man tried to avoid his eyes, he couldn't.

'You've been spying for the Nazis. You thought you were doing great work for the good old anti-fascist struggle, cocking a snook at the reactionary British upper classes, but what you were really doing was helping the Nazis, giving away our plans for a second front. How do you feel? Look me in the eye, you poor, poor dupe . . .'

Finch's eyes were moistening. His defences had started to crumble. Menzies smiled sadly and kindly down at him.

'Listen,' he murmured. 'Listen, there's a way you can make up for it. We want to salvage some benefit for the anti-Nazi effort from this mess, and for that we could do with your help. You don't actually need to name names or betray anyone. We just want you to do one more run for us. One more, and then the whole sordid business will be over for you.' 'C' paused for a moment. 'When the next warning comes and that traitor brings another wallet to the café . . . one more. It's all we need. After that, you'll be able to face things with a clear conscience, in the knowledge that you made up for your terrible mistake. Tell me you'll help . . .'

'It can't be true,' Finch said throatily. Tears were trickling down his face.

'I know it *is* true.'

Finch let out a long, aching sob, and Menzies knew then that he had him. The home flank was secure for the time being; almost certainly for long enough.

Therefore let SIGNIFY move ahead with all speed.

21

The trainees were allowed a bottle of lager each after lunch and an hour to take their ease. Since the day after April Fools' Day was sunny—warm as an English June—the three of them gravitated to the rear of the stable block, where there were views of the mountains and they wouldn't have to go far for the coming lecture on the political and ethnic make-up of Rhodes, courtesy of Elliot.

'By God,' said Jessup. 'We've been here three-and-a-half weeks. It feels like a year.' He pulled on his cigarette. 'I should think that people in our position end up grateful to be allowed to push off somewhere and get shot at.'

'That's probably the whole idea,' Meyerscough said loftily. He didn't smoke, as he informed the party from time to time with some pride. He stretched out his thirteen-stone frame on the grass of the bank behind the stables and compensated by drinking greedily from his bottle of beer. 'And, well, we have to get fit, don't we? Some of us have spent the war in drawing rooms.'

Knox looked for the smile on the man's face, but there was none. For Christ's sake, Meyerscough meant it. 'Or on the playing fields,' he retorted pointedly, remembering the talk about football. 'But then I forget: that's where wars are supposed to be won, isn't it?'

'The extraordinary thing is actually the smallness of it all,' Jessup mused, oblivious of the dark signals being exchanged between the two others. 'I know it sounds naïve. Nevertheless, one had always imagined these special ops units were . . . really rather posh and on the grand scale, eat, drink, and tomorrow . . . you know . . .'

'Come off it,' Knox said. 'The only place where they do that is well behind the lines. In the Long Bar and the Continental. I should damned well know. It was out of disgust with that kind of life that I volunteered for this mob.'

'You speak Greek, don't you, Knox?' Meyerscough asked suddenly.

'Yes.'

'Well, I suppose that's useful,' Meyerscough commented, as if nothing much else about Knox was. 'Where'd you get it from?'

Knox hesitated, just as he had years ago at boarding school in England when someone had asked about his unusual middle name. Then he said: 'My mother was Greek. From the islands, not too far from the Dodecanese. But I was brought up mainly in England.'

'Ah. So that's why you're here.'

'I suppose it must be part of the reason, yes. How about you?'

Meyerscough shrugged. 'Who knows? I haven't asked. I'd guess someone happened to mention my name. You know how it works,' he said, clearly doubting that Knox did.

'My father's a professor of Archaeology. He used to take me with him on digs before the war,' Jessup cut in, not to be outdone. 'I spent an entire summer holiday on Delos once, helping to excavate the big theatre. It was extremely hot. And the people were terribly friendly and hospitable—the local Greeks, I mean. Marvellous. I bet they're giving the Germans a really bad time.'

'In our case, of course, it will be Italians,' Meyerscough said. 'And I suppose this chap we're supposed to help the Greeks bump off will be a wop general or something.'

Knox thought he sounded disappointed. He was about to point out that Mussolini's soldiers did actually have weapons, and that everything he had heard about their behaviour in Greece and the Balkans indicated that they used them, when Elliot, the lecturer, appeared round the corner of the stables.

'Good afternoon, gents,' he said. 'I'm afraid that I've come to round you up for our afternoon talk. We might as well get started, because I think Sergeant Watts will be after you soon to spend some more time taking crystal sets apart.'

He had a bottle of beer, too, and he swigged at it while they got to their feet and filed round towards the lecture room. Decidedly louche, Knox thought; even dangerously so. He caught Meyerscough's eye, and from the coldly resentful expression there it was clear that they agreed on the qualities of friend Elliot, at least.

They sat down at their desks. Elliot, still finishing his beer, mounted the dais and looked at them, then at the large map of Rhodes to the right of the blackboard.

'Well, there she is again,' he said, setting his empty bottle carefully on the small table to the other side. 'Our little bit of Greece. Except that in international law you're not going to Greece, you're going to Italy. Understood? Just as—or so the wops would maintain—when you go to Gibraltar, you're not going to Spain, so when you go to Rhodes, or Kos, or Leros, you're setting foot on the sacred soil of the New Roman Empire. All right?'

Elliot waited for them all to nod agreement, then smiled evilly.

'This is, of course, bosh. When we beat the Italians and the Germans the whole operation will be handed over to Greece, because most of the inhabitants of Rhodes—apart from some Italian settlers and a small Turkish community left over from time when the place belonged to the Ottoman Empire—are a sort of Greek. I say "sort of" because they speak a pretty strange variety of demotic, and also because the Italian authorities spend a lot of time trying to persuade them that they're not Greek at all—to the tune of outlawing their language in schools and generally forbidding them to celebrate their traditional festivals, and so on. Mussolini, you see, wanted Rhodes to be a tourist centre as well as an Italian dagger pointed at the belly of Asia Minor. In neither case did a lot of scruffy, lackadaisical, fearsomely nationalistic Greeks fit in with his plan. Far from it. This has an advantage for us. Anyone?'

The ever-willing Jessup put up his hand. 'The Greeks don't like the wops, sir. Which means they'll be keen on us.'

'Absolutely! The moment you set foot on the island, you'll receive a rip-snorting welcome—as warm, if not warmer, than you could expect anywhere in the Aegean. The Rhodians have been under the heels of the Crusaders, the Knights of St John, the Turks, and now the Italians, and they're heartily sick of being occupied. They'll probably find a reason to object to being governed from Athens when that happens, but that's not our problem. Any more questions on the Baedeker level?'

No one spoke.

'Then on to the details about your hosts. It's time we got down to brass tacks,' Elliot said with relish, making it sound like they were all due for crucifixion. Everyone had to admit he was on good form today. There was an excitement about the way he spoke, an urgency that was infectious. 'The particular band you'll be meeting are based in the southern mountains . . . here . . . and are some three dozen strong. Such groups are usual when you get off the mainland. E.L.A.S. has some battalion-sized forces operating in the Pindus, but elsewhere it's small beer. You'll be delighted to know that the organization's basically run by the communists, which at least guarantees some degree of efficiency. The K.K.E. are generally much more reliable than the monarchist forces, though the powers-that-be would frown on me for telling you that. Nevertheless, I have, haven't I? Mainly because it happens to be true, and your lives could depend on the fact. You see,' he added with a grin, 'when you're actually there, you won't be able to ask my advice or anybody else's.'

'I say, I hope I'm not expected to act like a fellow-traveller,' Meyerscough said loudly. 'I abhor politics in general and communism in particular.'

'I shouldn't worry too much about that side of things. So far as they're concerned, we're their allies until the Party leadership—by which I mean Moscow—tells 'em different. Decadent imperialists you may be, but you've been provided with the status of honorary proles for the duration. You don't speak more than a few words of Greek, anyway, Lieutenant. Captain Knox is the one who's going to have to mind his Ps and Qs during the campfire indoctrination sessions. Now, a quick breakdown of the history of the Communist Party of Greece . . .'

Afterwards, when they had been dismissed for tea in the small sitting-room that served as their recreation area, Meyerscough managed to get Knox on his own.

'I say,' he murmured. 'You're not *left-wing*, are you? You'll be our link with these people. It's up to them, of course, what they choose to believe, so long as they kill the enemy, but I wouldn't like to have to rely on one of our chaps if he was like-minded.'

Knox rubbed the scar on his cheek, a reminder of his last night with Irene Kontiak, when he had finally got round to telling her that he was off out of Cairo to another posting with the 'bloody army'. Those long fingers of hers had long, painted nails.

'Don't worry on that score,' he said. 'My mother's family were Chiots, merchant adventurers. Capitalists of the worst sort. And I'm not interested in politics either.'

'Good-oh. It's just that Elliot had me worried. He knows his stuff, I'll admit, but he's a strange sort to find on an army training course, isn't he? Bloomsbury lounge-lizard. If you ask me, he's likely to be a bit of a Red himself. I don't like the cut of his jib. Bellingham's a much sounder type. Straightforward. And the sergeants are the salt of the earth.'

'Quite right,' said Knox with feigned enthusiasm. He had been a paid-up, though inactive member of the Labour Club at Oxford and was rather looking forward to meeting a genuine Greek communist.

Jessup, who had been out for a breath of air, came into the room wearing a hunted look. 'Off we go again,' he said. 'I met Watts outside. He wants us for a session with the radio. Says it's essential, because we have to do some sort of simulation exercise while we're on the island.'

'Politics. Fiddling around with radios,' grumbled Meyerscough. 'I thought we were supposed to be getting to grips with the enemy, giving him a bloody nose. Anyone would think we'd signed up to prepare a talk on the Home Service.'

'Now the Major says this is something you've got to have off pat,' Watts explained when they arrived, jerking one thumb at a brand-new radio transmitter/receiver that he had removed from its carrying case and laid out on a bench. 'I've got a list here for transmission. We'll be using the set we've just got from Cairo. Communications, the Major says, are essential. He's very keen on communications. Buggered if I know why, but he is . . .'

After two hours at the radio, Watts was reinforced by Darling and they went for an at-the-double march around the hills behind the villa with full packs, a brief but very exhausting burst of activity which Watts called 'our toddle round the olive groves'. The 'toddle' came whenever they had spent all day in lectures, and in some ways the trainees feared and hated it more than a twelve-hour session in the mountains; coming on top of a sedentary period, it hurt like hell.

Elliot was in his usual position, drinking red wine on the terrace, when they got back.

'Welcome back, boys,' he told the three trainees as they trudged into sight up the drive. 'I hope you're all feeling A1 and tip-top, because I have reason to believe that the Major has some news for you and that you won't be hanging around here much longer.'

No one said anything. They were too interested in hauling their sweating, aching bodies those last few yards.

Knox reached the house first, touched it like a tag-racer, then dumped his pack and Sten at the foot of the steps.

'Is it on?' panted Meyerscough, who had been only a foot or two behind him.

Knox was opening a fresh packet of Egyptian cigarettes. 'Either that,' he said dully. 'Or the war's over. Come to think of it, peace could have broken out days ago. How the hell would we know?'

Then Major Bellingham was in the doorway behind Elliot, bare-headed and looking masterful.

'All right, Mr Elliot. Leave the smarty-pants act,' he said. 'You three gentlemen be so kind as to step inside, and I'll tell you what's happening. We'll talk in my office, I think.'

He had put a couple of extra chairs in there in preparation, and a Johnny Walker bottle and four tumblers were ready on his desk.

'Make yourselves at home,' Bellingham murmured.

'Well, sir?' said Meyerscough, unable to contain himself. 'Is what he said true? Are we going?'

'Sit down, sit down, for goodness' sake . . .' Bellingham waited until they were all seated, busied himself pouring good trebles and distributing them. 'Yes,' he said then. 'As it happens, Meyerscough, "you"—singular—are going. In the case of "you"—plural—I'm afraid I had to make a choice, and Captain Knox will be accompanying you and Sergeant Watts.' He smiled apologetically at the third officer. 'Sorry and all that, Jessup, but someone had to fall out—orders from high regarding numbers—and I decided we needed someone who spoke the language fluently. Absolutely no reflection on the way you have responded to this course, none.'

'I understand, sir,' Jessup murmured manfully, managing to look both crestfallen and mildly relieved.

'Naturally we'll consider you for further projects. As a consolation prize, I don't see why you shouldn't be allowed a spot of leave in Beirut, or somewhere enjoyable on the coast, once we've got our friends here safely to their destination.'

'That's terribly kind of you, sir.'

'Good man. I knew you'd take it well.'

They sat in awkward silence for some moments until Jessup realized that he was supposed to leave at this point. Nodding sagely and at some length to cover his embarrassment, he downed his drink very quickly, stood up and saluted.

'Thank you, sir.'

'Er, thank *you*, Jessup.'

When he had gone, Bellingham looked solemnly at each of the remaining pair.

'Well, you two,' he said. 'This is it. How does it feel? Any problems? Sing out now, because from now on things get really secret, very secret indeed.'

'I'm fine, sir,' said Meyerscough.

'Yes.' Knox nodded slowly.

'Good. Our caïque leaves from Tyre first thing the day after tomorrow. It will hop across to Cyprus and then on to Rhodes by night, conditions permitting.' Bellingham smiled, topped up their tumblers. 'I'll be coming with you as far as the first stop, and after that you'll be in the care of a chap who's done the trip more times than he can count during the last couple of years, so I shan't feel I'm deserting you. Thought I'd tell you that much. We can discuss the details tomorrow. I intend to spend a good deal of the day with you.'

Bellingham's casual crispness was perfect; despite himself, Knox felt a shiver, a thrill. By caïque into Axis-occupied Europe, to an oppressed people who spoke the language of his mother and of his forebears. If all went well, it would be something to tell his grandchildren. If all went well . . . Knox looked at Meyerscough, saw that the other man's eyes were shining with simple delight, and felt a little ashamed of that final 'if'. Men like Meyerscough held nothing back; young Mark Knox always thought of the snags. But at least Knox hadn't pulled back at the last fence. He was *in,* he was going.

'Could we leave any practical questions until then, gentlemen?' Bellingham said. 'There's some cold supper for you, after that I think you should try to get some sleep. I have some important arrangements to put in train. We only received our final marching orders today, so I have to act swiftly.'

They saluted and filed out, leaving the major to his professional mysteries.

At supper they consoled Jessup, who had begun to look somewhat miserable now that the fact of his exclusion from the Rhodes undertaking had sunk in. After all, even if you didn't really want to join in a game, it was nice to be *asked*.

After the meal, the three of them sat out under the stars, finishing off a bottle of oily local wine.

'Goodness, we're getting out of here, we're actually

going to do it!' Meyerscough reminded them for the dozenth time. 'Begging your pardon, of course, old boy,' he said to Jessup yet again.

Knox stared up at the constellations, trying to remember which was which. The Plough was usually the easiest . . . it actually looked like its name . . .

Meyerscough, meanwhile, flowed on. The evening's news seemed to have transformed him out of all recognition. 'You see, I'd thought the war had passed me by,' he was saying. 'I thought that when they asked me: "What did you do in the war, daddy?", I'd have to say, I organized a great number of football matches . . .'

He laughed incredulously. The bugger was happy, mused Knox. Meyerscough had become like a man in love, a quiet, inarticulate type who falls for some girl and suddenly finds he can summon up words, feelings he never thought he possessed. It could be, from what he had pieced together about Meyerscough's background, that war was the only joy he was permitted. Fornication counted as a mortal sin, but for killing the enemies of the realm . . . well, a few Hail Marys and no questions asked.

Knox realized that Meyerscough was now addressing him.

'I say, I hope we get on all right with these people over there. Still, as Elliot said, they're bound to be friendly, aren't they?'

'Perhaps we should take some beads with us,' Knox suggested acidly.

'No need to be like that, Knox. I mean, I know you're—'

'Yes, I am. Look, I'm sorry. I think I'll take a bit of a stroll and then turn in. It's been a hard day,' Knox said, rising to his feet. 'Good night, you two. I'll be fine in the morning.'

He walked off down the steps from the terrace, hands in the pockets of his shorts, and made for the far corner of the villa. The prefabricated hut where the Sudanese troops slept was about fifty yards away, in the shelter of some poplars planted by a homesick Frenchman many years before. Knox stopped and listened. Talk came drifting on the breeze, conversation in a staccato, expressive language that he couldn't begin to understand, and laughter, full-throated and easy. It occurred to Knox that they might be mocking the white man and his rituals, which they were happy to go along with and perform in such a hilariously rigorous fashion. They might be trying to imagine why the white man had brought them here in the first place, weaving fantasies on the subject, each more extraordinary than the last. They might be—

Knox checked himself. He must not get carried away. His father had always warned him about that as a boy, when he had tended to become more excited than was seemly, to see things too simply, to laugh and to cry too often and too much. Gradually he had pushed that part of himself—the part that was like his mother's people—beneath the surface, hidden it where he could find it and take it out from time to time, to examine it like a dog with a buried bone. He had, in fact, become English. Even when the school bullies had called him a wop or a dago—most of them didn't have the wit to conceive a specific insult for Greeks—he had never risen to it. He had answered calmly: 'Come on, fellows. My dad's a Brit. He was in the war. And the Greeks were on our side then too!' And he had always worked hard at his games and his lessons, so that he had become a good all-rounder, so that no one could call him stupid or feeble as well as a mongrel.

He cut through a small archway that led into the courtyard at the opposite end from the stable block, paused to do some more stargazing. Two, three days, and he would be among mountains surrounded by sea, in the company of a bunch of anti-fascist brigands . . . and Meyerscough. Ah well. He guessed he could put up with that brave, blockheaded booby of a squire's son for a few weeks, though there would be a certain lack of intellectual stimulus.

After a short while, Knox gave up on Meyerscough as well as the constellations and decided to take a turn round the courtyard before bed, a self-imposed winding-down. He set off along the concreted path on a route that led him past Bellingham's office, where there was still the faint suspicion of a light, probably a desk-lamp. Of course, the major had said he was going to work; and as Knox drew level he heard Bellingham talking to himself, as many people did when drafting letters or reading through complicated memoranda. The window was slightly open, so the major's voice was quite audible; out of good manners, Knox quickened his step. Then, suddenly, his attention was caught by the noise of a hollow object, a glass or something similar, falling onto the floor in the office. Not breaking, but falling. Knox could no longer restrain his curiosity. He stopped and listened, and heard Bellingham's voice rise momentarily to growl a curse, the chair scrape the floor, as if he was having difficulty in retrieving whatever it was that he had dropped. After a few moments, a mutter of triumph, the chair moving back into its previous position, a pause, and liquid being poured into a glass. A smile of realization spread across Knox's face: the crafty old whatsit was sitting in his office getting quietly sloshed. Sounded like he was well on the way, too.

It was a moment later that he heard the major's voice very clearly saying: 'You're a bastard, Stewart. I know you don't give a damn about the little people, but I do. I do . . .'

Knox moved away in shocked embarrassment. Hanging around listening in on soliloquies, particularly drunken ones, was a thing characters did in plays by Shakespeare, where the rules were different from real life. But who on earth was this 'Stewart' character? Bellingham didn't sound as if he was on the telephone, and there was no one of that name around the villa. He was almost out of earshot when he heard Bellingham's voice grow louder again, with anger: 'And the other side'd better leave those boys alone. By Christ, they'd better . . .'

The major showed no sign of remorse or hangover the next day, however. He took Knox and Meyerscough, plus Watts, through an explanation of who would meet them, harbour them, guide them, get them off the island again. Bellingham also vouchsafed some hints about the 'Axis figure' they were to assassinate, and finally revealed how it was to be done: a section of mountainside was to be dynamited down on top of the unfortunate enemy bigwig while he was motoring up a certain stretch of road. Hence Watts. They might have known. There was also the matter of the radio transmissions, about which the major was more insistent and precise. Both the officers were very grateful that Watts was going to be coming along; he was a dab hand at almost everything.

By mid-day, their heads were spinning. Bellingham had promised he would go over the main points again in the afternoon, and then there would be the trip to Tyre and the caïque journey to Cyprus to really ensure everything was established in their heads and clear. Lastly, he said they should write any letters they might feel necessary—keep them general in tone—and . . . ah . . . they would be posted in a few days' time from Beirut. He hoped they had sorted out all the other legal things, wills and so on, as all serving officers should.

The session ended. They were to separate for lunch, because Bellingham had to work through the meal time. Knox picked up his cap and turned to leave, but Meyerscough stayed put.

'Sir,' he said stiffly, 'I have one thing to ask.'

'Fire away, Lieutenant.'

'The thing is, sir, that I haven't been able to attend Mass or to confess for some weeks now. Naturally, there are dispensations for soldiers on active service, but under the circumstances I would rather like to . . .'

'Very well, Meyerscough. We'll find out where the nearest one of . . . your . . . churches is, and Darling can drive you there. If all else fails, there's the cathedral in Beirut that the French built.'

'Thank you, sir.'

Bellingham coughed gingerly. 'You all right in that respect, Captain Knox?' he asked, including him in so as not to make Meyerscough feel like a freak.

'Fine, sir.'

They need not have worried, in any case. Meyerscough, in his piety, was used to such minor embarrassments. Having unburdened himself, he gazed on the major and the captain with a faintly patronizing smile, like a civilized man fallen among barbarians, who sees them struggling to speak his language in order to put him at his ease.

When he and Knox emerged onto the terrace, Meyerscough smiled again and said: 'I say, what was the chap's name again? The link-man, the one whose name we're not supposed to write down?'

''I-o-ann-ides,' Knox spelled out slowly. 'It's a very common Greek name. Like Smith or Jones in England.'

'Well, you can remember it. I'll call him Mr Smith, and you'll know who I mean.'

'All right. But you'd better be civil to him. He's going to be important to us at various crucial points.'

'Such as when we've knocked off our target. Very mysterious, isn't it? Total secrecy and whatnot. Any ideas?'

Knox shrugged. 'I heard a rumour some chaps once had a go at Rommel, landed a small party close to his headquarters. Heydrich was killed in Prague, of course. Hope we don't end up like the blokes in that case . . . Might just be some wop official or minister. Useful for propaganda purposes. Make sure they don't sleep too easy in their beds at nights . . . Anyway, you're right. We're going to be marked men when the fat makes contact with the fire.' He glanced at the big man. 'Scared?'

'Excited. Scared is included,' said Meyerscough without a moment's thought, and Knox realized that he was less stupid and insensitive than he looked. Or perhaps, by some esoteric process, they had suddenly turned into comrades. Yes, that was probably it.

'I'm definitely scared. I'll let you know about the excited later,' Knox confessed.

Meyerscough laughed, touched his arm.

At that moment, Jessup appeared around the corner of the villa, casually dressed and looking a good deal happier than he had at breakfast. Silence descended when the other two spotted him, but if he noticed the fact he seemed unperturbed. He gave them a cheery wave and strolled over.

'A break from your session with the Major?' he said. 'I've been talking to Elliot. You know, he's not such a bad sort when you can get him on his own. And it turns out he's due to go on leave about the same time as I am. He reckons he can swing it so that we're off the leash together down on the coast.'

Knox looked suitably impressed. 'I should imagine that brother Elliot knows where to find a good time.'

'Rather,' Jessup said. 'He's knocked around these parts before. Says he's brought his little black book with him, stacked with telephone numbers . . . you know . . . the sort of places that the tourists never find out about.'

His earnest young face positively begged for approval. Knox leered politely, while Meyerscough, his mind evidently still on much higher things, discovered an interest in the activities of a couple of Sudanese who were sweeping the terrace.

Jessup continued: 'Not a bad consolation prize, eh? Still, I expect you chaps will be in for a spot of the same when you get back. Returning heroes. By then, I'll be strictly nose to the grindstone . . .'

The archaeologist's son was to be proved right in his second assumption, though not exactly in the way he had thought. Elliot more than justified Jessup's faith, acting as a surprisingly congenial and helpful guide to many unusual and enjoyable aspects of the Beirut social scene. Thanks to his knowledgeable, constant companion, Jessup ate extremely well at a variety of excellent restaurants in the vicinity of Ain Sofar, where Elliot found them rooms; acquired a greatly increased capacity for hard liquor that was to remain with him for the rest of his life; and lost his long-suffered virginity to an agile little blonde at an establishment called the Mimosa, just round the corner from the *Hôtel Normandie*. His ten days' allowance of leave was almost up when he was astonished to receive a curt War Office telegram that ordered him to report immediately for ill-defined liaison duties in Tunisia. The Allies had set up a small unit to handle the restoration and preservation of ancient sites damaged during the recent fighting, and the archaeologist's son had been appointed its second-in-command. Under any other circumstances, Jessup would have been delighted at the transfer, but at that stage he felt that he had failed some obscure, final test, and protested to the sympathetic Elliot. His companion was equally disturbed, so he claimed, and made a number of telephone calls on Jessup's behalf. All in vain. The decision was final, Elliot said, and nothing could be done. However, he would ensure that Jessup's remaining belongings were sent on to him from the villa on the Beirut-Broummanna road . . .

22

The darkened Greek fishing boat hung a third of a mile out to sea, bobbing in a mild swell. The wind was picking up, but Captain Keflakis saw no cause for concern yet, and his passengers were prepared to trust him. They stared at the rolling waves, they gazed at the driven, silver-grey clouds chasing across the sky, but mostly they watched the coast of Rhodes and waited.

All three Englishmen had their faces blackened with charcoal, commando-style. Knox made nervous jokes about Sudanese customs' becoming infectious. Captain Keflakis, a fat, jovially foul-mouthed man of forty exiled from his native Cos, plied them with *ouzo*—not too little, not too much.

'You fucking drink,' he told them. 'We keep an eye on this island for you. Signal always the fucking same, any fucking place round Greece. You fucking well drink, you blokes.'

He had learned his English, of which he was inordinately proud, while ferrying stragglers to safety after the fall of Crete. He had perfected it—if that was the word—in the bars and cabarets of Nicosia, where the dregs of the Cyprus garrison congregated. Keflakis was a linguistic phenomenon and a darned fine sailor.

Towards 2 a.m. the skipper leapt excitedly to his feet. 'It come!' he said, forgetting the otherwise invariable adverb in his excitement. They all followed his pointing finger. A tiny point of light flashed on-off, on-off, among the cliffs a little way down the coast. A pause, and then a repeat.

'Okeydokey,' Keflakis declared. 'We go fucking shore. Hold on, blokes.'

Meyerscough saw Sergeant Watts about to shoulder the W/T pack as well as his rucksack full of lightweight plastic explosives. 'I'll take the radio,' he said quietly. Watts looked at him and nodded. It made sense in the water, because the lieutenant was far the tallest.

'And I'll remember Mr Smith,' whispered Knox.

Meyerscough laughed. 'Or was it Jones?'

And so the caïque moved in towards the cliffs where the light had been seen, her engines throbbing softly on low power, so quiet that she could almost have been gliding in like a trireme of old. Keflakis, though he had sail, declined to use it even under these circumstances. Like the majority of younger Greek skippers, he was a fanatical modernist; his father, the owner of a fine schooner, had joined most of the Cos traders in selling his ship to the British to use in the Dardanelles landings in 1915, and with his pile of gold sovereigns he had bought the *Makaria—Blessed Isle*—to pass on to his heir. Keflakis loved *Makaria* like the son he still lacked, and more than the wife whom he held responsible for this tragic state of affairs, and he maintained that the boat would do absolutely anything he asked. *Makaria*'s engines would lap like muffled oars, or bellow like a wild bull. Keflakis' contempt for the Italian coastal patrols was boundless and founded in experience: 'Fucking eyetie boat make noise like fucking racing car, Maserati. They hear nothing of us, so no fucking danger. Anyway, all eyeties at home in bed, net on hair, drinking fucking chianti muck.'

From a couple of hundred yards out they could see a small group of figures moving among the rocks close to the sea's edge, though still the only sound was that of *Makaria*'s slow, obedient engine. The air close to shore was warmer, as if the balmy atmosphere of Rhodes formed a cordon round the island.

'I hope it's the reception we're expecting,' said Knox. All three of the British had their Stens at the ready.

Keflakis made a dismissive gesture, chuckled, and told one of his crew to pour them a last, swift glass of *ouzo*.

'Fucking eyeties bulls in china shop. Those our people there. Never fear, you blokes, fucking good Greeks is here to meet you.'

The shore came slower. Another wink for luck from the reception party. There were three figures on the narrow strip of beach, the one in the middle working an Aldis lamp.

'Mebbe two more on cliff at top, keeping fucking good eyes skinned,' said Keflakis knowledgeably. He downed his *ouzo*, smiled, and tossed the glass flamboyantly into the sea, where it hit with a disconcertingly loud splash. Then he stepped over and took the wheel of the caïque, to bring them the last few yards. 'Plenty rocks. I take in a bit further. Then you fucking walk on water.'

'I expect Major Bellingham would dearly like to see that,' Knox murmured. It felt uncanny, coming into this ragged stretch of coast in almost total silence. The strangest thing was the group of three figures waiting for them on the beach, not speaking or moving, like dark creations out of ancient Greek mythology.

Keflakis either did not catch Knox's remark, or he had decided that the time for jokes was past. He stood whistling softly to himself while he manoeuvred *Makaria* towards the shallows. They felt a very light bump against her bows, and Keflakis abruptly shut off her engine. He turned, one hand still on the wheel, his face serious.

'You fucking well jump out. Fucking walk,' he said, and they each shook his free hand and received encouraging pats on the back from his crewmen. 'Fucking quick,' he urged the Englishmen. 'So I am in neutral water before day.'

'Thanks.'

'Good luck, you blokes. Fucking quick.'

They slid over the side by the bows into almost four feet of water. Knox went first, holding his Sten above his head in the way they had been taught, and then came Watts, with Meyerscough following at the rear, with the W/T kit in its waterproofed carrier hiked high on his back and his weapon brandished in one large hand. He had long legs; if either Knox or Watts had carried the radio pack, it would have got a ducking, but in Meyerscough's care it barely touched the surface of the water. Big fellows could be useful.

The wading was slow because of the rocks and the amount of equipment they were carrying. None of the men wanted to stumble or slip; but it needed an effort of will to push cautiously, almost sedately from the hips, because a heavily-equipped man in the water felt ludicrous, incompetent, horribly exposed doing that, Knox realized. A voice within him that he had never heard before, the speaker of his unconscious, inflexible will to survive, the warning-bell of the clumsy land mammal that was man, began to scream at him: hurry to the shore and safety, never mind the rocks . . . He, Meyerscough and Watts—he found out afterwards that the other men had felt the same powerful urge—resisted and kept putting one leg in front of the other, a half pace at a time, less than half a yard per waterlogged step. The shore approached with an almost unbearable slowness, and seemed to blacken as the moon disappeared behind a headland, delivering them completely to the shadow of the cliffs. Then, suddenly, movement became easier. They had sand under foot and it rose steeply, so that with a space of a few feet the water washed around their knees instead of their rib cages. They squelched out of the sea like grotesque amphibian monsters. Whispers from the rocks, and after all the silence someone laughed richly, and another clapped hands in recognition. They had arrived. No high drama: they could have been emerging from the sea off Margate after a prankish midnight swim if it hadn't been for the muteness of everything.

Once they had walked a few yards up on the dry sand, everything happened very quickly. The three figures came half way to meet them, with one, slightly to the side, signalling like a man possessed with his Aldis lamp, flashing the final all-clear message to Keflakis out beyond the rocks. Within seconds, embraces and slapping of soaked backs. One of the reception party was a big man, even taller and more impressive than Meyerscough. This one stepped back, grinning.

'An extremely hearty welcome,' he said in English. 'It has been a very long time since I set eyes on an honest English face. I am Stavros Ioannides.'

The moon came out again, and they could see him clearly. He was an extraordinary man: about fifty, bull-necked and bald and physically dominant in the most direct, unmistakable way. Knox felt dwarfed. Even Meyerscough seemed insignificant and somehow a waste of precious flesh in comparison, though there was little to choose between them in terms of height. Ioannides was all muscle, from the broad shoulders through the tapering waist to calves that rippled beneath his flannel trousers as he moved back towards them, hand extended in a formal greeting. The man's loss of hair seemed premature, but of course it was not; merely at odds with his appearance of youthful power and vitality. His face was the strangest part of him: almost unlined, as if its features had never expessed deep emotion. When Ioannides smiled, his lips were like servants performing their task. Once finished, it seemed to Knox, they would be rested until needed again.

They shook hands politely and introduced themselves. Ioannides pointed to his two companions.

'Marcos, one of my boatmen,' he said, indicating a fierce-eyed youth in a threadbare jersey and shorts. 'And Mehmet. Hey!'

The figure who had been signalling with the Aldis lamp turned. He was dark-complexioned, skinny, dressed in patched sailcloth trousers and a white shirt. His shyness, at first odd, became quickly explicable when the Englishmen realized that his sharp features were scarred by a grotesque harelip.

He greeted them in heavily-accented Greek. His deformity meant that he whistled as he talked, but Knox could understand him well enough. Each of them shook hands with Mehmet, too. For his part, Mehmet then retreated behind Ioannides.

'Excuse him. He is very ill at ease with strangers. An old family servant from the days when my people lived in Smyrna on the mainland of Asia Minor.' Ioannides smiled. 'Marvellous creatures, the Turks, so long as you don't rub them up the wrong way. Mehmet is very reliable. He has a secure job and a roof over his head, and he is grateful. Now, I think we should find a safer place to chat.'

At a signal from Ioannides, Marcos made to relieve Meyerscough of his radio pack, but the attempt was resisted. 'No. Sorry. Tell him, Knox . . .' Meyerscough protested in a baffled, strained voice. Eventually Ioannides called him off, and the party set off in the direction of the cliffs.

They made the ten-minute climb from the beach in near-silence. Mehmet leapt ahead like a mountain-goat, occasionally stopping and listening, peering into the darkness, while Ioannides trudged more companionably with his English, smiling a lot and urging them on. Marcos made up the rear. They reached the top, three or four hundred feet above sea level, and there were two more men waiting. They carried elderly shotguns. Only now did Knox notice that Ioannides had a pistol thrust into his trouser belt. A brief, swift exchange in Greek.

'We are safe,' Ioannides announced. 'Not a sign of any patrols, German or Italian. From here it is less than half a mile. Then we shall make you truly welcome to Rhodes.'

'When do we meet the partisans?' asked Meyerscough.

Ioannides pointed to the narrow path that led through the gorse into the interior of the island, then shrugged. 'Tomorrow. I brief you first, hide you during the daytime at my house here. Tomorrow.'

By the time they bedded down, close to dawn, at the little house in the hills above sea, Knox felt he knew Stavros Ioannides as well as he was ever going to. The man had been born the son of a prosperous merchant in Smyrna, Turkish Asia Minor, but he had been packed off to relatives in Alexandria to be educated. He had attended an English school, which accounted for the indefinably alien inflections and the occasional howlers that marred his otherwise perfect control of grammar and syntax. Meyerscough rather tartly described a conversation with Ioannides as like 'talking to a huge, pushy and well-spoken parrot'. The rest of Ioannides' personal history—or as much as he revealed—was typical of Smyrnan Greeks: expulsion as a result of the Graeco-Turkish war in 1920, destitution, escape to Rhodes, where the family had acquired property while it was still in Turkish possession, and gradual re-establishment of the family's fortunes by heavy investment in shipping. The price had been a curious position in the no man's land between the Italian authorities and the largely peasant and stubbornly non-cooperative native Rhodians, about which Ioannides was quite frank, indeed proud. He felt that his position made his work for the British so much less self-interested.

When they woke up towards mid-day, Ioannides was nowhere in sight. He and Mehmet had disappeared, leaving only Marcos, who supplied them with a simple lunch of bread, cold mutton and fruit. Knox spoke to the boy while Watts checked over the W/T to make sure that it hadn't been damaged in the water or during their climb through the darkness to the house.

Marcos was virtually a household slave, Knox quickly realized. He asked the boy how long he had been working for Ioannides. The boy said eight years, which since he was now just eighteen meant that he had been in this situation since childhood. His sister, who was a year younger, also formed part of Ioannides' entourage, but she was at the big house in Rhodes city where they lived most of the time. The boy refused to be drawn, but Knox guessed that the girl was Ioannides' mistress. When Knox asked him if he liked working for Ioannides, Marcos told him that he and his sister, who were orphans, felt safe and protected, because Ioannides was a powerful and rich man with many friends and much influence. He spent much time with Italians, was a regular guest at the governor's receptions in the castle, where he learned a great deal of useful information . . .

'Gossip is a vice, Marcos,' said a voice behind Knox. 'Harmless in this case, but as a general rule dangerous. I shall continue to try to teach you this simple principle.'

It was Ioannides, and he spoke Greek in the hard, slightly quaint accents of his native Anatolia. The boy looked very frightened, looked around the small courtyard where they had been talking, but the only way out was the doorway in which his master stood, square and massive.

Ioannides stared at him for a while, then moved aside sufficiently for Marcos to slip past him and out. He touched the boy's rump in passing, hissed something that Knox didn't quite catch but which made Marcos move very fast indeed.

'You speak excellent Greek. I was so fascinated and impressed that I had to listen for a while,' Ioannides said then, turning to Knox with a toothy smile. 'How is this? I expected an Englishman with perhaps a smattering.'

'My mother's family live in Chios,' Knox answered tersely, still wondering why the boy had looked so terrified.

'A beautiful, beautiful island. And Greek. Ah,' Ioannides sighed. 'If only that accident of history had not brought my family to Rhodes when we were expelled from Smyrna. This is why I am an Italian citizen, like it or not.'

'Presumably you don't.'

Ioannides traced an embarrassed figure-of-eight in the air with his powerful hands. 'As individuals the Italians are not so bad, but why do they not allow these islands to become Greek? I am one of very few Greeks who enjoy some status, as Marcos so indiscreetly told you. I have learned Italian, I go to social occasions, and all the time I watch and wait. I do jobs for the occupiers. It is, as the expression says, good cover. One day,' he added with a flash of self-pity, 'the people who attack me and spread rumours about me will realize what I have done for the cause of *enosis* with the mother country, while they sit and complain, or play with pop-guns in the mountains.'

Knox started. 'You don't approve of partisans?'

'I don't approve of some of the ideas that go with their activities,' Ioannides said smoothly. 'For the rest, they are admirable fellows. I spoke to one of their representatives in Rhodes town this mid-day. It was why I was forced to leave you here alone.' He offered Knox an Italian cigarette, which the British officer accepted out of curiosity. It tasted of herbs and sour, black earth. 'They are ready to fetch you later. Mehmet will take you to the rendezvous point.'

There was a certain fastidiousness in Ioannides' attitude towards the wild boys in the hills. Perhaps it was not so unreasonable; from everything Bellingham had told them, Ioannides' role was closer to that of a spy than a Resistance worker; he clearly had little in common with fighters. It was another small issue to be explained, however, another complication to be kept in mind. Knox filed it for future reference.

'I suppose it wouldn't be a good idea for them to come here,' he said.

'No. And there is no point, anyway.'

'I suppose not. So how do you intend to communicate with us in future?'

'I shall send Mehmet. He will bring you to me if need be.'

'And afterwards, when we have done what we came here for?'

'We shall rendezvous at the same place as this evening. I shall, I hope, have a boat ready to take you straight off the island. If not, I shall hide you here until one can be arranged. So long as nothing happens to connect me with the partisans, any house of mine will be as safe as your lodgings at home in London.' Ioannides beamed, pleased with the comparison. He looked at his watch. 'Ah. Sergeant Watts, he told me before I found you that you were to make a transmitting to your base at sixteen-thirty hours. Five minutes to go. Do you wish to be present when he calls home? He and Lieutenant Meyerscough both seemed to think it very important to have the message absolutely correct.'

'Yes. All right, I'll be there.'

'I will ensure that Marcos is hard at work preparing some supper.'

And if the poor little sod isn't, thought Knox, *God help him.* He forced himself to remember the first law of guerrilla liaison activities, as taught in the villa on the Beirut-Broummanna road: Don't Get Involved.

Ioannides didn't re-appear after they had made their radio transmission, sending the agreed first message to Bellingham. Nor did he join them for supper, which was a kind of poultry stew served by a cowed-looking Marcos. He finally deigned to drop in to announce that Mehmet was ready to guide them to where they would meet the guerrillas.

'Business, business,' he chuckled wryly. 'If I do not appear at my office, then suspicions are aroused. I have enjoyed our talks so much. It is a pity that we could not meet under more civilized conditions, but this is the penalty for living in such violent and uncertain times . . .'

'Yes,' said Knox.

'Great pity,' Meyerscough added.

Watts looked at him as if he were speaking complete gobbledygook. Travel had not broadened his mind. He had a simple attitude to foreigners: if you need something from them, shout; if not, ignore them.

'Mehmet!' Ioannides called through the bead curtain that divided off their small dining room from the rest of the ground floor of the house. He raised his voice only slightly, but somehow he managed to imbue it with an urgent note of command.

The Turk shambled into the room, and Ioannides fired off a stream of instructions, to which Mehmet answered with a gloomy nod.

'He will take you. We shall meet again in a few days, when I have our essential information, yes?'

'And it is essential,' Knox said, extending his hand.

Ioannides shook on that and looked pleased. 'It is because of my unique position that I can supply this information. If the Axis people suspected that I was not a whole-hearted supporter of the occupation, I would lose my status and therefore my usefulness. I am sure that your superiors understand this . . .'

'Of course.' Knox cut him short as politely as possible. 'Our superiors made their great admiration for you quite clear.'

More handshakes all round. Ioannides was quite beside himself with gratitude for Knox's words of reassurance.

Finally they trooped out into the darkening twilight and stood under the plane trees at the back of the house, where the path continued into the hills and they could look out over the slate-coloured sea a mile or so distant. They checked their packs, waved once more to Ioannides, who stood by the door with his arms folded, smiling. The Turk with the harelip moved quickly ahead when they had signalled readiness, and within one or two minutes they were in among thick oleander bushes, climbing quite steeply and out of sight of the house, though somehow it seemed as if Stavros Ioannides was still looking up after them, grateful and overbearing, generous and secretive, an enigma.

The march was half an hour, above the tree level, where gorse and pale alpine flowers spilled onto the ill-defined path. The Turk did not look round or speak, even when they saw a village way below them to their left, whitewashed houses sleeping in the shadow of a tiny orthodox church, a small community of Mountain dwellers. He kept on grimly, his agility belying the clumsiness and gauche uncertainty that he showed on level ground. Suddenly, for no apparent reason, he stopped.

'What is wrong?' Knox asked in Greek.

Mehmet just looked around, moving only his eyes, and said: 'Here.'

They waited. Then they heard the sound of a rifle bolt being drawn back in the stillness. Meyerscough unshouldered his Sten, braced his feet apart in a firing stance, but Mehmet simply shook his head. Someone whistled above them, roughly in the same place where the rifle sound had come from. Then a voice rasped in Greek, the Rhodian singsong that Knox recalled from his boyhood travels: 'Go back, Turk. Tell Ioannides we have taken over.'

Mehmet frowned. The rifle bolt clicked again. He shrugged, nodded shyly to the Englishmen, and scuttled off back down the hill whence they had come a few minutes earlier.

Suddenly the Englishmen could pick out figures all around them on the rocks. Maybe a dozen in all, obviously carrying weapons of various kinds. Two separated themselves from the circle, scrambled down towards the path, came to a halt a few yards from Knox and the others, peering at them in the near-darkness. Sizing them up? Deciding whether to cut their throats?

'Who is your leader?' In Greek.

'I am,' said Knox with a firmness of tone that was totally faked.

'English?'

'All three of us.'

The speaker moved closer. Knox noticed that he was carrying a rather smart, well-greased and polished Biretta machine-pistol, obviously the pick of the group's captured weapons. He wore a cap pulled down over his forehead and eyes. His companion wore a woolly hat against the night chill but had no apparent weapon.

'Code?'

Knox smiled. This was really too theatrical. 'Colossus,' he said. That had come from Major Bellingham. Rhodes = Colossus. It was also part of the messages they had to send. Theirs not to reason why.

'Correct.' A pause, and then the man moved forward, as if with violent intent.

'I say—' growled Meyerscough, pointing his Sten.

But the Greek had taken off his cap and was hugging Knox like a long-lost brother. Tears were trickling down his cheeks.

'English comrade. You have come to help us liberate Rhodes,' he sobbed. 'English comrades have come . . .'

Within seconds, they were surrounded by laughing, backslapping Greeks. It was like a bath of humanity. In the end, the spokesman had to bawl at his friends to give the British some air and space. He stood, still refusing to let go of Knox's hand, and grinned like a child.

'I—I—I am Panayiotis Chorakis. I embrace you. You are quite safe now. These men are partisans, and I am their elected leader.'

'Glad to meet you,' Knox said quickly. 'My name is Captain Knox. This is Lieutenant Meyerscough, and this is Sergeant Watts.'

At that, a ripple of excitement went through their new hosts once more, and the tide threatened to engulf them again. Chorakis beat his men back. Knox had noticed that the figure in the woolly hat was hanging back, not moving.

Chorakis saw where the captain was looking. He smiled, this time rather apologetically, beckoned to the reluctant one.

'Shy. Very shy,' he explained, miming for the benefit of the British who did not speak Greek. 'Come forward!' he hissed.

The figure walked closer, taking off the hat, then stopped. As Knox watched, a cascade of dark hair escaped and poured down onto a pair of broad but slim shoulders. Full lips parted. Fine teeth flashed in a self-conscious smile. And Knox looked into the kind of brown eyes that could make a man want to live, but be willing to die.

'This,' Chorakis announced, 'is our representative of anti-fascist Greek womanhood. Thea Chorakis. She is my sister.'

Knox uttered a polite, distant greeting, because he knew that one did not throw one's arms around a Greek's sister at first, or for that matter subsequent meetings unless one wanted to end up in very deep trouble.

'This is all obviously very emancipated,' he said feebly to Meyerscough and Watts, who were looking on, fascinated. And he was thinking: First rule again—*Don't Get Involved.*

The second part of their trek was long. Partisans were permitted to take turns in carrying Watt's case of explosives and the W/T, tasks that they took on joyfully. The column filed through olive groves, heard the faint protests of sheep below, moved up onto higher pastureland, stony and patched about with harsh, uneven grass. There were few buildings on their route. Occasionally Knox thought he glimpsed a low, whitewashed house on a hillside, but they were never close enough to make out detail. He asked questions sometimes in Greek, which Chorakis would answer and Knox would paraphrase for Meyerscough and Watts. There were not many people here on the south-eastern corner of the island, particularly in the mountains. That was why they had chosen this region; the fascists left it alone unless they were trying to impress someone, or unless the partisans made a particular nuisance of themselves. Around Attaviros, the peaks reached almost 2,000 metres high; there were few enough of them in the partisan band, and they could easily hide when need be.

The going became very hard towards the end, harder than it had ever been on those hikes in Lebanon. No mockery or jokes by Watts now, because this was the real thing. There were treacherous loose stones all over the path, and finally no discernible path at all, only crags and tiny, cracked plateaux, where it was a case of keeping grimly behind the shadows of their guides. Once Knox, beginning to become mesmerized by the sight of Chorakis's back, felt himself growing vague and dreamy. A gentle touch on his shoulder from the man behind pushed him to his right, almost putting him off balance. He swore in English, heard the Greek click his tongue, and to the left saw the slit of the chasm he had been about to stumble into.

'We are almost there,' announced Chorakis, hardly turning round. 'Go with care.'

They must be at least two thousand feet above sea level, Knox estimated, and possibly more. He knew that the heart of the island was high and without roads—good, uncomfortable guerrilla country. When they stopped for a rest, allowed by the Greeks out of politeness to their guests, the night-chill reminded him that winter had only just passed, and that he had had only a half-night's sleep. Better to keep moving.

Chorakis reached behind to touch Knox's arm, and nodded off to their right.

'Care,' he said.

They turned right, and suddenly they were in a tunnel where progress came by touch. Meyerscough caught his head on the roof and grunted stoically, too exhausted to raise a curse. Some thirty seconds later they were through, into a small natural theatre with the stars above them. A couple of men came down to greet them. Sentries carrying rifles. They had really arrived at last.

An opening at the far end of the theatre led into a smaller dish in the rock, perhaps ten yards round and to the mouth of a cave. There was a flickering orange reflection on the left-hand wall, where the cave curved. Deeper inside there was a fire, warmth and light, and something roasting.

'We have got some sheep,' Chorakis explained with a laugh. 'No roast beef like home. Sorry.'

He ushered them in past him, repeating his joke more loudly for the benefit of his men as he did so, and earning throaty laughter with nothing malicious in it, only gratitude for everyone's safe arrival.

The inner part of the cave seemed enormous. The light from the fire did not fill it, leaving three of the four walls ill-defined and hidden in darkness. The ceiling was twenty feet above them. That much Knox managed to establish before he was really surrounded, by a host of loudly chattering Greeks, by the smell of garlic and sweat and sheepskin, arms seizing him, warm hands trying to pump his. Now that the partisans were free to make a noise, they made full use of the opportunity; where there had been catlike reticence and caution, the atmosphere was suddenly transformed into that of a boisterous village wedding.

'The English comrades are tired and hungry!' yelled a thick-set, heavily-moustachioed man who had planted a great kiss on Knox's cheek. He swiped at his friends, clearing a path for them to the fire. There they were forced to sit down, and glasses of what they were told was cognac were thrust into their hands.

Bemused, smiling, occasionally going into an involuntary cringe when the din around them reached a particularly fierce peak, Knox, Meyerscough and Watts sat by the fire for some minutes without saying a word. Questions swirled around them: How long had it taken from their base to Rhodes? Had Ioannides treated them well? How old were they? Would the Axis be defeated soon? When would Rhodes be liberated from the fascists? Next month? Next week? What was the plan that involved the explosives?

Knox saw the woman again through a fleeting gap in the crowd. She was standing on the edge of the darkness, staring straight at him with a frank curiosity that to an Englishman would have seemed outrageously rude or provocative. Chorakis was next to her, talking excitedly, one hand on her shoulder. Both he and his sister were slight, almost willowy compared with the chunky peasants who made up the rest of the band. Knox smiled at her, and he fancied that she smiled back. Then a partisan moved into his field of vision, preparing to refill their glasses with the rough, home-made brandy.

It was a while before Chorakis restored some kind of order, a process that involved a good deal of bellowing and clapping of hands, pushing and shoving. The partisans' leader sat himself down next to the British in a defiant, determined fashion, continuing to shoo his men away until there was room to breathe and talk.

In the firelight Chorakis revealed himself as a slender young man of no more than thirty, with a short, curly beard and very serious, bright eyes. He was an educated man, having studied law in Athens before the war, and even had a tiny amount of English, which he now had the courage to try out. He referred to his guests as 'comrades', which Meyerscough, thank God, did not rise to, and Knox noticed that he affected battered knee-boots, like a Cretan mountain-man—or a Russian commissar. Nevertheless, Greek exuberance had the upper hand over politics at the moment, even in the case of Chorakis.

'You must be very tired,' he said. 'But you must eat. There is a lot to do. We are lucky that the Italians are so lazy. They do not move outside their fortresses at night. There are many garrisons . . . you will see them . . .' His voice held a pride that was almost proprietorial. To listen to him, you would think that the Axis strongpoints belonged to him and not to the despised occupiers.

Knox found his tongue more easily than he had with Ioannides. His mother's language seemed to trickle out of him easily, like a flow of water from a hidden spring. 'Thank you, thank you. Yes, there is a lot to do. But for tonight we shall enjoy your welcome and your food, get to know everyone.'

'So . . . you are here to kill important fascists?' Chorakis said, causing appreciative growls all round.

'Our orders are secret. But we are not here to play games.'

It was good enough. Several partisans let out whoops. The glasses were hastily refilled, with such enthusiasm that Knox's trousers were soaked with 'cognac'.

'The British are coming here.'

'No, first they will attack Italy. My cousin Socrates delivers vegetables to the fascist barracks, and he hears talk . . .'

'They will invade both places. Piff . . . paff. Now the Germans are beaten in North Africa. Nothing can stop them . . .'

'One thing is certain,' Chorakis confided above the babble of opinions. 'The fascist Admiral Campioni is frightened. Since this past month, a lot more Germans have come. He is frightened of them. The British wait in Egypt and in Cyprus and now in Tunisia. More and more security is being mounted on Rhodes. Something big will happen. Much Italian, German police.'

'Are the Italians frightened, or will they fight?' asked Knox, his head racing with the brandy and the sheer force of their welcome.

The partisans roared with laughter. Chorakis smiled, though with a touch of apprehension. 'The fascists do not like fighting. But maybe,' he said with a shrug, 'if the Germans are there with guns at their backs, and their leaders are resolute . . . But Rhodes is not their country, though Mussolini says it is. It is like this: you sleep with an absent man's wife and you enjoy her. But when he returns, if you value your life, you disappear very quickly . . .'

The food, hunks of roast lamb with coarse, flat bread, was brought by a boy and Chorakis's sister. Chorakis nodded to her to set the huge wooden dish so that the Englishmen could reach it easily.

'Comrade Thea,' Chorakis announced, 'is the new Greek woman. She fights. Very anti-fascist.'

He spoke the right, sternly socialist, 'modern' words, but they did little to hide the traditional Greek within him, the hot-blooded young Greek buck, the *pallikar* who would defend his and his family's honour with his life.

As for the 'new Greek woman', she was doing much what the old one would be doing, which was to neatly slice and distribute smaller, less choice portions of meat and bread to the rank-and-file ruffians. She might have been twenty-five, perhaps a year or two younger, and slim like her brother so that she was swamped in the man's shirt and trousers that she wore—whether as a revolutionary affectation or out of necessity it was hard to say. She seemed as serious as her brother, too, though there were dimples on her smooth olive cheeks that begged her to show happiness. She worked earnestly, with intense concentration, and she used a broad, heavy and wicked-looking dagger, which Knox noticed she stuck back in her belt when she had finished her task. It was then that she saw him watching her, and tossed her hair self-consciously. He felt a twitch in his groin. The old Adam. There was no escape from it.

'Thea!' Chorakis shouted.

She came over, stared solemnly at the British guests.

'Some words of welcome,' her brother urged.

The woman's hand went instinctively to the knife in her belt as she nodded and said with a shy smile: 'Welcome. I hope that together we shall kill many fascists.' She spoke in a low, pleasant, quite cultured voice without a trace of drama or cruelty in it, as if she were expressing a preference about the weather.

Meyerscough glanced at Knox. 'What did she say?'

Knox told him.

'Charming.'

'Just my type,' said Sergeant Watts, who was becoming rather drunk. 'My mum had a very similar attitude towards rent collectors.'

The carousing went on for another two or three hours, after which the British party were shown to a smaller, lower cave beyond the main vault, where they rolled out their sleeping-bags and settled down for a brief rest. They were due to make their second radio transmission at eight-hundred hours, Eastern Aegean Time.

Meyerscough was the first to wake. He roused first Watts and then Knox.

'It's just gone seven,' he said. 'I think we should get some fresh air and make sure the natives haven't been fiddling with the radio.'

It was cold in the cave, for the day found it hard to penetrate the rock. Their only light came from an ancient oil-lamp placed in the entrance to their sleeping-chamber. And the place was so silent. Chorakis had explained that in Byzantine times, Anchorite monks had come here to do penance for weeks, months, even years on end. The previous night seemed unreal now, and a thin atmosphere of loneliness filled the caves, as if with the party over the spirit of those ascetic refugees had seeped back into the air.

'I doubt they have. Not this lot. But all right,' Knox mumbled. He was hungover, but more than that he was shocked to realize that he had an early-morning erection. He recalled dreaming of women—of Irene, Thea Chorakis, and others—and of their stifling him in a most pleasant way, like velvet, living cushions. Meyerscough had cut into that dream. Damn Meyerscough. Nevertheless, this was all very unprofessional and unheroic. Somehow one expected the libido to switch itself off for the duration of operations such as this.

They had slept in their underwear, leaving their battle dress tunics and trousers to air by the fire. The clothes were folded on a rock by the chamber entrance, with a few pieces of bread and some olives in a small bowl.

After getting dressed and picking at the breakfast, they made their way out through the main cave, gingerly in the half-darkness like convalescents. A couple of Greeks, probably the ones who had stood guard all night outside, were asleep in one corner, swathed in goat skins.

Meyerscough saw their carbines propped up against rocks by their improvised beds.

'Goodness knows where they got those blunderbusses from,' he said. 'Positively antediluvian.'

'Turkish, by the look of them. There were sporadic rebellions against the pashas all through the last century, until the Italians walked in and took over. Your average Rhodian peasant is pretty well bound to have the odd liberated weapon from those days hanging around the house. They always did on Chios, I remember. And they knew how to use them.'

'Ah, yes. Good enough to see off a wop, eh?'

'Good enough to make a fair-sized hole in anyone, including the man who fires it, if he's unlucky or careless,' Knox yawned. 'Come on, let's go out and greet the morning. What with being cooped up in Ioannides' house yesterday, I don't feel we've said hello properly yet.'

Nothing can prepare anyone, but particularly an Englishman, for the light of the Aegean; it can be unbearable, but it is also addictive, a drug. The sun rushed in from Anatolia at dawn to assault the senses. In the early morning, it is stunning but still within reason. But the sun reaches a fiery noon intensity that leads even the modern Greek peasants to call mid-day the 'hour of Pan', when all activity must cease, leaving the Lord of Misrule to stalk a helpless earth. Only towards evening does sanity return completely, and then the light caresses the islands, gold and shot with red-orange, strokes them as if they were monsters asleep in the cooling sea.

'Oh, my eyes,' said Meyerscough.

Knox put up his hands for shade. He had forgotten. How could he have forgotten this?

No one seemed to be about in the clearing outside the main cave. Knox beckoned Meyerscough to follow and led the way through the tunnel into the natural theatre beyond. From its corner they gazed down towards the sea. There were a few clouds to the north-west, towards Chálki and Tilos, but between and beyond there was a sea like no other sea anywhere in the world, blue and glistening like a polished shield. The grey rocks sweltered under their blankets of lichen.

'The others are gone, some to find food, some to inspect

Italian positions,' a voice said. 'They will be back soon, *Kapetánios*.'

His military rank was pronounced with deep respect. Knox, still overwhelmed by the vista, turned and saw a young man standing twenty feet to their left, fingering yet another dubious carbine and smiling shyly. They had been introduced the previous night. Knox thought his name was George, but then there had been at least four Georges . . .

'We shall wait,' he answered politely. 'We must send a radio message in a short while. That is all.'

The man nodded. 'Yes, *Kapetánios*. I and a friend are on guard duty.' He gestured with one hand at the path through the rocks, with the other raising his rifle defiantly. 'Anyone comes, and they will be surprised at their reception.'

They discussed the island and the season with him. Yes, it was unusually hot for April. At Easter it had been cold and wet, which had meant that the feast time had been a muted affair. The Italians forbade the Greeks to celebrate their festivals, but usually the remoter mountain villages managed to put on something. This year there had been plenty over to feed the partisans as well as the priests. Good, yes? And when the liberation came—this month, next month, next year—all would change . . .

Knox added sagely when the guard spoke of the liberation, but he did not offer any comments. It was always difficult to do that without getting involved in Greek politics, which even when right and left were making common cause against the Axis could be reckoned to be remarkably bitter. He was justified by the turn the conversation took immediately afterwards.

'Soon we shall be free of the fascists,' the guard said, twisting his moustache vehemently. 'Then we shall deal with the collaborators and the capitalists. They are not much different from each other. Rhodes will be united with a socialist Greece, and then . . .' Words failed him; nothing could adequately express either the ease of his ideal's attainment or the bliss it would bring to all concerned.

Suddenly Knox found himself saying: 'This Stavros Ioannides, the patriots here in the mountains do not talk about him. Why is this?'

The guard frowned, then looked nervous. 'He is very rich. A bad man, who drinks the best wine with the fascist Campioni and talks with de Vecci in the governor's palace. Despite all this, some say he is a friend of the patriotic movement. This may be true, but I doubt it.' He spat neatly onto the rocks at his feet, to show the force of his scepticism. 'Ask Chorakis. Or better, ask comrade Thea. They will tell you. Ioannides is bad. After the liberation . . .'

His voice fell quiet. He was staring past them, towards the mouth of the tunnel.

Knox turned and saw Chorakis's sister standing by the tunnel entrance. Her face was a mask, empty of all emotion except a profound loathing. The young guard could not look at that face for long. He flinched, then looked back out to sea, as if returning to his watching task, and tried to continue: 'After the liberation . . .' he repeated, but his heart was no longer quite in it.

Thea Chorakis carried a basket of kindling which she had been gathering further down the mountain. Knox noticed that she was still wearing that wicked-looking knife in her belt. She continued to stare at them for a moment, until her face softened and she gently shook her head, shrugged and hurried off into the door in the rock that led into the main cave. It was as if she had been called out of a trance of hate.

'Does comrade Thea not like the English?' Knox asked the guard.

The man grinned and shook his head. 'She likes the English very much. She is anti-fascist. Two Italians have died this year because of comrade Thea.' He threw up his hand, formed its fingers into a blade and pretended to whizz it through the air at a soft target that succumbed with a fleshy plop when it hit home. 'She has learned to do it at a distance with the knife because her brother will not let her have a gun. Sometimes I ask myself: is it good for a woman to learn such things? I do not know. But after the liberation . . .'

Meyerscough looked pointedly at his watch.

'We'd better start checking the W/T over. Don't want problems. The major will panic if we're late transmitting so soon in the proceedings,' he said.

'All right,' agreed Knox. He took leave of his guard, retrieved Watts, who had parked himself on a rock to admire the view and smoke an early-morning cigarette, and walked back towards the main cave.

Meyerscough grunted. 'Pretty thing, Chorakis's sister. Seems like a nice enough girl, too, if you get her in the mood. Looked a bit sullen just now, though. And I'm not sure about the knife.'

'Perhaps she has a reason to be sullen.'

'Perhaps.'

They sent their second message spot on time, pleasing themselves and also ensuring that the good Major Bellingham need not fret at his cosy hide-away in Lebanon. So far they had seen neither hide nor hair of the enemy, his agents or his armed forces. Apart from Meyerscough, none of them particularly wanted to, either.

But within a day or two they would have to chance their hand and undertake some kind of a reconnaissance trip. The last reliable inspection of the spot earmarked for their projected assassination had been in 1936, and since then Rhodes had been fortified madly. The first thing that struck Knox was the way the partisans kept talking about the numbers of Germans on the island now. These past few weeks, they said. Suddenly Germans, Germans, everywhere Germans.

23

The heavy-laden Heinkel III transporter dipped its plump belly another few feet. Then the lowered wheels met the concrete runway with a jolt that made Bredow wince. His burns rarely gave him pain now, but the scars on his arms did not like to be disturbed. And he was frightened. He hated flying.

The Luftwaffe pilot, who had flown him from Athens as 'extra cargo', turned and grinned, relishing the sight of an Army Intelligence man rigid with nerves in his fold-up seat forward of the wing.

'Calm down, Excellency!' he bellowed over his shoulder. 'We've arrived: Kremasti airfield. Welcome to paradise! If you can stand the spaghetti-eaters' rotten conversation, you're in for the time of your short life.'

Bredow nodded queasily. The main Italian air base on Rhodes was squeezed into the narrow plain between the sea and the mountains; from high up a few minutes before, it had felt as if they were about to dive onto a postage stamp from the top of the Eiffel Tower.

'Thanks,' he said. 'It was a good trip.'

'Don't mention it. Any time the sun, the wine, and the luscious signorinas get too much for you, just shout and I'll run you back so that they can transfer you to Russia. I drop by once a week with goodies for the boys.'

They taxied in, and ground personnel directed them past ranks of aging Macchi fighters. A Kubelwagen was already on its way across the concrete, heading in Bredow's direction like an urgent little insect scuttling to get out of the heat. The pilot cut his engines and rested on the aircraft's control column for the moment, gazing balefully towards the approaching vehicle. When it stopped short of the Heinkel, he got to his feet and twisted his way through to where Bredow sat.

'We have a reception committee, Excellency,' he said, pulling off his leather flying helmet. 'Always security people around these days. SS and such. Miserable bastards. Still, these characters look relatively harmless. One Aryan gentleman of your ilk, the other highly un-Aryan. Your first encounter with a spaghetti-eater coming up, I'd guess.' He took out a pack of Greek cigarettes, tossed one to Bredow. 'Go on, have a smoke. Let the bastards sweat.'

Two or three minutes later, they emerged through the hatchway under the wings, and Bredow saw what the pilot had meant about Aryans and otherwise. Captain Huber was there to meet him, as arranged, but with him in the Kubelwagen sat a tall, grey-haired Italian officer in an elaborate white uniform and dark glasses.

Huber, bronzed and with his blond hair bleached almost colourless by the sun, waved to Bredow and got out of the passenger seat. The Italian sat for a little while longer, then climbed out onto the concrete, carefully patting the crease of his uniform trousers and straightening his cap before joining the two Germans over by the plane.

'Have fun!' the pilot called. He was on his way to the whitewashed control building, his cigarette still dangling from his lips.

Huber and Bredow shook hands.

'Glad to see you arrived safely, Oberleutnant,'' Huber said. 'Those transporter boys are mad bastards, but they can fly.' The Italian was hovering expectantly. 'This,' added Huber with a faint grimace, 'is Major Count di Pantanelli, my Italian counterpart and an officer of the *Regia Aeronautica*. He was most eager to make your acquaintance, and so I brought him along.'

'Indeed,' said the Italian in excellent German, with a sudden smile that made Huber's sarcasm seem churlish, which it was doubtless intended to do. 'As senior Intelligence officer to the garrison here, I shall do everything I can to make your stay on Italian soil as pleasant and fruitful as possible.'

Bredow glanced at the impossibly violet sea, the tiny white village nestling in the protection of the shimmering headland. 'It is delightful,' he murmured. 'Almost a shock to the system after grey, rainy Berlin.'

'It will be more beautiful still when the war is over. Rhodes will once more be the pearl of the eastern Mediterranean. You must visit us again then, Oberleutnant. We have built many villas and hotels along the coast, where our victorious heroes will be welcome to relax . . .'

'I'm sure he will be delighted to do so,' Huber interrupted on Bredow's behalf. His driver had put the bags into the back of the Kubelwagen. Huber began to ease Bredow towards the vehicle.

'Aha. But there is much to discuss now,' Pantanelli agreed with a sad shrug. 'I am told that you are considering the possibilities of Rhodes as a new outstation in case Turkey should enter the war. This eventuality is, of course, very improbable. Nevetheless, I should be glad to hear the details and give my opinion in the matter.'

Bredow caught a warning glance from Huber—not that he needed it. They immediately began jockeying for position in the cramped rear of the Kubelwagen, Huber trying desperately to ensure that he interposed himself between Pantanelli and Bredow. He failed. Pantanelli was prepared to be ruder, elbowing Huber to the far side of the seat while still wearing an entrancing smile. In the end they had to compromise: Bredow sat in the middle.

'I have found a room for you at the *Albergo della Rosa*. It's very comfortable, and you will have a base until we can find you an office and some more long-term quarters,' Huber told him when they were travelling north towards Rhodes city on the well-surfaced military road.

'There is space at the palace, and it would be convenient for liaison purposes,' Pantanelli said. 'I shall speak to my superiors immediately—'

The bizarre struggle lasted until they arrived in the town, a quarter of an hour's drive from the airfield. The ancient settlement, head and heart of the island, lay drowsy in the afternoon, its port still except for a pair of Italian coastal vessels chugging gently and apparently aimlessly round the Mandraccio harbour like tourist boats. Everywhere trees in bloom, riots of scarlet anemone and yellow wall flowers among the stone, their scent mixing with the tang of the sea. Narrow streets, a hint of three-thousand-year-old mystery, with the *Castello* of the Knights spreading above on the hill overlooking the harbour. It had been restored by the Italian governor to be his seat of power, oat-brown and theatrical as a filmset from a mediaeval epic.

The Kubelwagen stopped in a street lined with sycamores, and Huber ushered Bredow to the foot of a broad flight of steps.

'We must go now, Major,' he said to Pantanelli. 'The Oberleutnant must rest. He has had a tiring flight.'

'Tomorrow, then, I shall show him the glories of Rhodes,' the Italian insisted.

'Of course.'

They made their way slowly up the steps towards the *Albergo*, minus Pantanelli at last.

'Are all the Italians here like that?' asked Bredow incredulously.

Huber sighed. 'He is not so bad. But his job is to keep an eye on what we are doing on the island. His people are beginning to feel the wind of competition, I think. And he is wondering why there are so many German security officials arriving all of a sudden . . .'

'The Admiral told me that very few Italians had been told of the planned meeting. The SS insisted—justifiably for once—because the likes of our friend the Major there leak like sieves.' Bredow smiled. 'I should imagine that an Abwehr officer with my background is none too welcome. Pantanelli will be wondering who the hell is coming here next.'

'Let's hope he doesn't guess. At least until he's officially told. Avoid him if you can, and if you can't, then keep your mouth shut and enjoy your fate. The Major has an excellent taste in wine, keeps a personal chef, and—if you're interested—throws some of the wildest parties east of the Via Veneto.'

Bredow said nothing. Huber's driver put down the bags in the marble-floored lobby of the hotel, and the Luftwaffe Intelligence captain told Bredow to wait while he sorted out the room, which he did in very loud and heavily-accented Italian at the reception desk.

They agreed that Bredow would be fetched in the early evening for dinner at divisional headquarters in the western suburbs. Until then he really did need to rest. Huber was very sympathetic; it was easy to tell that someone had briefed him about how and where Bredow had acquired his injuries. After an *espresso* and some military gossip on the terrace, Huber and he exchanged restrained but very cordial farewells. The captain was a nice fellow, but he knew nothing of *Wintermärchen;* so far as he was concerned, Bredow was merely the Abwehr's warm-up man for the Hitler-Mussolini meeting and a sympathetic colleague, a change from Pantanelli.

Bredow's room on the second floor of the *Albergo* was small but furnished with the uncluttered good taste that had once been so typically Italian and here had survived even fascist pretensions. It had French doors leading onto a south-facing balcony, where the guest could sit and enjoy the fragrant breeze while he drank in the sight of the city, the sea and the hills. Bredow gratefully stripped off his tunic and holster, opened up the doors and went out to take a look. Across the rooftops he could see open country, green with spring, and mountains in the distance. He checked the map he had brought with him from Berlin and calculated to his mild disappointment that the high plateau where the Englishmen were hiding could not be seen from here; it was off to the southwest and forty, fifty kilometres distant. He would need a day or two to acclimatise, create a relationship with Huber and, God help him, Pantanelli, feel secure enough in his official cover to be able to give them all the slip. A telephone call to this man Ioannides would suffice for now. More important, both for his own peace of mind and for his real purpose on the island, would be to commandeer a vehicle of some sort and drive down the coast road to the wild, rocky south. The Admiral had instructed him to familiarize himself with the terrain, just in case.

A spick-and-span driver from divisional headquarters called for him at seven. He marched in through the glass doors, spotted Bredow waiting there, and sprang to attention.

'Obergefreiter Spatz. I request the Herr Oberleutnant to allow me to drive him to headquarters!'

The driver was a boy of perhaps twenty, with a strong Tyrolean accent and the sharp, almost Mediterranean looks of an Alpine peasant. There was, however, no sign of the notorious Austrian carelessness about him. General Drewitz, the Wehrmacht commander on Rhodes, obviously ran a tight operation.

General Drewitz's way of fetching his guests certainly possessed a certain style. Waiting at the bottom of the steps below the *Albergo* was a sleek, open-topped Mercedes staff car, leather seats and rolled-back hood, shining in the dull gleam of the solitary street-lamp like a rich man's toy. Perhaps Italian ways were also infectious.

Bredow sat in the back, and Spatz sent the Mercedes gliding towards the harbour. Until they arrived by the waterfront, the driver passed in silence. Then, without warning, the driver spoke.

'*Mandraccio,*' he recited loudly. 'Ancient harbour of Rhodes, famous for windmill tower and used to shelter the Knights' galleys.'

They carried on south along the harbour road, past great stone walls defying the sea.

'Old town of Rhodes,' Spatz announced, still gazing straight ahead. The phenomenon was very similar to ventriloquism. 'On our right, the Knights' Quarter; a little further on, the Turkish Quarter . . . notice the silhouette of the Mosque of Murad Reis, completed in 1532 to honour the memory of the Sultan's naval commander, who fell during the siege of the island ten years before.'

The car was proceeding at a sedate twenty kilometres an hour, fast enough to give a mild edge to the evening wind, sufficiently slowly for Spatz to perform his curious duty at leisure. When they met a small convoy of Italian lorries and had to wait for them to turn the tight right-angled bend by Emborio pier, the Mercedes stopped, but the driver continued relentlessly.

'This larger harbour takes the larger ships. An industrial shipyard has been constructed to the south of here . . .'

An old Greek in shabby trousers and a sweater, with a peaked cap on his head, sat mending a net by the entrance to the pier and watching with evident enjoyment as the horns blared and Italian army drivers leaned out of their cabs to gesture and shout at each other and anyone else who could be blamed for the temporary traffic snarl-up. The Greek saw Bredow; his weatherbeaten features opened up into a gap-toothed smile; he took off his hat, scratched his grizzled head, then replaced his headgear, grinning all the while. The small performance in no way implied approval of the occupiers, but in his way the Greek was prepared to admit that the scene was good theatre and to play his part. When a man's island has not been his own for a thousand years, Bredow thought, perhaps that is the only pleasure he has left—the secretive pleasure of the spectator.

When the way forward was free again, Spatz had fallen behind schedule. He picked up speed, turning right again to drive along the western walls of the old town, past a modern sports stadium and through suburbs of whitewashed houses. The tiers of dwellings rose steeply ahead, to a bare hill crowned with broken columns that glowed dull primrose, a trick of the dying sun on ancient white stone.

Spatz jabbed a finger towards the hill and the object on

its summit, simultaneously stepping on the accelerator again.

'The Acropolis!' he barked in desperate triumph.

They arrived at a rambling villa on the outskirts at twenty-eight minutes past seven. Spatz had been sweating visibly during the final couple of kilometres, occasionally cursing quietly, mentioning Jesus, Maria, and Joseph all in the same breath. His relief at being able to decant his passenger before half-past was evident, almost touchingly so. One of the sentries on duty at the gate checked Bredow's credentials and led him in through a small garden teeming with hibiscus and into a glass-windowed orangerie, where several officers, including Huber, were standing with aperitifs in their hands, waiting for the call in to dinner.

Bredow described the delay down by the harbour to Huber, who was hugely amused.

'General Drewitz is very punctilious,' he explained. 'The tourist route is Spatz's specialty, and he guards the privilege jealously. One condition: he must deliver the general's guests on time. Have some Campari.'

A sudden drop in the volume of the conversation signalled the stroke of seven-thirty. Huber glanced at the ornate Venetian clock mounted above the double doors at the far end of the orangerie, then said softly to Bredow: 'Now!'

The doors swung open as he spoke, and General of Infantry Heinrich Otmar Gustav, Graf von und zu Drewitz, strolled into the room. He stood tapping one elegant foot on the parquet floor, hands in the pockets of his breeches, approving the silence. A mess-waiter appeared, carrying a tray with a crystal glass containing a colourless, effervescent liquid. General Drewitz took it without for a moment removing his gaze from the assembled officers.

'Good evening, gentlemen,' he said then, in a voice as arid as the wind-swept plains of Brandenburg.

It was his only comment. He half-turned and began to sip from his glass as if he were alone in the room. The conversation picked up, but officers were discreetly hurrying to finish their own drinks.

Huber motioned for Bredow to do the same. 'We have exactly two minutes. It will not escape the general's notice if you are still holding a full glass in your hand when the call to dinner comes. He is drinking mineral water, for his stomach. A mess-waiter will appear to collect it when the time is up.'

The extraordinary thing about Drewitz was, actually, the fact that he looked so totally undistinguished. The uniform was impeccable, the precision intimidating, but the general himself was simply a tired-looking man in his middle fifties, of average height, with a widow's peak and a slight pot belly.

'He's all right,' Huber hastened to explain. 'I think the boredom here affects him. This ritual is a game, one way of passing the time until they send him back to the real war. Sometimes the general is almost human. You'll see.'

Bredow recalled that Drewitz had once been a hero of a kind. He had commanded with exceptional skill and daring during the campaigns in Poland and France, and had been considered for a major military position. He told Huber what he knew and expressed surprise to see the man here.

'Ah, you wonder why he is here, in charge of a half-strength division and subordinate to the whims of our glorious Italian ally?' Huber smiled grimly and answered his own question. 'I believe it arose from some unflattering remarks that he made to General Keitel last year, when Stalingrad was encircled. Keitel could have demoted him in Russia, but that would have caused unrest among his brother-generals. So a much more refined cruelty was devised. They sent Drewitz to the Aegean to rot in the sun . . .'

Drewitz drained his glass and replaced it on the tray that a mess-waiter held at his elbow. Without pausing, he walked over to the head of the long, polished table. His chair was pulled out for him and he sat down.

Bredow found himself propelled forward to the place on the general's right. Drewitz did not acknowledge his presence until the soup plates were being cleared away.

'We are honoured to receive a gentleman from the Abwehr,' he remarked to an adjutant on his left. 'Oberleutnant von Bredow is his name. Rhodes has suddenly become exciting to the pranksters at the Tirpitzufer. I tell myself that this is an interesting fact. Could it mean that we shall have to place certain restrictions on the use of bathing beaches; even fortify them a little more efficiently?

Or might a certain promise of a visit have something to do with the Oberleutnant's presence here?'

'It is possible, General,' answered the adjutant, a coot-bald major who wore a monocle.

'I think it is possible, too. I shall ask the Oberleutnant.' Drewitz turned and affected a look of earnest curiosity. 'Oberleutnant von Bredow, welcome to our humble patch of sun and salt sea,' he said. 'Tell me, if you can, precisely why you have come here.'

Bredow had a sense that his answer could be very important indeed. 'I believe that Admiral Canaris sent you a detailed communication some weeks ago, Herr General. However, if you wish me to refresh . . .'

'Yes, kindly do refresh my memory, Oberleutnant. One is so busy. We are busy, are we not, Falcke?'

The hairless major nodded gravely. 'This also is possible, General.'

'Very well, Herr General,' Bredow said. 'My duties are to observe the military situation and report on it to my superiors in Berlin. I am also to assess the prospects for setting up an extra full outstation here on the island—with the technical status of *Kriegsorganisation,* naturally, in deference to Italian sovereignty. The aim will be to . . . monitor the situation on the southern coast of Turkey more effectively than can be done at present.'

'And the—shall we say—high-level visit?'

'I have been briefed, Herr General. Clearly I shall be observing those arrangements also, although of course we would not dream of interfering with the duties of the . . . visitor's . . . own security people. I think we understand each other's meaning, Herr General.'

'We do. And congratulations on your skill at circumlocution, Oberleutnant,' the general murmured. 'As a reward, we shall afford you every assistance.' He raised a warning hand to prevent the waiter from piling too many boiled potatoes on his plate to accompany the veal in lemon sauce, then turned and resumed his apparently separate conversation with the adjutant. 'I told you, Falcke. Canaris has sent one of his young men here on holiday, for a well-earned rest. We must ensure that Spatz drives him round the island and supplies him with more information for his report to Berlin.'

Drewitz popped a piece of meat into his mouth. Bredow was forced to wait until he had finished chewing his food, and that seemed to take a very long time, for he performed the operation very thoroughly. Like the mineral water, for the sake of his stomach, perhaps.

'May I make a comment, Herr General?' Bredow asked before Drewitz could start on another forkful.

'By all means, young man. This is, after all, a social occasion.'

'Herr General, the Admiral placed great emphasis in his communication on the fact that the Eastern Aegean now has a high priority for all our purposes. I wish to reiterate this.'

'Reiteration noted. But Turkey will not enter the war on the Allies' side or anybody else's side. You are wasting your time so far as that matter is concerned.'

Drewitz had stopped playing. His eyes were shrewd as he gazed at Bredow, and the veal in lemon sauce lay forgotten for the moment on its gilded plate.

'But there are other considerations, General. As you must be well aware, the Anatolian harbours and inlets appear to be providing safe refuges for British raiding parties in the Eastern Aegean, despite Turkey's neutrality. This is a problem that we wish to investigate thoroughly, particularly since the level of enemy activity is increasing. It could indicate broader British ambitions in this area.'

'I am delighted to hear you express such concern, Oberleutnant,' Drewitz said after short consideration. There was a ghost of an approving look on his face. 'I have been indicating this in my reports to the Wilhelmstrasse, apparently to no avail. Yes, something should be done about the British and their friends on the Turkish mainland. Perhaps the . . . visit . . . indicates a new interest on Berlin's part.'

'I daresay, General. I am not privy to such councils.'

Drewitz stared at him levelly. 'I sense something in the wind, Oberleutnant. Why, two or three days ago we and the Italians both picked up coded radio messages being transmitted from the southern mountains, indicating a relatively sophisticated level of wireless activity unknown in these parts for some months now.' He turned to Falcke. 'When was the last British commando group heard of?'

'November-early December, General. Thought to have been a naval Special Operations Unit surveying the beaches.'

'Thank you. This may be just another reconnaissance trip, or a deliberate irritant to keep us and the Italians on our toes. We do not yet know.'

Bredow cleared his throat, trying to hide his nervousness. 'Have the security people in Berlin been informed, General?'

'Of course. With a recommendation that, for the moment, they do not fuss excessively. Nevertheless, we shall keep an eye on the situation.'

'I note that with special interest, General,' said Bredow. 'It is part of my brief to do so. Tell me, do these commandos have local support?'

'There is a small group of so-called partisans operating down there. Comic-opera stuff. It is altogether likely that they are aiding the authors of the radio messages. We do not usually bother with them—such matters are left to the Italian garrison. But perhaps—'

'Might I be allowed access to the intercept reports, General?'

Drewitz frowned, glanced at his bald-headed adjutant, then nodded. 'Detailed transcripts of the messages have been forwarded to the appropriate authorities in Athens. The code has not been broken, so far as I know. And the persons responsible are very careful to move around and to keep their transmissions very short.'

'May I nevertheless see them?'

'I don't think I could stop you, even if I wished to, young man.'

'Thank you, General.'

Drewitz inclined his head in response to an urgent whisper from his adjutant, then nodded decisively.

'Falcke informs me that my meat course will soon be so cold as to be inedible,' he announced blandly. 'You will excuse me? I am very glad that we discovered a topic of common interest, Oberleutnant, however inconclusive the discussion.'

Drewitz did not address Bredow again. Neither did he stay for the final course. He stood up, and the entire table rose with him. The General acknowledged first the assembled officers and then Bredow personally.

'I trust that you will work hard while you are with us, Oberleutnant,' he murmured. 'I ask only one thing: if the British are about to attack us here, then the Abwehr must tell me. I will do the rest.' He smiled crookedly. 'That is your function—though from what I hear, much else is discussed in Berlin these days. Good, honest operational Intelligence seems to have diminished in importance for you gentlemen, to be replaced by political parlour-games of a very dubious kind. Now, Major Falcke will entertain you. He knows many funny stories.'

With a stiff bow, he turned and walked out of the room.

Major Falcke sat down, waited for the buzz of conversation to reach a respectable level, and then smiled at Bredow across the table.

'Don't worry, Oberleutnant,' he said. 'I think that the General likes you.' Unnervingly, the left eye twinkled amiably while the right one behind the monocle remained quite lifeless. Bredow realized that it, too, was made of glass.

'I accept your assessment of the General's mood,' he said.

'Oh yes,' Falcke retorted firmly. 'The General is a man of very clear opinions. And he does not like political soldiers—the likes of Keitel or, for that matter, Canaris. He believes that between them such people got us into our present fix, and who can gainsay him?' He reached over and poured Bredow some more wine. 'Had he suspected you of wasting our time with the parlour-games to which he referred, you would have found yourself bundled onto the next plane back to Athens—or, indeed, to anywhere at all. As it is, you have convinced him that you may be engaged in at least marginally useful activity. Quite an achievement. Now, shall I tell you an amusing story while we enjoy excessive quantities of wine?'

'Why not?' said Bredow.

He arrived back at his quarters in the *Albergo* some time after midnight, more than a little unsteady after a heavy drinking-session with the bald, one-eyed Major Falcke, Captain Huber, and a group of other members of Drewitz's staff. To his intense relief, Driver Spatz had not insisted on repeating his entire tourist-guide performance during the return trip.

The chief thing, Bredow told himself before he lay down on his elegant brass bed and began the quest for sleep, was that he had secured his position on the island for the moment. More than that, he had gained access to the British party's transmissions and to reports on the commandos' activities in the mountains. He had also, it appeared, made a friend in the droll Major Falcke. In short, he had done all that Canaris had asked him to do: he was well established as good shepherd to the British end of the Admiral's *Plan Wintermärchen.* Once contact had been made with the double-agent, Ioannides, the preliminaries would be complete, and most of his task would consist of waiting and watching.

Bredow should have been able to sleep. A year, six months, the comfortable bed, the drink, the thought of a day's work well done would have ensured it. But he could not. Instead he felt a nagging sickness in his stomach that had nothing to do with the wine or the rich food. It was always there when he was alone and trying to sleep, and tonight, as every other night, he told himself that one day he'd be able to rest. Really rest. *Gisela, I'm so tired,* he whispered out loud to the Mediterranean night.

24

Knox handed the binoculars to Meyerscough and gestured down towards the coast.

'Take a look down there for yourself,' he told him. 'They're Germans all right. A motorcycle unit patrolling the field perimeter. Same goes for the artillery emplacement to the right of the Acropolis. Christ, only the bloody Germans could put an ack-ack nest there . . . Say what you like about the eyeties, but at least they've got souls.'

Meyerscough grunted in acknowledgment. 'Golly, I'd do anything for a mortar and a pile of fat shells.'

'Well, you'll have to be patient. Feast your eyes for the

moment. You can look, but you can't touch,' Knox said. He glanced at Watts, who was gazing keenly at the airfield and the road, keeping his own counsel as usual. 'Well, sergeant?' he asked. 'Reckon you'll be able to handle the job?'

Watts nodded thoughtfully. 'It'll be all right. Need about a dozen charges, properly placed in that outcrop that overhangs the road there. Timing'll be important, too. But I don't foresee any serious problems, sir. We'll have the bugger fair and square.'

The three Englishmen and an escort of eight partisans had tramped through the night to be here at dawn, perilously close to the Italian military road that ran down the east coast of the island to a point a few kilometres south of Lindos. From their vantagepoint between the villages of Kalathos and Pilon, Knox's highpowered binoculars gave them a fine view of the harbour of Lindos, its Acropolis, and—most importantly—the military airfield a short distance away. This was where their V.I.P. victim was going to land, and it was at this point approximately on the road that Watts was going to do his stuff. They had been shown models of the coast, pored over maps, heard descriptions. The reality felt odd; not unreal but unserious and placid.

'Awful lot of German activity,' commented Meyerscough as if to allay the peaceful impression by an act of will. 'Patterns indicate security patrols pure and simple rather than purposeful military manoeuvring. Fits in with what Chorakis told us about Jerry increasing his presence. This airfield's obviously important to him. I 'spose a lot of matériel and personnel comes in and out . . .'

'Including our proposed victim. Be interesting to get a clearer sight of the field,' Knox agreed.

Chorakis and the armed escort were sprawled among the grass-covered boulders behind them, conducting desultory conversations in dangerously loud demotic and waiting for something to happen. Knox turned, called for the partisan leader. He and Chorakis squatted together and smoked a cigarette.

'Dare we go in closer?' Knox asked.

The Greek looked uncertain. 'We would have to cross the tar road,' he said. 'And some of those farms down there belong to Italian settlers. But if you think you must do so . . .'

'It's all right. We mustn't take unnecessary risks. Sergeant Watts has managed to spy out the terrain through binoculars. We shall, of course, have to risk going very close to the road when we help him place the charges. Until then, there is no point in endangering ourselves or you. This is intended as an initial reconnaissance, after all.'

'Danger is inevitable. This is war,' Chorakis retorted stiffly, obviously relieved but at the same time uncertain whether or not his courage had been called into question.

'Yes. But we don't go looking for it. It's important that we survive to do what we came here for. I think we've seen just about enough under the circumstances.'

Chorakis nodded reluctantly, got to his feet and hissed an order to the other partisans, who began to prepare themselves for the march back across the hills to their hideout.

'All right, you two?' Knox asked Watts and Meyerscough. Both nodded, though the lieutenant continued to glance longingly down at the enemy forces in the valley. From up here it was easy to believe that you could squash them like toys. Watts had turned away and was ignoring the scene below. He had obviously had enough time to judge 'the job'.

They took their time to get back on the march, though everyone was aware that the walk would be a long one. The party had only just strung itself out into a single-file walking formation when from the other side of the island a light aircraft came into view, flying slowly between the mountains, weaving about in a leisurely fashion that seemed to indicate that it had no particular destination. As it came closer, Knox noticed that the aircraft was making little swoops, banking and going down to within a couple of hundred feet of the rocky peaks and slopes like a bee searching for honey.

Chorakis saw it too, but he expressed no particular interest or concern. 'Italian, German,' he commented. 'It doesn't matter. They patrol every few days in such a plane. It is unarmed. Routine.'

'Well,' Knox said, not entirely convinced, 'we'd better be getting back. Soon it will be starting to get hot.'

Chorakis indicated agreement and called his men to move off. Their projected stopping-point was twelve kilometres distant. They would spend the baking, noon hours there, resting in a high, cool valley, and then press on to the caves, which they were due to reach in the late afternoon.

Suddenly, as if summoned by Chorakis's hoarse shout, the aircraft changed course and moved south-east in their direction. It came in low towards Kalathos, appeared to be heading directly for the airfield to land, but then swung due south and came right over them.

'Keep walking,' Chorakis said. 'We could be farmers, or people gathering spring flowers. We could be many things. There are villages not so far from here, and there are few of us. If they are looking for freedom fighters they will expect to see a large column of men, perhaps running for cover, scattering.'

Knox had his doubts but decided to follow the Greek's advice. In the event, he was right. The plane buzzed down, throwing its shadow over them for the moment, then levelled out and began to climb away again towards the east coast. Perhaps it had been performing a final pirouette before landing, a case of some young pilot enjoying himself.

The reconnaissance party walked on into the dry uplands, covering the ground quickly, despite the growing heat, and shortly before noon they halted by the little waterfall that marked their pre-arranged spot and took shelter under a wooded overhang within sight of the tiny monastery of Aramatis. Watts, sweating profusely, slipped off the radio haversack and all three of the British dumped their Stens and got ready for a meal of goat's cheese, bread and black olives. Even the partisans spoke in relatively hushed tones, for the place was indescribably quiet. The only other sound for a great way was the distant, thin bleating of sheep on a lower pasture.

After the meal, Chorakis posted two guards on either side of the halting-place and the rest of them settled down to a short siesta, all the more welcome to men who had not slept for thirty hours or so. Watts, accustomed to living rough and aware of the value of even the briefest of sleeps, got his head down along with the Greeks, but Meyerscough and Knox forced themselves to stay awake; it was twenty-five to one, and transmission time was on the hour.

Meyerscough splashed his hands and face in the icy stream to cool off.

'You get on rather well with our friend Chorakis, don't you, Knox?' he said when he got back to where they had been resting in the shade.

'I rather like him. I like and admire the Greeks as a nation, on the whole.'

Meyerscough frowned, pursed his lips. 'They're likeable enough. Bloody disorganized, though. They're lucky the Italians are even more shambolic, or they'd have been flushed out of these mountains a long time ago.'

'Perhaps. But it would cost the occupiers quite heavy casualties—and probably a great deal of ill-will, because there would be trouble with the villagers, reprisals and counter-reprisals. No,' Knox said, 'I think they'd rather pretend that Chorakis's lot are no more than the usual brigands, occasionally causing a bit of bother up in the hills. Rhodes, you must remember, is the Italians' showpiece; before the war a lot of fashionable people used to come here. A nasty little guerrilla war would look bad.'

'Could it also be that our Greeks are none too effective either? I mean, they cut the odd sentry's throat on a dark night or get somebody's cousin to sabotage a vegetable shipment bound for one of the island garrisons, but they seem more interested in political fantasies—or Chorakis does, at least. I wonder sometimes if they realize what it'll mean when we actually bump off someone who really counts.'

Knox nodded by way of an answer. He preferred not to think of the retaliation that would almost certainly follow their assassination of the 'Axis official'. Chorakis and his innocent fellow-islanders would learn fast that life was much more unpleasant when people took you seriously. Instead of pursuing the subject, he responded to the first part of Meyerscough's comments: 'The scale of things here is very small,' he said. 'Tito in Jugoslavia, or Serafis on the Greek mainland, are waging full-scale war against their oppressors, with all that entails. Chorakis is a town-bred radical who's managed to persuade a few dozen disgruntled young peasants to join him in the hills. He'd probably be cooling his heels in Rhodes town jail on political charges if he hadn't.'

'Positively Ruritanian,' muttered Meyerscough.

'If so, it works in our favour. At least we're not being harried from one hideout to another. We can prepare our task under fairly peaceful conditions, can't we? I'm rather enjoying myself, personally speaking.'

'So am I, I suppose,' Meyerscough murmured. 'But it's tamer than I expected. More like a walking holiday in the Lake District so far.'

'May it continue along those lines. Come on, let's wake old Watts up and get transmitting.'

They were in the act of signing off when they heard the sound of feet slithering down the stoney path towards the stream. The partisan who had been taking watch above appeared, looking agitated. Chorakis woke with a start and leapt to his feet to receive the man.

'*Kapetánios,*' he called out after a hurried conversation. 'Christos has seen Italians coming up the valley.'

Watts was left to sign off. Knox and Meyerscough accompanied Chorakis and the guard to a narrow promontory which gave a view to the south-east and Knox focussed his binoculars where the Greek pointed.

There was something like a platoon-strength patrol of *Bersaglieri* in their bizarre plumed helmets struggling up the slope beside the stream half a mile below, led by an officer. One of the men carried parts of a heavy machine-gun slung across his shoulders.

'Do they often venture up here?' Knox asked Chorakis.

The Greek shrugged. 'Last time was when the Fascist Propaganda Minister, Pavolini, came. To impress him, the Italian military authorities mounted a sweep through the hills. They never found us.' He grinned. 'And neither will this bunch of tailor's dummies.'

'Where would they be based?'

'They will have come by truck from barracks in Rhodes town, up the mountain road through Laerma before climbing on foot. It is a very bad road, fit for donkeys and peasants' carts, and usually they avoid it. We are therefore to feel honoured that they are taking so much trouble, particularly at this hour of the day. And those men with the feathers in their helmets are special troops. To kill some would be an honour.'

Knox could see what Chorakis was leading up to. 'We'd better get out of here fast,' he said firmly. 'It looks to me as if this might be connected with the plane we saw this morning.'

'Maybe. They are not too many,' Chorakis said calmly. 'We have the advantage of surprise, and the cover up here is very good . . .'

'Please, no. Not now.'

'A pity. But very well.' Chorakis sighed meaningfully.

They turned round to watch as the rest of the Greeks came up the path from the stream, accompanied by Watts, who had packed up the W/T once more and loaded it on his back. Chorakis stabbed a finger to show they would be retreating once more before the might of the Axis, and told his men that they would also be heading straight across the top to home, avoiding the paths they had followed on the way here.

'I say, what's going on?' Meyerscough asked.

'I think those Italians are looking for us, you know. Interesting that Chorakis said the last time they ventured up here was when some other bigwig was visiting. Things could get a bit hot.'

'I got the impression our friend here wouldn't have minded having a go.'

'Chorakis wanted a dustup, but he knuckled under when I told him we were on orders to preserve our hides at all costs until the great day.'

'I take back what I said about those chaps,' Meyerscough said. 'It's we who are cramping their style, and not the other way round. Makes you think, eh?'

Watts, meanwhile, after pausing briefly by the officers, scrambled over the top between the jagged rocks, hunched under the awkward weight of the W/T pack. Knox and Meyerscough followed.

Bellingham had warned them that their radio signals would probably attract some unwelcome attention. Well, he had prophesied correctly. Knox hoped that Chorakis and his people would not be the ones who paid the final price for the Englishmen's 'walking holiday'. It did, indeed, make you think.

It was possible that Bellingham might have felt better if he'd felt able to leave the villa and the radio transmitter, but he doubted it. What else would there have been to do except lie in the sun, visit shabby night clubs down on the coast? Instead, he had started to live within hearing distance of the radio room. He had taken the tiny servant's quarters next door, set up a camp bed. Darling was supposed to do equal duties 'on call', but more often than not Bellingham insisted that he 'take the night off', 'get some air', or 'read a good book undisturbed'.

Elliot, the angelic corruptor, had brought him a whole crate of whisky from Beirut before flying off back to London to report to 'C'. At first Bellingham had rationed it strictly; then he had started to secretly drink the health of the boys on Rhodes; finally he had used it to get to sleep on the hard iron put-me-up, allowed whisky to rescue him from a constant fear that they might transmit one day or night *in extremis* and he wouldn't be listening.

'Sar'nt!' he bellowed, putting down the headphones. There was no need to shout, for Darling was just out in the garden, reading and enjoying a cup of tea in the late afternoon sun, but Bellingham felt the compulsion. 'Sar'nt! They've called in!'

'Excellent, sir,' said Darling, appearing in the door. 'That be all for a day or two?'

Bellingham nodded. 'If they transmit only according to the pre-ordained schedule, yes.'

'Sir. Want me to pass it on to London? You look a bit tired.'

'No, thanks,' Bellingham sighed. 'Did the job straight away. Best to get it over with.'

He ignored the comment about his 'tiredness'. He had a feeling that Darling was aware of the crate of whisky and the use his superior was putting it to. The sergeant had done some boozing in his day, but in early middle age and with a war to fight, he only touched beer now. Bellingham said with a stubborn quality to his voice: 'I think that deserves a drink. Beer?'

'All right, sir.'

'Very much all right, Sergeant.' Bellingham felt mildly sick at his own condescension, born of boredom and self-loathing. Darling didn't deserve it, heaven alone knew.

They walked over to the kitchen/mess and got two bottles of Black Label lager out of the refrigerator. As they sipped their beer, they could hear the Sudanese calling to each other over by their huts. The black guards, too, would be going as soon as this business was wrapped up. Elliot had left for London after ridding them of Jessup; with the three other ''IFCU'' men on Rhodes, the villa on the Beirut-Broummanna road was like a shell. What the hell. 'IFCU' was also a shell, waiting to be crumpled to nothing just a few weeks and days from now, its fragments scattered to the winds to leave no trace.

'Seems a bit ghostly here now, eh, sir?' Darling essayed when they were half way through the beers. He was tough and brave, the sergeant, but shy as a child with his social superiors, unlike Ron Watts. Bellingham loved him dearly and found him unbelievably boring company.

'Looks like Cairo's forgotten about us for the moment, it's true,' said Bellingham. He was dutybound to keep up the pretence about the expected new intake for 'IFCU' until London gave the word to dissolve it. 'Ours not to reason why.'

Good God, he thought. *And it's still only five o'clock in the afternoon.*

He wished SIGNIFY was all over and the lads back safely. He wished he knew what on earth Stewart Menzies was really up to—Elliot's statement about the arrest a couple of weeks back continued to trouble him. And most of all he wished he could get back to his lonely watch next door to the radio room and the whisky he kept in a little locked cupboard there.

25

On the evening of the third day after their big reconnaissance trip, and the ninth day of their stay on Rhodes, Knox saw Thea Chorakis smile, really smile.

Chorakis had taken them out for another look at the east coast and the airfield. This time, since there seemed to be very few enemy forces active outside the field perimeter, they had dared to cross the military road at a point where trees provided cover, and had ended up crawling to within a couple of hundred yards of an Italian coastal battery. They had watched for twenty minutes at their leisure while the enemy soldiers desported themselves among the spring marigolds that grew among the barbed wire and the concrete in perfect ignorance. The Italians had posted no sentries so far as anyone could see, though Christos and 'After the Liberation' George were sent off to check. Apart from the solid reality of the four-pounder in its pit, the scene could have been unfolding on a public beach at Ostia. To Knox, to observe the enemy like this felt like going big-game hunting with a camera. When he said so, Meyerscough complained that this was only too true, and that the wops seemed to be a protected species round here. He moaned with frustration when the Italian NCO and a pair of his men stripped off and went to bathe in the sea, leaving their emplacement almost completely unprotected. They were so close that they could eavesdrop on the jokes, the curses, the popular songs blaring out from the unit's radio. On the way back across the road, they had seen some Germans bivouacked among some rocks. They had been big, disciplined men in uniforms of olive green rather than the usual field grey, as Knox was able to see through his binoculars, and they had come here since the morning. It was clearly time that the partisans made for home and did not push their luck. Even Chorakis had a healthy respect for Germans.

The march back had been tough. A sudden storm blew in from the Aegean in the afternoon, bringing high winds and thundery rain that made the fields of flowers ripple and writhe like the sea, and by the time they reached the high ground the rocks were wet and treacherous. It made for a painfully slow climb back to the caves. A warm fire and hot food were the prizes, and both had never seemed so welcome. The basics of life, at least, had become very simple.

Towards the end of the trek, Knox fell into step with Meyerscough. The big man had been silent during most of the way, pretending to find the going arduous but in reality, Knox suspected, nursing some kind of worry or resentment. At almost any time in his life until now, Knox would have shrugged and reckoned a man's moods were his own business, but over the past few days his attitude had changed. It was crucial to know how each of them felt, he had realized. His new awareness, he suspected, had something to do with his own developing qualities of leadership, which meant thinking about other people and suchlike. He was not sure whether he was disturbed or relieved at his own transformation; perhaps a little of each.

'How's things?' he asked Meyerscough. 'Shouldn't have reckoned on us Brits being put off by a spot of rain.'

Meyerscough pretended that he needed to watch the rocks ahead, where they rose steeply and were covered in slimy lichen. 'Just needs a bit of concentration, doesn't it?' he mumbled.

Watts was well back, in the company of an older Greek with whom, despite their mutual lack of foreign languages, he seemed to have developed an easy, close friendship. Conscious that they would have little privacy once they were back in the cave with the entire partisan band, Knox decided to press his point.

'That's a lot of bilge, Meyerscough,' he said. 'You're fed up about something, aren't you? You could find your way back to the caves with your eyes shut and all four limbs in plaster. Come on, out with it.'

He found himself surprised at the steel in his own voice, despite his attempts to disarm the probe by giving it a jovial, public school surface gloss.

'Oh, for goodness' sake,' said Meyerscough, obviously also surprised. And he responded. 'I'm just a bit impatient, I suppose. I want to *do* whatever we have to do here. This wandering around the island is getting on my nerves. When are we going to see some action, Knox? You should ruddy well know. You're supposed to be in charge, when all's said and done.'

His broad face, pink from being whipped by the storm-rain, peered irritably out from under an oilskin hood like a character from *The Wind in the Willows*. Knox resisted the temptation to laugh out loud.

'We were told from the outset that we'd have to wait for

the word. When the powers-that-be have the information, we go into action. Ioannides will tip us the wink, and then—puff!' he exclaimed with passable conviction. 'Lord knows but we'll have enough on our plate once things get going. We'll be busy trying to get off the island alive, for a start . . .'

'I know, but—'

'Then cut it out, Meyerscough. This kind of work takes discipline and trust. The Major said the recceing and the radio stuff are also pretty vital to the war effort locally, though of course they're far from glamorous or exciting.'

Meyerscough swallowed hard, turned back to face the path. They tramped on in single file and lapsed into chill, wet silence. Knox himself was far from convinced by his own talk about 'discipline' and 'trust', though he saw the necessity of keeping Meyerscough on rein. He suspected, in fact, that even the big man, who thought, acted and talked like a schoolboy, was beginning to recognize a few sober realities—to wit that 'IFCU' had picked some strange and altogether unlikeable allies and often behaved in ways that defied any rational or at least favourable analysis. Major Bellingham, for example, was clearly being manipulated by some higher power, and he didn't much like the fact—or so his drunken mutterings that Knox had overheard that night in the Lebanon implied. And always Knox had the feeling that he and the other 'IFCU' recruits had been kept apart, isolated like a bacillus from the moment they had first driven through the gates of the villa on the Beirut-Broummanna road. Even here, everything was ritualized, put into compartments, with no room for individual initiative. Their movements had been predetermined, the radio messages were 'IFCU' issue, to be transmitted exactly according to orders, and even the assassination job seemed mechanical; a setting of explosives by a craftsman. Knox had the feeling that he and Meyerscough could have been *anybody,* anybody at all . . . In the meantime, however, they had to keep each other amused. Personally, Knox was coming to like the lieutenant, despite—or perhaps because of—the fact that he spoke, acted, and apparently thought like a fifth-former. Meyerscough almost felt like some kind of a lucky charm. His pompous habit of addressing Knox by his surname in true schoolboy fashion, which had been amusing at first, then irritating, counted as a comfort now. Chaps like him, dullards who excelled on the sports field or in action, always got through, didn't they? The conventions of their youth, which had conditioned so much of this generation's life, told Knox so. It was lesser races and beings who complicated things: Englishmen were straight, rather dull, but they won out in the end by sheer honest determination.

They reached the caves in premature twilight. Grey clouds masked the setting sun, though the storm was over. The ten men of the reconnaissance party, including the Englishmen, stripped to various degrees and huddled in goatskins and coarse blankets by the fire in the main gallery. Thea welcomed them like a housewife with many sons, plying them with bowls of hot chicken soup sharpened with lemon, to restore them. That morning they had wrung some hens' necks, and so the partisans' menus for the next days were set firm.

After supper, Chorakis clapped his hands and announced a political education session. 'You will join us, *Kapetánios*?' he asked politely.

'Of course.'

'You must be joking,' muttered Meyerscough, and asked Knox to plead exhaustion on his behalf. He took himself off to the adjoining cave, yawning theatrically.

Chorakis read for half an hour from a copy of Lenin's *State and Revolution,* which most of the partisans listened to with a respect that was almost as total as their incomprehension. His small library of Marxist tracts was faded and dog-eared with age—all the books had been printed in Athens in the early Thirties, before General Metaxas had taken over as dictator and banned left-wing writings—but loved and often read. The works were Chorakis's great support and joy. He insisted on reading them out loud to his men because, so he told Knox, it was necessary to impress them with the great quality of the thought of the founders of socialism. Afterwards they would discuss what they had heard and he would simplify the concepts for them so that they could begin to understand the real, historical reasons why they were here in the mountains. In mainland Greece, Knox learned, there were many well-schooled communists, even in the countryside, but here on Rhodes, where the people had been stupefied first by four hundred years of Turkish rule, then by the indignities heaped on them by the Italian fascists, where the priests held them in poverty and taught that this and the occupation were God's will . . . Chorakis had smiled helplessly. The Rhodians were politically backward in the extreme, which was why he had only thirty men here, while on Crete and in the mountains of Macedonia there were thousands waging the battle . . .

His duty done, Knox decided to stick his nose outside when Chorakis's reading ended and a desultory political discussion began round the fire. He suddenly felt a yen to smoke a cigarette in the fresh air away from the lingering smell of wet clothes, the reek of woodsmoke, food and goat.

On the mountain, the rain had stopped and the moon was rising. Knox stood and enjoyed his cigarette and the sight of the stars in a sky that was now as clear as only a Levantine sky can be. He was on the corner of the rock platform with the view of the sea, the other islands, and if he craned to the right, a finger of the Turkish mainland jutted into the margin of his vision. A shadowy movement ten yards or so away made him turn, so as to recognize and be recognized. He saw Thea Chorakis, also brooding among the damp rocks. She greeted him formally, with a woman's embarrassed gesture, a raising of the hand that was also a warding-off.

'Your brother is talking politics. I thought it was compulsory,' he said with a wry smile.

Thea moved a little closer, studied him with apparent suspicion. 'I know those books as well as he does. And he does not mind if I go away and pretend some womanly task needs to be performed. The men . . . are not used to having females present during their talks.'

'Their loss is my gain.'

That was when she smiled, stuck her hands in the pockets of her shapeless trousers and shook her head. Her eyes were sparkling.

'I have never spoken to an Englishman before,' she said then. 'I think I like it. But then you are not really English.'

'Oh? Gossip behind my back?'

'My brother told me about your mother, the Chiot. It did not surprise me. You were not at all as I would expect one from a cold country to be. You are warm. And your looks are those of a Greek.'

'Nice of you to say so. If you go on like this for much longer, you'll have your brother asking me what my intentions are. I know all about that aspect of life on a Greek island.'

She smiled once more, this time with a touch of mischief. Her shoulders were thrust back, and the wind sculpted her breasts through the heavy shirt that she affected. He had never seen her like this before: there had always been awareness of her as a potentially attractive woman, but now she was revealing a physical challenge, quite deliberately.

'One day, perhaps, it will be a Greek woman's own business what she does and who she meets,' Thea said. 'I can march, I can fight, and I can think and men can accept these things, though maybe reluctantly. But when it comes to the other aspects—' She shrugged in a way that wrote volumes of meaning. 'I can speak to you because you know the other ways of the world, the ways that my comrades here have never experienced and therefore do not understand. Tell me, in England can a woman do as she wishes?'

Knox tossed his cigarette onto the rock beneath his feet. 'That depends what her desire might be.' Deep water was looming ahead. Care was called for. 'In certain circles, I suppose very few things are forbidden. Among urban intellectuals, some of the rich and worldly. Whether this is a good thing, I can't claim to judge. I gather they're pretty equal in the Soviet Union,' he concluded rather lamely, thinking of the lady stevedores and road menders he had seen in the papers and unable to summon up much enthusiasm.

Surprisingly, Thea also failed to look keen. She was obviously not much concerned about the roadmending aspect of female emancipation, Knox realized. He had a feeling that a well-established pattern in his life was repeating itself yet again. She said nothing, just stared at him with eyes that were big but far from innocent. He had to look away.

'Anyway,' he said. 'You don't seem to be having any problems pulling your weight in the group. None at all. I'm very impressed at the way you wander around and take your duties just like anyone else.'

'Why not?' Thea retorted quickly. 'There are men all around, and in any case I can defend myself.' She tapped the knife in her belt meaningfully, just in case Knox had forgotten.

'Yes. You can do that.'

'I come out here alone because I like to think, *Kapetánios*. It is impossible to think in there.'

'I agree entirely. I could say that this is no life for a woman, but that is not entirely true. It is no life for anyone.'

She smiled faintly. 'It's not so bad. Better than the oppression and fear that we left behind in the town. Life is hard, but we have the basic requirements of freedom.'

'That's important,' Knox said, feeling that he had made a blunder. He did not know her, but what he had picked up about her life during these past two years was sufficient to understand why she preferred living rough in the mountains to the dangers of the city. 'After the Liberation' George had confided to him during one reconnaissance march that Thea had been in the hands of the OVRA, the Italian equivalent of the Gestapo, as a result of political intrigues to do with her brother, and that she had suffered in some unspecified and humiliating way. Knox was surprised that she was so level and . . . well . . . emotionally normal—for it was evident that she was more than able to look at a man. If it hadn't been for that knife, of course. That was an interesting detail. He suspected that, in fact, the reason why he knew relatively little about Thea Chorakis was due more to his own reluctance than any secretiveness on the part of the guerrillas. He had not pushed, or picked up hints. What Knox found difficult was living with the reality that in occupied Europe ordinary men and women underwent experiences such as Thea had undergone every day, and were fortunate to escape with their lives as she had. Not only that, but they then continued to think, live and act in ways that put them at risk again and again, though they knew the cost only too well. The knife at this woman's belt, the controlled violence inside her that had no right to be there, all reminded Knox that he had spent his war until now in the comfortable, artificial bosom of a machine. In a while, if all went well, he would return to that machine, perhaps enjoy some leave, and even if he were then sent on to Crete, or the Pindus, or some other remote fastness where guerrilla war was being waged against the enemy, he would know that the machine was there in the background, at his call, looking after him in its heavy-handed fashion. Thea and the rest of these people had no machine, no Major Bellingham on the end of a radio link, and if they failed themselves, then they had nothing.

'Will you be glad to go back to your headquarters after your task has been completed?' she asked gently, as if she had guessed his thoughts.

'In some ways,' Knox said. 'I feel that you may be safer without us. The level of enemy activity seems to have increased since we arrived. The fascists are aware of our presence.'

'Perhaps we shall have a chance to kill some more fascists. In which case we shall have good reason to be grateful to you, *Kapetánios,* I think. The closer they come, the better. We are ready for them.'

A few minutes previously, she had been flirting, and now she was a killer. Maybe what the cynics said about the aphrodisiac qualities of violence was all too true. Knox hadn't come across women who were directly involved before. Indirectly was different: he had known of girls in Cairo who hung around the places where the cloak-and-dagger boys were known to congregate; of course they would never admit it, but everyone knew they were after the vicarious thrill, even the risk of death mixed with the sex; much as a certain kind of female before the war had been attracted to racing drivers. Only then did it really occur to him that he now came into that category, and that this might be part of the undoubted appeal he had for Thea Chorakis.

'I dare say you are,' he said. 'Ready for the fascists, I mean.'

She nodded gravely. 'And ready to help you with your task. It will be an honour. You are still awaiting orders, *Kapetánios*?'

'Yes.' On impulse he added: 'The word will come through Ioannides the shipowner.'

It was as if he had sprayed her face with dry ice. Thea's features hardened into a frigid mask. Her eyes, which had been alive with interest, changed, became hard diamonds of old hatred. She said nothing, clearly could not.

Knox lit another cigarette, partly to give her a chance to recover. He had known the guerrillas' dislike of Ioannides and had been hoping to extract a little information about it, but he had not expected quite such an extreme reaction. Nevertheless, he knew that he had to find out more, particularly after Thea had responded in this way.

'You . . . you don't like Ioannides?' he asked as matter-of-factly as he could.

Thea shook her head vigorously, half-turned away. Her hand had gone to the knife when he had mentioned the shipowner's name, and the fingers had tightened since around the pommel, until Thea's knuckles were showing white in the moonlight.

'I'm sorry, Thea. Has he done something?'

A sour laugh. 'Panayiotis will be missing me. We all have to obey orders—and ours are to help you in whatever way you ask. We must accept the friends you choose, whatever our feelings.'

'Thea—'

'Please. There is no point. I must go now. It has been good, *Kapetánios,* to talk to an interesting man. In the old days, in my father's house—he was also a lawyer, a very good one—we would receive visitors from Greece and from other parts of Europe. To talk to you and to be with you reminded me of that.'

She smiled genuinely, though the muscles around the mouth were still tight with loathing of Ioannides, and touched his arm as she walked past him towards the entrance to the cave.

'*Heréte,*' she said in the local dialect, the tongue of the quiet, patient herder of sheep on the high hills. When foreigners first learned what it meant—having heard it and seen it inscribed on gravestones—they thought its layers of significance quaint and delightful. The word, used as hail and farewell in one, had survived two thousand years of oppression, siege, and massacre, and had lived on into the twentieth century, cruellest age of all. It came from the hearts of a people who lived in a paradise and yet knew everything about suffering. In its original meaning, the dead challenged the living with the simplest, yet most elusive task: Be happy.

Knox returned the compliment. At that moment he felt that to use such expressions was tempting fate, but if a woman like Thea Chorakis could wish such a thing, who was he to deny her? Perhaps it was the British side of him that refused to accept that a human being could be at war, and suffering, and endangered, and still strive for some kind of pleasure and contentment. Yes, and it could be also that the British had had it too damned easy. They had never had to try to square that particular circle; they on their cold, comfortable fortress island far from anywhere.

26

Bredow sat with Huber and Major Falcke on the terrace of a little Italian restaurant overlooking Mandraccio Harbour, passing the afternoon over glasses of locally-brewed beer. They were the only customers at this hour; the proprietor and his plump wife were huddled in the far corner, arguing noisily about the business's accounts. The woman was accusing her husband of being too timid to collect his debts, the unpaid bills that were mounting up, she claimed, from officers of the Italian garrison. No one paid cash these days, she said: not like the fine ladies, the *beau monde* and the milords before the war, who had always settled promptly and tipped handsomely. If he did not press the officers, if need be make representations to the military authorities, they would soon be bankrupt.

'Nonsense, it goes without saying,' commented Falcke. He took his monocle out of his eye and polished it thoughtfully with a napkin. 'They are making a fortune, as everyone here knows, if only because we Germans pay cash on the nail. I suspect that she wishes to have as much ready money as possible, so that she can put it to work, maybe buy some land back in Italy. Quite rightly, she feels insecure here. A shrewd woman, if a trifle loud.'

'Deafening,' Bredow agreed.

'The war situation, from their point of view, is none too hopeful,' Falcke continued, because he liked to develop his arguments at leisure and in crushing detail. 'Invasion rumours are rife. The Greeks are becoming quietly insolent, as is their way every couple of decades when they feel the call of the motherland and see an opportunity for *enosis*. If I were a spaghetti-eater—or, for that matter, a spaghetti-cooker—settled here, I would also be trying to hedge my bets, as a matter of common prudence.'

Huber shifted uncomfortably in his wicker chair. 'Falcke, I feel that even among friends . . .'

'You think I am a defeatist?' Falcke exclaimed with mock amazement. 'No, my dear fellow: I was merely attempting to explore a civilian's thought processes, such as they are. I myself am a soldier. We do not hedge, we do not even bet; we ride in the race and take the consequences for better or worse. If the Allies come here, we shall fight. The civilians will try to run away and save their skins, as is their God-given right. Such is the way of the world.'

The one-eyed major drained his beer and bellowed for more.

'And until the fighting comes, I shall drink beer, tell jokes, and help General Drewitz to keep his sanity here in our sun-kissed temporary home. I have taken the afternoon off from the latter task. Do I have to spend it mouthing death-or-victory slogans created by Reich Minister Goebbels?'

The *padrone*'s wife waddled over with a tray of fresh drinks, which she served with a professional smile.

'It seems inconceivable that this place should ever be fought over,' Bredow said, shading his eyes to watch a tiny fishing-boat manoeuvre into the shelter of the azure harbour.

Falcke snorted his amusement. 'That's why the General is threatening to lose his sanity. The Great Visit will perhaps give us some excitement when it happens.'

Der grosse Besuch—the 'Great Visit'—had become the

accepted euphemism for the proposed meeting between the Führer and the Duce. Everyone who was in on the secret on the German side used the term. It had become like the password to an exclusive club.

Bredow lit a cigarette and said casually: 'Has the General any special plans, Falcke? Any you can repeat to an Abwehr backslider, that is.'

'He intends, of course, to do his duty. No more and no less. The SS security people will be responsible for escorting the Führer around the island. They won't allow us poor Wehrmacht tin soldiers near that aspect of the visit. We shall merely parade around for the Great Visitor's benefit, looking, we hope, both decorous and effective. Suits me.'

'And might I be permitted to observe, if only the . . . ceremonial part? I understand, of course, that the SS would probably not find my presence too welcome, but that is their problem.'

Falcke smiled slyly back at him, understanding only too well what the Oberleutnant was saying. 'Oh, I can assure you that the General will not be intimidated by the SS's objections—precisely the contrary, in fact. You are quite right to assume that, Bredow. Alpha minus for that piece of work.'

'Only Alpha minus?' queried Bredow. 'Where do I lose marks?'

'He won't let you within two hundred metres of the Great Visitor, and he'll check all your weapons first and extract any ammunition.' Suddenly Falcke's good eye was as hard and expressionless as his glass one.

'The General is a very careful man. Presumably this precaution will apply generally.'

'No,' Falcke said blandly. 'Just to Abwehr Oberleutnants who are sent on vague personal missions by Admiral Canaris. The General is very well-informed, though fortunately his loyalty to the officer corps outweighs any other considerations. Now, shall we talk about something else?'

'I think that would be wise.'

Huber, who had been glancing around the terrace like a haunted man, mopped his forehead and nodded emphatically. 'Absolutely, absolutely. I suggest that we have drunk enough beer—perhaps more than enough—and that we should see some sights. The Turkish cemetery? I believe that you have not seen the stones there, Bredow. There is an old man who served with Germans in the Turkish army before the First War. For a few lire to supplement his pension, he will translate all the inscriptions in the most delightful and amusing fashion.'

'Well, I suppose it would add much-needed light relief to my reports,' Bredow said. 'A cemetery—'

'Speaking of light relief,' Falcke butted in, 'I spot Major the Conte Pantanelli labouring up the steps towards our refuge. For those of us who are in the mood, he should provide some innocent amusement. For the rest—among whom I include myself—this may be time to discover urgent business elsewhere.'

Huber cursed softly but at some length. The aristocratic Italian Intelligence officer, dark glasses and all, was jumping up the steps from the harbour two at a time. Seeing Huber glower in his direction, Pantanelli paused and waved gaily to the Germans, who were clearly so very glad to see him.

'Should you want to know the Italian governor's plans during the Great Visit,' Falcke advised Bredow, 'all you have to do is to ask the major. Even better, wait for him to tell you, because if he knows anything he will most certainly spill it for the price of a glass of decent-quality brandy.'

'No. I have suffered from his technique before,' groaned Huber. 'He will not make it so easy for us. *He* will insist on buying the drinks.'

'On credit, it goes without saying,' Falcke chuckled.

The Italian arrived breathless, gesturing wildly to the *padrone* for drinks all round, which were produced quickly and duly put on his bill. What surprised them all was that Pantanelli did not say anything at all for a few moments after he had recovered himself, just sat with them sipping with elegant greed at his Campari. The three Germans were beginning to exchange quizzical stares when, with excellent timing, he stuck out his chin and put down his drink. His eyes blazed like those of the much-imitated Duce, Mussolini.

'My comrades-in-arms,' he said, with a catch of emotion in his voice. 'The Great Visit has been fixed. In almost exactly one week's time, the genius of the Mediterranean will meet the genius of the North on this small patch of Italian soil.'

Even Falcke's jaw dropped. 'He is coming?' was all the bald-headed major found it in himself to say. The portentous absurdity of the Italian's phrasing attracted none of Falcke's usual ridicule.

'*He* is coming, yes.'

'This is definite?'

'I was at the governor's palace fifteen minutes ago when the news was announced, to a circle of key officers, intimates . . .' Pantanelli ran the last word gleefully round his tongue, enjoying himself hugely. He had really caught the proud Germans with their red-striped pants down.

'Good God,' murmured Huber, reaching for his cap and gloves. 'We should be at Headquarters.'

Falcke was also ready. He tossed a wad of notes onto the table, got to his feet. But Pantanelli was too quick for him.

'Gentlemen, a toast! To *il Duce* and *der Führer*!'

Falcke and Huber alike hopped manically to their drinks, desperate to escape but aware that to refuse to drink to such a toast would be considered unspeakably boorish, even subversive. The beers were downed in one.

'To them both,' they croaked in unison. 'To the Axis!' Then, grabbing their caps one last, definitive time, they turned and bolted off down the steps before Pantanelli could start working his way through the entire canon of inter-allied sloganizing.

This left only Bredow. It took him a good half hour to extricate himself from the clutches of the Count, and another five minutes to get to the telephone in the lobby of the *Albergo*, where he dialled the number given to him by Stavros Ioannides for use in this precise case.

He had to wait some minutes for Ioannides to be fetched from the grounds of his villa, and when they spoke it was in halting French; to have used English, though they both spoke it fluently, would have been too dangerous. God knows, the call itself was not to be undertaken lightly.

'So soon? I am at your disposal,' Ioannides said when

Bredow delivered the pre-arranged code phrase: 'I have news of the big consignment.'

'We must meet as soon as possible to discuss the landing formalities. Come in your car and drive yourself. Be at the foot of the steps near my hotel in half an hour.'

Ioannides' voice was silky and respectful. 'Yes. I can do that.'

'Good.'

Ioannides arrived slightly early in his second car, a ten-year-old Fiat saloon. It was a small runabout, less noticeable than the open-topped Lagonda that he usually drove. The German wore slacks and a white shirt, and the casual observer might have thought he was seeing a taxi driver pick up a fare, for Bredow jumped in quickly while Ioannides kept the engine running. They set off towards the outskirts of Rhodes town at high speed, causing loud complaints from the car's tiny engine.

'You seem agitated, Oberleutnant,' Ioannides said. 'The nerves before the big event? Or you are excited?'

'Perhaps a little of each.'

They spoke in English now that they were alone. The combination of Bredow's clipped, precise tone and Ioannides' caricature of a third-rate English public school accent was so bizarre as to be hilarious, had anyone in the Fiat been in the mood for jokes. Bredow certainly was not.

'Perhaps you could drive to some place where we could talk confidentially outside the car?' he said. 'We are so cramped.'

Ioannides shrugged his powerful shoulders. He seemed very easy, considering the magnitude of what was happening. The steering wheel looked absurd in those hands of his. 'All right, old chap. You're the boss.'

A kilometre or so outside the town, Ioannides braked and pulled off the road. They bumped along a rough track that ended in a glade of Aleppo pines overlooking the sea. Ioannides stopped where the way petered out. The two men stepped out into the cool, pine-shaded air.

'So. You need my contacts, Oberleutnant,' the Greek said heavily.

'Yes. I want word got to the men in the mountains as soon as possible. The target arrives at about ten hundred hours on Wednesday, and my information is that the route to be followed has not changed.'

'The . . . men in the mountains will be pleased. I suppose I'm still to be kept in the dark about exactly who the target is?'

'Absolutely. Sorry. Even the others will not know until the very last moment. It's a question of knowledge endangering the recipient. If—heaven forbid—anything went wrong, you would be glad that you weren't told.'

Ioannides frowned, obviously offended, and lit a black tobacco cigarette. 'I am in a curious position,' he said slowly, for effect. 'I feel that my German friends don't trust me, though it was their idea, all those years ago, that I contacted the British.' He made a patently insincere gesture of resignation. 'But then, I simply do as I am told and must not question my orders. Although I sense that we are all moving out of our depth. My expenses are already very high, Oberleutnant, and the risks—'

'Once this affair has been brought to a successful conclusion, you will be welcome to discuss some extra token of our appreciation with either myself or my successor as Abwehr representative on this island. Until then, kindly concentrate on informing our men in the mountains quickly and efficiently, and afterwards getting them safely off the island. That was the bargain, and you will be well rewarded for success—if such is your primary concern, Ioannides.'

The Greek had been resting one huge hand on Bredow's arm. He understood the international language of contempt very well, however, and released him immediately.

'I thank you, Oberleutnant,' he breathed, and sounded as if he wanted to choke.

'I do not wish to be harsh on you, for you have served us very well,' Bredow said, realizing that a little massage would be in order. 'But please: we cannot discuss expenses at this point.'

'I understand.' There was still a bad catch in the man's throat. Ioannides scowled and stubbed his half-smoked cigarette viciously against a slender tree trunk.

Bredow could see that the strain was really starting to tell on the Greek. Men like Ioannides divided their hearts again and again, until eventually the self-inflicted surgery took away so much that there was nothing left to cut. Bredow had met his type before: they were the trickiest to handle, but also very useful, so long as they were given the space to fulfil both their roles. Circumstances were forcing Ioannides into a corner, where he might soon have to make choices, and like any double-agent he did not like the fact at all.

'This matter is very, very important. If it were not, we would not make such demands on you,' Bredow added for good measure.

Ioannides suddenly moved closer, the soles of his shoes rustling through the dry pine needles, and took hold of Bredow's arm once more.

'You know, Oberleutnant, if you should ever need to go somewhere safe in a hurry. Turkey, for instance—even Cyprus or Egypt . . . I can negotiate special rates . . .'

Bredow could not answer that. But he asked himself if the Greek, who heard a lot of gossip around higher circles in the town, had picked up a whiff of Hitler's visit. Whether he knew anything, or had added the clues together, it was not possible to discern. One thing was becoming increasingly clear to Bredow, however: this man already knew more than enough about *Plan Wintermärchen* for anyone's good except that of Stavros Ioannides, and Bredow felt even on their slight acquaintance that the good of Stavros Ioannides was, at the very best, a suspect quantity.

Knox and Meyerscough were playing draughts inside the main cave by the light of a mutton-fat candle when Chorakis appeared.

'*Kapetánios*!' he bellowed. 'You are wanted!' He seemed tense; a façade of commanding arrogance was his answer to situations that he feared.

'You come too,' Knox murmured to the big lieutenant. Watts was off down the mouuntainside with his Greek friends, probably looking for Italian patrols, though that was strictly against orders.

Chorakis strode ahead of them through the theatre and the tunnel and out into the open in sight of the darkening sea and the stars. There sat a very crestfallen-looking Mehmet with two armed Greeks looming over him, kept right out here as if otherwise he might pollute the partisans' dwelling. There was no sign of Thea, though she was usually quick to turn out to view any unusual sights or receive news, for life up here was tedious enough to make almost anything of interest.

'He wishes to speak to you, he says,' Chorakis declared, addressing Knox for the first time since fetching him from his draughts game. 'Urgent news.'

The Turk was nodding frantically, supporting Chorakis's statement, muttering: 'Quick! Quick!'

Knox nodded, walked over to the Turk with Meyerscough close on his heels. Mehmet said simply, in his strangled singsong: 'Target. Speak with my master. Come now. Alone.'

He added detailed conditions, to the effect that they should wear Rhodian civilian dress and that he would guide them to the house on the coast, he alone. That way they would be safer.

Knox explained to Meyerscough, who looked positively delighted. 'So Mr Smith has news, eh? Fair enough. Lead me to it.'

'We shall come. Give us ten minutes,' Knox told the Turk, who immediately got to his feet, as if showing himself ready to leave when they were. One of the Greek guards growled something at him that Knox didn't quite catch, and Mehmet caressed his twisted lip nervously with his tongue. When asked what he had said, the Greek said: 'I told him to watch out when the war is over, because someday he will have to work for his living like a Greek, not help a man like Ioannides grow rich from exploiting the poor.'

'That was all?'

The man's eyes avoided Knox's gaze. 'All, *Kapetánios*.'

Chorakis, who had been listening to their conversation with Mehmet, had already ordered clothes to be provided for the Englishmen. Thea finally put in an appearance a few minutes later, carrying two bundles. She looked at Knox with steady, cold eyes, but she did not at any time so much as glance at Mehmet.

They simply put the clothes on over their service underwear. Knox looked at Mehmet, who was waiting where the path began twenty or so yards from them, and then at Chorakis. 'No one seems very tolerant of the poor benighted Turk,' he said.

'On the contrary,' Chorakis insisted. 'We are very long-suffering of him and his master. We put the cause of the anti-fascist struggle before private grievances.'

'Look, Panayiotis, the man is neither particularly attractive nor, I'm sure, very virtuous, but—'

'There are reasons from when we lived in the town. Not simply political. But for the moment we must work with him.'

'Well, we're under very clear instructions to do so, by people who ought to know. So we'll do exactly as he said.'

'As the *Kapetánios* wishes.'

They were unable to find a pair of trousers long enough for Meyerscough, and so he just wore his battle-dress trousers with a shabby, long jacket and a woollen cap to conceal his fair hair. Knox, on the other hand, dressed in a shirt and trousers belonging to Chorakis himself, looked almost startling authentic. 'My goodness,' commented Meyerscough. 'Don't go and get mixed up in a crowd, or I shan't be able to tell you from the rest of the peasantry.'

After that, they wasted no time. The grotesque little Turk smiled with gratitude when they indicated their readiness to leave. He moved off down the goat track wordlessly. Chorakis, who had produced his Biretta machine-pistol and had been making a great play of cleaning it while they put on their disguises, saluted with heavy solemnity and then went back to his work.

It was some four miles from the cave to the coast. They seemed to be going down most of the way, part of the time along paths that seemed familiar from their first climb into the mountains almost two weeks previously. Then they went off at a tangent, so far as they could tell to the south-west, along a meandering ravine for half a mile or so. Mehmet walked tirelessly and in silence, his sole acknowledgment of their presence an occasional glance over his shoulder to check that they had not fallen too far behind. Luckily for the two Englishmen, it was a bright night, cool and clear, and the path was fairly easy to follow. When they made their first brief halt, after an hour of walking, they were standing above a meadow, a huge bowl of coarse green grass that seemed to pitch headlong to the dark, silver-flecked sea.

'*Kondá. Kondá,*' he repeated, pointing with a sweep of one hand to their right. *'Plátanos.'*

'What on earth's the blighter saying?' asked Meyerscough. 'I've picked up a bit here and there, but that lip of his makes it ten times as hard to understand him.'

Knox watched the direction of the Turk's gesturing.

'He says "near". Then something about a plane tree or trees. Either it might be the name of the house, or he's talking about a copse a mile or so away. I can't see any sign of a house, so I suppose it might be tucked away down there in the trees.'

'Same place we were at before?'

'Could be. We might be approaching it from a different direction. Mehmet didn't say. Hardly seems important, anyway.'

'I suppose not.'

Mehmet seemed to be listening intently, with his head cocked at one side. At first Knox thought he was trying to make sense of the Englishmen's conversation, but when he twisted round and stared up the path behind them, he realized the Turk was checking their way with the only sense that was truly reliable at night. Finally Mehmet shrugged, waved his arm down the hillside to the right. They set off obediently down the grass slope, braking with their heels on the stony pastureland.

They came across the house quite suddenly, shortly after entering the copse. First Knox glimpsed a white chink of light, and then he saw the corner of a white-washed stone structure jutting out from the hillside. The building was the same one they had spent the night in after they had arrived on Rhodes, but somehow the night and the descent made it feel very different. They followed the path, which took them round the back; the chink of light disappeared as unexpectedly as it had first come, and the house seemed to be in complete darkness. Mehmet led them down the twisting, rough-cut steps, making his own strange clicking and hissing noises that were almost like a song of relief at their safe arrival.

'Wait,' he mouthed when they reached the rear courtyard. There was the low rear door straight ahead, which he strutted up to, very conscious of his own importance as their guide and guardian, and struck with the flat of his hand, just once. A few seconds passed before the door opened. Mehmet turned and nodded to the Englishmen.

Both Knox and Meyerscough had to duck to negotiate the doorway. They found themselves in a bare, white-washed scullery, and if they had expected Ioannides to be waiting for them in there, they were disappointed. Knox assumed it must have been Marcos who had opened up for them until he heard a rustling sound. By the light of the single oil lamp that lit this part of the house, he saw what looked like a slim, long-haired version of the boy slipping through a door to their left. Of course. Marcos's sister. Ioannides had brought female company on this trip, perhaps to while away the time of waiting.

'I say. What was that?' Meyerscough whispered.

Knox thought it wise not to reply. The absurd melodrama was becoming oppressive as well as faintly ludicrous. On cue, another door opened at the end of the corridor that ran along the right-hand wall, and a light so bright that it blinded poured into the scullery. Mehmet stepped back a pace and grabbed Knox's arm to push him towards the open door and the light.

'Do come in,' Ioannides' voice boomed. 'I'm sorry about the procedures, but one really can't be too careful.'

Knox waited until his eyes had adjusted to the conditions, then walked along and through the doorway. Ioannides was standing in the middle of the square little living room of the house, which was lit by a dozen or so oil lamps. He extended one hand and he shook formally with the two officers before offering them a seat on one of his cane chairs and moving into an alcove in the corner, where he had placed a bottle of *ouzo* and some glasses.

'No Sergeant Watts,' he commented, indicating that he had provided a glass for the NCO. 'Everything all right, I trust?'

'Fine. He happened to be out taking the air when Mehmet came. Since his presence was not strictly necessary, we didn't wait for him. Mehmet seemed to think that speed was of the essence.'

Ioannides handed out large tumblers of the fiery aniseed

drink, nodding vigorously. 'Quite right. The time has been set for your target's arrival on Rhodes. The sooner you were informed, the better.'

Both of them had gathered that something of the sort was coming, but all the same there was a joint intake of breath. Meyerscough gulped down his *ouzo* and smiled broadly.

'Yes,' Knox said. 'You were right. When's that date?'

'Wednesday. Ten-hundred hours, as the navy boys say, I believe. At the airfield. All is as you were taught, or so my source tells me.'

'I see. I say, are we entitled to know who your source is?'

'Please.' Ioannides spread his hands and smiled painfully. 'Let us describe him as an influential Axis officer who is in my debt.'

'All right.'

'It is one reason why I am forced to communicate with Chorakis and his men through Mehmet, a characterless servant. In order to gain the confidence of such individuals as the officer I mentioned, I have to pretend to be hundred-percent collaborator. If the occupying authorities suspected that I was anything else, well—' Ioannides rolled his eyes comically and made as if being shot.

'I understand that. I sometimes wonder if our other hosts do, though.' The words were out before Knox had time to consider. Ioannides had a certain talent for encouraging one to say things that would be best left unsaid. A professional skill.

In response, a shadow flitted across Ioannides' well-preserved face. It co-existed for an instant with a broad, Cheshire cat smile, then was banished as if by an effort of will.

'Captain,' he said with a sigh. 'Chorakis is a Rhodian. The islanders are delightful people, loyal and brave and basically very decent. But at heart they remain Byzantine peasants, creations of a thousand years of subjugation and poverty. If anything goes wrong in their personal or communal life, they blame a higher power. An ignorant shepherd will see the hand of the devil, or some malevolent *kauos*. Chorakis, being something of an educated man and interested in politics, imagines that all evil comes from prosperous, well-connected men—and he fondly imagines me to be both.' Ioannides paused to sip his *ouzo*, then asked with an ironical raising of the eyebrows: 'Does he have any particular . . . the phrase, I believe, is "bee in his hat"?'

'Bonnet,' Knox corrected him, wishing fervently that he hadn't opened his mouth in the first place. 'I can't really say, anyway. Just a general resentment as far as I know.'

'Ah.' Ioannides' breathy exclamation was finally judged to express dismissal, pity and contempt all in one. In this part of the world, a whole vocabulary could be contained in a sigh, a grunt, a heave of the shoulders.

Meyerscough, who had been letting Knox do the talking when it came to the practical issues, suddenly showed an interest. 'It's nothing more than envy,' he declared, reverting to the political framework of the Norfolk squire that he was. 'We have the same problems with such types in England.'

'Perhaps a similarity or two,' Ioannides answered, warming to his theme. 'But we Greeks take such matters a lot more seriously than you British. We accuse each other of the most frightful things, worse than any crimes we would credit to the enemy. When Rhodes—and Greece—are cleared of the foreign oppressors, we shall have to face that problem, perhaps as adversaries . . . but in any case, I am sure that good sense will prevail over anarchy. We are relying on your government's support at the time of the crunch . . .'

'First we have a war to win, I think, Mr Ioannides,' Knox interrupted successfully, and felt very pleased with himself.

'Of course.' The answer came back pat but somehow without meaning. Ioannides glanced at the gold watch strapped to his thick wrist. 'And this is why we are here, discussing such matters as the arrival of this person on the island next week. It is a very closely-guarded secret, you know. Even my source, who is usually "in the know", has not managed to find out the identity of the visitor. This leads me to believe that he must be a very important individual, for such security arrangements to be enforced. But then, your superiors know . . .'

'They must do, or they wouldn't have bothered with all

this. But they haven't told us, for the same sort of security reasons. And fair enough. Doesn't really make much practical difference, does it, considering the method of dispatching him that's to be used?'

'You are right, naturally. And now, is there anything you gentlemen need, or have you everything you require?'

'We're fine. We know where and when, and that's what matters. So far as you're concerned, Mr Ioannides, all we ask you to do is to get us off the island afterwards.'

'To which end, captain, you will come to this house as quickly as possible—one of Chorakis's band will guide you, I will allow that under the circumstances. Then you can leave the rest to me. I know how to move cargo around the Eastern Aegean without the authorities' knowledge, believe me.' Ioannides chuckled with deep self-satisfaction. 'And now another drink? I intend to stay the night here, for the Italian curfew will be in force on the road. If you wished, I could let you each have a bed . . .'

'No, thanks. We promised Chorakis that we would be back tonight. He would worry if we didn't return. More work for that chap of yours, I'm afraid.'

'But you will have one more drink, at least?' Ioannides asked, ignoring the reference to Mehmet.

'A quick one.'

They talked for another five minutes or so over a fresh glass of *ouzo,* until Knox decided that custom had been respected. Ioannides clearly had some unfinished business—perhaps with the long-haired 'boy'. He felt a momentary sense of distaste at the thought, but quickly suppressed it. None of his business. *Don't get involved.*

'Well, we must be going,' he said. 'It's a long march.'

'Oh, must you?' Ioannides said politely, draining his glass. 'But you have much to plan, to discuss, and a lot of work to do between now and X-Day. Good luck!'

'Thanks.'

'Very much,' added Meyerscough.

'I shall send Mehmet if there are any alterations in the schedule, by the way. If possible, I shall give him a brief message. We do not want to drag you up and down the mountains like this every time I have something to communicate.'

'I should say we don't.'

The Turk appeared. They shook hands yet again, and then he led them off through the back door and into the darkness.

Mehmet did not speak at all during the return journey. They climbed for what seemed like a short eternity, with the Turk stopping from time to time, more frequently than on the way to the house, to feel the air. He seemed not entirely content, but he continued to lead them as quickly as they could manage. The terrain became scrub, then mostly bare rock, and then they recognized the approaches to Chorakis's hideout. It was after two a.m., and the walk had taken them a round hundred and twenty minutes. And suddenly there was Chorakis and Christos, sitting on rocks by the side of the path with their weapons. Mehmet froze.

'Usual drama,' Meyerscough said. 'You'd think they could just meet us at the door like normal human beings.'

'Panayiotis!' Knox said, raising one hand in greeting. 'A welcome!'

Chorakis did not move, just stared at the Turk. 'Tell Mehmet he can go.'

Not that Mehmet needed asking. With a whistled farewell to the two Englishmen, his bony figure disappeared like a hunted animal off down the path.

Knox frowned. 'There was no need for you to come out and meet us like this,' he said to Chorakis. 'Mehmet was doing his job very well.'

'I did not come out to meet you, *Kapetánios*. We followed you all the way down and back, in case you met trouble on the path.'

'Now that was extremely good of you,' Knox said patiently. 'But, as I said, quite unnecessary. Whatever you may think of Ioannides, he has no interest in handing us over to the enemy or harming us in any way. He had vital information for us, in fact, for which he had already risked a great deal.'

Chorakis and Christos exchanged knowing glances.

'Look, can't you chaps discuss this back at the cave?' Meyerscough complained. 'I'd like to get some sleep. I don't mind telling you.'

He began to move off up the slope towards home. Chorakis made no effort to stop him, but when Knox tried to follow he put out a restraining hand.

'*Kapetánios,*' he hissed. 'Listen. There is something you should know, that we learned while we were waiting for you at Ioannides' house.' He paused. 'Someone else was present, without your knowledge.'

'I saw a young girl. I did not approve, but I thought it no concern of mine.'

Chorakis spat contemptuously onto the rock in front of him. 'She was his whore. He collects such women and discards them at will. I speak of another man, who was standing in the shadow of the far courtyard by a window, listening and waiting.'

'Who was that? Another employee of his?' Knox asked with growing exasperation.

'No, *Kapetánios,*' Chorakis said, drawing out the drama, savouring the moment of his supreme justification. 'He was an officer in a smart uniform. A German officer.'

27

Sir Stewart Menzies had not moved from the window of the third-floor flat since before first light, though the room was cold, with the chilling dampness that came at the end of an English night. Grainger had insisted on providing a high-backed chair for Menzies' use, but to take one's ease seemed indecent, unsporting, reminiscent of a party of Regency rakes gawping at a public hanging. Menzies stood with his hands clasped behind his back, erect and military in his dark coat and loosened scarf, and stared fixedly down over the waste ground next to the café three hundred yards away. Occasionally he would shiver. No one had thought to make up the fire.

'We snapped this place up in November, sir. Right at the start of the job,' Grainger explained. He had been chainsmoking as they waited for dawn. 'Slight strain on the departmental budget and all that, but worth it,' he added with a self-conscious chuckle. 'When you need to move at twenty-four hours' notice, as we've had to here, you're grateful to have everything already set up. As you can see, perfect view of everything, including the rear of the establishment, in case something went wrong and the subject decided to nip out through the tradesmen's entrance.'

Still with his eyes on the suburban sunrise, Menzies acknowledged the man's self-regarding patter with a cursory nod. Grainger mumbled something about 'more char' and went out into the kitchen, where it was warmer. Some half a mile north of the low, modern block where they were camped, the open fields of Hertfordshire began. Rows of sturdy, mock-Tudor semi-detached houses with pallet fencing marking off their tidy gardens stretched beyond the café to the rim of the city, where they stopped abruptly, like an army forced by exhaustion to rest, leaving the broad trunk road to carry the mission of concrete and tarmac into the rural unknown. Here lay the mediocre but hearteningly solid breeding-warren of lower middle class England sprawled out before him in the rosy monotone of dawn. Grainger probably felt at home. Menzies most assuredly did not.

'Be so kind as to leave the door open for a moment, there's a good chap,' he said. The room was filthy with cigarette smoke. 'Let in some air.'

'Righty-ho, sir.' Grainger prised the door open with his heel, then clumped over and set down the tea things with a clash of crockery on the table in the middle of the room.

Menzies eyed him expectantly. 'Well, how much longer?' he demanded.

'Another ten minutes or so, sir. It's just coming up to a quarter to six. He's usually extremely punctual.' Grainger was noisily setting out cups and saucers, diligent as a parlour maid, though a good deal clumsier. 'Would you care. . . ?'

'No. Not at the moment, thank you, Grainger. But do have some yourself, by all means,' Menzies murmured, returning to his cold vigil.

'C' thought about the man who was about to walk down this suburban road outside his window. There was an unspoken prayer that it would all go well at this end, for everything depended on success, and there was still the slight worry of the courier, the man they had captured and injured by accident, turned and then reconstructed like a Frankenstein's monster. If he did his job and none of his former colleagues smelled a rat, then this aspect of SIGNIFY was complete, but the courier was an imponderable, nevertheless . . . Under the circumstances, it had been advisable to tighten up on Rhodes. *Dancer*, the venal brute, had insisted on hugely increased expenses as the price of his undivided loyalty to Menzies, but 'C' had paid up willingly, for he needed to be as certain of his man as he could be, to know that his orders would outweigh any others. Just in case. In return, to give him due credit, *Dancer* had informed him promptly of Hitler's projected arrival date, giving Menzies six days to handle things here—not as long as he would have wished, but more time than he had feared he might be granted if the Germans had kept things under wraps until the very last moment. Once this business here had worked its way through the system, the main task for *Dancer* was to prove his dearly-bought loyalty by spiriting those three Army chaps off the island. Then SIS experts could debrief them in some carefully sanitized place where no one else could get at them, if necessary taking a hell of a long time to do so. Menzies' conscience had not, so far, allowed him to consider his share of the responsibility if by any chance *Dancer* didn't manage to evacuate the commando team before the storm swept them all away. That was an aspect that he had considered in theory a matter of months ago at the planning stage and had refused to look at since. The important thing was that SIGNIFY would succeed so long as this courier got through and the message went along the chain to the SD in Berlin to Brigadeführer Walter Schellenberg. All other considerations were luxuries of the individual, considering the scale of the project.

Grainger appeared at Menzies' elbow to interrupt his thoughts, squinting professionally in the direction of the parking area and still swigging his liquid breakfast.

'Four minutes,' he declared. 'If the underground's running on time. First train up here. In and out of the greasy spoon like a whirlwind.'

'I assume that Finch is also on his way.'

Grainger nodded. 'Daniels was on the blower a little while ago, chief. Confirmed that he let them out by the east gate at five-oh-three. We've parked his lorry ready for him in its usual spot, with a couple of reliable chaps already set up in the back to keep an eye on him during the solo drive. Been there all night, in fact,' he said with a grin. 'I should imagine they're thoroughly brassed off by now.'

To his left, south-east of their observation point, where the underground crossed the last bridge before the end of the line, Menzies noticed metallic, bright red movement on the line.

Grainger had seen the train too. He leaned forward onto the window sill and peered out, checking that everyone was in position, from the two regulars in workmen's clothes to their backup, apparently asleep in the cab of his lorry, the two lookouts crouched on the roof of the parade of shops on the way from the station, and the one more lounging near a bus-stop, reading a newspaper.

'We're ready when he is,' said Grainger laconically. A terse, professional persona had taken over.

Menzies nodded. He felt a relentless, private tightening in the gut that he had not experienced so strongly for a good twenty years, since he had last officiated at a full-dress field occasion such as this. Silly, of course, because it was all a charade—they were not going to arrest anyone or commit any violence or mayhem. The support groups had been put there chiefly to cover the courier, Finch. It was an act of vanity—or perhaps insecurity—on Menzies' part to have come here at all, but he would not have missed it for a dukedom. The climax of his part, the controllable part, of SIGNIFY.

The physical tightness lasted until Menzies saw *Turquoise*: a youngish man of medium height and build, dressed in a raincoat, trilby hat and striped scarf, carrying a briefcase. Ordinary-looking in the extreme, like any good spy. He was still a couple of minutes' walk from the café, approaching along the pavement in unhurried fashion, swinging the case gently as he strode past the sparsely-budded municipal trees set among the paving stones. When he came closer, the face looked early-morning haggard, no different to a million others that would stare indifferently at the morning on their way to work that day, except that in its way the face was both hard and rather dissolute. Such was the man. Menzies knew him well by now.

'He'll light up before he goes in. That's his routine. Calm his dear little collywobbles,' Granger murmured, piercing the hush that had fallen over the room. 'There . . .'

Turquoise stopped at the edge of the pavement, where it broke to provide the car park's entrance, put his case on the ground, and took out a packet of cigarettes. He extracted one and lit it with a lighter that glinted momentarily like a jewel in the pale sunshine. Then he strolled rather than walked towards the café door with the cigarette hanging out of the corner of his mouth like a Parisian *apache*, every inch a cocky bohemian.

The wait until he re-emerged some minutes later had its own quality of tension, but slowly everything seemed, for Menzies, to be dipping towards anti-climax. *Turquoise* came out of the café, buttoned his raincoat, put on his hat, sauntered back across the rough ground to the main road. Nothing about him seemed to have changed; he had even lit another cigarette.

'I think I shall have a cup of tea now,' Menzies said slowly. He watched the raincoated figure growing smaller again, making its way back to the station. 'I suppose we're in for another bit of a wait,' he added. 'Until our courier comes to pick it up.'

'About half an hour,' Grainger confirmed. He handed 'C' a cup like a relative comforting a widow, concerned but determinedly cheerful. 'Then, say, twenty-five minutes to the drop, and another half an hour or so until the villains come and pick it up. That's when we'll be able to relax.'

The tea was luke-warm now, but Menzies sipped it gratefully. The sun had climbed above the rooftops during the past few minutes: there was slightly more traffic on the road and on the pavement. An old lady walked a spaniel dog, which stopped to defecate by the bus stop where Grainger's man continued to wait with his much-read newspaper. Occasional early commuters hurried towards the underground, the system that had already swallowed *Turquoise* to carry him back to the city's congested heart. Menzies studied each movement, every traveller and stroller. It helped to keep at bay the slow, irrational sinking feeling, the premature *triste*.

At twenty-eight minutes past six, the lorry turned into

the café car park, bumped gently across the uneven surface and stopped at a spot that shortened the walk needed to reach the door. The driver sat for a moment in his cab—a very long moment, it seemed to Menzies, who could see only the rear bumper and the hunched back of the vehicle. When he swung himself down, it was with surprising gracefulness, though the limp was obvious and pronounced as soon as he began to make his way to the café. The bullet wound in his thigh was not yet completely healed, and for today he was fitted with a flexible elastic bandage, so that there would be no restriction of movement. The rest had been taken care of with a pain-killing injection, administered shortly before they left the country house prison. The driver's face showed no emotion, but then it never had, much.

'We've briefed him and rehearsed him until we're blue in the face,' Grainger said, as if to himself. 'He'll go through the entire routine, in case they have someone inside. We told him to do exactly the same as he always did, and our chaps in there know what it is. He's aware that he'll be under observation for every second, even in the . . . the outhouse . . .'

'Do you think the other side might have someone actually watching him?' Menzies asked.

'I doubt it, sir. They're probably even more short-staffed than we are. I suppose they might occasionally drop someone by to make sure, a sort of random quality control, but then they haven't had any cause to worry about his efficiency so far. Mind you, if anyone in there does look like one of them, it's a bit ominous, goes without saying. Means they might have smelt a rat.'

Grainger sounded cool, confident. He knew his job, whatever else might be said about him.

'Absolutely,' Menzies agreed. They had discussed that aspect in the planning stage, and hence the care taken to assemble the support group and the almost choreographic precision of the orders covering their dispersal afterwards, which was to be achieved casually and naturally. And still all one could do was wait and trust.

By the time it was Finch's turn to emerge from the café, Grainger had smoked his way through two more cigarettes and was puffing nervously on a third. Finch stepped down onto the cinders of the car park, hands in his pockets, and seemed about to make straight for his lorry when suddenly he stood quite still and stared straight ahead with a kind of dazed intensity. Menzies felt his stomach tighten again: what had attracted the man's attention, for goodness' sake? Grainger leaned forward and frowned, worrying at his moustache with his lower lip. It took a little while before they realized that Finch was not looking directly at anything particular; he had simply taken a last opportunity to experience freedom, even a counterfeit, temporary freedom. No one could make him move from that spot without making an unwelcome scene, and he knew it.

'Come on, man,' Menzies muttered.

Grainger shook his head in wonder. 'Bless him,' he said incongruously.

Finch stood there for a couple of minutes, drinking in the sunrise, defiantly gazing to his left and right, as if he intended to miss nothing. Then, just as unexpectedly as he had stopped, he heaved his broad shoulders in a faint shrug and hobbled towards the lorry, his eyes cast down among the cinders. The lorry started first time.

The first telephone call came shortly after Finch had driven away. The men placed in the café reported to Grainger that, so far as they could tell, there had been no one else watching the driver.

There was a twenty-minute wait until the second call came. The drop had been made, without incident and apparently unobserved by anyone else.

The third, the crucial call, was received after a further thirty minutes, and Menzies insisted on answering it personally. A voice wearied by long hours spent watching and waiting informed him that the 'usual villain' had collected the package from the safe house in Bedford. Everything had gone like clockwork. Finch had behaved beautifully throughout. He was now on his way back to the country house, where he would be held pending Menzies' instructions.

'We shall have to think about what to do with him next. I'll inform Captain Grainger accordingly. Fine job. No, just keep him under lock and key and treat him well,' Menzies said, becoming uncharacteristically garrulous in his excitement and relief. 'A fine, fine job you've done.'

He put down the telephone. Grainger smiled toothily

and offered Menzies his hand. 'I knew it would be all right, sir,' he said. 'I knew it would work out in the end.'

Menzies nodded. The two men shook on their success. 'Well . . .' 'C' said then. 'All I really need you to do is to hang on to Finch for a while, until we decide on ways and means of dealing with him. The other business . . . I mean, the final reckoning with the other chap who was at the café this morning . . . will be handled through higher channels. These matters are always delicate—you know, when they involve a member of the Service. All right?'

'Absolutely. Righty-ho, sir. Understood. If you should need us, though, all you have to do is holler. We've enjoyed being of service.'

Menzies winced inwardly at Grainger's choice of words, but he recognized the man's sincere devotion. 'I'll always bear you in mind from now on—and I think your departmental budget will reflect the fact,' he said. 'And now I'll be off back to my flat for some sleep,' he added cheerfully. 'I have a lot of tidying-up to do over the next few days. Loose ends and all that.'

Grainger beamed, happy as Larry. Of course, he didn't know the half of it. To him, SIGNIFY was about catching a spy or two, pure and simply. Just as to Jackie Bellingham it was principally about a commando raid, a radio game, and an assassination. Within a few days, as the plan progressed, each would be given reason to believe that SIGNIFY was concluded one way or the other, crowned with obvious success or failure, depending on one's point of view, or individual optical illusion. Only Menzies—and his Prime Minister—knew that SIGNIFY had merely completed its long, tortuous opening phase. And that the first priority of that phase was to keep the agent *Turquoise* not behind bars but firmly and unquestionably operational, whatever the cost.

28

As X-Day came closer, the fact of Ioannides' duplicity loomed larger. In the immediate aftermath of their visit to the house on the coast, there had been room for discussion about what to do, how far Ioannides might be prepared to go, for, after all, he hadn't actually turned them in to the Nazis when he had the chance. Then they had radioed Bellingham, breaking away from the ironcast format of the regular transmissions for the first time. He had responded at first with dismissive incredulity, then with a clear order for them to continue to obey Ioannides' instructions unconditionally. Just like that. Stone wall.

'I don't know what the hell's going on, but what choice have we got, for goodness' sake?' Meyerscough argued. 'Maybe Chorakis was mistaken, maybe Ioannides was playing some game . . .' His honest face creased in a sad frown. 'Knox, let's hear what you think again.'

They were sitting on some rocks under the shade of an overhand, for it was mid-afternoon and still broiling. Meyerscough had forgotten to shave, Knox felt that he had forgotten how to think. Watts just carried on checking the fuse and detonation equipment that he had laid out on a flat stone nearby and listened to the officers' argument with a kind of bland amazement that he had learned in the army, speaking only when he was spoken to directly by one of them and expressing no opinions about Ioannides or the famous German officer.

'The question is, why hasn't he turned us in if he's in cahoots with the enemy? They don't need to catch us red-handed, and there's little we know that they wouldn't already know if they've got Ioannides on tap.'

'Honestly, Knox. I ask for answers, and all you do is ask more bloody questions. I suppose that's a trick they taught you at the University. If so, it's not appropriate here, my good man. We need ideas and decisions.'

Knox lit a cigarette from the stub of its predecessor, realized vaguely that this must be his fifteenth or sixteenth of the day. 'All right,' he said. 'Point one: Chorakis tells us he saw a German officer listening in while we were chewing the fat with Ioannides about our target. Point two: We inform Major Bellingham of this fact, and he insists that the good gent is still just about their most trusted agent in this neck of the woods, bar none, to be trusted with the last of the family jewels, et cetera . . .'

'Though not with your sister's virginity, judging from what our chum Chorakis also told us!'

'No, definitely not that,' Knox sighed.

They knew now why Chorakis and his sister both hated Ioannides with such intensity. Thea had been detained by the OVRA the previous summer on information supplied by an unknown traitor—shortly after having refused the persistent sexual advances of one Stavros Ioannides, womanizer, ship-owner, and friend of the Italian authorities. The fascist secret police had given her a very bad time—Chorakis had not gone into details—but then had let her go, perhaps because they possessed some lingering sense of shame, but perhaps also because they hoped that if they kept her under observation in the town, then her rebel brother, Panayiotis, could be lured down from the mountains and arrested. She had given her watchdogs the slip, with the aid of some comrades, and fled to join the partisans, thus ensuring that the OVRA would have no opportunity to play at cat and mouse with the surviving members of the troublesome Chorakis clan.

'Well?' Meyerscough's abrasiveness was born of fear.

'Ioannides is an unsavoury character. We told Major Bellingham, and he continued to say: do what the blighter tells you, all will be revealed when we're back in Lebanon and guzzling Black Label in the Monastery Garden.'

'And without someone—Ioannides or another individual nominated by "IFCU", we don't get off the island, whatever we do. Checkmate. Trust him or stay here.'

Knox nodded. 'There you have it. I'm stuck. I dislike Ioannides as a man. I don't care much for his politics, or at least what I know of them; and if I were negotiating for a crate of oranges or my sister's virtue, I'd not give him an inch. The funny thing is, I'm inclined to feel he's not actually going to betray us into the enemy's hands—God, if it wasn't for Chorakis's tale about that bloody German—'

'So. We've got clear orders from our immediate superior, plus what your instincts tell you, Knox,' Meyerscough said deliberately. His slightly puffy, torid features seemed to sag a little further into his skull, as if the worry was physically draining him. 'Against those considerations we can set a Greek's vision of a Nazi in the shadows a couple of hundred yards from where he was watch ing. The moon had gone behind the clouds by that time, remember, and—I hate to mention the fact—Chorakis and his lads had been hitting the *retsina* just a bit at suppertime.' He shrugged. 'Know what I'm inclined to think?'

'Yes. You think we should go ahead and trust to providence, Major Bellingham, and the potency of Sar'nt Watts' plastic charges. Not forgetting Ioannides' and Co's trusty ferry service to Cyprus.'

'Bellingham told us Ioannides has got people out before, sometimes from very tight holes. Says his status as a so-called collaborator makes it possible for him to do these things. But, given the kind of chap he is, the likes of Chorakis aren't going to lose an opportunity to do him down, are they?'

Knox grimaced with the frustration of it. Everything Meyerscough said made sense, so far as it went. On the other hand, he didn't believe that Panayiotis Chorakis had been drunk or just plain mistaken when he had seen the German at Ioannides' house. He was beginning to suspect that the problem lay not so much in the events themselves but in his incomplete understanding of the context, the larger framework that was so infuriatingly hard to grasp. In short, there was a missing link somewhere, and he must be quite close to it. Bellingham, for instance, had to know a thing or two, or he wouldn't be so insistent in his orders to them to stay put and trust Ioannides. And what was it that the major had muttered back at the villa in his cups, the reference to 'the other side'? Suddenly Knox was feeling a glimmer of sense, and he had to share it with Meyerscough, however disjointed and far-fetched he might sound.

'What if . . .' he said tentatively. 'I mean, have you considered that this German—if that is what he really was—might actually approve of what we're doing, and that's why he's not interested in having us shot?' Knox laughed out loud, thrilled by the audacity and clarity of his own statement.

'Eh? He wants us to bump off one of his own bigwigs? Really, Knox! I know the enemy are a Macchiavellian crowd—the great rogue was a wop, wasn't he?—but I'm unconvinced that they'd go that far.'

'Why not?' Knox seized his arm. 'It's been known among gangsters, which is what these chaps are, more or less. Imagine: they find out we're coming here to kill—

Herr X, let's call him. They think: that might not be such a bad thing politically for us. So they do everything they can to smooth our path. In return, they get their Herr X out of the way, we British can be blamed, and they're completely in the clear. Ioannides may have realized this and is using the fact to give us extra security; he's probably arranged it with "IFCU" months before we arrived but didn't want us to know for fear we might get the wind up—which is, of course, what's happened.'

He sat back in triumph, beaming at Meyerscough. Meyerscough looked blank for a moment, then shook his head.

'Look, I don't care how you come to the conclusion,' he said coolly. Meyerscough had learned a lot in these few weeks. He was starting to grow up, too, and in a way it was a pity. 'The question, Knox, is: do we obey orders to go ahead, remembering that our superiors have instructed us to do so in full knowledge of the local circumstances? I'm for it personally, whether or not your little tale there holds water.'

'Then, yes.' Knox turned to the sergeant, feeling slightly chastened. 'Watts? Any objections?'

The sergeant looked up from his labours. His weather-beaten face expressed very little. He had been systematically lengthening all the SOE issue fuses on his charges. He claimed that these fuses had killed more of the saboteurs sent into occupied Europe than all the Nazi secret policemen put together. 'Take the SOE fuse allowance, add a couple of inches, light it and then run like hell,' he had told the officers in his usual casual, laconic way.

'We can press on,' he said to them now. 'It's all right with me, sir. Strikes me we're buggered if we do, buggered if we don't, so we might as well have a go at achieving what we came here for.'

'Well said. Then that's it.' Knox turned to Meyerscough with a crooked smile, began fiddling in his pockets for another cigarette, realized that he had smoked the darned lot. Watts promptly came up with one of his extra strength Capstans, one of a small horde that he had been trying to preserve since they had arrived. His swift offer of one to Knox was recognition that a crisis moment had been successfully negotiated.

He agreed that he would go and tell Chorakis. The Greeks would have to be given the option whether or not to continue to support and aid the British under the circumstances. He found the partisan leader sitting in the main cave, reading by the light of a tallow candle. Knox greeted him noisily from the far side to give him fair warning, then realized that Thea was asleep by her brother's side, taking an afternoon siesta, and regretted his haste. To tell the truth, he had been avoiding the girl for the past couple of days. She represented all the things Knox did not want to face, in light of the quite separate decision that he had to make about the fate of the commando party. Now he was trapped. There was no way out.

Luckily, Thea did not stir. Chorakis got to his feet, stood with his hands on his hips and watched Knox's approach with a level dignity. The partisan leader had read the signs; he knew the weight of the conversation that was about to take place between the two of them.

'*Kapetánios*, it is good that you seek me out,' Chorakis said, extending a hand in welcome. 'We have not talked together for some time. It is necessary that we do so, I think.'

'Yes. Decisions to be made.'

'In war there are many decisions. Life cannot be allowed to simply drift by us. That is a luxury for the civilian, eh?'

Chorakis was still keeping hold of Knox's hand. He had left his palm resting gently there, as if wanting to feel what the Captain said and felt in his fingertips.

Knox did not try to disentangle himself. It was neither wise nor necessary. Instead, he placed his own left hand on top of Chorakis's.

'Comrade Chorakis, we are going to carry out the task we came to perform,' he said. 'Our superiors have ordered us to continue, and we feel in our hearts that we must, despite all the doubt and confusion that the events of the past few days have created. The question is,' he added slowly, looking the Greek firmly in the eye, 'whether we can ask you and your brave friends to risk themselves with us. We must leave that decision to you, and we shall understand completely if you feel that you cannot. You have already done so much for us, faced so much danger for our sake.'

Chorakis's gaze was friendly but shrewd. 'Many aspects of what has happened are hard to explain,' he said. 'If, for example, Ioannides had wanted to have you killed, or had been prepared to betray our hiding place, then he could have arranged both things. You could have been ambushed on the night that you and the Lieutenant visited him, supposedly alone. But nothing happened. There was, I think, just one German, and he simply watched and listened.'

'We also asked ourselves that same question and arrived at the same conclusion, Comrade Chorakis.'

'One moment, *Kapetánios*. The truth is that I still do not trust Ioannides,' Chorakis said. 'There is always the possibility that he is biding his time and will betray us all when it suits him. But his treachery is no simple thing, that much is clear to me. What I really wish to know, *Kapetánios* my friend, is whether you are being completely honest with us.'

Here we go, thought Knox. *This is it.* Out loud he said: 'I am being absolutely honest with you when I say that I do not understand the full meaning of what has happened, any more than you do. All I can do is obey orders and trust, for the moment. I and my comrades are totally dependent on the people who sent us here. Unless some really immediate danger presents itself, we can only do as they say, in the assumption that they have full knowledge of the overall picture. The rest, these things of which you have spoken, are mysterious to me, as they are to you.'

Chorakis did not react for a moment. Then he gently curled his fingers turning the pressure to a slow handshake.

'I believe you,' he murmured. 'Now I must speak with my men. I cannot commit myself to anything without consulting them.'

He looked down at Thea, who seemed still to be sleeping, then back at Knox.

'Some of them will not be back for an hour or two, *Kapetánios*. I must ask you to wait until then. Now, please excuse me: I shall walk and think everything over. I shall do my best to persuade my comrades to help you.'

Knox watched him disappear out through the tunnel. He had not told Chorakis absolutely everything, but then what would be the point of that? He barely credited most of it himself. The important thing was that he had not lied, that he had behaved with integrity. God help them, though, if the partisans decided that the heat was too much and that they would rather stay out of this particular kitchen, because then he, Meyerscough and Watts really would be thrown back on their own meagre resources, and they would have no choice but to deliver themselves over to Stavros Ioannides body and soul.

'*Kapetánios . . .*'

Knox started, stared around him wildly for a moment, then recognized the voice as that of Thea Chorakis. She had shifted under her rough blanket and was looking up at him with eyes that were wide awake and very sharp. Knox suspected that while he and Chorakis had been talking, Thea had been no more asleep than they had.

'Hello,' he said.

She shook her head. Her brown eyes seemed to grow larger and brighter. 'I heard everything. You are brave to continue. And I think Panayiotis will persuade the comrades to help you until the task is accomplished. But first please look at something.'

'Yes?' Look at what?

'Look at me,' Thea said. 'I have been told that I am attractive, even beautiful.'

'The rumours are true,' Knox said, trying to make light of her words. He glanced around quickly. The nearest partisan was thirty yards away, cleaning his gun with his back to them. Most were outside or away at the moment.

Thea's hand went down to the buttons of the man's shirt she habitually wore, plucked at them, revealing an expanse of smooth, tanned skin and cleavage.

'Thea, for God's sake . . .'

'Look!'

Then he saw why she had insisted on showing herself. As she unbuttoned further, the silky, tempting skin was turning to blotchy scar tissue. She stopped. Knox could now see three or four clear areas of scarring arranged in a line down from the breastbone, each perhaps an inch square. The line obviously continued under her clothes.

'Good Lord,' he muttered. 'Somebody took some trouble to do that. Is there a lot? Thea . . .'

'As far as my waist,' she said. 'It was an Italian secret policeman, a lieutenant in the OVRA. He smelled bad and had eyes like a deep-sea fish. He sat one night for two hours with a succession of lighted cigarettes, taking frequent pauses between in order to let me consider what was happening to my body. He was very systematic, always going for the most sensitive skin. Otherwise, he showed no interest in me at all in the way of other men . . .'

'Thea—'

'To him it was another job. I never saw him again. When I had joined Panayiotis, we used our contacts in the town to find out who he was, but it seems that he was transferred soon after. Perhaps back to Italy. That leaves only Ioannides.' She brushed the shirt collar over so that it covered the skin, tossed her hair. 'One day I will be able to confront him. You see, I cannot really hate that cruel, ugly Italian lieutenant, because he was stupid, a bureaucrat who knew no better. Ioannides chose—and chooses—to commit such crimes. Remember that, please, *Kapetánios*. And remember also that once this task has been carried out, Ioannides is ours.'

Knox did not need to ask what she meant. 'I understand that. Anyone who could have delivered you up to such a thing deserves all he gets. But we need him.'

What a bloody, bloody mess, he kept thinking. Along with the persistent conviction that Thea Chorakis, scars or no scars, would have him eating out of her hand if he gave her the chance. This was the kind of situation where a man like himself badly needed to know who his friends were—and his potential lovers. Until they had completed their job the day after tomorrow, though, he dared not get involved; and afterwards—if there was going to be an afterwards—he was due to disappear from the island in a matter of hours. He was buggered if he did, as Watts had so aptly said, and buggered if he didn't. That might stand as the motto, not just of his limited relationship with Thea Chorakis, but of the entire, wretched operation.

God bless Meyerscough and Watts. All they wanted to do was to kill and go home.

29

There was a second vote on the next—their last—night. The partisans went back into council to decide how many of them were to go now with the British party to the east coast and how many stay behind. The three improbable assassins, for their part, sat in their own small sleeping chamber while the discussions went on in rapid-fire Rhodian Greek next door. With only eight hours before they were due to be at the spot overlooking the road and ready for Watts to lay his charges, each made his final preparations. The sergeant silently checked through his adapted detonators. Knox consciously psyched himself up for the assignment by repeating over and over to himself: 'It's just a walk in the hills'. He supposed that Meyerscough was praying: the big lieutenant sat quietly in the corner for some time, fiddling with what looked like a small set of beads and murmuring gently and rhythmically to himself. Knox found it hard not to be envious of that comfort.

Finally, when the fluorescent dial on Knox's Royal Marine-issue watch told him that the time was coming up towards midnight and he was beginning to fear that he would have to force the issue, Chorakis appeared in the doorway, carrying his beloved Biretta and with a knapsack slung over one shoulder. He looked haggard and subtly resentful.

'We are ready for you, *Kapetánios,*' he announced. 'Fifteen of us will come with you. You will see who we are. The rest will stay. Everyone chose themselves. I want you to know that.'

There was an implicit challenge in his final words that puzzled Knox. But the important thing was that a good support team had made itself available to cover their rear while Watts was planting the charges and deal with any accidental run-ins with Italian patrols—God forbid. Knox got to his feet, nodded solemnly and acknowledged the courage of the partisans who had taken it upon themselves to share the danger of the British as well as the glory.

It occurred to Knox that some of Chorakis's unease might stem from the fact that since the vote had been taken on the original issue of the German officer and whether they should continue helping, his control over his band had been slipping. The men were getting a taste for democracy, and like the anarchist militiamen in the Spanish Civil War, who had gone so far as to take a show of hands before every attack or retreat, they showed signs of carrying their mania for personal freedom to an extreme that threatened Chorakis's authority and the effectiveness of their fighting capacity. It was starting to look as though he might just be looking forward to the day when these troublesome Englishmen left and he could restore calm and obedience. On the other hand, perhaps there was something more . . . Knox caught a flashing of the eyes as the Greek turned away, beckoning to the British to come through into the main cave and prepare to leave. It was a jealous look, Knox noted with dismay; the look of a Greek man who had experienced the possibility that someone—not something, but someone—might be taken from him? But who?

Their equipment had been ready for hours. It was merely a question of collecting themselves and making their way through. Chorakis was waiting in the main cave, which was already half-empty. The last of the volunteers was filing out through the tunnel that led through into the amphitheatre and the open air.

'The volunteers are waiting outside,' Chorakis said dully, then looked away, refusing to meet Knox's eye.

One of the men who was staying behind, a farmer called Nicos, smiled in embarrassment at Knox. Then, when he met Knox's eye and realized that the *Kapetánios* felt no resentment, he grinned toothily and made a mocking gesture in Chorakis's direction, clearly a personal message for Knox.

Knox waved once, a dignified gesture to those men who had gone so far with them and now felt that they could go no further. But as he gazed at the group, he suddenly felt an incompleteness.

A moment later, he realized what the problem was. No Thea. Was she waiting a bit further away to say farewell, perhaps hoping for a modicum of privacy?

'*Heréte*,' he said firmly and with warmth. The men chorused back.

He followed the way out through the tunnel. No one there. Neither, when he got out and saw the escort group waiting, did he see anything but men armed to the teeth. Perhaps Thea had been unable to face the good-bye. He felt a rush of savage regret for time wasted, things unsaid.

'Comrade Chorakis,' he said slowly. 'We are missing someone. A special comrade. Could she not be here with us for this moment?'

'She is here,' said Chorakis, as if he were biting a brick in half.

'Then won't she wish us luck?'

'Good luck to you. And to us all. Even to me,' a voice said from the midst of the escort.

Thea Chorakis laughed loudly, took off the same woollen hat that she had worn the first night they had met among the rocks above Ioannides' house, and slapped the knife in her belt. 'It took some persuasion,' she said. 'But I am now equal. I shall not desert you.' She beamed a white-teethed, wide smile at her brother, who continued to look decidedly unhappy. 'And my comrade here allows that this is a very special occasion. He is gracious, is he not?'

'Yes,' Knox answered with a grin that failed to express the leaping joy he felt inside him. 'He is obviously delighted.'

'We must go,' Chorakis muttered darkly. Then he bellowed to the others to start moving ahead. Even in this first phase, they were to keep checking the terrain constantly, for the latest news was that the fascists had many patrols out. Even before they got into the vicinity of the airfield, there was the prospect of clashes with enemy units. If these came, they were to disengage and melt into the mountains as quickly as possible, and then try to find another way through to the east coast without losing too much time. They had to get the British to the spot overlooking the road by no later than seven the following morning, so that Watts had time to lay his charges and then allow them time to get out of the immediate vicinity before the explosion. That was why they had left themselves a few hours to spare by setting out at midnight.

All that was clear. But Knox understood now why Chorakis was so thoroughly disgruntled, even hurt. The partisan leader was not only losing control of his men, but his own, nubile sister had chosen to question his orders for the sake of another man. Until he and the British parted company, there would be no mending the damage on either front—and in the case of Thea, it might never be mended, whatever happened. After all, if a man could not control a woman, how could he lead other men?

30

For the past twenty-four hours, since breakfast time on Tuesday, Oberleutnant Bredow had been blessed with the company of a member of General Drewitz's staff, one Oberleutnant Winniger. Winniger had turned up on the General's orders, knocked on the door of Bredow's room at the *Albergo* and introduced himself, explained that he was to act as a 'companion' during the period immediately before, during and after the Great Visit. He had spent the entire day with Bredow, not moving from his side; even an angry phone call to Falcke had had to be made in his presence. He had listened impassively while Bredow vented his feelings, only to be told by his highly-placed friend that Winniger could not and would not move. If Bredow really wanted to be rid of him, the only method of effecting that was to leave Rhodes. On Tuesday night, Winniger had supposedly slept in the room next to Bredow's, though a swift clandestine check had revealed that he spent the entire night in an armchair on the landing of the third floor of the *Albergo,* thus preventing any possibility of Bredow's sneaking out for any reason. Now, as Bredow sat in a car being driven, with a party of other officers, down the east coast military road in the dead hour just before dawn, Winniger sat next to him, smiling pleasantly. It was like being shadowed by a large soft toy.

The car, a six-seater Mercedes, was forced to stop at the end of a long queue waiting in front of the gates to the Italian air base near Lindos. There were truckloads of Italian troops in full dress uniform, SS security men in Kubelwagens and riding motorcycle combinations, and the Wehrmacht guard of honour, to which, technically at least, Bredow and Winniger were attached. The other three officers in the car with them were men with whom Bredow had met in the Mess with Huber and Falcke, but he did not know them well. They were all badly hung over, in any case, and so they all sat in suffering but moderately amicable silence until they reached the queue and the Mercedes stopped dead.

'Dear God,' said one, the commander of a Luftwaffe anti-aircraft battalion. 'This is like being trapped among the grandmas trying to get into the winter sale at KaDeWe,' he growled. 'Security must be tight as a whore on holiday. I trust we feel honoured, gentlemen! Do we?'

There was a general chorus of ironical approval, even from Winniger, who was probably quite a reasonable human being when he wasn't being a watchdog.

'I see you have a sense of humour,' Bredow said wryly.

Winniger nodded. 'I suspect that is why the General chose me for this job,' he said. Then he added, just in case Bredow had misunderstood his meaning: 'He was certainly also aware that my sense of humour is totally subservient to my sense of duty. Cigarette?'

Bredow took one and stared gloomily out of the window. He found the man's company oppressive, but in fact it made no difference to him. All he wanted was to be here and observe; the British in the hills would do the rest. From here, in fact, he could see the slate-grey rocks littering the hillsides a couple of kilometres distant, glimpse the twisted ribbon of the steep road in the very first rays of the rising sun. That was where the British would be busy very soon. Bredow fancied he could even see the overhang where the charges would be placed, according to Ioannides, but then at this distance all overhangs looked roughly alike.

'Impressive, isn't it?' said Winniger conversationally. Drewitz—or had it been the affable but two-faced Falcke?—had deliberately picked a man of equal rank for the task of sticking to Bredow, so that there would be no rank-pulling, no problems about who orders whom.

Bredow realized that Winniger had seen his interest in

the mountains. 'Eh?' he said with feigned vagueness, as if he had been daydreaming and taking nothing in. 'Oh—the landscape. Yes. This lush plain, and then the untamed crags. An extraordinary contrast. Of such contrasts is true scenic beauty composed, Winniger. But for that give me the Rhine Gorge any time. The peaceful river valley, the rocks rearing like crazed animals . . .'

He continued in that vein, taking a malicious delight in boring the wretched man back to sleep and causing puzzled smiles from the other officers, who had never heard him talk like this, until they reached the gates. Two eagle-eyed SS security men in full uniform peered in through the driver's window, demanding to see everyone's papers, which had to include specific permission to be here on this day. An Italian OVRA officer hovered ineffectually behind them trying to push himself forward from time to time, while another German, an SS Oberscharführer, wandered round the car, ducking to look underneath, checking the boot, scribbling notes on the vehicle and its occupants.

The SS officer in charge of the gate inspections eyes narrowed when he saw that Bredow was attached to the Abwehr. The Oberleutnant's papers were absolutely in order, including a lengthy *laissez-passer* dictated and signed by General Drewitz himself, but the SS man was obviously determined to have his pound of flesh.

'One moment, Herr Oberleutnant. A routine check on such credentials must sometimes be made,' he said, with a tight smile that left no doubt that the check was by no means routine—or if it was, the routine applied only to his organization's Abwehr competitors. Then he marched slowly and with great deliberation to his gatehouse. The OVRA officer scuttled after him like a pet dog.

They sat and sweated, grumbled and sighed, while the SS officer made a lengthy call from the telephone in his gatehouse. A motorcyclist revved his machine irritably behind them: truck drivers began to hoot.

'I don't think he likes you, Otto,' said the talkative Luftwaffe officer. 'I vote we throw you overboard. You're a jinx. Nothing but trouble.'

'My apologies, gentlemen. There are often problems when one insists on associating with persons beyond one's normal social sphere, as you are now learning. It if difficult to accustom oneself to the special treatment, such as the officer in the gatehouse feels constrained to bestow upon me. However, I must beg you to be patient.'

The Luftwaffe officer chuckled. This was a standing joke—Bredow would play the haughty Abwehr officer, he the combat commander with a chip on his shoulder.

'Kiss my arse, Otto. We'd be in there scrounging some breakfast if it weren't for your running feud with the boys in black there.'

'Ah, but you would have missed this magical feeling of *specialness*!' Bredow riposted. He had learned to be good at banter. To engage in such talk was like switching off one's mind and emotions and coasting down the hill of the day's problems in neutral gear. He did not need to think of anything, and at this moment he did not want to.

The SS man returned after six or seven minutes. 'All right, Oberleutnant von Bredow,' he grated, emphasizing the aristocratic *von* with obvious distaste. 'The General wishes you to be confined to the guard-assembly area, and this also suits us. Report there.' He glanced at the driver of the Mercedes, who happened to be Bredow's old friend, Spatz. 'Deliver the Oberleutnant straight there, eh?'

Spatz nodded. 'Guard-assembly area, Standartenführer!'

The SS officer let them through, though he continued to stare balefully at the retreating rear of the car as it passed him and continued into the airfield. It clearly hurt for him to let Bredow through with such relative lack of delay, but they had the traffic flow to consider, since the Führer was due in five hours.

Bredow and Winniger breakfasted with Falcke and Huber under a canvas awning that had been constructed for the occasion. There was cheese, sausage, coarse, grey rolls, and acorn coffee. As they ate, the major pointed out to Bredow where he was allowed to go, just in case the faithful Winniger forgot, which was unlikely. At no time was he to be allowed to within two hundred metres of where the Führer was due to disembark, greet the local commanders and inspect the guard of honour before proceeding to the villa in the mountains for lunch and a nap in preparation of his first session of talks with Mussolini. The Duce would be making the much shorter hop by plane from Brindisi that afternoon.

Bredow could see enough to estimate that there must be upwards of five hundred German security personnel—SS men imported from the Reich, plus experienced Wehrmacht *Feldpolizei*—without even starting to count the Italian contingent, who were noisily obtrusive in their brash uniforms and streamlined patrol vehicles. There would be more out on the road and at the villa. They would be protecting Hitler against mines, assassins with rifles, bombs, simple ambushes—anything but a former quarryman who knew how to tip over a mountainside with a bagful of explosives. With that thought lingering in his mind, Bredow decided that he should relax and enjoy the anticipation, the occasion—even more historic than anyone else here could guess—while he waited.

'Fascinating,' said Falcke, appearing at his side, sipping a mug of coffee. 'Did you know that in the building behind us is a full SS Brigadeführer with a staff of twenty, all manning telephones, radio telephones, wireless telegraph apparatus, and so on? To ensure that at no time do they lose contact either with Berlin or the Führer's aircraft. If one means of communication should fail, they will switch to another. Taking no chances, eh, Bredow?'

'They would be unwise to do so. It is their job to prepare for the unexpected, the far-fetched. Just as it is my job in the Abwehr to dream up schemes that are both things. In fact, the possibilities for disaster in any given situation are always infinite, Major.'

'Oho. Do I sense a touch of professional pique there, my friend? A little bearing of the fangs?'

'It has been my experience that the SS are sometimes efficient, but never lovable. This seems to me to be self-evident. I would be less than totally honest if I said I wish them well. Perhaps a small disaster . . .'

Falcke burst out laughing. Then he sucked in his cheeks, glanced around to ensure that none of the leather-coated tribe were in the vicinity. 'My dear Bredow,' he confessed, 'I couldn't have put it better myself. This may be why I and so many other Wehrmacht officers are here and watching the proceedings with such interest—apart from being granted the opportunity to see our beloved Führer in the flesh for those magic few moments between the aircraft and the limousine, that is.'

'Yes.' Bredow thought that he had struck just the right note of professional bitchiness mingled with professional concern. He had known about the communications centre. It would be part of his job later today to get access to a phone or a W/T and contact Berlin to make sure that the Admiral and his co-conspirators there knew that the British strike had been successful. Then they would be able to move against the SS. After all, who had been so fully in charge of the Führer's safety but Himmler's apes? And who else could be held responsible—even culpable—for Hitler's death?

'But the wait is long,' Falcke continued. He looked at his watch. 'I make the time five-twenty-one. Good God, that means we still have almost five hours to wait, to be herded around this forsaken place like so many cattle.'

'Relax and enjoy it,' Bredow said. He winked at Winniger. 'We shall have even more time to get acquainted.'

It was Winniger's turn to look perturbed. The smooth façade almost cracked for a moment at the thought of what this Abwehr officer could do if he really wanted to make life awkward. But the moment of concern passed. Bredow soon settled down. In fact, Winniger observed, he seemed far more concerned with the view of the mountains and the high road that the Führer's car was due to pass along than with the frenetic activity at the airfield. Everyone, Winniger reflected, had their own way of switching off when under pressure. The Oberleutnant obviously liked to commune with nature.

Franz Wilhelm Canaris stirred on his steel-framed cot. The telephone in his office next door was ringing persistently. He started, almost tipped off the familiar bed, but habit made his movement stop short of that. A moment later, he rolled off and shuffled towards the door. There was the palest of lights coming in through the window on what he prayed would be the most significant day in German history, the day he had worked, cajoled, schemed, lied and loved for these years past. X-Day. The climax of *Wintermärchen*.

It was his private telephone that was ringing, a scrambler line that he kept for close friends to use in emergencies. The realization brought him to full consciousness within a fraction of a second. He moved quickly, picked it up with a snatching motion, a sudden, untypical fear and panic.

'Canaris. Yes?'

A screaming, undulating burst of static. Then a voice that he recognized as that of Arthur Nebe, the conspirators' inside man at Gestapo headquarters in the Prinz-Albrecht-Strasse. 'Admiral, this place is on fire,' the voice said. 'It has erupted. The Führer's plane has been instructed to stop when it reaches Belgrade for refuelling in ten minutes' time. The meeting with Mussolini is to be aborted.'

'Why?' Canaris knew the risk that the man was running at this moment by making this simple telephone call.

'Information. The British are planning to kill the Führer shortly after his arrival on Rhodes. They have received this knowledge overnight. Schellenberg is rushing around, acting the hysterical prima donna. Kaltenbrunner is planning what to do next.'

Canaris's right hand, the one that held the receiver, was starting to tremble gently. It was the only outward sign of his pain and fear. '*Turquoise,*' he whispered. 'It can only have been *Turquoise.*'

'Yes, Admiral. We have scored an own goal. We have well and truly backfired . . .'

As Canaris replaced the telephine, his mind was rushing forward to what he was going to say to the others as the morning went on and the disappointment turned to anger. And he thought, just once but very clearly, of Otto von Bredow. God grant that Bredow would be able to get news to the British in time. And God grant, too, that *Turquoise* hadn't given the SD complete chapter and verse, because then Kaltenbrunner would have them all where he had Oster and Dohnanyi.

Canaris shivered, though it was a mild spring dawn and the Tirpitzufer's heating was the most efficient in Berlin.

A man came running out of the communications building with a piece of paper in one hand. He was quiet, pale, and Bredow realized immediately that he was in the grip of a deadening, all-consuming panic. A description took shape in Bredow's mind of the man with the paper: a Signals

Unterscharführer wearing SD shoulderflashes on his pale khaki uniform, fair and in his late twenties, slight build for an SS man. A man with something to say, something he would rather not have to say.

Bredow moved closer, thanking providence that he had not accepted Falcke's offer of a camp bed in one of the tents close to the airfield perimeter. All the staff officers except Winniger had sneaked off to grab a spot of rest, in the assumption that nothing would really happen until it got fully light.

'Bredow!' Winniger was with him; a little slow off the mark, for tiredness was starting to affect him, but only a few feet behind him, making his presence known, showing he was a good boy and carrying out orders.

'Come on, then!' Bredow hissed with a glance over his shoulder. Suddenly he felt brutal. Just before the SD signals NCO had emerged from the building he had been daydreaming of Gisela. For the first time since her death, he had been able to picture them making love the way they used to, slowly and with a lingering concentration, as if they had all the time in the world. That dream, and the contrast with this grey, dangerous reality, made him feel like striking out. Winniger was the nearest target.

The SD NCO had stopped and was talking quickly and excitedly to a tall, jowled man in a trenchcoat who Bredow recognized as a high-ranking recent import from the Prinz-Albrecht-Strasse, one of Kaltenbrunner's troubleshooters. They were both so involved in what was being said that neither noticed the Abwehr man.

'Führer plane turning back . . . Belgrade . . . Information . . . Plot against his life . . .'

At that moment, Bredow knew why the signals NCO had looked the way he had when he emerged from the communications building, because he felt the same sensation that the man must have felt. A sudden, aching blow in the diaphragm, a throat emptied of moisture as if someone had turned a blowtorch on it. This couldn't be. He wanted to run, hide, tell everyone to do the same before it was too late, but he knew he had to stay exactly where he was and gain as much information as he could.

'Orders following, Gruppenführer Kaltenbrunner . . .

Counterstrike against British bandits . . . Commando Order applies . . .'

So they were going to sweep into the mountains to catch the British group red-handed. Just as long as they didn't catch Ioannides and through him learn about the Abwehr connection, Bredow and the others would be physically safe, but first it was essential to get word to the British, ensure that they kept as far away from the airfield as possible. There was still time, if they were lucky; if Ioannides could be contacted and a message dispatched within the next half-hour or so, before the security men began to move up into the hills above the airfield.

Winniger had heard what the SD men were saying as well, but he didn't yet seem to have got the message. All the better.

'Winniger,' Bredow said quickly. 'There is no point in our staying here. Get me out and to a place where I don't have to be with these people. Find Driver Spatz!'

'But—'

'I'll stay here. You have my oath as an officer and a gentleman. And I am both those things when it comes to dealing with a fellow member of the German Army. Find Spatz! Otherwise, a lot of us will have reason to regret it!'

'Bredow, the General said I must stay with you. Until the Führer has gone from the island.'

'The Führer isn't coming to the island, you oaf! Don't you understand?' Bredow screamed at him, until a couple of the SD men who had now grouped around the original recipient of the news glanced irritably in his direction. 'Visit aborted! Nothing! There's been an assassination scare, so he's not coming!'

'I see, but—'

Bredow took him and pushed him towards the huts where the various Wehrmacht support teams were being housed, growling: 'I'll see you in five minutes! The worst I'll do is make a phone call! All right? I don't need to be nursemaided any more, Winniger! Now get Spatz and the car if you value your hide, before they seal off the place and we're stuck here all day!'

Winniger only looked doubtful for a moment. Then the common humanity in him showed through and he nodded.

The prospect of being wound up in an SS security panic was too much. Another moment and he was haring off in search of a driver. Not necessarily Spatz, but any driver.

Once Winniger had gone, Bredow forced himself to assume a majestic calm, to return to the arrogant insouciance that was expected of him and upon which, he knew instinctively, his life might well depend. Wearing that mask, trying to extend it to his whole body and way of walking, he made his way over towards another, smaller building that had telephone wires coming out of it. He had seen it earlier and earmarked it as his fallback, in case he failed to gain access to the more sophisticated communications centre. Under these circumstances, it would do very nicely.

When he walked in through the door, there were only two or three bored-looking Wehrmacht NCOs sitting there, smoking and drinking acorn coffee. The growing alarm outside had not yet penetrated here. Bredow decided that it was time it did so.

'Sergeant! You two corporals!' he bellowed. 'Something's up out there, an emergency! I'm not allowed to say what it is, but we need all the help we can get! Do you have a civil line to Rhodes town? I need to contact a very important member of the military administration!'

The sergeant was still standing to attention. He made a stiff gesture in the direction of one particular phone and said: 'This serves the civil switchboard, sir!' Then he hesitated. 'I don't like to leave the switchboard unattended, Herr Oberleutnant.'

'I'm ordering you to do so. I'll mind the store here and make absolutely certain that no one abuses your precious phones. Now move!'

The sergeant looked unhappy, but he moved, taking the corporals with him.

'Report back as soon as you are no longer needed, understood?' Bredow called out after them. 'I don't want to have to stay here all morning!'

Then he headed for the phone, got the emergency number for Ioannides. Perhaps the man had sixth sense, for this time he answered the phone personally and sounded completely awake.

'You sound tired,' Bredow said before the Greek could come out with anything that would identify or incriminate them. 'Don't speak. I'll just tell you what I want to tell you. We can discuss it later.' He was working hard to keep up the voice of the languid Abwehr aristo who didn't intend a little local difficulty to ruin his social arrangements. 'We were going hunting with those friends in the mountains today, but that's not possible now. The visitor hasn't arrived and there's a big panic on. Looks like the mountains are going to be full of other hunters, and we don't want ourselves or our friends to risk getting mixed up with them. Do you understand?'

Bredow was relying on the fact that Ioannides could understand a lot more German than he could speak. He waited for the man's reply. Finally a slow, soft *ja* came over the line. 'I understand,' Ioannides said in painful, self-conscious but very careful German. 'I will tell the others on your behalf. Another day, perhaps.'

'Yes. Another day. Meanwhile, they can go home.'

'Of course.'

An SS officer with wild eyes crashed into the room, glowered at Bredow and grabbed a phone, indicating for the Wehrmacht Oberleutnant to make himself scarce. Bredow carried on in his best playboy voice, even though Ioannides had put the phone down at his end.

'Fine, then, *signore*. We shall hunt together sometime. Bad luck that today is not possible, eh? Perhaps we could meet for a drink?'

Two more SS men entered. The officer on the other phone snapped: 'Cut him off!' and one of the men came over and wrenched the receiver out of Bredow's hand. 'Total communications blackout except for authorized personnel!'

'I say. It's four hours until the Führer is due to arrive. I have important arrangements to make . . .'

'Out!' the senior man, a tough young Standartenführer, barked. 'History is in the making here, Herr Baron!'

'I shall complain to the appropriate authorities!' Bredow whined. 'Who are you to order an Army officer about in this fashion?'

Two burly SS men already had him under the arms and were dragging him towards the door. Within seconds he found himself, to his relief, pitched outside the door and left alone. He picked himself up and looked around. Winniger had not found Spatz, but he had commandeered a motorcycle combination from somewhere and was sitting on the cycle with the engine revving noisily.

'Good man, Winniger!' Bredow said. 'Let's get through that gate, quick!'

The adrenaline kept pumping all the way back to Rhodes town. Soon after they arrived came the bitterness, the anti-climax, and the raw, insistent fear. *Wintermärchen*, the Winter's Tale, had suddenly taken an unexpected twist. No one could know what lay waiting for them on the next page. To assuage that fear, Bredow rang Ioannides again. Mehmet had been dispatched into the mountains minutes after their dawn telephone conversation. Whether or not he managed to find the partisans before the SS did was now in the hands of an inscrutable God.

31

They had made slow but surprisingly steady progress, stumbling through the night like blind men following a guide by touch. At least it was cool and silent in the hills. Once they had stopped, watched and listened to the signs of a German patrol more than a mile away; it had been possible to see men lighting cigarettes, make out barked orders through the clear night air. Sounds carried easily, which was both a boon and a danger. Chorakis had ensured that each of the quite heavily-laden British soldiers had an 'anchor-man' to hold on to during the rocky parts of the march, so that they would not lose their footing or mistake the path in the darkness.

As dawn approached, they found themselves moving in and out of drifting sea mists that had crept up into the coastal parts of the mountains. By six, with the coast only half an hour away, the sun was beginning to pierce the mist and hazily pick out fingers of coarse grass and lichen among the rocks. Soon they would be descending again onto pastureland, preparing for the drop onto the coastal plain. It was then that Meyerscough, of all people, spotted the figure approaching from the north, working its way upwards as if it had come not from either coast but from a point nearer to Rhodes town.

'Hey!' he bellowed, and then lowered his voice, for in his excitement he had forgotten the instructions about patrols. He stage-whispered: 'There's a man down there. About half a mile away.'

Knox stopped, causing some concern to Christos, his 'anchor-man'. The burly young Greek held onto him for a moment, thinking that the *Kapetánios* might have been about to faint from weakness or illness. Knox smiled at him in what he hoped was a reassuring fashion.

'Can't be,' he said, shading his eyes with his right hand. Then he grimaced. 'You're bloody well right. Comrade Chorakis!'

Christos seized him fiercely, since he was now absolutely certain that there was something wrong with the *Kapetánios*. It took several seconds for Chorakis to react, however. The guerrilla leader was leading his sister by the hand up ahead, talking with her earnestly, which helped to explain why he had not seen what Meyerscough had seen. Once he realized that a stranger had been spotted, he rushed back to where the two British officers were standing, with Thea following close behind. In the grey light, their olive skins seemed the colour of slate, which lent Chorakis's features a rigid, sculpted look.

'*Kapetánios?*'

'There's someone coming along that path there to the north. Can't see who, or even if he's alone.' Knox fiddled with his binoculars, trying to focus them more keenly, cursing quietly in Greek under his breath. 'Every time I think I've got him, he's lost behind a rock . . . ah . . . It's not a German or an Italian—or a Greek. For God's sake, it's Mehmet!'

A ripple of surprise and apprehension spread among the Greeks, who were now all peering north from their various vantage points. Several drew the bolts of their rifles, muttered insults.

Chorakis gestured for the loan of Knox's binoculars, glanced through them and curled his lip. When he had finished, he handed them back to Knox and picked out Christos, 'After the Liberation' George, and a serious-faced young man whom everyone had dubbed 'the priest' to go and fetch the Turk. They should first make sure that he had brought no Axis troops with him—perhaps lurking a few hundred yards behind him or following further up the mountainside, where there was more cover from big rocks. The three partisans moved off quickly and with an unquestioning readiness that Knox continued to find moving. These Greeks would always argue, demand their 'rights'—and in the end they would always do the brave thing.

Thea had sat down and was hugging her knees to her chin like a child. She was not looking towards the north, but one hand had crept to her knife.

'Presumably he has a message from Ioannides,' Knox said in an attempt to help her through her fear. He knew that anything associated with Ioannides was liable to put her heavily on the defensive.

Thea continued to stare down at the ground. 'I know we must work with him because it is necessary, but I can only feel what I feel.' The last words were spat out like poison being expelled from the system.

'Try,' Knox said. 'Try hard. We can't afford any passengers.'

She looked up at him again, and to his surprise there was gratitude in her eyes. Perhaps no one had spoken to her like that about it before, sharply and equally, as if she were a man.

Knox looked back up the mountain. The three had reached Mehmet. The Turk was trying to press on past them, but they were insisting on making up an escort. Against his natural inclinations, Knox decided to wait, and signalled for Meyerscough and Watts to do the same. Best to let the Greeks feel that they were in control of as much as possible; later, when it might be really crucial, he would start giving orders if need be.

A few feet from Knox, Chorakis watched the scene. He had unslung his Biretta and had tucked it under one arm like a shooting-piece. The intended impression of casualness was belied only by the gentle, tell-tale tapping of one booted foot on rock and the tension in the set of his shoulders.

As Mehmet came closer, with the accompaniment of the odd shove from Christos and 'After the Liberation'

George, Knox could see the fear, but also the harsh determination on the Turk's face. Whatever he had come here for, it had cost him dear. He looked exhausted, but there was a kind of fevered fire in the man's eyes. Knox wished he could know what went on in the mind of such a creature. To struggle miles through rough mountain country at dawn with enemy patrols about, and to do it on another man's business, was something that the educated, western European mind found harder to grasp. And yet as Mehmet picked his way down the goat path towards them now, Knox sensed in his body posture a kind of repressed nobility that had survived other men's ridicule, disgust and hatred and the cold disciplines of a master like Stavros Ioannides.

'A strange meeting, Turk,' Chorakis said when Mehmet was almost level with them.

Mehmet's features were rigid with exhaustion, but there may have been just a hint of a triumphant smile when he shambled the last few feet to Knox and handed him a note that he produced from inside his jacket. He waited then, panting very gently and ignoring the partisans. His business was with the English *Kapetánios,* and not with the Rhodian Communist trash.

The note was a page torn from a cheap accounting book, and the message was written in pencil in a surprisingly neat, copperplate script, the kind of faintly archaic handwriting taught in British schools in the colonies before the First War:

> *Please cancel your plan,* it read. *You have been betrayed and the target will no longer come. Instead, patrols are being sent into the hills to look for you. Come immediately to my house with Mehmet. You must leave the island as soon as possible.*
> *Your friend,*
> *S.I.*

Knox read it twice, found it hard to think anything when he handed it to Meyerscough, who had been waiting expectantly at his elbow.

'Just like that, eh?' Knox said when a sharp intake of breath told him that the big lieutenant had reached the end of the note. 'Pack up and go home, he says.'

Meyerscough shook his head violently, glared at Mehmet like a kid who has just been told that the Sunday treat's been cancelled for no good reason.

'Damn it, Knox. It can't be.'

In a faintly ridiculous acting-out of the British Army pecking order, Watts had now been handed the note and was reading it impassively. Neither did the sergeant's expression change when he gave it back. He simply muttered, 'Fuck', and looked away.

Knox also looked at Mehmet, but with a quizzical expression. 'Who can have betrayed us?' he asked in Greek. The partisans gasped. Now, for the first time since Mehmet's arrival, they were realizing the purpose of his mission.

The Turk frowned, obviously wanting to tell Knox but unable to conceive of the ramifications. He waved one hand feebly, hissed: 'Very, very far, I hear my master say. Men in far country. Visitor very important. He hear things very far away.'

'Important? Who?' Knox realized that Mehmet was truly innocent. He would tell no lies, except if Ioannides had specifically instructed him to do so.

'Very important. My master get very angry if—'

'Who?' Knox snapped.

Mehmet closed his eyes. It was cool in the mountains here, though the sun had come up, but he was sweating suddenly. Now Chorakis was also in on the act. Before Knox could stop him, he had launched himself at the Turk and had him by the shoulders, shaking him and saying: 'This fascist? Who? You tell the *Kapetánios*!'

The Turk shook his head, half-opened his eyes and mimed the writing of the note to Knox, shrugged, as if saying: 'The note tells all. I am merely the servant of the man who wrote it.'

It was not good enough. Knox had suddenly realized that the identity of their victim might not have been important a little while ago, but it was very important now, because that identity might well have a direct bearing on Ioannides' motivation for trying to warn them off at this very late stage.

'We must know,' he said.

And then Chorakis hit the Turk, sending him off balance and arcing over in a slow, inevitable fall that left him sprawled in the gorse. Adding indignity to the violence, the partisan leader spat on Mehmet to the general approval of his comrades. Knox groaned inwardly, but he resisted the temptation to tear a strip off Chorakis on the spot. This blasted feud was getting in the way, that was for sure. The one thing Mehmet wasn't going to respond to was a smack in the mouth from a Greek.

Knox went down on one knee, put a hand on the bemused, angry Turk's shoulder. Mehmet was still lying on the ground, shaking his head in an attempt to clear it, hissing obscure Turkish curses or prayers under his breath. The blow from the edge of Chorakis's hand had caught his harelip and bruised it, though it had not drawn blood. It was like hitting a man on his sore spot, literally.

'Pay no attention to the Greek,' Knox said very gently, with just some slight pressure on Mehmet's shoulder to stop him from getting to his feet and reciprocating the violence. 'I am a *Kapetánios* in the British Army, and I will protect you from everyone, both these people and your master. Do not fear. And tell me who the visitor is.'

The Turk looked reluctantly at him, and at that moment Knox was struck with how clear and almost childlike his eyes were when they met yours directly—which they hardly ever did. He and Mehmet gazed at each other for some moments, ignoring the chattering, jostling partisans all round. Then Mehmet said very softly but to Knox's ears more clearly than he had ever heard him speak: 'German. Hitler German. Bad man Hitler.'

'Adolf Hitler?' Knox asked again, to make sure. He and Mehmet were in a private world of their own on the mountainside at that moment. 'That Hitler?'

Mehmet nodded. 'Hitler. My master spoke of it. I see, I hear much. I understand more than anyone knows, *Kapetánios*. Much more.'

'He says that our target was the Führer himself. Adolf bloody Hitler,' Knox said, looking up at Meyerscough. 'Are you thinking what I'm thinking?'

'I'm certainly wondering whether this stuff about the whole thing's being called off is true, I can tell you that. I mean, if he was on their side, he would say that, wouldn't he? We have to trust him, and at the moment that isn't easy.'

'An understatement. I believe this poor chap as far as it goes, but Ioannides is obviously up to his neck in some sort of skulduggery. I don't know any more. What if we head for the house and there's a Nazi reception party waiting for us? What if we turn back now, thus sparing Hitler, and get bushwacked on the path? On the other hand, we could also land in hot water if we press on . . .'

'We're stymied, Knox. I understand that much.'

Two of the Greeks had possessed sufficient self-discipline to stay at their guard posts while the fascinating encounter between the Turk and their comrades was unfolding. One of them now whistled a warning. For an instant, the Turk and his message were forgotten, and everyone looked in the guard's direction.

The man was waving frantically, pointing in the direction of the east, which meant the coast. Knox and Chorakis moved a couple of paces and hopped onto rocks to see more clearly. Both saw immediately what the guard meant. From the direction of the coastal plain, a column of field-grey figures was winding up a path. From here it looked like a company-strength patrol, and it was moving with speed and an air of determination, as if it knew what it was looking for. They had been betrayed, it was true, but precisely by whom was something that perhaps only Mehmet could tell them . . .

All eyes were on the German patrol less than a mile distant. For that moment, every man who had set out from the partisans' cave shortly after midnight was drinking in the bitter reality of disappointment and treachery, adjusting to the imminence of danger and death. The shot that rang out from a few yards away came as an intense shock.

'Jesus—' Knox whirled round in time to see something writhing in the gorse and a man standing nearby holding an old firing piece. Smoke was wafting out of the gun's barrel. It was 'After the Liberation' George, he realized, and he also realized at that moment that George had shot Mehmet. The Turk kicked with a horrendous energy once more as Knox stood rooted to the spot, watching. Then he lay still. A brittle silence descended. It lasted for about five seconds, until they heard shouts from down below, where the German patrol was advancing. The shot had been noted and would be acted upon very quickly.

'He is dead,' said 'After the Liberation' George with a combination of pride and fear. 'He tried to run off while we were watching the enemy. I had no choice.'

A check on the Turk's pulse showed that George was right. The bullet from the venerable Ottoman Army carbine had smashed into the spine and carried on into the chest. The shock alone of such a large bullet entering a man's body at short range would have been enough to kill. Knox suspected that the shot had also taken away part of the lung. He turned Mehmet over, looked one last time into the dead eyes that a few minutes previously had been open and direct as a child's, and closed them. He got to his feet and said to Chorakis: 'The time for discussion is over. Whatever the reason, we are being hunted. We had better get out of here.'

Chorakis continued to stand where he was. He looked at Knox, then down the hillside, and still he did not move. At first, Knox thought that he was frightened for his personal safety, but then he realized that Chorakis was simply paralyzed with indecision, with the weight of his personal responsibility. Chorakis cared little about whether he himself lived or died, but when it came to caring for fifteen others, the strain told.

'Comrade Chorakis,' Knox hissed urgently, seizing him by the arm. No response except a bemused, faintly irritated stare. 'We must go.'

He realized that Thea had risen and was at his side. She had been watching the entire pantomime with Mehmet and had shown nothing more than a kind of sullen indifference, but now she was alive and diamond-hard in her resolve. Knox could feel the heady energy of leadership emanating from her as she said clearly and crisply to her brother: 'Panayiotis. We move. We go to the cave and collect our equipment and possessions. Then we look for a new hiding-place, where the patrols will not find us, even with the aid of traitors. Come!'

'Thea—'

'Quickly!' She was staring skywards now, as were the rest of them. From the direction of the airfield some four miles away a group of planes was approaching, heading inland over the mountains. In fact, they were already starting to swoop; the realization came, hard on all the others, that the patrol down there had radio and would have been able to summon air support at a few moments' notice, that, in fact, the aircraft were probably already in the air when the searchers had found their quarry.

By the time everyone had started to scatter, the first of them was screaming down low over the hillside; they were Junker 87s, the infamous Stuka dive-bombers, with wicked pointed noses and sirens on the wings that picked up the wind and howled terrifyingly as the planes went in for the kill.

'Move!' Thea screamed once more, motioning to Knox to grab her paralyzed brother by the arm. Chorakis was staring up at the approaching Stuka with a kind of fixed, cold hatred, as if he were not actually in this lethal, all too real situation but watching something he loathed from the safety of a seat in a cinema.

Together, Knox and Thea pulled Chorakis to one side and threw him down among the gorse. Thea rolled over in one athletic, powerful move and lay with her body covering that of her brother. Even before they had managed to force Chorakis into cover, tracers had started zinging and thudding around the hillside, and a couple of rockets had hit further down, showering up dust and slivers of rock but falling short of the main concentration of guerrillas.

Knox lay a few feet from Thea and her brother. He was surprised to register how little he actually felt; there was neither the often-cited adrenaline of action, nor the paralyzing bite of fear that had so clearly affected Chorakis at the crucial moment. He felt calm, perhaps a little too calm. He found himself thinking over and over again during those moments with the bullets flensing the earth all around him that Thea Chorakis was very physically strong, far stronger than she looked, and that he liked strong women. Thoughts of Thea were driven away only when, after a brief pause, another aircraft howled down and this time the spray of bullets found some targets. Knox heard a very loud, long scream, the sort of expression of pain and horror that could only come from a human being's awareness of irreparable injury. Then the hillside shook, as if it had been punched by some huge fist in its softest part, and Knox felt a wave of hot air pass above his shoulders and head so that for a moment he dared not breathe. This was followed almost immediately—the time-lag was strange—by an ear-splitting explosion and an overwhelming scent of cordite that clawed its way into every particle of a man's mouth and nostrils. A rocket close by, he realized dimly. The German pilots had their measure, and this hillside could only become hotter from now on. The only advantage was that with this kind of a bombardment from the air in progress, the German patrol on the ground wouldn't risk coming too close—in fact, it might even pull back a little to avoid stray tracer and rocket fire.

The second plane was beginning to climb away. There would be a ten, fifteen-second respite before the next really got into its descent. Knox raised his head like a small, furtive animal snatching a glance at a predator, saw Watts crouched to his right, Meyerscough next to the sergeant. Meyerscough, bless him, had managed to set up his Sten and was blazing away for all he was worth at the sky, leading several of the partisans on that side of the path in a brave, if almost certainly futile, attempt to shoot down the approaching Stuka.

'Let's get out!' Knox bellowed. He saw a glum nod of agreement from Watts who, he now realized, was clutching his left arm. The good sergeant was phlegmatic to the last. Meyerscough waved with his left hand, continued firing away with the weapon held in his right.

'You all get out! I'll supply covering fire!' he yelled to Knox before the Stuka's shriek began to drown all possibility of communication.

'Bloody fool! You can't cover us against those things!'

Knox's advice was lost in the din, and perhaps his last couple of words were chewed off into the ground as he buried his face back in the harsh gorse and rock.

Another twenty seconds of pummelling to hell, two rockets this time among them, more shrieks and moans. It was break for it or die. The second Stuka's engines changed from a howl to a rasping growl as the plane bottomed out a few yards above the ground and began its climb, banking off back towards the sea.

Knox rose to a crouch, resting on the balls of his feet and his palms, glanced around. Watts' partisan friend had the sergeant secure and was supporting him under the arms. Either Watts' initial injury had been worse than it looked, or he had been unlucky enough to be hit during the last attack as well. Knox waved to him but left the Greek to help him to safety. He looked down, saw Thea still on the ground.

'Come on. Bring Panayiotis and let's make a run for it!' he snapped. 'To stay here is suicide. At least if we head back into the hills, there's a chance . . .'

She looked up at him. There were tears glistening around her dark eyes, and she was stroking her brother's shoulders with both hands, as if vainly trying to expel water from the body of a drowning man.

'Yes,' she said then, and got up. 'He is dead, you know. Just as we reached cover, a bullet took him. Stupid.'

Knox looked at her hands, realized that they were covered in blood. A swift glance at the body of Chorakis revealed a spreading patch of dark red between the shoulder blades.

'Tell the others to come, too,' he said almost brutally, surprised at the hardness of his own tone.

She nodded. 'Retreat to the hills!' she shouted in a clear voice. 'Bring only the walking wounded, or the Germans will catch up and take us all!'

One or two of the men who emerged from gorse bushes or from behind rocks, or limped out into view from no apparent cover, looked surprised or even slightly resentful, but most simply obeyed. Watts' friend hauled the sergeant across his broad shoulders and began to take the path to the interior like a goaded mule, oblivious of his burden. Two men, Christos reported to Thea as he hurried back from his vantage point, would have to be left behind, and they had been allowed to keep their guns so that they could give a good account of themselves—and perhaps save themselves from the ministrations of the Gestapo or the OVRA. Within moments of Thea's shouted command, eleven men were heading away from the coast with hardly a glance for the body of Chorakis or any other fallen comrades. Later there might be time to weep, to drink a toast to their courage, to sentimentalize.

Knox turned, ready to follow Thea, for the third Stuka

was already beginning its attack run. And then he saw Meyerscough. Somehow he had taken the big lieutenant's indestructability for granted, and he had been right. The trouble was, Meyerscough had not turned back during the respite but had used the opportunity to move forward to a spot where he could command both the German patrol's approach route and also get a good view of the Stukas. For Christ's sake, he was now a hundred yards from the rest of them.

'Meyerscough!' Knox bellowed. 'Come back! We need you here!'

The figure of the lieutentant was standing absolutely upright in the gorse further down the hill with his Sten crooked under one arm. He might have been out rough-shooting in Norfolk for all the tension that showed in his body. He turned when Knox called out, smiled and gave a thumbs-up. He was happy as a sandboy, there was no doubt.

'Meyerscough! We're making a run for it! Come on!'

The figure continued to smile, then waved the Sten like a favourite toy, as if to say: 'No, I want to stay here and play some more'.

'Meyerscough!'

Thea was pulling him. Knox knew he would not and could not go and get Meyerscough. The man had made a choice. If he went down the hill, all it would mean would be two deaths.

'M-e-y-e-r-s-c-o-u-g-h!'

'Byee, Mark!'

That final, drifting shout came as a shock. The casualness, the use of the Christian name. Meyerscough had relaxed completely for the first time since they had gathered at the villa on the Beirut-Broummanna road. He was happy. Circumstances such as these were made for him.

'Good luck, Gerald!'

The last sight he ever had of Meyerscough was of his turning back to face the oncoming Stuka, raising his Sten and letting out a hearty cheer that was a cross between a war-cry and a muscular prayer. His tousled fair hair looked at that moment as if it had been painted with gold, for the sun had burst through the clouds to flood the hills with light. Then Knox ran, stumbling after Thea Chorakis and the others, to begin running the long gauntlet back to the cave, thinking: 'It can take a man strange ways.'

For a fact had just sunk into his consciousness. The fact was that they had just been given the opportunity, and had failed, to assassinate Adolf Hitler. Someone, somewhere, had betrayed them.

So where did they run to now?

PHASE THREE:

'SIGNIFY'

April—May 1943

32

Shortly before midnight, Beirut time, when Bellingham was thinking about his fifth large whisky, the telephone rang. He reached for it with a grunt of relief.

'Villa office,' he answered. It was all he was allowed to say at this stage.

Menzies' voice was faint and distorted, but there was no panic in it. In fact, had Bellingham been facing him across a desk in London, he supposed that 'C' might have sounded crisp and incisive. Only the long-distance line, filled with vague chatterings in the background, tranformed his tone into that of a saloon-bar bore unsuccessfully shouting to make himself heard.

'Be careful,' Menzies crackled. 'Use only agreed terms, no names. Can you hear me?'

'Just about,' Bellingham said. He shook the old-fashioned French receiver, unleashing a rush of static.

'It'll have to do, old boy.' A short pause. 'Have you made contact with *Tweedledum* again since the first report?'

Bellingham tensed. 'No. Your telegram told me to wait, so I didn't try to get in touch with him. He's made no effort since then.'

'I see. All right.' Another gap. Stewart did not like telephones, for a number of good reasons. 'Do you think he knows?'

'Knows what?'

'About the ramifications of SIGNIFY. What else?'

'I'm not so sure that I bloody well do. And I can hardly ask him outright—he's in a shocking enough state anyway. What on earth do I say?'

'Sweet nothings,' said Menzies. 'Keep the channel open, by whatever means present themselves, and make *Tweedledum* feel loved without being too specific. This sort of reaction is not uncommon when something goes badly wrong in the field. Chaps decide they can't trust anyone, refuse to move. One has to go softly-softly with them . . .'

'But what practical advice can I offer? Can't we send a sub to pick him up, to show we care?'

'No,' Menzies answered quickly. 'You know how delicate things are. It must be *Dancer*. We can salvage the situation there so long as *Tweedledum* can be persuaded to trust *Dancer*. I want your help to turn *Tweedledum* round.'

Bellingham sighed in exasperation. 'But *Dancer* and his bloody friends are the main problem!' he bellowed, refilling his glass from the bottle with his free hand. 'I'm not so bloody sure about that particular situation myself!'

'Look, Jackie, trust me. Please. There's always a risk involved in these projects. We did all we could to ensure the safety of the men involved. *Tweedledum* lost his nerve, disobeyed instructions. But if you turn him round, he can still make his way to safety.'

'Stewart, I don't know if I can.'

'If you really care about that young man and his companions, you'll be able to,' Menzies snapped. There was something peremptory in his tone, as if any challenge had to be warded off at all costs. And when he raised his voice on this terrible telephone line, it made him sound fighting drunk. Perhaps he had realized it, because he changed his tone, becoming gentle, a little penitent. 'I really need you to help, Jackie,' he said. 'Things this end are bad. We are barking completely up the wrong tree. *Turquoise* has given us the slip. I'm still wondering about the . . . other side's role. So tell *Tweedledum* that everything will be all right so long as he co-operates. Tell him *Dancer*'s a good boy really. Everything else will follow, believe me.'

'I still don't think it will work.'

'It will. We must ensure that he doesn't fall into hostile hands. His life is not just his own responsibility. We can't let the Nazis have him.'

'You said *Turquoise* is still at large. Good God, Stewart, that means failure all round. Can't you explain a bit more?' Bellingham said, frightened and bewildered. Trust Stewart to show no emotion, not even a little simple regret.

'This isn't the place. Get *Tweedledum* to trust *Dancer*.

Then come back to London and all will be explained. Really, Jackie.'

'But I ought to know!'

'Later, Jackie. Good luck. And goodbye . . .'

'Stewart! Listen! I have a right to—Stewart!' Bellingham bawled into the receiver, forgetting basic security in his rage and frustration. But the line had gone dead. There was only a distant rushing, like a message from a sea shell. And Menzies, he suddenly realized, had never even said he was sorry. Not before, not now, not ever.

Bellingham sat at his desk overlooking the Persian courtyard for some time. The hand that had held the telephone was shaking. All of him was shaking, he realized, and took a sip from the glass of whisky. It was bitter as aloes. The emptiness in his stomach had not been filled, and never would be by that stuff. It was the waiting . . . he had been on alert by the telephone here since four in the afternoon, when Menzies' second, longer telegram had arrived, and for what? Instructions to a long-distance nanny: keep Knox happy with a pack of lies and damn the rest, because Uncle Stewart knew best.

The biggest 'might-have-been' in the whole affair had, of course, been the decision to press on even after Knox's panic call of a few days back, with its reference to the German officer in Ioannides' back yard. Menzies had sworn that they had to continue, and Bellingham had obediently worked to persuade Knox, because there seemed no alternative and Menzies insisted that Ioannides was wholly reliable, despite all appearances to the contrary. He was still insisting that, for God's sake, and he might even be right. Who knew? The fact was that Knox was now refusing to have anything to do with Ioannides, and that put them right in it . . .

Darling had been on duty in the radio room the previous afternoon while Bellingham took a siesta on the camp bed next door. Knox had transmitted to tell them that the whole bloody issue had gone awry and that Meyerscough was presumed dead in an air attack on the commando group. Bellingham, when fetched from the bed, had not been able to persuade him to obey orders and head for Ioannides' safe house, ready to be whisked back to Cyprus by sea. The lad had had enough by then, and who could blame him? A flurry of carefully-phrased wires to and from London had ensued, outlining the scale and manner of the disaster, resulting eventually in this midnight telephone conversation and now a terrible silence.

Because Bellingham had been forced to wait for the call from London, Darling was taking radio watch again tonight. It would be best to go and relieve him, see if he couldn't perhaps will something to happen, for Knox to change his mind, whatever a poor old man with a bad conscience could hope for.

'Good luck, laddie . . .' Bellingham murmured, raising the whisky to his lips. He suddenly had a shockingly vivid image of the three men who had gone to Rhodes as he had last seen them, hopping on board that caïque in Nicosia harbour just a few weeks previously, cheerful and businesslike, courageous and trusting. And he remembered one of the last things he had said to Knox . . . or had it been Meyerscough? . . . anyway, it had been about the fact that if they got into hot water, they'd organize them off the island in no time, no matter the price. *Good Lord,* Bellingham had joked, *if all else fails, I'll nick a dinghy and sail over and get you meself* . . . He wished he could remember whether he had said it to Knox, or Meyerscough, or even whether he had merely wanted to say it to Knox, or Meyerscough, or even whether he had merely wanted to say it but never managed to get the words out . . .

'You're a bastard, Jackie,' he said out loud to himself. 'You've got something like a score of years to go, mouldering in retirement—less if you carry on hitting the Bell's at this rate—and you're prepared to sacrifice those young men for your pension and the continuing good will of that other bastard, Sir Stewart bloody Menzies.'

He stared balefully down on the three quarters-full whisky glass, then leaned slowly over, picked it up, and poured the dun liquid out of the open window, heard it splash against the paved stones of the garden walk below. With a kind of unsteady dignity that was a precursor of the real thing, he took up his jacket and cap. He had to fumble to find the left arm-hole, but finally he got the jacket on and plonked his cap on his head. Then he made his way to the door of his office. 'Out on a bloody limb,' he said. 'Right out and no mistake. But all is not lost. You may not like what Jackie's decided, but you're going to have to lump it, Stewart.'

Darling was perched on the little canvas stool when Bellingham walked into the radio room.

'Er, morning, I think, sir,' he said, getting to his feet. He marked his place in the detective novel he had been reading and placed it carefully on top of the locker that acted as a filing cabinet. 'Helps to pass the time, sir. Rubbish, of course,' he added shyly, excusing the fact that the book had a noticeably lurid cover.

Bellingham felt as though the brief walk through the garden had cleared his mind. He sat down on the only other piece of furniture in the room, an old wicker chair that creaked dangerously beneath his weight.

'Nothing from Captain Knox?' he asked the sergeant, fiddling with his pipe but making no move to fill it.

'Not a peep, sir.'

Darling was looking at him questioningly, and so Bellingham decided to give him an amended account of his telephone conversation with Menzies. The man was entitled to something; there were friends of his involved, after all.

'Well, I spoke to the powers-that-be,' he said. 'Orders are to do our best to persuade Captain Knox back to his senses and to keep communication channels open. I may have to do a bit of travelling about to that end,' he added, still rather surprised because the audacity of what he had decided to do was quite terrifying really. 'I'll need to get in touch with *Dancer* shortly, make some fresh arrangements. We'll do what we can—everything we can—to help Captain Knox and Sergeant Watts, don't worry.'

'I know, sir,' Darling agreed with a nod of his cropped head. 'I'm sure the captain'll be all right, once he's had a chance to get his bearings. We'll get him away somehow, and when he's back over here he'll be able to see it all in the right light. He'll probably end up laughing about it—excepting the business with poor Lieutenant Meyerscough, naturally.'

'I'll transmit at the scheduled time in the morning—assuming he doesn't get in touch first, that is,' Bellingham qualified hastily. 'Keep things as normal as possible. Rather like when fellows get trapped in a mine shaft. Send messages through to cheer 'em up until the rescue party breaks through from the far side of the workings.'

Darling seemed pleased and comforted by the image. 'Thank you, sir,' he said, and grinned. So far as he was concerned, Meyerscough's death and the circumstances surrounding it had unhinged Knox, made him imagine phantoms. If the bizarre details of Knox's radio message of the previous day had disturbed him to any appreciable extent, he had managed to rationalize them out of existence.

That was precisely the problem, Bellingham thought. Darling, who knew nothing, was happy enough, while Menzies, who knew everything, had the broad view to sustain him. Old Jackie Bellingham, though, the man who knew only the half of it and who got more confused by the minute by what he did know, he was in trouble. Pig-in-the-bloody-middle. He wondered what his Prussian was up to.

'Yes. So long as we keep our heads, sir, he'll keep his, eh?' Darling murmured. 'That's the answer. Usually is, in my experience.'

'Absolutely, Sergeant.' Christ, but Bellingham could have done with that whisky now. And he wasn't going to touch any more until Knox was back on a caïque and on his way to Cyprus; and perhaps never. He was going to need every iota of clearheadedness, physical strength and animal cunning over the next few days the way his plans were suddenly taking shape.

'Why don't you get some rest, Sergeant?' he suggested. 'Go to your quarters, get right away from this place and give yourself a real break. You'll be worked hard enough over the next few days if I have to spend prolonged periods away from here.'

Darling, who knew a drunk when he saw one, looked doubtful. Then an ingrained habit of deference won out. Officers, even ones who hit the bottle at critical moments, were officers.

'Thank you, sir. You'll . . . er . . . be all right, won't you?'

'Never better, ta muchly.'

'Good.' Darling picked up his mystery novel, the packet of 'Victory V' cigarettes and the box of matches next to the W/T set. 'You know I don't mind being woken if you're tired, sir, don't you?'

'I know. See you in the morning, Sergeant.'

Darling walked slowly out of the room, nodding in that way people use to express disagreement that they dare not show openly. He said 'good night' four times.

Bellingham sat down on the radio operator's stool, braced himself against the table. He remembered that he was still wearing his cap, and so he took it off and placed it carefully next to the W/T. It would take him a couple of hours to sober up sufficiently to be really on-the-ball about things, he reckoned from long experience. Until then, he could draft a few ideas, make some rough notes on what he was going to need and how he was going to neutralize London while he did what he knew he needed and wanted to do.

After less than an hour, Bellingham had covered ten sheets with reasons, projections, plans. His mind—or the part of it he was using—had moved into high gear; he felt as if the whisky was being squeezed into the inessential areas of his brain, like raw sewage being left to rot in the insalubrious slums, and that soon it would all decay and be washed away.

On the top of the first page of his notes he had written in a slightly unsteady but quite legible hand:

> *First steps. Get Keflakis's boat. Leave contacting Ioannides until the last moment. Meditate on Prussian, because he's in there somewhere. Don't give Stewart a chance to stop you. This last vital.*

33

Grainger was waiting up for Menzies in the next room, drinking tea by the log fire. The men of his team had been busy all day lugging wood into the fuel store, because Sir Stewart had remarked on the chill in the air.

'All right, sir?' he asked, rising with heavy deference to greet his chief.

'Yes, thank you,' Menzies said.

'Tea, sir?'

Menzies nodded absently. The hot, sweet drink typified the standards of life in wartime England: it was cheap, uniformly mediocre, healthy, and thoroughly democratic. A body fuel for all seasons and for all—or nearly all—men.

'Did you manage to telephone abroad, sir? I know it can be difficult, and I'm afraid the situation's getting worse rather than better.'

'Thank you, Grainger. I had a short wait. But it wasn't too time-consuming.'

Grainger was, of course, fishing. Menzies had actually made several calls apart from the one to Bellingham. The house here had its own small exchange that bypassed the village telephonist and linked directly to the military network, so doubtless Grainger would be able to find out all the details if he was prepared to bend the rules a little, but Menzies was darned if he was going to start chattering about his conversations with Bellingham at this stage in the proceedings.

'How's Finch?' he asked, pushing the conversation gently in another direction. The courier was no longer relevant except as a source of harmless diversion at times like these.

'Very fit, sir. Bored, unsure of what's going to happen with him. Apart from that, all right. Anything's better than the old eight o'clock walk, I suppose.'

'Yes.'

The 'eight o'clock walk' was Service slang for an execution, since hangings were usually carried out at that time in the morning. Grainger picked up on the non-committal nature of Menzies' reply and shrugged. 'Of course, he's still a naughty boy, sir. Always a price to be paid in the end, isn't there, sir?'

Menzies drank his tea in silence, in the knowledge that Grainger dared not challenge him openly on this or any other issue. Why SIGNIFY had suddenly been re-activated twenty-four hours previously, for instance, when all had appeared settled. And why 'C' was constantly making telephone calls, sending and receiving coded messages, dashing around like a blue-arsed fly. Grainger just did as he was told. It was what he and his people were good at; paid to do their job and keep quiet. None of the high-fliers from Broadway ever talked to them; some of them had probably forgotten their existence. Grainger was as useful and as inconspicuous as an Untouchable, and that was why Menzies had chosen to establish his operation headquarters for SIGNIFY here at the house in Hertfordshire. Grainger could even supply a reliable courier to bring up the transcripts of the radio transmission that came from Rhodes via Bellingham, so that they did not need to pass through the usual Service channels before Menzies had them for his use. So long as Grainger felt that his little department, so often under threat when the budget came in for review, had been granted Menzies' special protection, then he would be the absolute soul of discretion. He would kill for 'C', literally and gladly.

'I would be grateful if I could be woken at seven,' Menzies said when he had finished his tea. 'I have some telegrams to dispatch in the morning, some for embassies abroad included. Could you have priorities cleared and two couriers ready to go first thing tomorrow?'

'Yes. Of course, sir.'

'Then I'll be off to bed. One has to keep the Service ticking over even at a time such as this. Can't be cut off completely. I'm sorry to say that it means a lot of work for you, Grainger,' he added with calculated grace.

'Oh, I don't mind a bit, sir. We're always ready to rally round, as you know. Muck in and all that. A nightcap before you turn in, sir?'

Menzies shuddered faintly at Grainger's minor public-school phrasing, his pathetic eagerness to please. 'Putney-gone-Mayfair' was the damning description he had heard applied to such individuals, and Menzies had to admit that there was no one so subtly obnoxious as the tradesman's son with pretensions.

'Thank you, no. Not tonight. Goodnight, Grainger.'

'Jolly good night, sir.'

As Menzies undressed in his small, unheated guest bedroom at the back of the house, he mulled over his conversation with Jackie Bellingham and told himself very firmly that any feelings of guilt were quite misplaced. Knox would be spirited out in some way that did not compromise the Service or SIGNIFY—by drastic means, if he persisted on behaving like an ass—and the Service's skilled debriefers would then provide him with an explanation of the fiasco that should cover most of his doubts—enough, at least, to ensure that he would cause no embarrassment. Meyerscough's case was sadder and a lot easier: his family would receive a notice from the War Office to the effect that he had been killed 'while on active service of a secret nature in the Mediterranean theatre.' The same would go, if necessary, for the wounded NCO. Good God, of course one was happier when things went completely smoothly and without loss of faith or life, but then they so rarely did. The principle was to carry on with one's projects so long as the price remained acceptable. In the Service's accounts, and therefore in Menzies', the balance that mattered was the balance of individual lives against the lives of thousands and millions. One accepted that way of thinking, or one did nothing. Outsiders, of course, could never understand that. Not even a man like Churchill, with his curious mixture of cynicism and sentimentality, fully grasped the arid realities that the Service had to confront daily.

Having thus dealt with his guilt feelings while removing his day clothes, reaching the inevitable conclusion at the same time as he reached for his pyjamas, Menzies dressed for bed and performed his ablutions to the accompaniment of a brief mental soliloquy regarding the nature of panic. Bellingham's initial, highly alarming communication the previous evening had caused 'C' distress and great confusion, but the crisis of self-confidence had passed quickly. First, Menzies had realized that SIGNIFY could not now fail, whatever happened. Second, he had weighed up the true significance of the fiasco on Rhodes and had concluded that it held few dangers for anyone, except possibly the Abwehr. Provided that the surviving officer and his sergeant were kept out of trouble until they could be spirited away, all would be well. Third, the death of one officer was an acceptable cost for such a project; one had only to look at the casualty rates on such undertakings as the Dieppe raid to realize that it was only a question of scale, and in terms of effectiveness against lives risked, SIGNIFY could have cost a thousand deaths and it would still have been worth it. Menzies and Bellingham—poor Jackie—had made every attempt to ensure that when the payoff came, those involved would be given as much protection as possible. In the event, *Tweedledum* and his colleagues had done what no agent in the field should ever do, which was to refuse to obey a direct order from his controller while in hostile territory, no matter how little sense it appeared to make, and they had paid the price. Even now, for goodness' sake, Menzies was doing his best to get them back to Allied territory, though in some ways it would be better if everyone concerned disappeared off the face of the earth . . . That would be the last resort, Menzies thought, and for the first time a shiver ran up his back. It was all very well to risk men, but to cold-bloodedly eliminate them went against the grain. Nevertheless, the calculation of a few lives against SIGNIFY's success still held, and if it became necessary, Menzies knew that he could and would have to issue that order. But a last resort, a last resort of all.

Menzies sighed, shook off his thoughts of death and picked up the copy of Trollope's *Barchester Towers* that lay on his bedside table. He opened it to the page indicated by the leather book mark. Then he read, as was his habit, for thirty minutes, a total, one-pointed immersion in harmless Victorian intrigue, before switching off the light and enjoying his usual excellent night's sleep.

One of Grainger's men brought a pot of strong tea and some toast to Menzies' room at seven the next morning in accordance with 'C''s request. He breakfasted alone at a small table by the window that overlooked the flat, almost fenlike countryside of north-east Hertfordshire. The weather had suddenly taken a turn for the worse; East Anglia could be terribly cold well into the spring, and today it had reverted to type. Menzies gazed sadly out across the drizzle and the creeping mist and allowed himself in that moment a longing for a kinder, wiser world than the one he had been granted a place in, one in which young men did not have to die or be murdered on strange islands, and in which old friends such as he and Jackie Bellingham could really be friends, not manipulator and victim. Then, putting such thoughts aside along with his empty tea-cup, he made a harsh decision that had been pressing him, if he was honest, for twenty-four hours now. The result was a draft telegram to a man attached to the British consulate in Smyrna, on the Turkish mainland not too far from Rhodes and the Service's nearest outstation. It was to be translated into a military rather than a diplomatic code, and it read:

> *Endeavouring persuade Tweedledum emergency exit via Dancer. Chances success most uncertain. Dancer to hire helpers case failure. Ultimate extreme may be necessary. Only on direct orders from me. Hold ready await further instructions.*

Captain Knox, Menzies said to himself, please believe what Bellingham tries to tell you, because to all intents and purposes it happens to be the truth. If you do, then this unpleasant business won't be necessary and I shall be a happier man as a result. If you don't, however . . . Menzies was glad at that moment that he had never met the young man and the NCO concerned. That made such thoughts easier, much easier than they must be for poor Jackie. It briefly crossed his mind that Bellingham had sounded very annoyed on the phone, and perhaps hurt. It was possible that he had been away from this profession for too long, tending his Portuguese garden, and that Bellingham also no longer fully understood the realities of the situation. Luckily he was old school Service, and his kind were made of stern stuff.

Shaking his head in gentle exasperation, Menzies read the communication through once more, marked it with the name of the man in Smyrna and the instructions PERSONAL, MOST SECRET. After some short consideration, he added an exclamation mark. The Gods had been kind to SIGNIFY, but one couldn't be too careful.

Keflakis reckoned on twelve hours' sailing time to Rhodes, if the weather held. So far as Bellingham was concerned, everything was taking too long, but he knew he had no choice but to trust the skipper of the *Makaria*. He had got Knox and co. safely to Rhodes; now he would get whoever had survived back to safety. Just so long as Bellingham could get them onto his boat.

He had snatched a couple of hours' sleep shortly after they had left Nicosia the previous lunchtime. Now it was pushing towards the small hours of the morning, and soon they would begin to hug the Turkish coast for the last stretch through neutral waters to Rhodes. Bellingham sat out on deck, luxuriating in the hosts of sharp, tiny stars in the night sky, feeling the wind on his face, and cleaning the Smith & Wesson that he hadn't used since 1917—September it had been, in a petty fracas on a beach near Cadiz with a party of German saboteurs who had been dropped from a U-boat. The weapon, which he held in enormous affection, had been kept in thick cloth and oiled, locked away in a drawer at Bellingham's villa, since he had retired from the Service twelve years ago.

'You fucking well drink, Major sir.'

Bellingham looked up, saw Keflakis clutching two glasses of *ouzo* in his plump paws. The Greek skipper's face was expectant, respectful, almost nervous.

'Thanks, but no. Not at the moment. Afterwards, on the way back.'

'Is good for you, *ouzo*.'

'It's a rule. Don't be offended. Actually, I'd really like some coffee now.'

Keflakis met his eye, nodded, then shrugged. 'You are a man with some experience of life, Major sir. I accept your decision. Those young officers I bring here, they drink. They fucking well drink and no mistake, my God in heaven.'

'I'm sure they did,' Bellingham said with a tight smile. 'But at the moment I need to think, above all else I need to think. Coffee, please.' Since Keflakis remained standing and staring in that amiable, uncritical way of his, Bellingham asked: 'Did the young officers . . . have a good trip to Rhodes?'

The Greek thumped his own chest, chortled. 'With me, Major, everyone has fucking good trip. Never lose fucking no one at sea, me. Not like those fucking bastards on fucking land. I know what I fucking doing.'

'I'm sure you do. I mean that.'

And Bellingham did. Keflakis was a wholly honest, admirable man, despite all his smuggling activities, his womanizing and his boozing, his foul-mouthed self-assertion, because he was innocent and he kept his promises. He was the kind of man who had to exist in order for the Canarises, the Menzies and the rest to get their jobs done, for if the whole world were devious, then their schemes would never work.

Seeing Bellingham's Smith & Wesson, Keflakis went to fetch his own weapon and brought it—and the requested coffee—to Bellingham so that they could talk in comfort. His gun was a hand-crafted special Lueger that he had found on the corpse of a German officer during the fighting for Crete, when he and his crew had not only picked up Allied soldiers from the rocky coves and beaches, but had made sorties into the hills above to find them, a task that had taken them into the thick of the hand-to-hand battle raging just short of the shore. Keflakis was proud of the gun, because it was beautiful and also because, he claimed, he had checked the German officer's identity papers and found that he had just robbed the body of a member of the aristocracy, a man with a brace of 'vons' to his name and a 'zu' or two to match. They talked guns, reminiscences of soldiering and sailoring, adventuring and smuggling—Keflakis's main source of income before the war—until it was the captain's turn to take over the wheel. By then there was the tiniest warning of light on the eastern horizon, back in the direction of Cyprus. Keflakis would stay at the helm until they were secure among the many inlets that made ragged the coast of southern Anatolia. Then they would talk some more, he assured Bellingham.

Bellingham had found the talk exhilarating. Keflakis was a pirate, a man who lived wholly by his own standards. For thirty years, Jackie Bellingham had lived according to other people's, and only now was he breaking out of that pattern, in order to save a young man for whom he felt a clear moral responsibility. It felt like a liberation. Let Sir Stewart Menzies argue about it when they got back to Lebanon, or back to London.

Before Bellingham settled down under the awning that Keflakis had laid across the deck for his use, he thought also of Ioannides. The man they called 'Dancer' had not questioned Bellingham's simple command to be met at the usual rendezvous point on the coast of Rhodes. On the other hand, Bellingham suspected very strongly, from what Menzies had said over a period of time, that Ioannides was also in contact with a British source in mainland Turkey. Ioannides certainly passed out information via agents there, using his cargo business to make clandestine trips across the narrow straits to Anatolia. That was an element that would have to be borne in mind. The essence was speed. But on the other hand, speed had to be combined with a job well done, and for the new, free Jackie Bellingham, the job could only be deemed fully completed if he managed to contact someone else who he now knew was on Rhodes and finally get to the truth of what had happened to SIGNIFY. That somebody was a young Prussian who had crossed Bellingham's path in Portugal and who, like Bellingham, had been charged with organizing the Rhodes end of things too. It had all begun to fall into place, you see: the officer at Ioannides' house that disastrous night when the Greek had briefed Knox and Meyerscough; Menzies' reluctance to discuss the practical details of co-operation with the Germans; and the way that no one had given the British or the partisans away to the enemy in any direct fashion. It all added up to a man of Canaris's choice on the island, trying to keep an eye on things, and that young Prussian would be the logical choice, for—like Menzies—Canaris would not use two men for a job like this where one absolutely trusty would do.

Hey-ho. Bellingham reflected that, since he had blown his pension and probably his entire future by acting on his own initiative like this, he might as well go the whole hog and bloody well get to the bottom of things.

He really was beginning to feel twenty years younger. The Smith & Wesson rested against his body like a familiar item of luggage. The water stayed calm the whole way along the coast to Rhodes. It was all deceptively like a holiday.

34

They had buried 'After the Liberation' George that morning at first light. He had been counted among the walking wounded during the retreat from the east coast, but he had deteriorated slowly afterwards from the pressure of a bullet lodged against his lungs. In the end, as the foreign body dug deeper, he had drowned slowly in his own blood, lucid and aware almost to the last, and thoroughly terrified. He would never see that wonderful future he had talked of so often; that was a minor extra cruelty.

Thea Chorakis sat a couple of feet from Knox, with her dead brother's Biretta cradled on her knees. She and Knox had granted themselves the luxury of a short walk in the woods that surrounded their new hideout, a strange patchwork of shallow ravines some kilometres to the south of the now unsafe anchorite caves. Four of the surviving guerrillas had volunteered to hazard a foraging trip down to a village in the valley. The rest were either asleep or on guard or taking turns to watch over Sergeant Watts. Their contacts with local shepherds told them that the hue and cry after the English assassins was dying down; the Germans and Italians claimed to be carrying out 'exercises' which had served their purpose and were now being phased out.

'Mark,' she said when they had been by the stream in silence for some time. 'I don't want you to go. But I think that if you feel you should, then you must. Never mind what happened for me and Panayiotis in the past.'

He grunted. She had a way of looking at him, like a dog that is hungry but has been trained to eat only when ordered to do so; he knew that he had only to give the word, weaken for a moment.

'If it were just a radio message from Lebanon and a question of shaking hands with that bastard Ioannides again, I wouldn't consider it. I'd rather take my chances on waiting until we could organize a boat to Turkey, or failing that, hang on here with you until the hour of liberation really does come.'

Knox fell silent, picked up a small sliver of rock and tossed it into the stream. The water was swift and cold; during the summer it would probably all but dry up, but at this time of year it chuckled over the rocks with an infectious lack of economy, as if the supplies of melted winter snow would last forever.

'You trust this major?' Thea asked thoughtfully after an interval. 'You don't believe that he might also betray you?'

'I trust him as much as I feel I can trust anyone in this situation.' Knox paused, took a breath. 'Except perhaps for you. You and the comrades. And I'd be doing you a favour by disappearing off this island, that's for certain.'

As he spoke, he was looking not at Thea but down into the water, and remembering how he had scribbled down Bellingham's message by flickering light of a rusty oil lamp. The impersonal tapping of a metal key four hundred miles to the east had told him: 'Coming personally arrange exit by sea—Whether you like it or not—Will guarantee Dancer OK—Please co-operate—Save my grey hairs—' The message had been repeated half a dozen times, and Knox had been able to absorb it completely, pick out the component parts, distinguish between the stilted orders and the fatherly pleading. He could see the major even now in his mind's eye, with his briar and old-fashioned moustache, frowning over the morse patterns sent out into the unresponsive ether. The image still moved him surprisingly powerfully. Major Bellingham had, after all, shown he cared. If only Knox could trust the system as completely as he felt he could trust the major's humanity.

Thea did not comment on his last statement, about disappearing, but there was a silky rustle of pine needles, as if her hand was clenching on the floor of the wood.

'You never had a father,' she said suddenly.

'What do you mean? Of course I did. He married my Greek mother . . .' Then Knox realized what Thea had really been saying, and he tailed off in embarrassment. Perhaps his feelings for Major Bellingham were his Achilles' heel, and then again, perhaps they would prove a saving grace in a world where he had only his instincts to go on. It was surely true, in any case, that he would have preferred to be the son of a Bellingham than of an affable, cool diplomat who somehow never had the time, or the energy, or the simple humanity to show he cared.

'Will you tell your superiors the story of the betrayal when you return to England?' Thea said then. 'Ensure that the traitor is punished?'

'Of course.'

'It may be that punishment will be decided here, before the liberation. But I would still like your superiors to know what happened.'

'Thea, we don't know who did it. The whole thing's an incredible tangle. I don't understand it. I'm pretty sure Major Bellingham doesn't. Or anyone else. It doesn't make sense, so don't jump to any conclusions,' Knox said. 'Perhaps one day we'll unravel the reasons. One day.'

'There is a bad smell,' Thea persisted. 'You and your comrades are . . . were . . . good men. This Major may also be good. But everyone else, everything else—' She made a face indicating extreme, childish disgust.

'Nothing's simple.'

'Death is simple. One day you are alive, the next, you are where Panayiotis and George have gone—and where your Sergeant is going. Mark, understand that, will you?'

The look of disgust had been replaced by a gaze of such urgency that Knox could hardly meet Thea's eyes. There was the shock of realizing that she knew Watts was dying, and that there was nothing to be done. And there was also a physical tremor running through his body that was close to excitement. A phrase flashed into his mind, a re-arrangement of the usual phrase from the funeral service. *In the midst of death we are in life*, he found a voice in his head repeating. Thea had taken off her shoes while they had been talking, and had rolled up her baggy trousers to the knee. She had beautiful, long legs, lithe and well-shaped.

'Yes,' he said dully. 'We only get one chance.'

'Then we should take it. Mark, we are alone here—'

He reached out and took her hand. They struggled for a moment for the privilege of initiation. Finally his strength prevailed, and it was he who pulled her gently but inexorably over into the cover of a budding bush. He pressed her down, felt her body soft under him except for the delicate hardness of the mountain of Venus between her legs. She placed his right hand there and whispered: 'One chance, perhaps. Take it quickly.' Knox was hardening too, and she was reaching for that.

Sergeant Watts, they realized later, must have died at just about the time that they reached their climax there by the rushing stream. It was as if he had been holding on until that moment, for reasons best known to his Dorset peasant soul. They didn't know it, but also at about that time, Jackie Bellingham entered the house of Stavros Ioannides and began issuing orders.

35

The Admiral insisted on standing facing the mass-produced portrait of Adolf Hitler on the wall nearest the door. From time to time, as he and Bredow reached some particularly distressing part of their conversation, he would lift his eyes to the picture and grimace meaningfully at it. The message to Adolf was: You may have escaped this time, but we shall keep on trying.

In fact, Canaris seemed to Bredow surprisingly, perhaps unreasonably positive in his approach. He did most of the talking in the pleasant little room at the Abwehr's outstation in Athens, and almost every other sentence contained another insistence that all was not yet lost. The British, he maintained, now needed the Abwehr more than ever, because of—not despite—the failure of *Wintermärchen,* for it must now be clear to Menzies that he had a uniquely powerful and dangerous spy inside his own organization. All the Abwehr needed to do was to keep in touch with Menzies, keep showing good faith. If they could help the surviving British escape from Rhodes, then how could Menzies fail to respond in kind?

'I plan on your remaining where you are for another two to three weeks, even if the British are evacuated in the near future,' Canaris told Bredow. 'Firstly, in order to monitor the winding-down of the security effort. Secondly, to keep you out of harm's way.'

'I gather Berlin is still dangerous, Admiral.'

'Yes.' Canaris sighed, fixed the portrait with another baleful stare. 'Dohnanyi is holding out, but only just. His latest ruse was to have his wife smuggle a cotton wad infected with a typhoid bacillus into his cell. With this he has made himself too ill to be interrogated.'

'And Oster?'

'He has disappeared. The High Command refuses to acknowledge that his whereabouts are any of its concern. He has been dismissed from the Army and is therefore no longer a fully-functioning human being. We can only conclude that he, too, is enjoying the hospitality of our friends at the Prinz-Albrecht-Strasse.'

'It sounds like I would be advised to stay away for as long as possible, Admiral.'

'I shall see what I can do. And meanwhile, I have a job to do, and so do you, Otto.'

'I understand that, Admiral.'

In a way he was glad to be returning to Rhodes rather than accompanying the Admiral back to Berlin. Everything down here reminded him of their failure with *Wintermärchen,* but at least there were no air raids, no Gestapo interrogators on his track—yet—and, above all, no reminders of Gisela and the baby. As for the distant future, beyond the early summer, no one could guarantee anything. Tresckow and company might succeed with one of their bombs. In any case, it felt as if the anti-Nazi conspiracy was starting again from square one, and the fact weighed heavily on him. To add insult to the injury, the latest news from Russia was that Field Marshal von Kluge, the wooden titan of the Eastern Front, was in hospital recovering from a car crash, and in the meantime he had been replaced by a man whose loyalty to Hitler was totally unquestionable.

'So,' Canaris growled. 'Ioannides is still clean, usable, despite his involvement in the disaster?'

'I was taken to the scene twenty-four hours later by Major Falcke, a member of von Drewitz's staff with whom I am on cordial terms. I was relieved to discover that no one had identified the corpse of Ioannides' Turkish manservant who, as you know, carried the message to the British shortly before they were due to attack. I was shown the bodies and recognized the trousers and rope-soled shoes that the Turk habitually wore, but naturally I did not identify him. His was one of six bodies that had been badly charred by rockets.'

Canaris snorted approvingly. 'Nice to have some luck for a change. Any other loose ends in that quarter, Otto?'

'No partisans were captured alive. It appears that two wounded men shot themselves rather than be taken by the SS. The investigating commission—led by Standartenführer Dickel, by the way—has therefore not been given the opportunity to interrogate anyone who witnessed the Turk's visits to the partisan camp. It is my reluctant conclusion that Ioannides will remain safely in operation until hell freezes over. The swine seems to lead a charmed life.'

'His kind often do,' Canaris observed placidly. 'The saying that the good die young is substantially accurate,' he said with a sardonic little chuckle. Then he saw the look of anxiety on Bredow's face, reached forward and touched the young Oberleutnant on the shoulder. 'I, of course, am in my fifties!' he said with a rather laboured jokiness. 'Draw what conclusions you will from that!'

Bredow nodded. 'The important thing, Admiral, is that I and Ioannides put our heads together and somehow remove the British officer and his wounded sergeant from the island, deliver them safely to Sir Stewart Menzies or whoever his representative may be. Is this correct?'

'It is.' Canaris pressed a button on the desk to his left and waited until an orderly appeared. He asked the man to bring a bottle of schnaps and two glasses for himself and the Oberleutnant. 'Otto,' he continued when the drinks had come, 'I cannot emphasize sufficiently strongly the importance of our keeping well in favour with the British. Kluge is out of the running, but Stauffenberg and some others have already begun to put out feelers to Field Marshal Rommel. Rommel is perturbed by the defeat in North Africa, and he now has time on his hands, to brood and make plans. We shall therefore be working on him over the next weeks and months. A revival of *Wintermärchen,* perhaps under some other guise . . .'

For the next half an hour, Bredow let Canaris's talk wash over him, answering from time to time with a polite *Yes, Admiral* or *No, Admiral,* but his heart was not in it. In his mind's eye, he imagined himself back on Rhodes, standing on the balcony of his room at the *Albergo,* staring out to the clear blue horizon south-west of him and the distant mountains, knowing that somewhere out there were two British soldiers, an officer and a sergeant, who had survived the slaughter on the hill above the airfield. He felt a sinking in the gut when he considered the implications of a connection being made between the British, the partisan group, and Ioannides. More often, he chose to cut off completely when such thoughts came, and he suspected that the Admiral was doing the same. They had to rely on luck.

Thirty minutes and three glasses of schnaps later, they parted. The Admiral had ordered a plane to take him to Brindisi at two-thirty that afternoon, and Bredow was due to go with the regular Ju 88 leave service to Rhodes at about the same time, though from a different airfield. Canaris was fulsome, even a little manic, in his thanks and praises. Had *Wintermärchen* succeeded, he would have been more his usual self, more reticent, Bredow strongly suspected. The last view he had of the Abwehr chief as he was driven away from the outstation building was of a small, prematurely white-haired figure, a square elf, standing in the doorway and waving farewell. Canaris's face was smiling, but the shoulders were braced, even while he waved, as if the weight of the world were crushing down upon them. His body revealed what the Admiral's subtle, tough mind and tightly-controlled emotions had tried to hide: a pressure that one day soon would break either Hitler's régime or the men who opposed it into so many pieces that History would never find them all again.

The flight to Rhodes left late, and the slow transport aircraft was overloaded, but the journey was otherwise uneventful. Darkness had fallen when they touched down on the island. Bredow had been away for slightly less than twenty-one hours, but he noted with interest that the security activity at the airfield was already being scaled down. Platoons of SS security troops were hanging around with their belongings, waiting to be flown out back to Athens, Rome, and Berlin. He forced himself to take a beer and a sausage in the officers-only canteen in order to gauge the temperature of the place, and found that the SS types and the *Feldpolizei* heavies were all beginning to drink heavily out of boredom. When that was the case, it meant that the emergency had been all but ended. He heard one SS officer comment boozily to a companion that the birds had flown, and if they hadn't, then why not let 'em stew in their cages? It was the same thing . . .

Bredow walked into the *Albergo* at some indeterminate time after midnight, took his key from the night porter and stumbled up to bed. All he wanted to do was to wipe it all out of his consciousness, clean the slate before the charade began again, under whatever name the Admiral chose this time. He opened his door, flicked on the light, glanced gratefully at the neatly-made bed in the far corner of the room. Then he saw the figure on the balcony, the outline of a big man.

'Who is that?' Bredow snapped unbuttoning his holster. A general had been kidnapped in broad daylight on Crete not so long ago. But they would not have Otto von Bredow without a fight. In any case, it could only be one person if it was not an assassin. When the big man stepped in, smiling in his controlled way and with his hands up in a theatrical gesture of surrender, Bredow took his hand away from his holster and suddenly felt very awake indeed.

'Ioannides,' he said, uncertain whether to be awed or furious. 'You have the gall to come here?'

The Greek shrugged, clearly unapologetic. He was in command. 'I had no choice, Oberleutnant. It was too dangerous to telephone, and in any case the hotel would not tell me when you were due back. So I was forced to draw on some of my more . . . disreputable . . . experiences and secure entry to your room. I have something very important to tell you. But first may I put my hands down and have a cigarette?'

'For God's sake!' Bredow almost laughed but not quite. He pulled a pack out of his tunic pocket and tossed one to Ioannides. 'Now, what the hell is it?'

Ioannides bowed, playing his game to its full conclusion.

'First,' he said, 'I can tell you that there is a very strong chance that Captain Knox will leave the island during the next couple of days. So long as we handle him carefully.'

'What about the wounded man, the sergeant?'

'He is dead. That simplifies things, doesn't it?'

'I suppose that is one way of looking at the situation. And what else? A first implies a second.'

Ioannides' smile was clamped back. His eyes seemed to petrify into a look of opaque devotion, that looked out but let nothing in.

'Oberleutnant, there was the sergeant's demise to simplify things. Now a complication. I have to tell you that a certain Mister Bellingham, who knows you, has arrived on the island and has made himself my guest. He has two aims: to persuade Captain Knox to trust sufficiently to rely on me to get him off the island; and to have words with you, personally. No references to chiefs yet. Informal. He emphasized that very strongly.'

Bredow sat down on his bed, lit himself a cigarette and drew on it hungrily, for the comfort.

'All right,' he said after a moment's reflection. The Admiral would forgive him. For God's sake, he'd probably not be able to find Canaris, even if he wanted to. The man was going to be in permanent transit for the next twenty-four hours. Bredow had to make his decision now.

Ioannides was clearly relieved. 'I'll tell him, Oberleutnant, and arrange a meeting. He is talking with Captain Knox at the moment, I believe. It is a delight to play honest broker in such a good cause.'

And it must be a hell of an effort to keep so many balls in the air at one time, Bredow thought. In fact, precisely how many balls Ioannides was juggling with was by no means clear. One of these days, they might find out, and the knowledge might come as an unpleasant shock.

'You've met?' Bellingham said rather stiffly.

Knox nodded, smiled at Marcos. 'For a short while. Soon after we arrived. He's Ioannides' general dogsbody, and a pretty hard time he has of it.'

Bellingham could see, even in the darkness, that the boy

was grateful for Knox's words, though he spoke no English. The hunger for security, affection, in him understood the tone of voice.

'Shall we get down to business, then?'

'All right.'

Bellingham sat on one small hillock with Marcos, his guide, while Knox was cross-legged on another a few yards away. A tall, slim type with a woolly hat that obscured most of his face hung about by the trees behind him. They had agreed on one companion/guide each, as a mark of trust.

'I feel a bit silly. And sorry,' Bellingham began. 'The whole thing was a glorious cockup, and I'm the first to admit it. Can you accept that, Captain?'

'If I hadn't been half-prepared to accept it, I wouldn't have considered seeing you. And this lad here wouldn't have got past the edge of our woods without having his scrawny throat cut from ear to ear, Major. Sir.'

The new Knox was disconcerting. He had no one to reflect himself back at this moment, and so Bellingham was uncertain what kind of impression he was making on Knox. Not much of one at the moment, it seemed.

'I understand your bitterness, I really do. I feel pretty sick myself when I think of what happened, the way things went wrong.'

'The betrayal, you mean, Major.'

'Oh, I'm not sure we can put it that strongly. There's still a lot of clarification needed.'

Knox laughed bitterly. He was wearing a peasant's shirt and trousers, tied with twine at the knees, and a rough cloth cap pulled down over one ear. There was something pagan and ruthless about him. Yes, he had changed a lot.

'I thought your way until quite recently, Major,' he told Bellingham. 'Then I decided that the whole business was like a big game of "Find the Lady". Three cards, one a queen, shuffled between turns, and whichever card you chose, you never catch up with her. There used to be spivs who worked that one in Oxford on market days, fleecing the bumpkins in from the hills and the richer, wetter sort of undergraduate.' Knox's eyes were glinting dangerously in the velvet dark. 'What I'm saying, Major, is that you'll look and you'll look, but whoever's controlling the cards will never let you turn up that queen. If it comes to the crunch, they'll simply change the rules of the game.'

It would have been an odd conversation under any circumstances. On a mountainside in occupied Rhodes, conducted between a failed amateur assassin and an expatriate wine-shipper-turned-spy, it could be reckoned totally outlandish.

Bellingham felt squashed. He had a feeling that Knox was right, but he also knew that if he admitted it, he would probably never get the man off this blasted island. And the more he thought about the consequences of all this, the more it occurred to him that he was going to need to produce this young man as part of the explanation of what went so horribly wrong with SIGNIFY. Stewart might carry on, apparently not caring, but Bellingham didn't intend to. He had a duty. Everyone involved had a duty.

'It's an invidious comparison,' he said pompously. 'There are several individuals who might have weakened sufficiently to let the secret out of the bag.'

'Quite so, Major. But before Mehmet was killed, he told us that this was all a result of something happening a long way away, that even his master didn't fully understand. We were to kill the Führer. A German was watching us, but didn't have us arrested. Your behaviour is also inconsistent, Major—much as I respect and like you, I have to tell you that—and in your cups back in Lebanon, I heard you say things that also fall into place.' Knox spread out his hands. 'I'm not saying I understand. I'm just saying that so many things don't fit, and they're not necessarily here on Rhodes. I want to know as much as you do.'

'Damn it, will you come back to civilization with me and help share your knowledge with the people who really ought to know about what's been going on?' Bellingham snapped. 'That's all I want to know. Then you can go back to your bloody hills and wait until I get a boat for you. I can see you like the life!'

Knox said nothing for a long moment. Then he asked quietly: 'Do you think anyone will listen, really want to know?'

'I've got contacts.' Bellingham was improvising as he went along, but he was improvising his own life as well as

Knox's. It had just occurred to him, in a bolt of inspiration, that the man to go to was Colonel Dulac in Cairo. If he and Knox could talk to him before Menzies' people scooped them up, then there was a chance that something might be done. He told Knox about Dulac, and the young captain seemed to take it to heart.

'So . . . when would you want me to take ship with you? Presuming that I decide to come with you, that is,' Knox qualified hastily.

'I'd reckon a couple of days. I'll send Marcos with any messages.'

'I see. I'd like a day or two, so that's good.'

Bellingham noticed a slight stirring on the part of Knox's companion. There was definitely something strange and unaccountable there. It seemed as though, whoever they were, they were getting the gist of the conversation and were not entirely happy with it. A pair of dark eyes narrowed under the hat, and the head sank more deeply into its muffler. The Biretta light machine-gun that the escort held rather inexpertly quivered as a few words of dialect Greek were hissed in Knox's direction.

Knox shot something back, without taking his eyes off Bellingham, and held out one hand as if warding his companion off. He and Bellingham stared at each other in silence.

'That seems to be it,' Bellingham said, aware that anything more they said might lead to renewed suspicions. Best to get out while you were winning, as the saying went. 'I believe you'll come with me. Together we can help shed some light on things. And if I have anything to do with it, you'll be a hero.'

Knox nodded mutely. Heroism was clearly the last thing that interested him at this stage. Residual patriotism. A sense of justice. Those were the spurs, Bellingham guessed.

They got up, stepped towards each other and touched for the first time since Bellingham had arrived on Rhodes. The handshake lasted ten seconds or so. Then they broke, not unlike boxers, and went their ways: Knox up into the hills with his mysterious bodyguard in the woolly hat, and Bellingham back to his hiding-place at Ioannides' safe house by the sea, led by the unhappy boy, Marcos.

The affair was rapidly going beyond reasonable bounds, Bellingham decided during the clamber down the mountain. It had acquired a momentum of its own. And, by God, Stewart was not going to like it one little bit.

36

The initially brief exchange of telegrams with their man in Smyrna had, like Topsy, growed and growed. And by some inverse law peculiar to SIS, the messages had become less and less explicit, at least so far as an outsider would see; in fact, the entire correspondence had become banal in the extreme. For instance, the telegram lying on Menzies' desk at the moment had been decoded as:

> *Dancer on the razzle tomorrow evening, with friends. Everyone invited and will be given the full treatment, no expense spared. No one will want to leave. No one will be able to.*

Menzies had to confess that he found his man in Smyrna's sense of humour rather distasteful, but the telegrams did at least have the virtue of being incomprehensible to anyone here at Broadway, even when decoded. *Dancer*'s codename had been carefully removed from the files weeks ago, and anyone who had ever heard the name would probably have forgotten it long since, or could be persuaded that they had. Stavros Ioannides was about to cease his recorded existence. Others were to follow him, except that in their case the demise would also be very actual and real.

Menzies read the telegram through again, sighed, then rose and walked to his window overlooking the park. He had been forced to switch on his desk lamp, for today was one of those unaccountable English spring days when clouds stubbornly blanket the sun and winter creeps back like a murderer revisiting the scene of the crime. It matched his mood. He dared not have feelings at this moment. Rationally, he had to blame himself, for not picking up on the danger signals from Bellingham on the telephone the other day. He had dismissed the man's anger, though he had never experienced him in such a rage, not even when things had gone wrong during the first war—the time they had lost track of Canaris, for instance, at Algeciras a quarter of a century previously. There had been no casualties then, it was true, but one had been prepared for bloodshed and losses, for one always was . . . it took only one wrong move at the crucial moment, one chap to lose his head, or a slip by an untrustworthy or incompetent locally-recruited agent . . . just as had occurred, when all was said and done, in the case of Knox, Meyerscough and Watts—or, as he would rather remember it, of *Tweedledum* and friends.

You bloody, bloody idiot, Jackie, he said to himself, because the regret wouldn't go away, or the sadness for what had been and might still have come about. Bellingham had had to decide to be a romantic, a knight on a white charger, and Menzies couldn't help but admire him. And he also knew that in his capacity as 'C', he had to sanction treating Bellingham like a mad dog.

A glance at his watch diverted him momentarily from his own feelings, and also told him that he had six minutes or so to collect himself for his appointment here at four. His eyes were warm and prickly, as if they were in strong sunlight, but he knew the sensation was that of tears and that they came from within. For sweet Christ's sake, there was no point in pretending to himself . . .

Menzies moved across the carpet, grabbed his onyx paperweight in the shape of the sphinx from the desk and, taking a deep breath, hurled it at the leather-padded door to the back stairs, through which he and Jackie Bellingham had passed all those months ago on their way to lunch at White's and the true commencement of SIGNIFY.

'It's not fair! It's not bloody fair!' he screamed, as he hadn't since he had been at school and his best friend had been beaten for a trivial offence. For that moment he allowed himself to hate Churchill, the Service, the war, and the human race. 'Damn! Damn! Damn! Damn!—'

Then he subsided into silence and stared down at the paperweight, which lay on its side, looking smugly straight back at him by a trick of its angle. Sir Stewart

Menzies stopped resisting. He let himself go limp, felt a breath come up from deep inside him. He sighed a long, long sigh and began to weep softly for friendship, for chivalry, for kindness and loyalty and all the other values he had shared with Jackie Bellingham. And he wept, too, for the affectionate, good, rather absurd physical presence of the man, which would soon be no more. He wept until there was a knock on the door.

Menzies checked his watch. His shoulders tensed. He shifted position so that he was looking out of the window, a habitual stance and one that did not show his face directly to the door. He wiped his face once with a handkerchief, blew his nose, and put the handkerchief back in his pocket.

'Come!' he called out in a slightly fuzzy voice.

The newcomer obeyed. Menzies heard him walk in and stand easy on the carpet just inside the door, waiting for his acknowledgment. 'C' breathed in, turned and smiled, though at this stage he kept his distance. The visitor, a man in his early thirties whom Menzies had last seen leaving the café in Stanmore, seemed nervous but pleased with himself. When he saw Menzies' face, he became mildly concerned.

'Are you all right, sir?'

Menzies winced inwardly. Clearly he had not left sufficient time to cover his feelings about Jackie completely. Outwardly, however, he managed a chuckle and forced his smile to become even broader. 'Fine! A spring cold, you know . . .' In a clearcut case of defending by attacking, he sprang forward across the room and seized the man's hand.

'My dear fellow,' he said. 'Congratulations! SIGNIFY is a success, a rip-roaring triumph. Victory from the jaws of defeat! We've had word via the Vatican source that Schellenberg's the hero of the hour in Berlin. He's the chap who saved the Führer's bacon—he and *Turquoise*, that is!' Constant pumping of the man's hand was bringing some semblance of life back into Menzies, and he kept repeating almost foolishly: 'Congratulations! Congratulations!'

Finally he let *Turquoise*'s hand go.

'A drink?' he asked, indicating the well-stocked cabinet

in the corner. As an ex-journalist and well-known socialiser, his guest was known to celebrate his successes in an explicitly liquid manner, so the Service grapevine had it. At least he was no secret drunk. Unlike old Jackie.

'Rather, sir. Whisky and water, and easy on the water, as the Yanks say.'

Menzies filled the next few moments with gossip about alcohol. Algerian plonk was flooding the market, almost literally, since the Allied landings there the previous November. Some of it was all right, but even the best of the locally-distilled pseudo-cognacs were muck, no substitute for the real thing from metropolitan France. That would have to wait for the day we landed on the continent, a red-letter day for lovers of decent booze all over the free world. This conversation, light and mildly obsessive, continued until Menzies and his guest were sat down in armchairs near the window.

There was a pause for ritual sampling and silent admiration of the whisky. Menzies knew how to keep a malt, and his guest knew the way to show his appreciation, which was to drink it slowly and with respect.

'Well,' Menzies said then. 'We've done it. The danger's over now. Moscow and Berlin alike are still pulling hard on the line, as firmly hooked as ever they were. Here's to you . . .'

'To *Turquoise,* sir!'

'Turquoise!'

It was permitted, just this once, to down what their tumblers contained in one gulp. Menzies strolled back to the cabinet for refills that could be lingered over. As he did so, he spoke over his shoulder in a casual way, the manner of the man who is first among equals.

'We've had our nasty moments in the past day or two. I won't bore you with the details, of course, Suffice to say,' Menzies told him, 'that your credentials have cost a little more to re-establish than we had hoped would be the case.'

'Oh dear, sir. Anyone I know?'

'No. One man temporarily attached to the Service, plus some of the commando team. We tried to minimize the loss of life, but it just didn't work out as we would have wished.'

'Rotten show.'

'Fortunes of war.'

Menzies decided that this would be the last word about the Rhodes element to SIGNIFY. *Turquoise* was a valuable man, perhaps the most valuable agent controlled by any of the world's Intelligence establishments, and it would pay to keep him happy and relatively free of the morbid guilt that could gradually ruin a man undertaking a long-term and very devious penetration task such as this. Menzies frequently asked himself how one could have the career that this man had behind him at thirty-one, and still stay sane, which *Turquoise* had so clearly succeeded in doing.

The man drinking companionably with Menzies in his office this spring afternoon was a supreme tightrope-walker, a triple agent. *Turquoise* had started his career in espionage when he came down from Cambridge almost ten years previously. Known in those days for his left-wing affiliations, he had spent that year in Europe opening up channels to the Russian-directed Communist underground. Within two years, he had become a fully-fledged Soviet spy—and all the time he was reporting to SIS at Broadway, who had got in before the Russians and recruited him during his last year at university. It was from SIS that he had got the name *Turquoise,* which he had kept throughout his career. The crucial twist in his career, however, the shift that had brought him to the pampered 'star' status that he enjoyed now, had come in the summer of '39, when two things had happened. First, the Russians had signed a friendship pack with Hitler on the eve of general European war. Second, at Menzies' urging, *Turquoise* had given up his job as a journalist and formally joined SIS as part of the huge intake when war broke out. He was thus well-placed to offer really high grade material to Moscow. And because of the Nazi-Soviet Pact, he could—and did—make a highly plausible suggestion. *Turquoise* convinced his Soviet controller at a meeting in November 1939 that a great deal of his information could be slanted to be of use to the Germans, and that it could be passed through specially created channels to the SD—the newer and therefore more gullible SS Intelligence service in Berlin. The plan worked. Schellenberg, on the look out for a spectacular coup, was rapidly convinced that he had acquired a highly-placed source inside SIS, whose reports came via a corrupt Swedish bank official. The bank official was indeed a bank official, but he was also a Communist underground worker of some twenty years' experience, the last link in a chain that started with the driver at the North London café and went with the aid of the Soviet diplomatic pouch to Stockholm.

The Russians' aim in agreeing to *Turquoise*'s clever suggestion had been to help the Germans unobtrusively while at the same time penetrating the SD's foreign espionage network. This was fine, if hardly moral, so long as Nazis and Communists were *de facto* allies. The extraordinary thing was that the dramatic events of June 1941, when Germany had invaded its 'ally', had changed the situation not one jot. *Turquoise* had been ordered to continue to report as usual to the Russians on British military planning, particularly regarding the Balkans, and Moscow had continued to pass it on to the Germans through the Swede, despite the fact that the two totalitarian empires were engaged in a no-quarter struggle for survival. The reason was extremely cunningly-calculated. Stalin and his Intelligence chiefs had an interest in the defeat of Nazism, but also wished to gain victory on their own terms, and to face the postwar world with maximum material gain and territorial advantage. They were therefore willing, even while at war with Germany, to let the SD have information on British military plans for the invasion of the continent, either via the Balkans or in North-West Europe. Stalins' dream was of Germany and the Anglo-Americans bogged down in a bloody stalemate on the English Channel while his own Red Army steamrollered across Europe from the East. To this end, Moscow was prepared to pass on anything that *Turquoise* would give it. *Turquoise*'s controller had recently begun to press him for details of the plans for the cross-channel invasion that everyone expected the following spring.

But Menzies controlled what *Turquoise* gave the Russians, and therefore what the SD received. He had done so since November 1939 and continued to do so. His object was that Moscow—and therefore the SD—would get what they asked for. But the invasion plans they received would be fakes. Their trusty *Turquoise,* who had so often been proved right, would feed Berlin the information that the invasion was coming in the Pas-de-Calais region of northern France, whereas Eisenhower's hordes would actually descend on the coasts of Normandy, several hundred miles to the south. When it really mattered, *Turquoise* would let his masters down with a bump, and the chances of the Allied landing's success would be greatly enhanced. It was a beautiful triple-cross, and all but foolproof.

Then Nebe had decided to raid Schellenberg's safe and had found the *Turquoise* material there, which he had passed on to Canaris. When the anti-Nazis in the Abwehr had approached 'C' with this material and offered a deal, the neat plans of Menzies and his protégé had been thrown into utter confusion. Menzies had wavered briefly, had been tempted to take the chance to kill Hitler and reach some kind of accommodation with his successors, while *Turquoise* had been dead against involvement with the plotters from the outset, claiming that Fleet Street and the British people would never stand for it if they ever found out, which they probably would. Nevertheless, Churchill had put out feelers to Roosevelt regarding co-operation with Canaris and a possible separate peace, only to be brusquely rejected—in fact, it seemed likely that FDR's Unconditional Surrender speech at Casablanca had been part of America's response. After a short period of excited, even hysterical debate, during which even *Turquoise,* usually so cool, momentarily lost his nerve and made wild suggestions about faking his own suicide, the plan that was dubbed SIGNIFY came into being. There would be no Abwehr-assisted murder of Hitler by a British squad—the risks of breaches between the Allies and the peoples of the great democracies were too great, and the rewards uncertain, for no one could know who would actually succeed the Führer or what that successor would do. Menzies and *Turquoise* between them had hatched the details of the plot: to appear to fall in with Canaris's proposals and to follow them right through, even down to sending a commando team of sorts to Rhodes to 'assassinate' Hitler—and then for *Turquoise* to warn Berlin of the plan. With that single stroke, *Turquoise* had proved himself to be the most precious agent that the SD possessed—

the spy who had saved the Führer and therefore the Third Reich, who was invulnerable and impeccable and whose information therefore would count as gospel from that moment. By the spring of '44, no one in the Nazi leadership would dare question *Turquoise*'s version of the Allied invasion plans. Whole army groups would be set in motion at a whisper from the SD's favourite agent in London. And the Germans would end up with egg on their faces and a quarter of a million Americans and Englishmen successfully landed on the continent of Europe. That was SIGNIFY, the most crucial charade of the war, and they were now drinking to its fruition.

'And the "good Germans"?' *Turquoise* asked. He didn't trust Canaris and company. He always referred to them sarcastically as the 'good Germans' or 'the *vons*'. The SD were 'the blackshirts.'

'Oh, so far as they're concerned, we just made an enormous blunder. Our fine-toothed comb obviously failed to reveal the real culprit, or their information was inaccurate in the first place . . . it doesn't actually matter. *Turquoise* managed to remain at liberty and put the kaybosh on the assassination plan—also, conveniently, proving that we'd marked the wrong fivers.'

'Well, I'm sorry about our own chaps, sir, but I can't say I'm weeping any tears for Canaris. Personally, I wouldn't have put it past him and the *vons* to have continued the war once they were in power . . .'

'Er, quite . . .' Menzies said. *Turquoise* could become rather pompous on this subject, and it was best to guide the conversation into other channels. 'You know,' he continued, 'I'm going to tell you something. I have a feeling that your career has scarcely begun, young man. Once the war is over, there's still the Russkies to be dealt with. We tackled them before and we'll be facing them again. *Turquoise* will still have a very important part to play. We may even promote you! Officially, that is.'

Turquoise chuckled modestly and busied himself with his whisky. 'Luck's played its part, sir.'

'And nerve. You kept yours, and we've ended up better off than when Canaris first set the cat among the pigeons. The uses of adversity, as the Chinese say.'

'Thank you, sir.'

Menzies smiled graciously. Then he moved a little to one side, made an awkward gesture that indicated he was about to put a slight damper on the proceedings.

'The . . . ah . . . courier, Finch,' he said. 'Can you assuage the Russians? He's going to have to disappear, you know.'

Turquoise nodded blandly. He had a pleasant, open face and a good, square jaw. 'I took the precaution of complaining about him at my last meeting with my controller, sir. I said Finch had started drinking a bit too much and was turning into a ruddy menace with that lorry of his. Unreliable type.'

'I see. You hinted at the fact that he might have an accident in the blackout?'

'Something like that, sir. Soon. If the situation continues as it is now, there's the possibility that one of the comrades will smell a rat. I think, with respect, that we should get out while we're winning in that respect. They'll find a replacement for him soon enough.'

'You can nominate someone.'

'P-perhaps.' *Turquoise* had a slight stutter which women found irresistible, so Menzies had heard, and which he also exploited in order to avoid answering challenging questions. 'I don't know very many lorry drivers, socially or otherwise.'

They chuckled at *Turquoise*'s tart little joke. In a world where whole classes and nations had been tossed into the melting-pot, and where morality counted for precious little, it was comforting to share a background, a way of looking at life and expressing one's thoughts. It cut out so many of the complications. At their simple level, these common assumptions allowed trust to develop.

'Ah . . . Kim,' Menzies said, suddenly moved to use the name by which *Turquoise* was known to most of his friends and colleagues. 'If I may . . . It's just that I want you to know that you can always unbend, be yourself, around me. I realize that it must be a trial playing all these different roles, and to have no one with whom one can really talk without inhibitions. Please. I'm available as friend and father-confessor.'

'Thank you. I suppose I've got used to the life I lead, but it's very nice to know the offer's there.'

Menzies sipped some more malt. 'Which reminds me, speaking of fathers and confessors. How's that old rogue, St John P.?'

'Oh, on riproaring form, sir. Pa sent you his regards in his last letter, actually. Says your decision to employ me has made a man of me.'

'Little does he know. Your health—and his, Kim!'

Turquoise's father was a well-known Arabist, traveller and writer who before the war had acted as an adviser to King Ibn Saud of Saudi Arabia. Eccentric, erratic, but with all the right credentials, St John Philby was one of God's own Englishmen. His son had been christened Harold, and the nickname—as in Kipling's story, of course—had come from the family. 'Kim Philby' had a bizarre ring, a combination of the exotic and the stolidly English. Menzies could only suppose that it arose from a passion for oriental mystery, the lure of the East. Appropriate, really.

37

Bellingham worried at his glass of *retsina,* giving it enough attention to keep his host happy, not so much that he felt woozy. It helped that he didn't much like the acrid, oily Greek wine. That way there were no temptations.

In the main taproom of the *taverna* below him, he could hear the undulating rumble of conversation. It was the same the world over; a quiet night in a village inn, where locals came for the company and the talk. Bellingham had been given a snack of bread and cheese when the boy Marcos had brought him here, served to him in his attic. He suspected strongly that animals had been kept here until relatively recently, for there was a lingering after-odour that felt as if it had been absorbed into the walls and the timbers. Three hundred years of goats, sheep and chickens.

It was shortly before eight. The meeting was due to start any time about now, depending on how easy it was to ensure discretion. Ioannides had sworn that the *taverna* and its owner were totally secure. The place was certainly off the beaten track; an Italian patrol would stop by, it was said, for wine and a meal once every few weeks, and attempt to molest the landlord's stocky daughter. The last one had been by a few days previously, and they would not be back in a hurry.

Bellingham tapped his briar out on the edge of the rough pine table, blew through its stem, then settled down to filling it. He could see the Aegean stars, or at least a tiny patch of them, through a half-open skylight in the roof. The sky was a deep shade of mauve tonight, like a fine, rich robe. Pure theatre, as if it had been designed by an expert.

He was settling into his first few puffs when there was a respectful knock on the door, a gruff Greek voice: 'Mee-sterr Bailingham . . .'

'Come in.'

The low doorway swung open. It needed a slight push, for it was stiff, and so Bellingham had plenty of time to prepare himself in the small ways that people consider necessary, pushing his chair back slightly, running his finger through his hair, illogically taking a sip of *retsina* to show that the landlord was a good fellow, and clenching his pipe firmly between his teeth in a characteristic pose. He rose, leaning on the table with his knuckles resting against the bare wood.

Ioannides' man came in first. There was no sign of Marcos, who had been last seen being given a square meal by the landlord's wife, enjoying the fuss the woman was making of him. This was one of Ioannides' boatmen whom Bellingham had never seen before. The man looked quite normal, of average height and build and highly deferential, but there was a subtle arrogance about him, perhaps a defensive pride, that Bellingham had learned to categorize as the mark of the collaborator.

'Mee-sterr Bailingham,' he repeated with a wave of the hand and a smile. He did not introduce the man behind him, partly because he did not need to, and partly, perhaps, because he had been warned to be as close-mouthed as possible by Ioannides.

Otto von Bredow had to duck to enter the room behind the Greek. It made his entry mildly ludicrous, as if he were participating in a party game, but when he straightened up and looked at Bellingham, his gaze was direct and shrewd, and also affectionate.

'Herr Bellingham,' he said, and held out his hand. They shook.

'Whom do I have the honour of addressing?'

For a moment the young man was taken aback. Then he shrugged and grinned. 'Von Bredow, Otto. Oberleutnant. That is all you get under the Geneva Convention, my good man.'

'It's all I need. We know who we are, I think.'

'We do,' Bredow said with a nod. Ioannides' man had poured him a *retsina* to match Bellingham's. He accepted it and took a swig, shifting from foot to foot in slight uncertainty. He was wearing a sheepskin coat over slacks that were incongruously well-pressed and expensive-looking. But then, Bellingham reflected, a German Oberleutnant had a perfect right to wander around this island in any garb that he chose, or at least at the moment he did. Bredow was not hunted; under any other circumstances, he would have been doing the hunting.

'Cheers,' said Bellingham. 'Take a seat.'

'Thanks,' Bredow answered, returning the informal toast.

They arranged themselves on opposite sides of the small table with their glasses in front of them and the open bottle of *retsina* between them.

'I am still not sure how we came to be here together,' Bredow said. 'We must be crazy. That we both ended up here, for a start . . .'

'I'd guess because your chief's mind works much the same as mine's. They'll work chaps like us to death, matey. And why not? Why let two chaps in on the secret when one will do? I guessed at a fairly early stage that you'd probably been turned into a good shepherd, just like me.' Bellingham paused. 'Not much fun, as jobs go, is it? I mean, sitting haggling in hotels in Portugal was rather preferable, wasn't it?'

'I agree absolutely.' The German made a face. 'Gambling with men's lives under such pleasant circumstances, discussing things in theory, was fine. Taking direct responsibility for just a few human beings is more difficult and fraught with problems.'

'I'll drink to that,' said Bellingham. He pretended to, but he didn't. There was still the difficulty of giving in to the urge for intimacy with a man like Bredow. They had so much in common, but it was their very common experience that made them chary of each other. Perhaps they could be close so long as they never had to demonstrate the fact.

There was a short silence that hung very heavy. Then Bredow said what he had to say.

'Why are you here, Mister Bellingham?' he asked baldly. 'I know why you might come to Rhodes, but why do you want to see me? You do not have the air of a negotiator any more. You have changed.'

'Ah . . . I suppose that I have nothing to offer from on high, from my chief. That's true. No . . . forgive me, but I wanted to see you and talk to you. I suppose, in a way, that I wanted to clear the air, apologize. A bit of a self-indulgence really.'

'A bit.' Bredow was avoiding Bellingham's eyes. 'But I think there is a point where some self-indulgence is the last remaining mark of human dignity. A desire for truth, perhaps?'

Bellingham nodded slowly. Rather heavily philosophical and teutonic for his taste, but well enough put. You could wriggle on the end of the puppeteer's strings for years, but somewhere within you was the need to discover what was behind the stage of the marionette theatre of life, to actually gain some inkling of why, really why, you did the things you had always done.

'Truth might be putting it strongly, but I wouldn't mind knowing more of what was really going on all the time, particularly in view of the eventual cockup.'

'Cockup?'

'Shambles. Disaster, Débâcle . . .'

'Ah yes. I see. Please, do not bother with the lexicon. I am also concerned about the cockup. So is my chief, though he finds it hard to admit the fact. Yours?'

'Haven't seen him. He smiles and whistles under all difficulties, it seems, like all good scouts.'

'Well, you have come to pick up the pieces. A disaster

for the British Secret Service, and one that we would not have wished to see.'

Bellingham grimaced. 'It's certainly been a disaster for those poor bastards in the hills.'

'Our situation has not improved either,' said Bredow defensively. 'We are coming under a lot of pressure from our enemies in Berlin.'

'Sounds like you were lucky to get away in one piece. Could have been worse.'

'And it could have been better. I think that the advantage to our enemies—and to the enemies of humanity—will become clearer as time goes on and we are able to count the full cost of failure.'

Bellingham felt the depths of the man's bitterness and could not find it in him to deny it. 'In fact,' he agreed, following up the thought, 'the only ones really sitting pretty are the Führer, the SS and . . .'

'Yes. And?'

'Well . . .' Bellingham hesitated for a moment. 'Their spy in London, I suppose. The sickening thing is that he's none of the chaps my chief thought he was. We were so busy concentrating on the fellows we'd narrowed it down to that the spy, whoever he may be, was able quietly to find out about this plan and slip it to his SD controllers. We start again at square one, that's for certain. I mean, if I didn't know the stake that men such as you have in overthrowing the Führer, I'd suspect a bit of jiggery-pokery. When someone's always a move ahead like that, there's usually a reason.'

Bredow looked at him levelly. '*Turquoise* has undoubtedly proved himself to his controllers beyond all reasonable doubt. Certainly, beyond all reasonable doubt that the Sicherheitsdienst might be capable of. Their standards are not, in my experience, high. I can tell you that if he were my man, *Turquoise* would find life both more interesting and more difficult. I should want to know a little more about him.' He paused. 'Mister Bellingham, have you read any of the works of Lenin?'

'No. His kind of politics are not mine.'

'Nor do I much like them. However, the point is that he once very wisely said that when you are looking for the underlying realities in an apparently complex, even inexplicable situation, and you are confused, then there is one simple solution, and that is to examine the *who whom*. In other words, who is actually the subject, who is the object, and why this is so.'

'Also, who has something to gain, I suppose.'

'This is often the next conclusion, yes. Now,' Bredow continued, 'if I were a controller, and I had managed to infiltrate into a foreign Intelligence organization a spy whose every piece of information was treated with total trust, awe and respect, I would have every reason to be very pleased with myself. It would put me in a position where I could determine what that foreign Intelligence organization was fed, and therefore what was passed on to its government, thus contributing to major political and military decisions; then I would be a very happy controller indeed. I would not allow anything—or anyone—to stand in the way of my continuing with this arrangement. Do you start to see what I am talking about?'

'I don't want to, but I do.'

'I know that you are not directly involved. But could you describe to me what steps Sir Stewart Menzies took to track down this *Turquoise*?'

'Hum. Not specifically. He showed me photographs of some suspects, made general remarks. He's not a man who likes to make a great fuss . . .'

'Or at least, he doesn't like to appear to be such a man.'

Bellingham bit his tongue. He had been about to say that he knew Menzies, had known him personally for thirty years, but at that instant he realized that it was not true, any of it. He had known what Menzies had chosen to show him, a fraction of the real, whole human being.

'One gets on with one's own part of things, leaving the chief to co-ordinate, as they say. It's his job, after all, and his responsibility,' he said, aware of how prim he must be sounding.

'As I said, I know that you are not directly involved. But I am sure that your chief has betrayed us. It is the most reasonable explanation. We have been duped. I mean we, on the German side of things, and I think I also mean you, Herr Bellingham. I find this very sad and it also makes me angry.'

'Understandable,' admitted Bellingham. 'I'm going to

have a few awkward questions of my own to ask when I get back home. What else is there to say? It sounds as if you've got your own problems communicating with Admiral Canaris.'

Bredow nodded. 'Correct. My chief's weakness is attachment to the conviction that he and Menzies speak the same language, that if only they were to thrash out their differences, then all this war nonsense could be concluded in a civilized fashion.'

'A gentlemen's agreement.'

'Yes.'

Bellingham looked at him sadly, then at his watch. They had gone as far as they could, or as far as made sense. The German had obviously thought a lot of things out; with any luck, there might be changes on both sides in the months to come, and out of the ashes of this disaster might come something more hopeful, for Britain and Germany, for the whole of Europe. He didn't like to consider the detailed implications, because the more he did that, the more the enormity of what he had involved himself in came home. SIGNIFY was so clearly far more than a few men on an Aegean island risking their lives and their freedom. Bellingham's obscure sense of having been cheated was slowly coming into the open, finding a vent in the form of good, old-fashioned anger. And it would have to wait until he got to Egypt, or England, or wherever.

'I wish I could be certain that the characters concerned lived up to the description of "gentlemen",' Bellingham said. 'In the world I was brought up in, it had a number of very clear associations, and they did not refer simply to social background. To tell you the truth, I've come across Portuguese fishermen who fit the description better than our superiors. And now I've got that off my chest, I'd like to ask your help in getting away from Rhodes in one piece, complete with Captain Knox.'

'First point taken. On the second point, I will do all I can to help you without intervening directly. I think that this would be tempting fate, yes?'

'Yes.'

'Then,' Bredow said with a shrug. 'I will let Ioannides know of any possible problems. In return, I would like to think that you are standing up for us back in London, at

SIS. We get very lonely, Mister Bellingham. I realize that you are just one man, but we need friends—for now, and also for the time when Germany is trying to make a fresh start within the community of nations. It is good that you, at least, know that in this very darkest of hours, there were those who didn't despair, who tried to change things.' He smiled self-deprecatingly. 'But that sounds terribly self-important, even heroic. You know that the reality is also very prosaic.'

'Of course I know that. And there is bravery, too. Everywhere. Hand in hand with the evil and the manipulation. Probably inseparable, but at least we can try to make distinctions.'

They leaned across the table to shake hands. Bellingham reached out on impulse and put one hand on Bredow's shoulder. The German, after a moment's hesitation, returned the gesture. They stood for a moment like that, two men from cold countries making a clumsy attempt to show closeness. Then they pulled apart and made for the door.

'Yes,' Bellingham said casually. 'One forgets that wars end. You'll be getting back to your wife and young family . . .' He stopped. Bredow's face had gone a shade of cream, like an eggshell that's had all the yolk and white sucked out of it, and before he looked away, Bellingham noticed that his eyes had narrowed with pain. 'God, I'm sorry. All right?'

Bredow looked at the straw-strewn floor. 'You can't help it. She was killed in an air-raid in Berlin, some months ago now. I was very fond of her. It still hurts.'

'God.' The main burden of the air war against Berlin and other major cities was being carried by the British at the moment. It was almost certain that the RAF had been responsible for the death of Bredow's wife and unborn child. 'God, I must apologize.'

'I do not apologize for everything my side does, so please don't feel obliged to do the same for yours. So far as finding reasons and scapegoats go, she might as well have been hit by a truck. No mass guilt is involved.'

It was true and yet not quite true. Bredow would have felt better, in fact, if he had been able to say what he really felt, and then he and Bellingham might have been able to become real friends, but they had neither the time nor the occasion on their side.

Bellingham nodded, opened the door and looked down into the courtyard below, to check that there were no strangers around. Ioannides had kitted him out in Rhodian peasant's gear, but it paid not to take chances. Bredow, as usual, looked extraordinarily large, fair and German, despite his feeble efforts at concealing his nationality. Everything was quiet.

'All right,' he murmured. 'Good luck . . .'

Then Bellingham saw a match being struck underneath the balcony opposite. He stiffened, waited. A man drawing on a cigarette he had just lit, and waiting for something or someone. He moved forward slowly and cautiously on the balls of his feet, looked over the rail of the balcony outside. In fact, the man down there looked just like . . . couldn't be . . .

'Knox!' he hissed. 'Is that you?'

A difficult pause, then from below: 'Who's that? Ioannides?'

'No, you idiot, it's Major Bellingham!'

They met halfway on the wooden steps that led up the outside of the building. Bellingham was horrified, and Knox was extremely puzzled.

'What the hell are you doing here?'

'Got a message from Ioannides for me to be here to discuss arrangements. Good Lord, I've spent the past few days learning to trust the bugger, and you've been persuading me for all you're worth. What's going on?'

'Never mind that. The point is, I don't know what you're talking about. We're due to leave in twenty-four hours. You know the drill.'

'Christ. Hey, who's that?'

Bellingham glanced guiltily up the stairs, then smiled, resigning himself to the situation. 'That's the nigger in the woodpile, Knox. The joker in the pack, whatever. He's an acquaintance of mine. Come upstairs.'

They went back up to the balcony and Bellingham ushered Knox inside the upstairs room again.

'This,' he said, 'is Oberleutnant Otto von Bredow of the German Wehrmacht. Don't worry. To all practical intents and purposes, he's on our side.'

To his credit, Knox nodded and said: 'Good evening, Oberleutnant. For some time now, I've had a feeling that someone very like you existed, and I'm glad to meet you. It's a pity, though, that we didn't make each other's acquaintance a week ago.'

'Captain Knox, a week ago you might well have shot me. You certainly would not have listened to what I had to say,' Bredow answered.

Bellingham nodded. 'It's a long story. I don't think we have time to dredge it all up now. Something's telling me that we shouldn't hang around here for too long.'

'A pity,' said Knox. 'Did you want to see Hitler dead? That's what I really want to know.'

'I wanted Hitler dead more than anything else in the world. I still do, Captain Knox.'

'Thanks. I just needed to know that.' Knox turned calmly to Bellingham. 'So what do I do now?'

'You must have misread the message. Ioannides isn't here. He told me he was staying the night in Rhodes town, dealing with some business so that he would have tomorrow completely free. He won't be back at the house until lunchtime,' Bellingham said. 'I suppose we just carry on as previously agreed. You meet us at the rendezvous at midnight. Ioannides says he's got a beautiful boat for us, a smuggling boat. Goes like a bomb.'

They had gravitated out onto the balcony again. Bredow was nodding approvingly as Bellingham spoke, but he was ready to leave the two Englishmen to their misunderstandings and their sailing arrangements.

'Gentlemen,' he said, emphasizing the word in deference to his and Bellingham's earlier conversation. 'I must go. I am sorry that our meeting has been so brief. Though I feel we know each other well . . .'

Bellingham shouted when he saw the flash of a gun opposite. The sound that emerged from his mouth almost beat the weapon's report.

'G-e-t- d-o-w-n!' he bellowed, and pushed both of them hard, one with the flat of each of his hands, so that they careened off in different directions along the balcony. As he did so, he felt a sharp pain in his arm, a wetness against the cloth of his peasant coat. He sat down abruptly on the stone floor, saying: 'Shit. I've been hit.' It was his left arm, he thought. Lucky. With his good right he was wrenching his Smith & Wesson out of his belt. It had six bullets in its magazine; enough to deliver a useful counter-fusillade that would buy time for him to bandage the arm.

Bellingham crawled to the rail, peeped over. There was movement by the stables twenty feet or so across the courtyard, and probably also at the corner of the *taverna* building itself. Six or eight men, perhaps, by the feel of them. With a start, he realized that the ambush party had almost certainly been watching, waiting and listening while he and Bredow had been inside, and inevitably had taken in every step of Knox's arrival and greeting of the two other men. This had been set up, in fact, and only one person could have done it.

He loosed off four, five shots in rapid succession, fanning out round the edge of the courtyard as he fired. No hits, but an intimidating effect. Then he heard shots from close by, turned and saw Bredow likewise shooting into the darkness with his Walther.

'Got much ammo?' Bellingham hissed.

'Very little,' answered Bredow with a slow shake of the head. 'Not sufficient to last through a siege, which I think may be what we have on our hands. I do not see the man who brought me here. I fear there may be a number of good reasons for his disappearance, none of them very healthy from our point of view.'

'I've got about fifty rounds. I've also got to bandage up my left arm. A bullet passed right through it. It's Ioannides, isn't it?'

'Yes. Captain Knox?'

Knox was crouched a few feet to Bellingham's left, looking angry rather than frightened. 'Yes, Oberleutnant Bredow? You seem to be trouble for me!'

'Has it occurred to you that things might work the other way round?' Bredow shot back with a humourless smile. 'My life was fine until I became involved in this business. Do you have a gun?'

'No.'

'Can you use one?'

'Quite well.'

'Then I suggest you use Major Bellingham's until he manages to put a cloth or a bandage to his arm. After that, we shall have to try to get out of here and reach a safe place. Don't ask where that is at the moment, please.'

Bellingham put his gun on the floor and pushed it across to Knox, skating it on the stone. Then he pushed over six boxes of magazine clips and settled down to bind his left arm with a piece of shirt. There were isolated shots coming from the besiegers, but no concerted effort yet. They must be Greeks. A military patrol might not have taken them on by now, but it would have shown a good deal more cohesion of approach.

'Save your ammo until the buggers try something,' Bellingham said as he worked on his arm, knotting the grubby cotton around the wound. The bullet had fortunately passed right through, and since he was still in shock the pain was relatively slight. In anything between one and three hours from now, he would be in agony. He could see himself and his body quite clearly and objectively as factors in the situation, elements to be taken into account.

A flurry of shots below. Bredow and Knox answering sparingly. Then silence, some murmuring.

'Major Bellingham! Oberleutnant! Captain!' A voice boomed out in the darkness. The intonation was that familiar but slightly alien, public-school English gone a degree or two wrong. Ioannides.

'Ioannides? You bastard!'

'Major, I want only Captain Knox. Really. This is all a terrible mistake. If you and Oberleutnant Bredow come out peacefully, you can go. I have orders, from where I am not at liberty to say. Believe me.'

Bellingham snorted angrily. 'You can't allow us out of here. We'd spill the beans. You can't have Knox. He's mine.'

'Ours,' added Bredow.

'Trust me,' Ioannides called out. 'We have worked together. I know that this is a bad business, but there is no need for a lot of bloodshed.'

'Get stuffed!'

An object suddenly came sailing over the top of the rail, bounced once. All three of the defenders knew what it must be, and they barely created the time to make themselves small and huddle against the side wall of the building. The hand-grenade exploded, showering pieces of stone, splinters and dust across the balcony. Bredow and Knox crashed into each other as they crawled towards the steps through the smoke, guns at the ready. They had both seen the same danger.

There were two men with carbines at the top of the steps, moving quickly, climbing like monkeys towards the balcony. Knox shot one in the face, registering only an amazed and frightened look before a red hole appeared just above the upper lip and the man disappeared from sight. The second attacker was quicker and, within limits, luckier. He managed to loose off one shot, which hit Bredow at hip level as the German tried to jump into an upright position. Knox, moving his gun round easily and feeling no panic, only a lust to make these animals disappear from his life, also shot the second man. Two bullets from the loaned Smith & Wesson ploughed into the man's chest. He rolled over, head over heels, down the steps and rolled all the way to the bottom, grunting very loudly all the time. There may have been a third on his way to the upstairs balcony, but if there was, he retreated very quickly.

'So much for trust,' said Knox, turning to see how the others were. He might have expected to find grimly expectant faces, even perhaps a little hardbitten approval for what he had done. There was only Bredow a short way behind him, clutching his slacks to the right of his groin, where there was an ominous crimson patch that seemed to be spreading with incredible speed, as if it were a living thing. No one else. 'Major Bellingham? Sir?' he said anxiously. 'Where are you?'

Bredow, his face distorted with the pain, opened his eyes for a moment. 'I think the grenade got him,' he said. 'We were lucky it did not kill us all three. Although luck is relative.'

Without answering, Knox crawled back towards the door to the upstairs room. The smoke had cleared now, and he could see the outline of Major Bellingham very clearly, sitting by the opening that led inside, still and hunched over like one of those comic Mexicans taking a siesta in Western films. Knox came closer, could still see nothing wrong with the man. 'Major?' Darkness round the neck was the only strange sign. A couple of feet away and he could see the sliver of metal embedded in Bellingham's neck on the left-hand side, a half-inch or so beneath the jaw. Blood was flooding out. The shrapnel had obviously cut deep into the carotid artery. At his age, Bellingham might well have died of shock; a wound like that might have allowed a young, fit man a few minutes while he experienced bleeding to death, but Bellingham must have gone instantly or near enough so.

'Sorry,' Knox said, and turned away. He had no time for anything beyond the briefest of looks at the half-turned face, the slightly droopy moustaches. He wondered if Bellingham had stayed alive long enough to hear his last remark about trust, and he decided that he probably hadn't. There was only Bredow now, and only one place where they could go. Knox wondered vaguely how far he would have to get clear, then rejected the thought. Whatever his plan, the first priority had to be to get past the courtyard and out into the oleander bushes on the hillside beyond. He had walked the last mile here on his own, against Thea's protests, and he had kept a careful note of the terrain. Beyond the bushes was a ravine that narrowed down to a yard or so in width and ran several hundred yards, rising steeply until it came out on much higher ground. If he could get to that, they could only follow him singly, and he would bet that he could outrun them. He was nothing if not fit, thanks to the late Sergeant Watts.

Bredow was sitting on the top of the steps still, leaning against the railing with his gun on his lap. He looked horribly pale, but he smiled when he saw Knox.

'Had it?' he said.

Knox nodded. 'Poor sod.'

'I think perhaps he had a good life. Like most of us, he did not generally appreciate the fact at the time, but nevertheless he didn't do so badly.'

'He should have got out while he was winning.'

'Pardon?'

'Got out while he was winning—cut his losses, not pushed his luck with this last project.'

'Perhaps. I don't judge such things. Now run, Captain. I will cover you.'

'We could hold them off for a bit longer. Hope someone hears what's going on.'

'Pointless. Ioannides has arranged things well. I suspect he has paid the *taverna* owner or has some kind of a hold on him. Debts. Favours with the authorities, who knows? I can assure you that if there were an alternative, I would seize it. But as things are, you must make the attempt.'

Knox looked at him, saw the wry acknowledgment in the German's pale blue eyes. In his way, Oberleutnant von Bredow was asking for forgiveness.

'You're right,' Knox said quietly. 'And the sooner, the better.'

'Before we run short of ammunition, and before I bleed so much, my friend, that I cannot shoot this gun.' Bredow forced his right leg, which was now drenched in blood and quite useless, over against the stone base of the railing. He was clearly finding the gun heavy, though it was not a large weapon, and it took him a couple of seconds until he had it resting on his good knee, ready to fire down over the courtyard. 'Go!' he bellowed with surprising force.

Knox ran without questioning the why. He bent low and hopped down the steps two at a time. He remembered to watch out for the bodies at the foot of the staircase, and remembered also that when he cleared them he would become plainly visible from where Ioannides and his men were concealed around the stables. The sound of pistol shots was audible from the balcony now; Bredow had left it until Knox would be visible in any case, so as to avoid giving Ioannides extra warning of the breakout attempt. He was keeping up a good, steady fire by the time Knox reached the middle of the courtyard and began to switch his direction, aiming for the gap between the stables and the corner of the main *taverna* structure and the quickest route to the hillside and a chance of freedom.

There were one or two seconds when he had a marvellous sense of physical power, of flow, and of everything going his way. He was running as if he were in the hundred yards dash at school, not bothering to shoot, only swinging his arms and covering the distance. As if by magic, the gunfire all around him seemed to be drawn to the balcony where Bredow was pouring fire down on the stables. During those moments, Knox felt a leap of invulnerability. *No one was going to kill him. He was the centre of the universe, and he was going to survive . . .*

Suddenly the firing from above stopped, and Knox felt bullets hissing through the air around him. Really, like insects. Except that insects didn't punch you in the shoulder. The blow did more than just hurt him physically: it shattered his fragile runner's euphoria. He stumbled, felt another blow to his leg, and fell. He rolled, alienating himself from the pain as much as he could, and had the presence of mind to raise the Smith & Wesson and shoot. It must have surprised the ambushers, and frightened them, for the firing eased off and he was able to roll further without feeling any more bullets hitting either the ground or, mercifully, himself. But he was weakening. Knox managed to sprawl on his stomach, splay his feet apart, hold the gun between his two hands, and shout: 'Fuck you!'

His fury kept him going. Knox was so enraged at everything that had happened and was happening now, that even when he had fired all the bullets in the magazine, he kept on squeezing the trigger and shouting repeatedly that schoolboy 'Fuck you!' Until his vision began to go and the world began to tip like a yacht in a storm, and the pain in his shoulder began to spread through him like a poison. Then all he could do was to lie there, panting, muttering thick, largely incomprehensible oaths to himself. Dying, he decided, was very painful but very physical and ordinary, like an appendix operation. Absurd.

On came the surgeon, as Knox dubbed Ioannides when he saw him, continuing with the wild analogy. The big Greek had jumped down from the stable roof. Surprisingly, he also looked sad. There was little triumph about his broad face, not even much relief; only the grim determination of the born survivor, the man who was always prepared for others to go before he did, and who if necessary was willing to give them a push.

'Bastard,' spat Knox, making a great effort. 'You bastard.'

Ioannides had a shotgun in his hand. It was light to him, and familiar. He was pointing it at Knox.

'*Kapetánios*, as they call you,' he said. 'You are a brave man. I salute you. But you must die. Orders from very, very high up.'

He braced his feet apart, aimed. There was going to be no further comments. Ioannides was not a sentimentalist.

'Bastard—'

Ioannides' face, indistinct as it was, then seemed to screw up in a rictus of effort that surprised Knox. The weapon was clearly no trouble to him, and it was late in the day for the agonies of conscience . . . Nothing happened. Then Ioannides took a step forward, another, and the steps were unsteady. He was trying to say something, but he failed. Then he dropped the shotgun, and Knox knew that something had actually happened, something violent and decisive. Ioannides turned on his heel, contorting his body so that his arms were twisted behind his back, like a man trying to scratch an unbearable itch there. In fact, his strong hands were plucking at a knife that was solidly implanted between his powerful shoulder blades, and the look on his face was now one of beetle-browed irritation. He continued standing for some ten seconds, while all around, Knox thought, there was the sound of guns being fired, shouts in Greek. He looked up once more before he passed out, and above him he saw Stavros Ioannides, who had blood dribbling out from his mouth. He had ceased his futile contest with the knife in his back and by some massive effort of will had picked up his shotgun again. He was looming over Knox, raising the weapon above his head to use it as a club. He bawled 'Kill!' in heavily-accented Greek, the Anatolian dialect of his childhood. His voice was terrifyingly loud, magnified by a final, awesome inrush of strength that could not last. Ioannides swung the heavy makeshift club back, but he could not bring it forward again. Instead, the shotgun veered off over his shoulder, and the knife must have moved in him, for the trickle of blood out of the corner of Ioannides' mouth turned to a flood, a last rush.

Thea Chorakis dropped down from the flat roof of the *taverna*, landed like a cat and moved quickly over to the two men lying in the centre of the courtyard. She knelt by Knox, felt his pulse, waved frantically to the two men with guns who were also climbing down from the roof.

The other men, Ioannides' thugs, had fled after a very

short exchange of fire. When men were paid, they did not risk themselves as comrades and freedom fighters risked themselves, or as lovers did.

Thea spent several minutes in bandaging up the wounds on Knox's shoulder and leg with strips of cotton from her own shirt, which she took off and ripped up quite shamelessly in full view of the two men partisans. They neither leered nor were embarrassed. As she did what she could for the *Kapetánios*, they moved among the dead, collecting documents and weapons. They even treated the body of the German with respect; they had seen most of what had happened, and they knew he was a good man. He had saved the *Kapetánios* while they had waited, unable to intervene until they had gained a commanding position on the roof. Comrade Thea had judged her moment perfectly when, seconds after they had reached their vantage-point, she had thrown her knife. If Ioannides had not come out into the open, it would have meant a shootout that the partisans might well have lost. They had been lucky. One of the partisans, good Communist though he was, fingered something beneath his shirt as he moved among the dead. The books that Comrade Chorakis had read to them assured them that they would win the struggle because History was on their side and on the side of deprived people everywhere. He, however, found it very hard to believe that History saved individuals from devils like Ioannides; a much more likely explanation lay in the power of the crucifix that he kept hidden against his bare skin as an insurance policy.

When she had bandaged Knox to her satisfaction, Thea kissed both his wounds and his face, and called to her two comrades. She supervised the two of them as they lifted Knox into a chair position between them.

'We all do some lifting. You begin. First . . .'

She went over to where Stavros Ioannides lay and, with some tugging and grunting, managed to turn him over onto his front. As if he were a huge slab of meat, she put one foot on his back and the other on the ground, grabbed the hilt of her knife, and pulled. The blade came out slowly, with a sound like a gentle, rasping sigh. She wiped it on Ioannides' shirt and stuck it back into her belt without another glance or word.

'Come on,' she said to the two carrying Knox. 'We have a long way to go tonight. We must go where no one can find the *Kapetánios*. No one, no matter how clever or powerful. No one.'

And they began to move upwards, towards the oleanders and away from the *taverna*. Thea Chorakis said nothing. She walked beside them, occasionally leaning over to wipe Knox's face and eyes.

They really did have a long way to go.

38

After a comparatively light supper, Sir Stewart Menzies and his Prime Minister strolled in the summer twilight, brandies and soda in their hands. The air in this particular part of the grounds at Chequers was dense with the creamy, slightly sickly scent of meadowsweet. They stood and stared over the smooth foot hills of the Chilterns towards the spire of Little Kimble church less than a mile away. There was magic in an English evening such as this one, and they were both silent for some time in respect of the fact.

'Next year in France!' Churchill toasted self-consciously, breaking the spell. He swallowed some brandy. Menzies followed his example. The Prime Minister hated to drink alone.

'We have laid the foundations, sir,' Menzies said. 'The work with the Americans in KOSSAC, the new training programme . . . and SIGNIFY.'

'Ah, yes. Your precious one, your crown jewels.' Churchill, who was ever so slightly drunk, and could be cruel at this stage of the evening, looked slyly at 'C' and wagged a finger. 'There was good and bad luck, my friend, in the final decision. I would rather that neither was involved.'

'Sir, then it would be a rare case indeed.'

Churchill laughed. 'You are our rare case, Stewart. You must be reckoned an amiable soul, but a sense of humour is not among your virtues.'

Menzies made no reply. When the Prime Minister ribbed a cabinet colleague or an official in this way, which he did often—especially after a good, well-wined dinner—it was wisest to rein one's tongue and play along until he became tired of the sport. To evidence either one's sense of humour or one's lack of it was equally fatal.

'Stewart, you're incorrigible, but I adore you,' said Churchill, rubbing 'C's shoulder playfully until it began to become quite painful.' He used words such as 'love' and 'adore' with an old-fashioned abandon, just as he cried in his intimate circle completely without hesitation. Having exhausted the limited possibilities of fun in the situation, he sighed heavily. 'You said your favourite spy is going to be up for promotion? Am I expected to rubber-stamp your decision? Is it all cut and dried?'

Menzies smiled. 'Nothing is ever cut and dried. But I think Philby deserves it. And there is another advantage. He will become even more precious to precisely the people we wish to value him. In fact, I've had an idea, Prime Minister. Rather a good one, actually.'

'Oho. Tell me more.'

'Well, sir, I intend to set up an independent Russian section later this year. I'd been thinking of Felix Cowgill for it, but frankly, for all his talents he'll hardly bring a fresh approach. So I hit on another candidate: Philby. Imagine the Russians' delight: *Turquoise* becomes head of the Russian section!'

'Superb idea. He is young, he is hardworking, he is devious in the extreme,' Churchill growled thoughtfully. A gentle breeze momentarily ruffled his sparse, white hair, and he shivered. 'Someone walked over me grave, Stewart. Perhaps this young man, Philby. Sounds like the type who'd ambulate on a whole cemetery of worthy gents without a qualm . . .'

'You know our work, sir. It requires a particular type of person. Able to sacrifice a good deal, to do things that most ordinary chaps wouldn't countenance for the sake of his country. But at heart, sound and decent. I'm convinced that Philby has those qualities. He certainly has the background.'

'His father's mad, but he has a certain style, it is true. Yes, I rather liked him the time I met him . . . not one of your weak-kneed advocates of dam projects and university bursaries for the natives. Wants to keep his favourite wogs as wild as possible, far as I could tell, which is in my opinion precisely the correct approach. Western civilization'll be the death of Africa, Arabia, Asia, the lot. Look at India . . .'

Menzies waited patiently while the Prime Minister spent a short while riding his hobby horse about the threat to the Empire from native education. When Churchill paused to down some brandy, he moved in with a skill born of experience.

'Canaris, sir, seems only slightly deterred, by the way. He put out some new feelers through the Vatican source a week or so ago. I propose to continue to play him, though from now on without committing us to specific courses of action. He will become very annoyed, and probably even more suspicious, but there is actually very little he can do to prevent us from having our cake and eating it too.'

'He needs us,' Churchill said. 'He and his friends cannot live without us, poor boobies.'

'There is more. We have learned, through leaks in the Italian High Command that Canaris has had conversations with Rommel, using intermediaries who served with him in North Africa. Could be the hero of Africa's the mount he's putting his shirt on now that von Kluge's out of the field, sir.'

Churchill pondered the implications and frowned. 'I don't like that combination, Stewart,' he said. 'We didn't like von Kluge much as a replacement for the Führer, heaven knows. But . . . Canaris's brains and the Desert Fox's aura of glory. Dammit all, but that sounds like a team that could actually win the blasted war if they managed to get Adolf and his thugs out of the way! We were right to fight shy, you know. May the Führer live for ever, or at least until we've finished with him!'

'Of course, Canaris's position will have been undermined by the SD's success with *Turquoise*. In a way, that may be no bad thing.'

'But if the underdogs should succeed in overthrowing Hitler after all, without our help, and Canaris becomes the kingmaker?' Churchill asked shrewdly.

'Nothing will have changed.' Menzies was smooth and

assured. 'Any new government in Germany will have only two alternatives: to fight on, or to talk to us and anyone else who will listen about peace. Actually, we can't lose, sir.'

Churchill nodded. 'Next year, we shall land in France, and friend *Turquoise* will have sold the SS and Hitler a fine pup.' He laughed drily. 'There is no alternative, I fear, Stewart, but for me to congratulate you handsomely, much as it goes against the grain.' He raised his glass, which had been generously filled before they left the house, and noted that there was still sufficient left for a toast or two. 'To you and your young Macchiavelli! Here's hoping you learn the error of your ways!'

Menzies smiled. This was the way he liked the Prime Minister. Rollicking, easygoing. But one never knew from one moment to the next, of course.

'And here's to the poor wretches who paid the price,' growled Churchill throatily, moving in a few moments from apparent geniality to the edge of tears. 'Lord help 'em.'

Menzies felt an ache in his chest, as he had from time to time over the past few days. Sooner or later, he would see his doctor about it. Not that conventional medicine would be able to do much, he suspected. Glancing at Churchill to judge precisely what was going on in that quarter, he saw a faint glistening in the corner of the old man's eye. 'Yes, sir,' he said with difficulty. 'Here's to them.'

They stood for a moment longer in silence, watching the sun hanging over the flatter land to the north-west. Churchill shook his head. 'Another drink, Stewart,' he said, and shook his head once more, as if freeing himself from some trivial but troublesome pest. 'Time to talk about the Yellow Box. We shall spend a jolly hour in discussion of its latest secrets. There is a war to be won, man. Isn't it wonderful? And we're darned well winning it!'

With a releasing guffaw, Winston Churchill took his spymaster by the arm and they began to walk back towards the ugly, tranquil little country house in the bosom of the hills. Menzies chuckled in response, for the great man's enthusiasm was infectious. For a while to come, his secret ache could be forgotten, and it was good to be winning a war on a fine English summer's evening.

Epilogue:
April 1979

The *taverna* that had once hidden among the hills, accessible only on foot or by donkey, now sat by the side of a good, wide tourist road. Here the Germans, the Scandinavians, and even the newly-impoverished British would come by in buses, on hired motorcycles and in rented cars, and frequently they would stop for a meal or a drink. The *taverna* had changed accordingly; it was now painted pink and boasted a car park and a garish sign proclaiming the virtues of its 'international' menu in several European languages. It always puzzled the present owner, a young businessman from the town, why the distinguished-looking old man and his handsome wife came here every year towards the end of April. They would come each spring in their little car, the man leaning on a stick, for he had a bad leg. It was a diverting mystery to the owner.

The couple never said much to their hosts, though they were always pleasant; the woman in a quietly forceful way that showed a hint of steel beneath the surface, and her husband with a twinkle in his eye, an occasional quip in an accent that was certainly Greek but not quite Rhodian. They would always order lunch and then sit for an hour under an umbrella on the far side of the courtyard, talking intensely but softly, occasionally pointing to this or that feature of the house. Once the owner came out the back and found both of them at the top of the steps that led up into the upstairs room, which he now used to store furniture. They had seemed embarrassed when he spoke to them, and had passed some comment about having known the place many years ago and wanting to see if everything was still there. The owner had told them that, yes, everything was still intact, mainly because he was too poor to extend his property and put in some more modern accommodation. Had he been completely truthful, he might have confessed that what he really wanted to do was to knock the whole place down and rebuild it as a good-class hotel for the richer tourists, but since he was a kindly, sensitive man and not just a moneygrubber, he realized that this would not be diplomatic. And so he left them to enjoy a drink after lunch, on the house, and went back to ogling a pair of half-naked Swedish girl hitch-hikers who were sitting out by the road.

'I have a sense that this place will soon change,' the old man said. He was about sixty, with a beard now almost completely grey, and he wore a light suit of good cut. 'One year we'll come here and it will all be gone. The memories of everyone who died here: Bellingham, Ioannides, that German . . .'

'Perhaps those who lived will be free then,' his wife said gently.

'I'm free enough. I've got used to it. I could even travel to London, cause a lot of trouble, as a number of old men seem to be doing at the moment.' He smiled and tapped the table, where he had set down his sunglasses and a newspaper. Then he picked up the paper and stabbed a finger at the front page. It was a week-old copy of the London *Times,* featuring a story about the newly-discovered Soviet spy, Anthony Blunt, the so-called 'Fourth Man'.

'Do as you wish, Mark.' She made a face. 'I shall not get you out of trouble this time. I am too venerable and dignified for such things.'

He grinned like a naughty boy spiting his mother. 'Burgess and Maclean; Philby; Blunt—and how about Mark Patos Knox, coming back to haunt them?'

'You did not betray your country,' Thea said. 'That is the difference. Your country betrayed you. A long time ago.'

'I suppose so.' He looked around to ensure that there was no one at a table within earshot and said out loud in English: 'Everyone thinks I'm dead. What fun!'

It was Mark's annual self-indulgence. When the fear and the bitterness had subsided and the war was long over, he had started to see the ironies that he had lived through as tiny, component fragments of a huge, universal irony. And by the time a man was sixty and had been living as someone else for almost forty years, and the men he mourned were that long dead, it was hard to keep things grim-faced. After all, Major Bellingham of the wondrous whiskers and the whisky would be in his nineties now, in the unlikely eventuality that his liver had not pickled itself thoroughly. As for the young German officer, Bredow, Knox saw him reflected in the fit, bronzed young Germans who came to Rhodes to enjoy themselves in the easy, democratic way that united modern-day European youth. They were a little earnest, perhaps, and sometimes heavy going—as Bredow had also appeared to be from their brief acquaintance—but to Knox they were a particularly piquant example of the ways in which this new generation enjoyed the trivial, essential freedoms. If he tried just a little, he could change the face of any young German and superimpose the features of Bredow. A young Wehrmacht Oberleutnant in a T-shirt and patched jeans, swigging coke from a can . . . When he came on his annual visit to the *taverna* from their home near Rhodes town, he liked to indulge himself in small fantasies such as that one, for he knew they had a potency that went beyond the now and permeated the atmosphere. He was getting spiritual in his old age, imagining beings still hovering here around the courtyard . . .

'It's actually impossible to regret anything,' he said to Thea in Greek. 'There is a certain sadness, but that's all. For people I would have liked to enjoy more, but who were taken from me. Otherwise there is only the life I have lived—before in England and in the Army, then here with you. At least I never had to divide myself as those men did, do so many things they didn't want to do in their hearts.'

'You have been allowed to be alive, Mark. Fully alive. And so have I. But first we had to die here, almost as completely as the others died.'

He nodded, recognizing what Thea was saying to him, but his eyes were closed. Knox was concentrating on the feeling of this place, of all the memories that it crystallized for him, of the people who had once lived, acted, talked and walked here and who for a moment came back to him so clearly and poignantly, then suddenly became vague and dark again. Just shadows of recollection in the mind. Walking shadows.